TWILIGHT'S LAST GLEAMING

TWILIGHT'S LAST GLEAMING

John Michael Greer

AEON

First published in 2014 by Karnac Books. This new 2019 edition published by

Aeon Books Ltd
12 New College Parade
Finchley Road
London NW3 5EP

British Library Cataloguing in Publication Data

A C.I.P. for this book is available from the British Library

ISBN-13: 978-1-91159-776-6

Typeset by Medlar Publishing Solutions Pvt Ltd, India

www.aeonbooks.co.uk

CAST OF CHARACTERS

United States of America

Executive Branch
William Stedman, Secretary of Defense
Paul Gregory Barnett, Director of Central Intelligence
Admiral Roland Waite, Chairman of the Joint Chiefs of Staff
Leonard Gurney, Vice President
Ellen Harbin, national security adviser to the President
Jameson Weed, President
Claire Hayes Hutchison, Secretary of State
Lloyd Schumacher, Secretary of Energy
William Honnecker, Ambassador to South Sudan
Stanley Fukuyama, CIA station chief, Juba, South Sudan
Jeremiah Parks, Ambassador to the United Nations
Frieda Thaler, presidential press secretary
Barbara Bateson, acting Secretary of Defense
Beryl Mickelson, Secretary of the Treasury
Emil Pohjola, operative, Executive Special Projects Staff
Janice Kumigawa, legal adviser to President Gurney
Blair Murdoch, Secretary of Homeland Security

Congress

Senator Pierre "Pete" Bridgeport, chairman of Senate Armed Services Committee

Leona Price, nonvoting delegate to the House of Representatives for the District of Columbia

Joseph Egmont, Senator Bridgeport's political strategist and adviser

Nora Babbitt, researcher on Senator Bridgeport's staff

Senator Michael Kamanoff, majority leader

Senator Rosemary Muller, chair of the Senate Armed Services Committee

Senator Nancy Liebkuhn, majority whip

Military

Colonel Melanie Bridgeport, commander, 33rd Logistics Group, US Air Force

Brigadier General Michael Mahoney, commander, 33rd Fighter Wing, US Air Force

Colonel Edward Watanabe, commander, 33rd Operations Group, US Air Force

Colonel Arnold Biederman, commander, 33rd Combat Support Group, US Air Force

Rear Admiral Julius Deckmann, US Navy, commander, Joint Expeditionary Task Force Three

Captain Samuel McCloskey, US Navy, captain of USS *Ronald Reagan*

Commander Philip Johnston, US Navy, executive officer of USS *Ronald Reagan*

Brigadier General Jay Seversky, commander, 101st Air Assault Division, US Army

Colonel Joseph Becher, chief of intelligence, 101st Air Assault Division, US Army

Colonel Benito "Benny" Martinez, commander, First Brigade, 101st Air Assault Division, US Army

Colonel Jason "Ish" Isherwood, commander, Third Brigade, 101st Air Assault Division, US Army

Major James Kroger, 509th Bomb Wing, US Air Force

Captain Philip Bennington, 509th Bomb Wing, US Air Force

Rear Admiral George D. Wanford, US Navy, commander of US forces on Diego Garcia

Major Roy Abernethy, US Army National Guard

Sergeant Howell "Chip" Lansberger, US Army National Guard

General Ralph Wittkower, US Army, Deputy Chairman of the Joint Chiefs of Staff

Corporal James Wallace, 101st Air Assault Divison, US Army

General Alberto Mendoza; Commandant, US Marine Corps

Admiral Willard Gullickson, Chief of Naval Operations, US Navy

Other

Alexandra Weed, Jameson Weed's wife

James Lattimer, mayor of Trenton, New Jersey

Terence McCracken, Governor of Texas

Bryan Tuckerman, television reporter

Theodore Pappas, chief of derivatives trading for a major New York investment bank

Loretta Wallace, waitress

Leonard Wallace, her younger son

Julia Gurney, Leonard Gurney's wife

Robert Price, Leona Price's husband, professor of history at Georgetown University

Daniel Stedman, grandson of William Stedman

Representative Deanna Bickerstaff, Arkansas House of Representatives

Bayard Haskell, House Majority Leader, Arkansas House of Representatives

Mary Brice, House Minority Leader, Arkansas House of Representatives

Clyde Witherspoon, office manager, Oklahoma Independence
  Party
Suzette Delafarge, President, Oklahoma Independence Party
Michael Capoblanco, Mafia don
Maria del Campo Ruiz, Speaker of the Texas House of
  Representatives
Thomas Pettigrew, Texas Senate majority leader
Philip Briscoe, Texas Senate minority leader
Harriet Elkerson, delegate to the US Constitutional Convention
James Owen, veteran, US Army Rangers
Ray Muldoon, county sheriff, Lamar County, Mississippi
Gretchen Hayes, Melanie Bridgeport's campaign manager

People's Republic of China

Wen Shiyang, assistant vice president, China National Overseas
  Oil Corporation (CNOOC)
Jun Yinshao, Chinese ambassador to Tanzania
General Liu Shenyen, Vice Chairman of the Central Military
  Commission
Fang Liyao, professor of strategic studies, Academy of Military
  Science, Beijing
General Yang Chao, commander of People's Liberation Army
  ground forces
General Ma Baiyuan, Vice Chairman of the Central Military
  Commission
Chen Weiming, President
Liu Meiyin, wife of Liu Shenyen
Major Guo Yunmen, air defense commander, Lingshui Air
  Base, Hainan Island, China
General Cai Tungshao, Hainan Military District commander,
  People's Liberation Army
Major Chung Erhwan, commander, Unit 6628, People's Libera-
  tion Army Special Forces
Captain Kuo Lienmen, commanding officer, *Zheng He*, People's
  Liberation Army Naval Force

Captain Kwang Wenshang, People's Liberation Army Air Force

Russian Federation

Gennady Maksimovich Kuznetsov, President
General Mikhail Alexeyevich Bunin, Minister of Defense
Colonel-General Lev Arkadyevich Myshinski, Army chief of staff
Igor Ivanovich Vasiliyev, director of foreign intelligence

Islamic Republic of Iran

Ayatollah Husayn al-Jahrami, President of the Expediency Council
General Farzad al-Zardawi, commander of the Revolutionary Guards
Ayatollah Saif al-Shirazi, member of the Expediency Council
Colonel Hassan Gholadegh, Iranian Air Force
General Abdulhassan Birjani, Revolutionary Guards

United Republic of Tanzania

Joseph Matenga, chief petroleum geologist, Tanzanian Petroleum Company
Elijah Mkembe, President
General Mohammed Kashilabe, commander, Tanzanian Army
Private Kwame Mtesi, Tanzanian Army
Private Moses Olokumbe, Tanzanian Army
Colonel Mohammed Ilumubeke, Tanzanian Army

Republic of Kenya

Mutesu Kesembani, President
Corporal Hassan Omumberi, Kenyan Army

Other

Thomas "Tommy" McGaffney, Australian freelance journalist/
  author
Hafiz al-Nasrani, reporter for al-Jazeera News
Yamagushi Fumiko, freelance news photographer
Prince Khalid ibn Saud, Saudi ambassador to the United States
General Hassan al-Sharif, Saudi Arabian Army
General Mehmet Burzagli, commander, Turkish expeditionary
  force in Saudi Arabia

PART ONE

HUBRIS

ONE

*29 August 2028: thirty kilometers
off the Tanzanian coast*

"Keep going," said Joseph Matenga. The driller gave him a dubious look, but turned back to his console. More than six kilometers below them, the drill bit chewed its way through rock.

Matenga turned away from the console, though there wasn't far he could go. Windows on three sides of the cramped little control room showed the girders and gear of a drilling platform and, beyond them, blue ocean out to the horizon. The fourth side looked down on the drill floor, where the roustabouts were hauling another length of riser pipe to add to the drill string—the long shaft of hollow steel connecting the drilling rig with the bottom of the ocean and the hole he'd spent years convincing the onshore execs to drill.

Down there, past a thousand meters of sea water and more rock than Matenga wanted to think about, there should be oil, plenty of it. Blurred patterns deep down in the seismic surveys, biomarkers in the scant oil from that fault zone further west: all of it spoke to him of black gold somewhere down below the Upper Cretaceous plays they'd been drilling for years, trapped under a fold of impermeable shale that might stretch for a hundred kilometers or more, a petroleum geologist's dream if it told the truth. If not—well, with drilling costs well on the upside of five million renminbi a day, and two months of that already spent, the chance that he would be given another try was really too small to worry about.

He heard the driller's breath catch, turned back. Half a dozen computer screens faced him, but the one that mattered showed data from instruments downhole, just behind the drill head. Porosity was up, electrical resistance headed the right way, hydrocarbons detected—

"There it is," Matenga said. "Now, a core sample."

"Yes, sir." That meant pulling up all six thousand meters of the drill string so a coring bit could go onto the business end, but the driller didn't argue. Back in the bustling ports of newly oil-rich Tanzania, they said that oil came to old man Matenga in his dreams and told him where it could be found. The driller knew that such things didn't happen, or so he would have said most other days. The numbers on the screen whispered otherwise.

It was noon before the first fragments of rock from the new formation had come back up with the drilling mud. By then everyone on the drilling rig, from the company men all the way down to the roughnecks who hauled trash and chipped paint down in the pontoons, knew that something was up. As he stood in the geology lab, waiting for his assistant to wash the last of the drilling mud off the rock chips and get them under a microscope, Matenga could hear muffled voices outside the door. He bent over the microscope when the assistant waved him over, saw what he'd hoped to see: porous sandstone with the sheen of oil on it.

Another three hours passed before the core sample came in, and by then the whole rig was tensed, waiting. Matenga was waiting on the drilling floor when the drill string came up. When the sample reached the geology lab minutes later, he slid it out of its tube and let out a long whistle. It was everything he'd hoped for, a good coarse sandstone full of pores, with the

4

sweet stink of crude oil impossible to miss. As soon as he finished examining it he was on the radio with corporate headquarters back in Dar es Salaam to give them the news, and get the core flown in right away for laboratory analysis.

It would take many months and much more drilling, he knew, before anyone could be sure just how much oil was down there, but it was good to be proved right, good to know that his luck had not yet turned its back on him and that his career would end with a success and not a failure.

"God grant that there be much oil," he murmured, turning back to his work.

It would be early the next year before he found out just how abundantly that prayer had been granted.

6 February 2029: Dar es Salaam, Tanzania

The customs clerk finished with the papers and smiled a broad insincere smile. "Welcome to Tanzania, Mr. McGaffney. I hope you enjoy your stay."

"Thanks, mate." Tommy McGaffney nodded to the man and left the visa desk.

A few minutes later he was crossing the main concourse at Julius Nyerere Airport, shapeless leather bag swinging from his shoulder as he weaved through the crowd. After a dozen years chasing news across the hot crowded belly of the planet, it was a familiar drill: travel light, move fast, have everything settled beforehand and then don't be surprised when it all goes blue on you the moment you get off the plane.

A quick glance up at the sign showed that they'd moved the zone for the hotel shuttles since the last time he'd been through Dar es Salaam: more construction, a fourth terminal going in. He headed for the doors.

It was hot enough inside the terminal, but outside the heat came crashing down like a falling wall and then bounced back up hard from the pavement. The hotel shuttle was where it should be, thank whoever, with a gaggle of Chinese business-men in black suits and red ties sweating bullets as they climbed aboard. McGaffney evaded a clutch of Russian tourists and made for the shuttle.

"Mr. Thomas McGaffney?" the driver asked. "Please, make yourself comfortable."

The van's feeble air conditioning tried to make good on the offer and failed. McGaffney got his bag settled on the overhead rack, plopped down on a seat, and only then noticed that one of the Chinese businessmen was looking at him.

"Mr. McGaffney," the man said. "The journalist, perhaps?"

McGaffney turned in his seat. "That's me."

"Wen Shiyang." They shook hands. "No doubt we will be at the same place tomorrow."

"Then I'll guess that you're with CNOOC," McGaffney said, as the van lumbered out onto Pugu Road and headed toward downtown. The guess was safe enough; the Chinese National Overseas Oil Corporation had its people all over most of the African petrostates these days, with Beijing's money and mus-cle to back it up.

Wen smiled. "Exactly. I hope you had a comfortable trip here?"

"Not bad, once I got out of Spain."

That got a startled look from Wen. "You flew out?"

"Not a chance, mate; the Catalans are too bloody good with rockets these days. Got a boat to Morocco and flew from there."

"Ah." Wen shook his head. "A bad situation, the Spanish war. Still, I gather you are used to that sort of travel."

"Comes with the job."

They kept up a string of small talk as the van wove through heavy traffic, while the other Chinese in the van sat and said nothing. Every few blocks they passed another construction site: here a terminal for the city's brand-new light rail system, there an apartment complex or an office park, with Chinese

6

firms as general contractors and Chinese banks as funding sources. Closer in, office towers loomed over the street, more markers of Tanzania's new prosperity.

The hotel was a bland faceless building just south of downtown. McGaffney checked in, caught the elevator up to his room, showered, and then parked himself at the bleak little desk next to the windows and powered up his tablet. A few quick jabs at the screen brought up a page of links he'd made with all the media stories so far on the new deepwater find, a few background pieces on the Tanzanian oil industry and the latest annual report on worldwide oil production from the International Energy Agency.

The oil was what mattered, here in Tanzania and around the world: the black gold that fueled planes and ships and trucks, and kept a faltering global economy from pitching forward onto its face. Countries that produced more of it than they used got rich, countries that used more than they produced got poor, and those that couldn't produce any at all got thrown to the wolves. Tanzania had been a modest exporter of oil for years, enough to balance the budget decades earlier when oil was cheap, enough to cash in handsomely once the price of oil broke out of its last slump in 2021 and started the ragged climb that had kept economies struggling ever since. If the rumors about the new find were true, though—

McGaffney leaned forward, propped his chin on his hands. After a dozen years chasing the news, he knew a crisis in the making when he saw it. If the rumors were true, there was going to be a hell of a fight over all that oil.

7 February 2029: TPC headquarters, Dar es Salaam

The taxi rattled to a halt, and McGaffney paid the driver and got out. Reflected sunlight nearly blinded him: the building in front of him, all glass and aluminum, mirrored sun down onto the street with terrific force. Through the glare, he managed to recognize the new headquarters of the Tanzanian Petroleum Corporation.

Except for the brightly colored tingatinga paintings on the walls, the conference room on the fifth floor might have been anywhere on the planet. McGaffney took a seat toward the back, got out his tablet and waited. Around him, the room filled: reporters on the East Africa beat, diplomats, oil industry people. He knew maybe half of them, nodded greetings to those, watched newcomers find seats. One of the newcomers was Wen Shiyang, though there were plenty of other Chinese present, CNOOC officials and media people mostly. The Chinese ambassador wasn't there, though that didn't surprise McGaffney; he'd get his own briefing, no doubt.

Twenty minutes late, bustle behind McGaffney announced the beginning of the press conference. A middle-aged woman walked up to the podium and introduced herself as a TPC vice president, then introduced the country's Assistant Minister of Energy, a rotund gray-bearded man who just then looked jolly enough to be East Africa's answer to Santa Claus. The assistant minister spent five minutes saying very little in the most graceful way imaginable, then introduced the petroleum geologist they had come to hear. McGaffney sized up the man—lean as a crane with a white crest of unruly hair to match, the sort who'd clearly spent much more time handling rocks on drilling rigs than giving speeches in conference rooms—and noted the name down carefully: Dr. Joseph Matenga.

The room darkened and the inevitable PowerPoint image came up: a map of the Tanzanian coast and the Indian Ocean's western edge. "Gentlemen, ladies, let us go straight to the point," said Matenga. "You have no doubt heard rumors and media reports about our new deepwater drilling project. We have confirmed the presence of a very large oil deposit in Tanzanian territorial waters, far beneath our existing offshore fields. I will not trouble you with the fine details of the geology, but as you see, it underlies a great deal of sea floor." A black

8

elongated blob appeared on the map, nearly a third the length of the Tanzanian coast and vaguely parallel to it. "The field is a little less than three hundred kilometers long and between thirty and fifty kilometers wide. Of course there is much more work to be done to find out for certain, but our initial estimate is that it will yield more than eleven billion barrels of crude oil."

7 March 2029: The Presidential Palace, Dar es Salaam, Tanzania

The Honorable Elijah Mkembe, President of the United Republic of Tanzania, rose from behind his desk, extended a hand. "Thank you for coming, Ambassador."

"Thank you, your excellency." Jun Yinshao was a professional, no question; his handshake and fractional bow communicated the perfect blend of friendliness and deference, a polite fiction Mkembe appreciated. The president knew all too well how completely his survival and that of his nation depended on its Asian patron. The presidential office around them was paneled and furnished in dark native wood, and the chandeliers overhead were ornamented with local gold, but all the electronics were Chinese; so was the glass case on one side of the room with a rock from the Moon, brought back after the successful Chinese lunar landing in 2025; and so was the antique scroll painting, a gift from an earlier ambassador, on the other side: a quaint fifteenth-century ink painting of an elephant, an edgy reminder of just how long China had cultivated an interest in East Africa.

"Permit me also to congratulate you on the latest oil discovery," said Jun then. "I was filled in on yesterday's briefing. Eleven billion barrels—that is astonishing."

"If the estimates are correct," Mkembe said. "We will see."

"Of course. Even a smaller find will be excellent news."

"True."

Jun considered him for a long moment. "I gather from your tone, your excellency, that you don't consider it excellent news."

Mkembe allowed a nod. "Very good. You will forgive an old man's worries, I hope. I am concerned that there may be trouble over this new find. If it had been more modest—well, that belongs to the land of might-have-beens, but I seem to recall something one of your philosophers said: 'Too much success is not an advantage.'"

"Lao Tsu," said Jun, smiling in response to the reference. "Yes."

"Thus my desire to meet with you privately, as soon as possible."

"Of course." Jun paused, then: "I'm sure you know that my government is well aware of the potential for trouble from—foreign powers."

Mkembe chuckled. "May we be frank, Ambassador, and say it out loud? The Americans."

"As you wish." Again the fractional bow, conceding. "I will be sure to communicate your concerns to my superiors, and to our intelligence agencies."

Mkembe kept his face calm with an effort. Chinese diplomats never said anything by accident; he'd learned that decades ago and used it to his advantage more than once, sensing some shift in Beijing's mood long before his political rivals got wind of it. An issue that didn't matter in Chinese eyes got referred to "my government" or "my superiors." A reference to the huge but highly secretive Chinese intelligence community was another matter. That meant—Mkembe was sure of it—that the danger he sensed was real.

7 March 2029: The Durban hotel, Dar es Salaam

"It is a delicate line that we walk here," said the Assistant Minister of Energy, and leaned back in his chair. The table between them had the remains of a very good dinner on it, and the latest of several rounds of whiskey. All of it was on McGaffney's tab, and worth it at twice the price. He'd done a standard interview at TPC headquarters earlier in the day, guessed that the man might have more to say after hours and off the record, and suggested a meal. Whether it was McGaffney's reputation or something else entirely, the assistant minister had taken the bait.

"I believe you know Africa quite well, Mr. McGaffney," said the assistant minister. "You have perhaps been to Nigeria?"

"Couple of times," McGaffney answered.

"A very sad situation. Oil companies from Europe and America moved in, developed the country's oil resources, saw to it that nearly all the profits went back home with them, and spent just enough in bribes to officials to make sure nothing would be done about it. Today the oil is gone, the country is bankrupt and falling apart, and the officials who took those bribes? Those who are still alive, and they are not many, are in hiding abroad."

"You don't want that to happen here."

"It must not happen here. So far, it has not happened here. It is a good thing, I think, that we did not make this latest find until now." The assistant minister leaned forward. "A great many of us here in Tanzania have been looking north, toward the Persian Gulf. We watch billions upon billions of renminbi flow into those nations because they have control of their own oil production. No one talks about a resource curse there. We see this and we ask ourselves, why should we not do the same thing here in Africa? Now, perhaps, we can."

"Because of China," McGaffney said.

The assistant minister said nothing for a long moment, and sipped some whiskey. Then: "Since this is off the record, I will be frank with you. The Chinese are not here out of charity. We have much that they want, though oil of course heads the list, and they have many things we need very badly. So we bargain. With the Americans—as you say, you have been to Nigeria, and perhaps other places where the oil is controlled by the Americans. How many of them have prospered? So we

11

deal with the Chinese, we get the things we need, and perhaps one day we will be a wealthy nation and no longer a poor one.

"See, Mr. McGaffney, the United States itself was once like Tanzania. It was a colony of Britain, and like any other colony of hers, its farms and forests and mines made money for rich men in London, not for Americans. So the Americans had their revolution, they took their own resources and their own destiny in their hands, and became a great nation; and not so many years later, the British empire was gone and it was the United States and not Britain that had its navy visiting every port and its garrisons all over the world."

"You think," said McGaffney, "they've forgotten where they came from?"

"No, no, not at all." The assistant minister took another sip of his whiskey. "I think they remember it too well. They know that sooner or later some other country will replace them as they replaced the British, and so they see every rising nation as a threat to them. So we walk our delicate line; we deal with the Chinese and try not to offend the Americans; and we hope—I hope—that this new oil discovery will not cause us to lose our balance. Or, shall we say, cause the Americans to lose theirs."

McGaffney nodded. "And if it does?"

The assistant minister gave his whiskey glass a long morose look, and then downed the contents in a single swallow. "Mr. McGaffney, I pray to God every night without fail that that does not happen."

TWO

8 March 2029: The White House, Washington DC

The meeting was in the Roosevelt Room: a nice touch, Bill Stedman thought, and very much the new president's style. Flames crackling in the fireplace took the chill off the air, and a portrait of Teddy Roosevelt on horseback over on one wall did much the same thing in a slightly more metaphorical sense. After eight years of National Security Council meetings in the Cabinet Room under Abraham Lincoln's morose gaze, the less imposing setting promised well.

Stedman pulled out a chair at the long mahogany table that filled the center of the room. He was nearly the last there, which rankled, or would have if the only one who hadn't arrived yet wasn't the only one who mattered. The Secretaries of State and Energy were bent toward one another over one corner of the table, talking. Stedman didn't interrupt them; he nodded greetings to CIA director Greg Barnett and Admiral Roland Waite, the chairman of the Joint Chiefs, and shook the hand of Vice President Gurney, then turned to the remaining person there. "Good morning, Ellen."

Washington gossip had it that Ellen Harbin wanted his job, wanted it badly, and wasn't happy at all that she had to make do with the lesser title of national security adviser. She looked up through her frameless glasses, smiled her bright cold smile. "Good morning, Secretary."

Stedman sat down, pulled papers out of his briefcase: the latest news from Spain and the Balkans, none of it good. He was less than halfway through the first paper when the door opened and the president came in.

"Oh, sit down, sit down." Jameson Weed waved them back to their seats. Pushing sixty, he looked barely fifty and still moved like the athlete he'd once been. "Everyone's here? Good. Anything else on the list before this Tanzania thing? Bill?"

"Nothing critical," Stedman said. "More of the usual from Europe; it can wait."

"Claire?"

Claire Hayes Hutchinson had broken off her conversation with the Secretary of Energy when Weed entered, and tilted her head to one side; the gesture made her look like an inquisitive bird. "What Bill said. Thank God for quiet Saturdays."

That got a laugh from several others, and an "Amen!" from Barnett. "Okay," Weed said, laughing with the rest. "Lloyd, what have you got on this?"

Lloyd Schumacher, the Secretary of Energy, clicked the remote in his hand. A screen came noiselessly down above the fireplace, and the lights dimmed. Another click brought up the first image: a map of East Africa and the western Indian Ocean, with the new oilfield marked off in black. "Not much more than the media. If the Tanzanians are telling the truth, they've found the biggest new oilfield anywhere in a couple of decades. Eleven billion barrels of proven reserves puts it in the supergiant category."

"Are they telling the truth?" Weed asked.

"Looks like it. They've got their people out leasing every deepwater drilling rig they can get, cash up front."

Weed nodded. "And the Chinese are all over it."

"Like ugly on an ape. Tanzania's been in their pocket nearly since independence, and there are CNOOC people all over the place right now—Dodoma and Dar es Salaam, but also out on the drilling platforms."

"Is it close enough to Kenyan waters—?"

"Not a chance. The north end of the new field is almost two hundred nautical miles from the disputed zone."

"Kenya wouldn't intervene even if the oil was practically in their pocket," said the Secretary of State. "That last clash with the Tanzanians isn't something Nairobi wants to repeat."

"Dammit, we need that oil." The president stared at the screen for a long moment.

He was right, Stedman knew, and "we" didn't just refer to the United States. Weed had won the White House the previous November with a campaign that focused with laser intensity on getting the US out of its long economic slump. With the once-huge shale oil deposits out West nearly exhausted, winning a bigger share of imported oil was the key to making good on that promise, but that was easier said than done; behind what was left of the polite fiction of a free global market in petroleum, most oil that crossed national borders did so according to political deals between producer countries and those consuming countries strong and wealthy enough to compete. These days, more often than not, the US lost out—and the impact of that reality on Weed's reelection campaign was very much on the minds of everyone in the room.

"There's one option," said Harbin. "Regime change."

President Weed turned to face her. Stedman cleared his throat. "In theory, maybe," he said. "In practice, it's expensive and risky. We could end up with another Iraq or Venezuela way too easily." He leaned forward. "And sooner or later, the Chinese are going to stand and fight, and eleven billion barrels might give them enough of a reason."

Harbin gave him a contemptuous look. "They won't dare," she said. "It's too far for their force projection capacity, anyway. They'll back down the way they did in Gabon."

The president glanced from one to the other. "It's an option," he said. "I want a detailed plan on my desk in two weeks."

10 March 2029: Russell Senate Office Building, Washington DC

Pete Bridgeport stepped into his office and went straight to the wet bar tucked in one corner. Two hefty shots of decent bourbon over ice promised some relief after a bruising afternoon in committee. Drink in hand, he crossed the room to his desk, gave the computer screen a weary look, and reminded himself that delaying just meant that he'd be home even later.

In theory, he knew, he should be pleased with himself. He'd landed the chairmanship of the Senate Armed Services Committee with the new year—a dud assignment, or that was its reputation, but he'd done his homework, read up on its history, and knew that a good chairman could turn it into a significant force on the Hill. When the media started claiming in January that the new Army antimissile system wasn't half as good as it was cracked up to be, he'd jumped on the issue, scheduled hearings, and kick-started the process of sorting out which of the claims were true and which were scare stories churned out by rival manufacturers.

Watching the CEO of United Ballistics sweat bullets on the witness stand was a definite pleasure, and seeing news websites chatter about the hearings for two weeks straight offered a different and more practical payoff, one that might matter come election time. Still, trying to pry loose anything useful from a closed circle of Pentagon procurement people and defense industry executives was exhausting work, and it didn't help that two members of the committee came from states that would lose jobs if the program got cancelled. All in all, Bridgeport was glad the hearings were finally over.

He slumped into the leather chair, tapped the trackball to wake the screen, sipped bourbon as another click brought up the news feed his staffers had prepared for him. Most of it was chatter about the big new petroleum discovery in East Africa and the latest word from the civil war in Spain: nothing relevant. He closed the feed, opened his email, filed the messages that could wait, clicked on one from his daughter Melanie— a quick little note updating him on her move to Elgin Field down in Florida, her new position as head of logistics for the fighter wing there, and the latest Air Force gossip—and then on another that might matter.

The sender was a minor Defense Department official he'd known since college, the email ostensibly chatter about the man's kids and their Little League teams, but Bridgeport set down the glass, got up, and crossed to the tall bookcase on the other side of the office. The book he wanted was behind a photo in a silver standup frame: a picture of Melanie, though it could almost have been one of her mother before the cancer sunk its claws into her.

He moved the photo, pulled out an old leather-bound volume of Gibbon's *Decline and Fall of the Roman Empire* and took it back to his desk. Snooper programs these days could break just about any form of data encryption, or so rumor had it, but a code with a completely arbitrary key was another matter. Bridgeport wondered now and then if anybody else in Washington remembered the old trick of using numbers in a text to refer to pages and words in an agreed-on edition of a book; still, it seemed to work. He started flipping through the book, turning baseball scores and kids' ages into words on a very different subject.

It was a familiar drill. Article One, Section Eight of the Constitution of the United States reserved to Congress the right to declare war, but like many other provisions that inconvenienced the executive branch, that one had been honored in the breach for many decades; the last time Congress declared war on anybody was back in 1941. Since then, American troops had gone charging into action around the world over and over again without so much as a nod to Congress or the Constitution.

Most members of Congress grumbled about the metastasis of presidential privilege now and then. The smart ones figured out ways to put themselves back into the loop, at least to the extent of finding out what the executive branch was doing in advance of official announcements. Like most of his colleagues, Bridgeport had his own network of informants scattered through the federal bureaucracy, and now and then got tipped off to something that made a difference.

Like this time.

The words on the notepad were: *Caesar consideration regime change eastern Africa oil.* "Caesar" was Weed, of course, and the meaning of the rest was clear enough. Bridgeport opened the news feed again, read the stories on the Tanzanian find, and then took a good long sip of the bourbon and sat back. Eleven billion barrels of crude oil would make quite a difference to the US economy, he knew—if Weed and the Pentagon could pull it off.

After a long moment, Bridgeport tapped the intercom. "Anne, I need to talk to Justin as soon as he can get free. I've got a project for him."

"Sure thing," Anne's voice said. "I'll send him right in."

"Thanks," said Bridgeport, and closed the connection.

12 March 2029: The Pentagon, Washington DC

The lights went down in the conference room, and a map of East Africa came up on the screen. "Here's the target," said the general at the front of the room; a dot of green light from his laser pointer glowed in the middle of the map. "Tanzania—the United Republic of Tanzania, for purists. The official capital's

18

here at Dodoma." The dot of light touched a city inland, near the center of the country. "The old capital's here at Dar es Salaam." The dot moved out to the coast. "The Presidential Palace and most of the executive branch are still at Dar, and so's our embassy. The legislature's at Dodoma. In theory, the whole government will be in Dodoma one of these days. In practice—well, this is Africa, so don't hold your breath.

"Form of government? Constitutional republic. One party, the Revolutionary Party—the CCM—has been in the driver's seat since independence; there are three small parties with about a quarter of the legislature between them and a bunch more with no seats at all. The CCM's presidential candidate—that's the guy in office now, Mkembe—won almost seventy percent of the vote in the last election."

"Rigged?" asked a voice in the back.

"Not particularly. The CCM's good at staying popular. That's not going to help, I know."

"What's the military like?" This from another voice.

"I was about to get to that. They've had a major buildup under way for more than a decade now. They had plenty of oil money even before this latest business, and the Chinese have been helping them too—hardware, but not just that. The PLA's had training cadres there, lots of them, since we popped Kenya out of the Chinese orbit in '23."

The general clicked a button, and the map zoomed out to take in the whole continent south of the Sahara. "These days Tanzania's a big regional power, as influential as any nation in Africa. South Africa's maybe a little stronger, but there's a tacit agreement between Pretoria and Dar es Salaam—maybe more than tacit. Both countries have their own spheres of influence; where the spheres overlap, they're careful to avoid conflict; other than that, Tanzania doesn't mess with South African client states and vice versa. They were on the same side in the last two Congo wars, remember.

19

"Here's what they've got." Another click brought up names and numbers. "Army, just over 100,000 men, mostly motorized infantry—what's the word for the pickups—"

"Technicals."

"That's it. You know about those? No? Take a small pickup, mount a fifty cal machine gun on the roof of the cab, stash a couple of grenade launchers somewhere, load the back with soldiers and gear, and you've got your standard African fighting vehicle. Don't laugh; they're fast and they can handle any terrain; the only thing that's sure to stop them is air superiority or a solid defensive line. Tanzania's got maybe two thousand of them ready for service.

"Other than that? One artillery brigade, mostly obsolete; one armored brigade equipped with Chinese armored cars, Type 92s, which are pretty good; and an airborne battalion with some old Russian helicopters and some new Chinese ones. Both those saw plenty of service in the Congo. The police force gets some military training, and there's a national militia. Give 'em time to prepare, and they could mount a pretty fair defense.

"The Navy's not an issue, though—it's a glorified coast guard. Three destroyers that used to be Soviet Navy, a dozen cutters with fifty cal guns, and a two-masted square rigger they use for training cadets. That's it. Nothing to worry about."

Another click brought up a new list. "Air defense is a mixed bag. They've got around sixty planes, nothing close to new technology—twenty J-7Bs from China and a few old MiGs is as close to a fighter force as they've got. On the other hand, they've got decent air defense systems, not state of the art but only a couple of generations back—Russian S-400s, six of them. Those'll have to be taken out early on."

"Shouldn't be too hard," someone toward the front said.

"Yeah, but it's got to be in the plan. Last thing we need is Congress on our case because a couple of our planes get shot down."

A murmur of agreement went around the room. "Okay," said the general, and clicked the control again. A map of Tanzania appeared, marked with the location of military bases. "The only friendly state we've got anywhere close is Kenya, and they've clashed with the Tanzanians a couple of times recently, so a lot of the Tanzanian forward bases are along the Kenyan border, and four of the six S-400 systems are there. That means there's going to be some fighting when the troops go in."

That set off a murmur through the room. "Any chance we can avoid sending in the troops at all?" someone asked. "Get an insurgency going with special forces and mercs, slap on a no-fly zone, take out the government that way?"

The general shook his head. "We can't risk the kind of stalemate we got in Syria, and if we don't get boots on the ground fast, the Chinese could probably give us one."

"Any chance they'll try anyway?" This from the back of the room.

"Hell of a risk for them to take," said the general. "Still, we can get an intel assessment on that. One way or another, the plan is to get it done fast and clean."

"Before the 2032 primaries," somebody added.

There was a moment of silence, and then the general shrugged. "You know the score as well as I do. What's that bit from Clausewitz? War is an extension of politics by other means? I don't think he was talking about election campaigns, but you never know." Another click, and the lights came up. "Any more questions? Okay, let's get to work."

21 March 2029: The White House, Washington DC

"Fair enough," said President Weed, and set the briefing papers down on the table in front of him. "Any more discussion?"

Half a dozen glances flicked toward Stedman, but the Secretary of Defense was silent, his lips taut. He had spent the previous half hour arguing against the proposed invasion of Tanzania, and lost.

"No? Okay." He flipped through the papers to the executive order authorizing the project, signed it. "Let's get this thing rolling. Is there anything else on the stack?"

"No, sir," said Stedman. No one else contradicted him.

"Fair enough," Weed repeated. "Nine o'clock Monday, unless something comes up. See you then."

Stedman got up and headed for the door. "Bill," Weed called after him. "If you've got a minute."

He stopped, waited while the other members of the National Security Council left. "Bill, I know you think this is a bad idea," said the president. "I hope you'll still help make it work."

"You're the boss," said Stedman. "If I ever get to the point that I can't do my job, you'll have my resignation."

"If you ever get close to that, you come talk to me. I value your experience—hell, all of us do."

Stedman gave him a bleak look, thinking of the obvious exception. "I'll do that."

"Thank you." Weed cuffed him on the shoulder. "Take a break this weekend. You look like you could use it." He turned and left the Roosevelt Room. After a moment, Stedman followed.

THREE

24 April 2029: Arusha, Tanzania

McGaffney came out of the door of his hotel, glanced up at the gray wet sky, and started up Sokoino Road. After two months in Dar es Salaam, interviewing politicians and TPC executives about the new oil discovery, he'd been ready to head just about anywhere else, but the editors back in Brisbane wanted more on the story, so he'd compromised and gone inland for a bit. Arusha, right up against the mountains and the usual starting place for Serengeti tours, was always good for a travel section story; he'd made arrangements to stay there for a couple of days, get something written to pay the bills, then go somewhere less crammed with tourists and try to find a story that mattered.

First things first, though. Thursday night meant there'd be a café concert on the grounds of the old German fort; that would be worth a paragraph or two, maybe a few leads, maybe someone to keep his bed warm for a night or two. A few minutes of walking got him there, and a smile and a few bills slipped into the palm of the maître d' got him the table he wanted, a little two-seater with his back to a corner and a good view of the whole place.

He settled into the chair, ordered a local beer—you could tell the Germans had colonies in East Africa back in the day, the beer was that good—and then took in the crowd. Arusha drew a lot of tourists and it also was where most of the big international charities had their East African offices. Still, that didn't explain the men two tables away, dressed like civilians but sitting like soldiers, who were downing beers and talking to each other in American accents.

The art of observing while looking intent on something else was one that McGaffney had mastered years and continents earlier. He plopped his tablet on the table, started typing, paid for his beer distractedly when the waitress brought it and ordered a meal in the same something-else-on-my-mind style. All the while, as his face imitated the frowning and fretting of a writer busy with his story, his attention was on the Americans. He couldn't hear what they were saying, but that didn't matter; he could see their faces clearly enough, and they weren't the faces of men who were kicking back on holiday.

Another American came into the café. He spotted the others, came over. Just then the waitress brought McGaffney's dinner, and he remembered to look distracted. By the time she was gone, the newcomer was sitting with the others, leaning forward, saying something in a low voice.

Screw the travel section story, McGaffney said to himself. This is worth looking into.

5 May 2029: The Presidential Palace, Dar es Salaam

"You are certain of this?" said President Mkembe.

"As certain as a man can be." The director of the Tanzanian Intelligence and Security Service tapped the papers he had placed on the table. "One: our highest level source in Nairobi says that Kesembani's signed a secret agreement with the Americans. Their idea, not his, and he's not happy about it. Two: three newly minted nongovernmental organizations with

US funding have opened new offices here in Tanzania in the last three weeks, and they're getting into contact with leaders of the other parties. Three: close to a hundred Americans have been seen in the middle of nowhere in southern Kenya, near Narok; they're out of uniform but they look and talk like soldiers. Four: a corporation we know is owned by the CIA has leased a great deal of land south of Narok, chattering some nonsense about an industrial park. Five: our people in the United States are convinced that something is up; soldiers' leaves are being cancelled, units are being sent to Texas and California for special training—"

"Where the climate and landscape are like ours. I know." Mkembe sat back in his chair.

"Exactly," said the director. "And now these reports."

"From bars and whorehouses."

The director shrugged. "When men relax, they talk freely—especially when they think nobody around them can understand their language."

The president picked up the last packet of papers, leafed through them. Each reported a conversation overheard in some Kenyan tavern or brothel, where some of the Americans who looked like soldiers happened to spend an hour or an evening. Oh, they were careful enough not to speak too openly of what they were doing, but this turn of phrase made it clear there would be many more Americans coming soon, that one hinted at a big airfield being built in a region where an ordinary dirt landing strip had been adequate for many years: put the pieces together and it was impossible to ignore what they were saying.

"Are you prepared to present this to the cabinet?" the president asked.

"Absolutely."

The president reached for the phone on one side of his desk.

The next two hours were chaotic, as cabinet ministers and the chiefs of the Tanzanian armed forces broke off whatever they were doing, hurried to the Presidential Palace, and were briefed on the news. Finally, though, Mkembe had all of them together, the last briefing was finished and the last question asked, and he had their agreement for the step they all knew he would have to take.

Only then did he have a call put through to the Chinese embassy.

Less than thirty minutes later, the phone rang to tell Mkembe that Jun Yinshao had arrived. He was shown immediately into the presidential office. After the ordinary pleasantries, Mkembe handed him the same briefing papers the cabinet ministers had seen, one at a time, and watched the man's face as the pieces came together.

Finally Jun glanced up from the last page. "This is very serious."

"Quite so." When the ambassador did not say anything else, Mkembe went on. "Since we won our independence, China has been our closest friend among the world's nations. We owe you much already, and it is an embarrassment to have to turn once more to one's constant benefactor and say, 'Please help us again.' But—" He leaned forward in his chair. "If you abandon us now, we are lost."

Jun considered him for a moment. "All I can promise is that I will relay this to the highest levels as soon as possible." Then: "But that much I promise you."

6 May 2029: The August First Building, Beijing

General Liu Shenyen got up from his desk and walked over to the windows. His office, high up in the headquarters building of the People's Liberation Army, had an unsurpassed view of central Beijing: the Forbidden City lay spread out before him, with the walled Party enclave of Zhongnanhai full of trees and blue lake water beyond it. After a decade of stringent antipollution campaigns, the air was almost clear enough to see the suburbs further out. The spectral shapes of wind turbines rose through the haze in the middle distance, wheeling silently against the pale sky.

He stood at the window, barely noticing the landscape before him, and then turned back to his desk, picked up the stack of papers: the long message from China's ambassador to Tanzania, two briefing papers from the intelligence department of the People's Liberation Army, and a third from the Ministry of State Security, China's principal intelligence agency. All four documents told the same story, freighted with grim implications and dazzling possibilities.

Liu considered the papers one more time, then went to his desk phone, picked it up, punched a number. Two rings, and then a familiar voice: "General! A pleasure to hear from you, as always. What can I do for you?"

Liu wasted no words. "Are you available for lunch today?"

"Of course. A game, or …"

That earned a fractional smile. "In a certain sense."

A brief silence, then: "Excellent. I will look forward to it."

They settled on a restaurant, ended the call. Liu glanced at the clock on his computer screen, then sat down with a sigh and spent the next hour taking care of routine business. In theory, a vice chairman of the Central Military Commission should not have had to worry about routine business. In practice, there was always something the Party or the General Staff Department wanted done at the highest level, and that usually meant one of the vice chairmen got tasked with it, no matter how easily it could have been done by some staff officer a dozen floors further down. Now that China's military concerns circled the globe, that happened more and more often.

An hour later, after wading through reports on the upcoming joint naval exercises with Brazil, Liu shook his head, left his desk and headed for the elevators. Guards saluted smartly as he headed for his car; he told the driver the name of the restaurant, got in back, let himself relax for a moment against the leather seat and then took the reports on Tanzania out of the portfolio he'd brought with him. He reviewed them again, frowning, while the car pulled out of the August First Building's huge garage and threaded its way through the noisy chaos of Beijing's lunchtime traffic.

The restaurant was a few blocks from Zhongnanhai and drew nearly all its business from within the walled Party enclave; it had no sign and no name, just a street number. The doorman and the hostess both recognized Liu at once and greeted him effusively. He chose a table for two in a secluded corner, next to a window overlooking the little walled garden in the center of the restaurant compound, and sipped tea while waiting for his guest.

He did not have to wait long. "General! I trust I have not kept you ..."

Liu got up. "Not at all, Fang. It's good to see you."

Fang Liyao, professor of strategic studies at the Academy of Military Science in western Beijing, beamed. "Likewise."

The waitress appeared the moment they both sat, and for the next hour the two men ate dim sum and talked about irrelevancies: the doings of their wives, the latest projects at the Academy, the latest gossip from the upper circles of the PLA. Finally, when the meal had reached that pleasant moment when two cups of green tea made everything perfect, Liu reached for his portfolio and said, "By the way, I would be grateful for your advice on something."

Fang considered him. "Ah. I wondered how soon you would move your chariot."

Liu smiled; the chariot was a piece in xiangqi, the Chinese variant of chess, which both men played avidly. "Good. Very good." He handed Fang the briefing papers on the situation in Tanzania, watched while the other read through them.

Fang finished the last briefing paper, handed them back to Liu. "Fascinating," he said. "Do you think it's at all possible that the Central Military Commission might be willing to take certain risks over this?"

Liu smiled. "You see it too."

"Of course. The Americans are immensely vulnerable if they go ahead with this."

"My thoughts precisely." He leaned forward. "I need a plan of campaign that I can present to the other members of the Commission. If you need time off …"

"That won't be necessary." Fang's face took on an abstracted look. Liu knew the look well; he had seen it many times across a xiangqi board, the only warning he could expect before some dazzling series of moves that left his position in tatters and his general in check.

"That won't be necessary," Fang repeated after a long moment. "I can have something suitable ready within three days."

"Thank you."

"Thank you, General," said Fang. "I welcome the chance to be of service to the Motherland—and it is a fascinating problem. A most fascinating problem."

7 May 2029: Stone Town, Zanzibar

McGaffney let the crowd carry him off the ferry and through the terminal into the narrow streets of Stone Town, the old capital of the island chain. Clouds piled up over the Tanzanian coast behind him, brought by the *kusi*, the southwest monsoon that made April and May the wettest months of the year. Still, the trip across from Dar es Salaam had been fine, with barely a drop of rain, and sunlight splashed across the old stone houses that gave the town its name.

This was familiar ground. McGaffney had been to Stone Town half a dozen times, most recently to cover the riots in 2023. The cause of the trouble, a big bronze statue of Zanzibar's most famous son, looked sardonically down at him as he crossed the street near the Big Tree. FARROKH BULSARA, the pedestal said, and below in smaller letters for the tourists: FREDDIE

MERCURY, 1946–1991. The old quarrel between Muslim morals and local pride had broken out into five days of free-for-all when that was unveiled.

This time he was looking for riots that hadn't happened yet. He considered the options and headed deeper into Stone Town.

He knew exactly what to look for, since the American way of manufacturing insurgencies had been glued in place since the 1990s and the post-Soviet color revolutions in Eastern Europe. Once the target for regime change was picked, it was targeted by nongovernmental organizations—the title was a joke, since the organizations in question got all their funding from the CIA's black budget, but that was always the official label—with the cover story of promoting democracy and the real goal of stirring up trouble for the offending government.

Locals with grievances provided deniability, but mercenaries brought in from the nearest US-friendly nation provided the muscle for the riots that followed. If the target government didn't send in the tanks, the mercs and the locals brought the country to a standstill with one swarming attack after another, and tried to force the government to panic and accept exile. If the tanks came rolling in—and they usually did these days—the local cadres called for American help, which was normally right there on the borders waiting, and that was the end of it.

Once the riots started, media people from all over the planet would head for Tanzania, and only the idiots among them would have any doubt about what was happening. McGaffney was there first, though, and didn't mean to miss the chance to grab the story and follow it all the way down, get a series of lead articles, maybe a book contract. That meant Zanzibar, for starters; there had always been strains between the once-independent islands and the mainland, exactly the sort of thing the Americans liked to target.

He spotted the first handbill a couple of blocks into the maze of narrow streets: Swahili but written in Arabic letters, an

30

old Zanzibar habit, ranting about something the government in Dar es Salaam had done and tossing around phrases like "occupied Zanzibar." There was another one a few blocks further on, and another one a block after that; he stopped at the third to snap a picture and take some notes.

"Well, well!" said a voice behind him. "What brings you here, Tommy?"

McGaffney turned, putting his best bland expression on his face. He'd recognized the voice at once: Hafiz al-Nasrani, a stringer for al-Jazeera who worked most of the same beats he did. "Looking for a tourist story. You?"

Hafiz smiled, tapped his ear twice, and said, "I'm sorry, what was that? My ear doctor tells me I have a terrible time hearing bullshit."

"Bastard," McGaffney said appreciatively. "Willing to trade?"

"Of course."

There was a café a few blocks away, a cramped little place with a few old men sipping tea out front. McGaffney ordered a local beer, Hafiz asked for tea and murmured something in Arabic to the proprietor; McGaffney didn't catch much of it, but "infidel" and "doesn't know any better" were in there somewhere. The drinks came, money changed hands, the proprietor vanished, and McGaffney leaned forward. "You saw what I was reading. Recognize the style?"

Hafiz nodded. "Too well."

"What got you down here?"

"Rumors in the Gulf. Nothing too specific, but put them together and it means the Americans are getting ready to invade somebody. With the new oil find, it wasn't too hard to guess where. And you?"

"Head up Arusha way sometime," McGaffney said, "and start counting military haircuts."

"Most interesting." Hafiz sipped at his tea. "Have you gone to Kenya?"

"Good God, no. With my reputation? They'd scoop me up and rendition me as soon as I got across the border."

"I went." Another sip of tea. "Nowhere near the place that matters, which is south of Narok. There is, you'll be interested to hear, an industrial park being built there."

"By an American corporation, I bet."

Hafiz nodded. "You'd recognize the name."

McGaffney took a long pull of his beer, then stopped, and set it down next to his chair where it couldn't be seen from the street. The background of street noise outside the café had taken on a raw and ugly tone, which turned moments later into running feet and shouting voices. The mob wasn't far behind it, maybe fifty young men, running down the street toward the center of town. None of them paid any attention to the café and the people in it.

When the mob was gone, Hafiz frowned. "I didn't expect that to start this soon."

"They're on a tight timetable," McGaffney reminded him. "Dry season's coming, and you can bet that Mkembe and his people are going to catch on right quick, if they haven't already."

"True." Hafiz sipped more tea. "And they won't be alone, I would guess."

11 May 2029: The August First Building, Beijing

"This is insane," said General Yang Shao, looking up from the briefing paper. "You cannot be serious."

"Quite the contrary." Liu glanced at him, then around the table. From their expressions, most of the members of the Central Military Commission agreed with Yang: no surprises there. Now, to convince them otherwise—

"Unacceptable." This from Ma Baiyuan, a gray-haired old warhorse who served as the other vice chairman of the Commission. "You risk gambling away some of our most important strategic advantages on this plan of yours. We cannot afford that."

"If not now, when?" Liu asked. "Year after year, decade after decade, we have poured more money than the Motherland can easily afford into gaining strategic and tactical parity with the Americans, and now we have it. You have all seen the same intelligence reports I have; you know how much real strength they have left, and where their weaknesses are. This situation in Tanzania is a golden opportunity to take advantage of those weaknesses."

"There will be other opportunities," Yang said. "We gain nothing by haste."

"I beg to differ." Liu leaned forward. "Sooner or later we will have to go to war against the Americans. They know that just as well as we do. The only question still to be settled is whether it will begin at a place and time of our choosing, or of theirs. The longer we delay, the greater the likelihood of the latter. That is why we should strike now."

"I am inclined to agree," said a voice that had not yet spoken.

Heads turned abruptly. Chen Weiming, President of the People's Republic of China and chairman of the Central Military Commission, considered them, tapped one finger on the table.

"We must never forget," he said, "not for a moment, that political power comes from the people. They lend it to us, that is all, and the term of the loan lasts only so long as we provide them with the things they want and need: order, prosperity, the chance to hold their heads high in the world. If we fail to give them those things, nothing else matters.

"Do you know what they are talking about on the street corners all over China? They are talking about Tanzania—about the oil and the prospects for jobs overseas and here at home. The internet is buzzing with it. If we let the Americans take that plum from our hands and walk away with it, how will the people react? And how will our allies in Africa react if we show

33

them that we will do nothing for them if the Americans decide to attack them next?"

"And if the Americans attack our interests elsewhere, or assault the Motherland directly?" Yang asked.

"As Liu has reminded us," the president responded, "there will be war sooner or later, so those risks cannot be avoided."

"Unless," said Liu, "we can prove to the Americans that they have nothing to gain by such actions. My plan suggests a way to do that."

The president turned to him. "That is true. You have made us a tempting proposal. My question now is whether you are willing to set aside your other duties and take personal responsibility for this project."

The room got very quiet. Liu nodded. "My intention, should the Commission accept this plan, was to offer to do so."

Yang gave him a long dubious look across the table. "I am still opposed to the project, but if the other members of the Commission support it, I will not stand in the way."

"Does anyone else wish to speak?" the president asked, glancing around the table. No one did, and he turned back to Liu. "You will take charge of this project immediately. If the reports are correct, there is no time to waste. Keep the rest of us informed of your requirements and actions. Anything else?" He glanced around the table again. "Let us proceed, then."

16 May 2029: The Presidential Palace, Dar es Salaam

"Yes, of course," said President Mkembe. "Please send him up at once."

The days since his last conversation with the Chinese ambassador had been the most difficult he'd ever known. Not that anything bad had happened, quite the contrary: Life went on as usual, and that was exactly the problem. His oldest granddaughter had just announced her engagement to a charming young man who was, not coincidentally, the youngest son of a close political ally of his; the bid to host the African Games in Dodoma in 2036 was proceeding well; the latest monthly petroleum production report from TPC was as good as anyone could have hoped—and all the while, he knew that the United States would shortly sweep all this aside, and everything else, with a torrent of planes and bombs.

He shook his head, waited for Jun Yinshao to come in.

When the two of them were alone in the presidential office and had finished the pleasantries, Mkembe considered the other man. "You have a response from Beijing?"

"Of course," said Jun. "And one that you may find encouraging. We will be intervening in this situation."

When nothing more was forthcoming from the ambassador, Mkembe said, "I would be interested in the details."

"I have not been told them. Neither has anyone outside our Central Military Commission." Jun leaned forward. "One of the vice chairmen of that committee has been released from all other duties to take charge of our response."

"I seem to recall that such a thing does not happen often."

"It is very nearly unprecedented," said Jun.

Mkembe considered him again for a long moment. "What you are saying," he said finally, "is that for the time being, we will simply have to take it on faith that China will do something to stop the Americans. So be it. Perhaps, though, you might communicate to the vice chairman that the Tanzanian government and Army will be most ready to assist once we know what it is that we are supposed to do."

"I believe," said Jun, "that your excellency will be fully informed when the time comes."

19 May 2029: The Kremlin, Moscow

"So." Gennady Kuznetsov, President of the Russian Federation, pushed the printout across his desk. "What do you think of this?"

35

The man on the other side of the desk took the paper, glanced at it. "Curious."

Kuznetsov chuckled, a little dry sound like paper crumpling. "No, Misha. I mean it. What do you think of it?"

They said in the Army barracks that you could break a bottle of vodka over Mikhail Bunin's head while he was thinking, and not a muscle in his broad plain peasant's face would stir until he had decided how to respond. Years ago, when he was a junior officer, they said the same thing to his face, and Bunin's unchanging reply was, "Try it." No one had ever quite dared, and now that he had the four stars of General of the Army on his shoulder straps and the reins of the Russian Federation's military in his massive hands, it was safe to assume that no one ever would.

Kuznetsov sat back, folded his fingers together, and waited as Bunin read the printout a second time. "The Chinese are planning a war," the general said at last.

"Exactly. A week ago, everything was proceeding in the normal way. Now they want to reschedule the summer exercises, and send someone here to arrange, at the highest levels, for aircraft they won't specify to make flights they won't specify over territory they won't specify, except that it isn't ours. They are indeed up to something. The question is what."

"I don't know," Bunin said.

"Understood. I want your best guess."

"Tanzania," Bunin said at once.

In the silence that followed, the tick of the clock on the far wall seemed loud. Kuznetsov leaned forward. "Do you really think they will risk intervening?"

"I don't know," Bunin replied. "You asked me to guess."

The possibility hovered in the air, uncertain, dazzling. "If that's true," Kuznetsov said then, "if it might even possibly be true, there should be no hindrance to it from our side. And the Americans—" Old and bitter memories stirred; he silenced them. "The Americans must not find out about it."

FOUR

20 May 2029: The August First Building, Beijing

"That is the situation," Liu said. "The only question is how China will respond."

The men listening to him in the cavernous meeting room were the best of China's best, tough, capable, and patriotic. He'd spent most of three days searching through the PLA's huge personnel database to find the people he wanted—the people who could make Fang's plan a triumphant reality.

"For decades now we have dealt with such events by biding our time, trusting to patience, minimizing our losses and pursuing our goals by other means. The Americans were strong and we were weak; the Americans had the technology and we were struggling to modernize—you know those words. At the time, they were good advice." Liu considered the officers before him, then: "But that time is over."

He could see eyes light up as the words sunk in, and went on at once. "During the next few months, the Americans will provoke an insurgency in Tanzania, prepare an invasion force and send it into action. They expect to brush aside Tanzania's armed forces and set up a puppet government that will pour Tanzania's oil into American tankers, not ours. That is their plan. We know it, and the Party leadership has chosen to act decisively in response.

"The war that is about to be fought will not merely be about Tanzania's oil. What is at stake is the global hegemony of the United States. The Americans do not know this. They do not know that I have been authorized to make use of some of our most advanced weapons systems and some of our most secret strategic advantages to stop them. They do not know that Tanzania will not be left to resist them alone. They do not know that the initiative has already slipped from their hands.

"The Americans must remain ignorant of all this. They must not know when and where the first blow will fall, or the second, or the ones after that. They cannot even be allowed to know for certain whose hand is delivering the blow, not until very late in the struggle. That will not be accomplished easily; it will take the utmost exertions of every one of you in this room."

He nodded to his aides, who began handing out color-coded folders to the listeners. "Each of you has been selected personally for this project. You have been assigned to working teams, each of which will be responsible for one part of the plan.

"One more thing. What we do must remain unseen and unknown until the moment we choose to make it visible, and I have named this project accordingly—Plan Qilin."

That got appreciative smiles from the officers. The qilin, the Chinese unicorn, was supposed to be able to walk on spring grass without bending a single blade.

"So." Liu considered them, nodded once. "We have little time and a great deal to do. You will begin work at once."

21 May 2029: Russell Senate Office Building, Washington DC

"Anything new?" Senator Bridgeport asked.

"Leona Price called," Nora told him. "She'd like to talk to you about something in the appropriations bill."

"Of course. See if she's free for lunch any day next week."

"Sure thing."

Bridgeport thanked her and went into his office. Price was the District of Columbia's nonvoting delegate to the House, a member of Congress in all but name, and a genius at the old-fashioned politics of favors, compromises and backroom deals. If the District needed something, Leona could usually find some way to make it worth your while to vote for it: that was one of the things old hands explained to newcomers on both sides of the Capitol dome.

Bridgeport scrawled a note on the notepad on his desk, reminding him to follow up with Leona. That done, he woke his computer and checked his email.

There was something new from his source in the Defense Department, the same one who'd alerted him to the Tanzania business in the first place. He went to the bookshelf, got Gibbon's *Decline and Fall*, then sat down and started translating the numbers—golf scores, this time—into pages, lines and words. The message took shape on his notepad: *Africa war on for July heads up thirty three fighter wing going.*

That stopped Bridgeport cold for a moment. The 33rd Fighter Wing was his daughter's new assignment down in Florida. He reached for the keyboard, then stopped. He'd resolved years before not to interfere in her career unless she asked for help, and knew better than to think she ever would. He compromised by closing the email, bringing up a browser window, and going to a news site.

The news from Tanzania was about what he expected. Riots against the government had broken out in Dar es Salaam two days earlier, after scuffles between protest marchers and police turned ugly. Somebody at State had gone in front of the media this morning, criticizing Mkembe for, quote, standing in the way of the Tanzanian people's quest for freedom, unquote. There had already been trouble in Zanzibar and a couple of inland cities; a spokesman for the Tanzanian government blamed those on foreign troublemakers. Bridgeport had seen the same things happen in half a dozen other countries where the United States wanted a change of government, and shook his head.

One of these days, he thought. One of these days that sort of thing is going to land us in a world of hurt.

22 May 2029: Expediency Council Offices, Tehran

The concrete office building was indistinguishable from hundreds of others in central Tehran, gray and water-streaked, with curtained windows turning blind eyes to the surging traffic below. Every reference to the building in print or on the internet assigned it to a minor religious charity funded by the Islamic Republic of Iran; it would not be prudent for infidels to know where the Expediency Council, the effective center of power in the more than Byzantine complexities of Iranian government, held most of its meetings.

Inside, in a tightly guarded meeting room, the ayatollahs, bureaucrats, and military officers who made up the Council listened attentively as Ayatollah Husayn al-Jahrami, president of the Council, read the message from China aloud. After he was finished, he set the paper down on the low table in front of him, and said, "I trust no one has any doubts about the point of this request."

"No," said General Farzad Zardawi, the commander of the Revolutionary Guards, who sat next to Jahrami. "None at all— though I admit I am surprised."

"Why?" This from another officer, in the uniform of the regular army. "The Chinese are going to have to challenge the Americans sooner or later; everyone knows that. This is as good an opportunity for them as any."

Jahrami held up a hand. "Whatever their reasons, the Chinese are going to fight, and wish to use our airspace to get their planes to East Africa. You are all aware of the risks we would run by accepting their request—and of the potential advantages."

"To see the Great Satan humbled," said the regular army officer, "it would be worth taking a great many risks."

Zardawi considered him, nodded. "I am inclined to agree."

Jahrami glanced around the room. The oldest of the ayatollahs present, Saif al-Shirazi, a white-bearded veteran of the Khomeini years, cleared his throat. "It is not," he said, "as though we have not been taking such risks all along. The United States will threaten us again, or maybe send cruise missiles or bombers, as they did when we humbled them in Syria. So? Those who are killed will see heaven—and those of us who are still living, we may see something almost as enticing."

"The Americans humiliated?" Jahrami was smiling.

"Or more than that," said Shirazi. "Possibly much more than that."

24 May 2029: PLA facility 2821, Beijing

"The crucial detail," Fang explained, "is the targeting of each blow."

The conference room was small, barely large enough for the eighteen PLA officers who were to be briefed on the overall strategy of Plan Qilin, and located in an out-of-the-way military base in the western suburbs of Beijing. Everyone except Fang, Liu, and the eighteen officers had been told that the afternoon briefing was on the latest inservice training program the PLA was providing for its officers.

"You will all be familiar with the old debates over the proper goal of military action: whether the target is the enemy's will to resist, the mind of the opposing commander, and so forth. All such theories are partly right and partly wrong, as different nations and different eras have their own distinctive strong and weak places. The question is what target is most relevant in any specific case—and with the Americans, that has an unexpected answer."

He clicked the control in his hand, and an image appeared on the screen behind him: a US Navy aircraft carrier with jet fighters taking off from it. "The American military is the most technologically complex in history. The vast majority of American military personnel spend their days operating technologies of one kind or another. That gives them immense advantages, but every advantage comes with a corresponding vulnerability.

"It's one thing to be empowered by technology. It's quite another thing to be dependent on it. The Americans long ago crossed the line that separates those two. Every aspect of their military doctrine and practice depends on the relatively smooth functioning of dozens or hundreds of highly complex technological systems, and most units have no training at all in how to keep fighting should a number of those systems fail."

He clicked the control again, bringing up a map of western Venezuela. "How many of you remember the battle of Maracaibo, early on in the Venezuelan war?" Nods answered him. "Good. The American strategy was predicated on using drones for battlefield reconnaissance and precision strikes. They failed to consider the possibility that some other power might have worked out a way to interfere with the drones' communication links—or that such a thing might be handed to the Venezuelans. It took days for the Americans to regroup, and by then the Venezuelans were able to get forces into the highlands to the west, putting the Americans in an untenable position.

"That was one interference with technology. The plan I have proposed does not stop with one." Fang paused. "Before I go on, are there any questions?"

"The technology of theirs that concerns me most," said one of the officers, "is the one you showed a moment ago. An American carrier group is not a small challenge."

"True," said Liu, who was sitting in the back of the room. "Nonetheless we have certain options there as well. I'll be going to Taiyuan in a few days to see just how ready one of them is to deployment."

25 May 2029: Dar es Salaam

McGaffney sniffed the air, caught the familiar tang of tear gas. Around him, protesters hurried past, wet bandanas over their faces and improvised weapons in their hands. It was going to get ugly right quick, he knew, and crossed the street.

Directly after that first riot in Stone Town, protest marches on the mainland followed like clockwork—marches that turned violent as soon as the police showed up, and it wasn't the police who started the violence, either. There were plenty of ordinary Tanzanians marching, but the professional rioters were easy enough to spot if you'd seen a few canned insurgencies, and McGaffney had been on the spot for more than a dozen. Plenty of hired thugs, and plenty of money going on other things as well: full-color posters accusing Mkembe and the CCM of selling out Tanzania to the Chinese were all over the place.

"Look in the right place, and you will see the future before it happens." An old man in a Johannesburg slum, probably a healer, a *sangoma* though nobody in the neighborhood quite got around to saying the word, told McGaffney that most of a decade ago, and it was good advice. Now, for example: look on the right websites and you'd learn that the USS *Ronald Reagan* had gone steaming out of the Mediterranean via Suez with carrier group in tow. The official version was that they were going to make threatening noises at the Iranians over their involvement in the civil war in Kurdistan. The Iranians had been up to their armpits in Kurdistan for the last three years, like the Turks, the Saudis, and everyone else with an interest in the Kirkuk oil fields, and they hadn't done anything out of the ordinary this summer. There wasn't any real doubt where the carrier group was actually headed and what it would do when it got there.

More protesters ran past him, heading toward the center of town where the action was. Off that way, a dull *whump* sounded, and over the next few minutes the smell of tear gas got stronger. Time to move, McGaffney knew.

He started down a narrow side street as more tear gas grenades sounded behind him. The fast drum-sounds of a 'copter in flight followed, and then another, sharper noise that rang off the walls of the buildings around him: gunfire. McGaffney looked back over his shoulder, saw clouds of tear gas billowing down the street he'd just left, and dim figures running through it, still heading toward the trouble. A moment later, a lone figure came hurrying down the side street, wiping his eyes with a wet bandana.

"G'day, Hafiz," McGaffney said, turning to face him.

The al-Jazeera stringer blinked, grinned. "What a surprise to see you here, Tommy."

McGaffney laughed. "Sure thing. Anything in the Quran about getting struck by lightning for telling lies?"

"Close enough." Hafiz finished wiping his face. "I don't recommend standing here, though. Some of the protesters opened fire on the police, and they returned the favor with interest."

"I bet." They started walking. "A hundred yuan says Weed makes a speech this week denouncing the government here for shooting unarmed civilians," McGaffney said.

"I can't think of a safer bet," said Hafiz. "You've heard about the *Ronald Reagan*?"

McGaffney nodded. "Straight out of the playbook. You wonder why everyone in the world doesn't already know what's going on."

26 May 2029: CIA headquarters, Langley, Virginia

The analyst frowned, scooped up the photos and walked over to his supervisor's desk. "Jamie? If you've got a moment ..."

"Sure thing. What is it?"

He handed her the photos. "These just came in from NRO." The National Reconnaissance Office was the branch of

America's sprawling intelligence establishment that received and processed data from the nation's spy satellites. "It's the PLAAF base at Kashi."

"Western Xinjiang?"

"That's the one. Look at the planes."

She did. "They've got some J-20s forward based out there."

"Not that many, and not these planes. Look at the tail numbers in this one." He tapped one of the photos, a blowup of an angle shot that allowed the serial numbers on the planes' vertical tails to be read. "Those planes are Fourth Fighter Division, out of Liaoyang. Any idea what they're doing on the other side of the country?"

She considered that for a moment, picked up the phone and dialed. After a moment: "Fred? Yeah, it's Jamie. Can you come over here when you have time?"

He walked up to the desk three minutes later. "What've you got?"

"Do you know any reason why J-20s from the PLAAF's Fourth Fighter Division would be in western Xinjiang right now?"

He blinked, and then broke into a broad grin. "You guys are on the ball. Yeah, we just got the decrypts. Beijing's gearing up for a big exercise with the Russians and the rest of the SCO in Kazakhstan, air and ground both."

She nodded after a moment. "Okay. I figured it was worth asking."

"Oh, no question. Good job catching that." He turned and walked away. She gave the analyst a silent thumbs-up; he grinned, went back to his cubicle, and put the photos into a folder in a locked filing cabinet.

At that same moment, on a different floor of the same building, another analyst in another CIA directory pushed a stack of papers across a table. "This is the fourth one this week," he said to the three others in the conference room. "Three from our people in Tanzania, one from South Sudan. Groups of young Chinese men, civilian IDs, civilian cover stories—"

"PLA tattooed all over 'em," the section head said, nodding. "Go on."

"Thirty-one of them that we're sure of, and we've probably missed some. Arriving by commercial airlines, no two with the same itinerary."

"The Chinese aren't dumb," said the section head. "They've got to have some sense of what's coming down in Tanzania. The question is what they plan on doing about it."

"I can think of two possibilities." The analyst tapped the table with a finger. "One, they might be military observers out to get a good look at our tech and operational doctrine in action. In their place we'd jump at the chance to do that."

"Granted. And the other?"

"They might be there as technical advisers to the Tanzanian military. They know who's going to win—as you say, they're not dumb—but they might want to make it messier and more expensive for us."

The section head considered that. "Unlikely, but you're right that it's possible." He pushed back his chair. "I want all three of you to track this, and get our people on the ground following up on it. If these guys are talking to the Tanzanian military, we need to know that right away. If not—hey, if they want to see just how hard the US kicks ass, let 'em."

Over the days that followed, more J-20s appeared in China's far west and more young Chinese men surfaced in various corners of East Africa. None of the latter showed any sign of contacting the Tanzanian military, so no one at Langley gave them a second thought.

28 May 2029: Military aerospace testing facility, Taiyuan, Shaanxi Province

"This is—" Liu found himself briefly at a loss for words. "Impressive."

"Thank you, General," the facility head said, beaming. "We are of course grateful for the constant support the Commission has given to this project."

The cruise missile in front of him was five meters long, and every millimeter of it from the bulbous nose to the angular geometries of the tail fins was shaped to evade radar and fly at supersonic speeds. Stubby wings amidships folded into the body until launch. Liu raised his eyes from the missile to the one behind it, and the next, and the next: there were more of them in the cavernous hangar than he could count.

"Truly a revolutionary weapon," said the facility head. "Every major power these days has supersonic cruise missiles. But a supersonic cruise missile that can be unloaded from a shipping container, armed and targeted in a few minutes using satellite data, and launched from any flat surface? That is quite another matter."

"My one concern," Liu said, "is the targeting process. How safe is that from detection?"

"That's the beauty of it, General." The facility head's smile broadened. "There are no signals from the missile at all—not during targeting, not in flight. One burst of encrypted data from a satellite or a drone, and the onboard and launch site computers do the rest."

Liu considered the missiles again, began to nod. "And active radar countermeasures?"

"One missile in ten contains those instead of an explosive warhead—we used the same countermeasure device that's in the Yingji-90 cruise missile. Size and weight limits don't allow us to put both in the same weapon, not if it's going to have carrier-killing potential, but we've calculated that one radar-countermeasure missile per nine warheads will keep losses to antimissile fire within acceptable levels."

"Very good." Liu turned to the man. "How many of them can you have operational within two weeks?"

"We can provide ..." The facility manager pursed his lips. "If needed, up to two hundred seventy-two missiles in that time, fully operational and loaded in shipping containers. Possibly six more, depending on how readily we can get certain parts."

"You'll have them. Get them ready at once; my staff will contact you to arrange the transport."

The man's eyebrows went up. "All of them, General?"

"Yes." Liu glanced back at the missiles. "We will be confronting the world's best navy. We can't afford to leave anything to chance."

28 May 2029: 33rd Fighter wing headquarters, Eglin air force base, Florida

Colonel Melanie Bridgeport came into the meeting room with a binder tucked under one arm. The other lead officers of the 33rd were already there—Brigadier General Michael Mahoney, the wing commander; Colonel Ed Watanabe, who headed the Operations Group, which ran the flying squadrons of the wing; Colonel Arnie Biederman, in charge of the Combat Support Group, which included engineers, communications people, and other ancillary services. She closed the door behind her, nodded greetings to the others, crossed to her usual chair.

"It's our baby," Mahoney said as soon as she was seated. "Officially, we're still going to Nellis for the Red Flag exercises next month. In fact, we'll be in Kenya, running air cover for this business in Tanzania. The orders just came in: they want two squadrons there and the third here on standby."

"Anything out of the ordinary?" Watanabe asked.

"Nope. SEADS—" The acronym meant Suppression of Enemy Air Defense Systems. "—and air strikes against government and military infrastructure, then air support for the Army as they go in. If everything goes according to plan, we'll be home sometime in August." Mahoney turned to Biederman. "They've got a Red Horse battalion in Kenya already, but you'll want to get your own people over there soonest to make sure we get what we need on the ground."

Biederman made a skeptical noise down in his throat. "Shared base?"

"Yeah, with the Army. At least it's the 101st."

"Good. I can work with those guys." Biederman made a note on his yellow pad.

"Mel—" The general turned to Bridgeport. "What about the planes?"

"Two squadrons won't be a problem," she said. "Three might be. 58th and 59th Squadrons are good to go, but we've still got field mods to finish on nine of the 60th's planes, and some of the parts are backordered at the factory. Binghamton has everyone he's got working on that."

"The usual," said Mahoney.

"Pretty much. If we need another squadron in a hurry, you may have to get one chopped from another unit."

"If possible," Watanabe, said, "not Lardbuckets."

Mahoney scowled, but didn't argue. "We've got the world's best pilots here at Eglin," he liked to say, and it was true, or close enough as didn't matter. What the 33rd didn't have was the world's best planes. Lined up on the concrete a short walk from the HQ building were sixty-two F-35s, the current problem child of American military aviation.

Mahoney was still in the Academy in Colorado Springs back when the F-35—they called it the Joint Strike Fighter then— was being pitched to the media as the next great revolution in military aviation: one plane that could carry out the whole range of air combat and ground support missions, and do them all better than anything else that flew. He'd been based out of Bahrain, flying F-16 patrols over the Persian Gulf and waiting for the Iranians to try something stupid, when troubled flight tests and spectacular cost overruns started casting a shadow over the program. He'd been dodging ground-to-air missiles in an F-22 over Syria when the first F-35s were delivered to training squadrons stateside, and turned out to be—well, not a bad plane, but not a good one: too heavy to be really fast, too low a thrust-to-weight ratio to be really maneuverable, too loaded with cutting-edge technology to be as reliable in service as a frontline fighter needed to be. The attempt to make it a jack-of-all-trades had succeeded in making it the master of none.

Most of America's allies had already wiggled out of buying the thing by then, and after the media and a Congressional subcommittee got through with the program, production of new F-35s had been stopped at a fraction of what was originally planned. Now all the scuttlebutt out of the Pentagon was about the F-43, which might be ready for service by 2038 if everything went well—but in the meantime Mahoney was stuck with the F-35, and so were his pilots. The plane's official name was the Lightning II, but everybody at Eglin called it the Lardbucket.

"We use the tools we've got," he reminded Watanabe. "It's not as though the other side has anything like a modern air force."

FIVE

"Operation Blazing Torch," Jameson Weed said aloud. "Nice."

Ellen Harbin smiled her tight little smile. "Thank you. One of my staffers suggested it."

Weed nodded, picked up a pen, signed the final orders for the Tanzanian operation. Outside the Oval Office, roses glowed in the bright June sun.

Stedman looked on from the other side of the room with a silent frown. He'd tried several times over the past month to bring up the small but real chance that the Chinese might decide to intervene, and had his advice dismissed by Weed and mocked to his face by Harbin and Gurney. The minute this thing was over, he told himself for the fifteenth time, he would hand in his resignation.

"Anything else?" Weed asked. "Okay, keep me posted on the preparations." He tapped the comm button on the desk. "Margie? Tell the Brazilian ambassador I'll be with him in ten minutes. No, make that twenty. Thanks." Another tap of the button silenced the comm, and he turned to the national security adviser. "Ellen, I'll want an update on the situation in Spain first thing tomorrow. Can you do that?"

"Of course." She waited for a moment longer, then turned and left the room with the others. Stedman moved to join them, but Weed said, "Bill."

Stedman stopped, let the others go. When the door clicked shut behind them, Weed went on. "I know you still don't support this thing."

"I don't see any point in discussing that further," Stedman said.

Weed got up from his chair. "Bill, we don't have a choice. Take a look at this." He pulled a report in a red binder out from a drawer of the desk, waved it. After a moment, Stedman crossed the room, took it and opened it.

"I asked Lloyd for a confidential review of our energy situation back in February," Weed said. "Not just the usual how do we get through until the next election sort of thing—a review in depth, going ten, twenty years out. The short version is that we're screwed."

Stedman looked up from the report. "That's been in the classified part of the Pentagon's annual threat assessment paper now for years."

"I don't mean screwed someday." Weed turned abruptly away, went to the window, faced out into the rose garden. "Everybody who's sat in this office since Nixon has been told that, and spent his time here kicking the can four or eight years down the road while the scientists tried to come up with something to keep us afloat once the shale fields run out. You know the score: ethanol, wind, solar, fusion, hydrates—one goddamn subsidy dumpster after another. None of it's lived up to the hype—for God's sake, none of it's even paid for itself, and we can't kick the can much farther because we're running out of road."

"I know," said Stedman.

"We're down to the dregs," Weed went on, as though Stedman hadn't spoken. "Mexico's down to the dregs. The North Sea's down to the dregs. Canada's got tar, Venezuela's got tar, but who can spare the natural gas to process it into oil any more?" He turned around, faced Stedman. "Oil hit $200 a barrel again this morning. That's bleeding our economy dry."

"Jim," said Stedman, "I know."

"Then why can't you see that we've got to go ahead with Blazing Torch?"

Stedman considered him. "Tell me this," he said. "Eleven billion barrels sounds like a lot, but that's not going to last forever. What happens when it's gone?"

"That's why I've asked Congress to triple the Department of Energy's research budget for next year."

"Jim," Stedman said then, "that's not an answer."

Weed said nothing for a time, and his face tautened. "It's not going to happen on my watch," he said finally. "Not if I can help it. Not if all it takes is knocking over a goddamn Third World country that doesn't have enough brains to sell their oil to us instead of the Chinese. Once that's done, we'll have a little more breathing room to figure out our next step."

Stedman didn't answer. After a moment, Weed turned away.

"You think I'm just kicking the can again," he said. With a bleak little laugh: "You're probably right. After the shit I had to eat and the deals I had to make to get into this goddamn office, though, I'm not going to be the one who's holding the bag when the bottom falls out." He walked over to the window again, and stared out at the roses. Stedman waited for a while, then turned and left the Oval Office.

6 June 2029: The Presidential Palace, Dar es Salaam

"This is …" President Mkembe tried to find an adequate word, failed. "Ambitious."

"But well within your military capacities, I believe," said the Chinese officer. He had arrived that morning from Beijing, in civilian clothes, under an assumed name, and with a cover story as a cultural-exchange official. "If there is anything that seems unreasonable …"

"Not at all." Mkembe considered the plan outlined in the papers before him. "I notice, though, that nothing is said here about the American navy and air force."

"That is quite correct, your excellency. You need not concern yourselves with those."

Mkembe gave the man a long, steady look. "Very well," he said finally. "We will leave those matters in your hands."

"Excellent. I have one more favor to ask, if I may. I will be presenting similar plans to several of our other African allies. If someone from your government could accompany me and assure them that Tanzania is already preparing to follow these plans, that would be very helpful indeed."

"I trust that our deputy minister of defense will be adequate," said Mkembe. "As you know, we are facing a crisis here."

"Of course," said the officer. "If it will be possible for me to brief him this evening, we will proceed to Lusaka tomorrow."

"Certainly," said Mkembe. He picked up his phone, asked the secretary to get a message to the deputy minister, exchanged a few more pleasantries with the Chinese officer, and wished him a safe trip as he left the office. Once he was alone in the room, he read through the papers again and shook his head. Then, on an inspiration, he pulled open his desk drawer, took out a well-thumbed Bible, and with eyes closed and a brief muttered prayer, opened it at random and put down a finger.

7 Lo, this is the man that made not God his strength: but trusted in the abundance of his riches, and strengthened himself in his wickedness.
8 But I am like a green olive tree in the house of God; I trust in the mercy of God forever and ever.

Mkembe drew in a deep breath, let it out. There was no question in his mind which of the players in this game was trusting in the abundance of its riches, and if invading another country to steal its oil wasn't strengthening itself in its wickedness, he couldn't imagine anything that would qualify. Very well, then: he would trust in the mercy of God.

Which, at the moment, seemed to be taking the form of the Chinese.

19 June 2029: South of Narok, Kenya

Melanie Bridgeport shouldered her duffel and went to the door of the C-130 transport. Outside was darkness, with the lights of the new base scattered here and there like stars; the air smelled of fresh damp dirt.

When she got down to the tarmac, an Air Force staff sergeant came up to her. "Colonel Bridgeport? Welcome to Camp Pumbaa."

She grinned, catching the reference to the old Disney film. "Thank you."

"General Mahoney wants you at HQ at seven, so—" He glanced at his watch. "You've got two hours. I can drive you to your quarters, get you anyplace else you need."

"That'll be fine." She followed him to a Humvee, threw her duffel in the back and climbed in as the engine roared to life.

Her quarters amounted to a trailer most of two miles from the airfield, lined up with others in long monotonous rows across the flat and mostly treeless ground. She got her gear stowed, took the time to wash and change clothes, and had the driver take her to the mess hall for coffee and a couple of doughnuts before getting to HQ with a few minutes to spare. By then the sun was up and she could see Camp Pumbaa in all its rawness—she remembered from briefings that there had been nothing but empty savannah there, and the Red Horse air base construction battalion and their opposite numbers in the Army had to start from bare ground.

The HQ building was one more big blocky prefab structure. She thanked the sergeant, got out of the Humvee, went inside.

"Mel!" General Mahoney's face lit up when he saw her. "Good to have you here. I hope the flight down from Bahrain wasn't too bad."

"Slept through most of it," she told him, "so I guess so."

"Good," he said, abruptly serious. "You're going to have to hit the ground running. It's—" He shrugged. "The usual. Tight schedule, plenty of fubars, and just try getting enough air transport."

"I'll see what I can do. Martell's still scrounging trucks stateside; I'll tell him he needs to steal us some C-130s while he's at it."

That got a grin from the general; Major Jack Martell was in charge of the 33rd Transportation Squadron, and his talent for getting access to trucks and planes technically assigned to other units was legendary. "Anything he can get, we can use," Mahoney said. "You gotta wonder sometimes what planet the Pentagon thinks it's on."

24 June 2029: Dar es Salaam

Engines roared and voices shouted as the first of the shipping containers came down onto the dock. The CSC *Hainan*, the ship offloading them, was just one of half a dozen huge container ships moored at the Dar es Salaam docks, packed with Chinese consumer goods for the booming Tanzanian economy. There was no record of the fact that twenty-eight of the containers originally loaded on board in Guangzhou harbor had been replaced at night, under cloud cover, during a stop at Sittwe, Myanmar's main port and the location of a big Chinese naval base.

Like the thousands of other containers aboard the CSC *Hainan*, those twenty-eight were hauled to the storage yards and signed over to the trucking firms contracted to take them to their destinations. The riots in Dar es Salaam stayed well away from the port facilities, which would be needed later by the Americans and the new government they expected to impose; the security guards around the storage yards carried automatic weapons, but that was to prevent ordinary theft. The only signs of trouble that reached the containers were the smell of smoke and the drumbeat sounds of government helicopters circling the center of town.

One by one, as trucks could be found, the containers found their way to commercial districts in a dozen ports along the northern Tanzanian coast, and went into warehouses rented by an assortment of little import-export firms. No one had any reason to notice that the employees at these particular warehouses were all young Chinese men who had recently arrived from overseas, or that whatever arrived in the containers stayed out of sight inside the warehouses as the last of the rainy season ended and the cool dry weather of July began.

Those containers were only the first of just over two hundred that would find their way to Tanzania in the month before the fighting began, all in small batches mixed into the cargoes of ordinary container ships. Each of them arrived and found its way to a warehouse or a storage compound somewhere in the country. Another two hundred containers found their way to South Sudan during that same month, offloaded at a dozen East African ports and hauled to the Nile valley like any other freight. The CIA agents in Dar es Salaam, watching for signs of a conventional military response, missed them completely.

11 July 2015: Academy of Military Science, Beijing

"They can't possibly be that foolish," Liu said.

Fang smiled. "Quite the contrary. They are Americans; they have no other choice."

They were in Fang's office in the Academy of Military Science complex, a spare little room with bookshelves lining the walls on three sides. The final preparations for Plan Qilin were well under way.

Liu gave him a baffled look. "Perhaps you can explain."

"Of course." Fang waved the general to a chair, and perched on the corner of his desk. "Do you know what makes America different from any other country in the world?" When Liu motioned for him to continue: "They have never lost a war."

"Vietnam, Iraq, Afghanistan, Syria, Venezuela," Liu countered, but Fang shook his head at once. "There's a difference between losing a war and being unable to win one," he said. "In each of those, they decided when to withdraw, and under what terms. They have never been beaten, never been forced to accept whatever terms the other side chose to offer."

Liu nodded, granting the point. "Go on."

"They literally can't imagine losing a war, and that affects their thinking in ways that are hard for us to imagine. You know that they fought a civil war at the same time as the Taiping Rebellion? Very similar, really; a region tried to break away from their national government. Your family's from Nanjing—do you happen to know if any of your ancestors fought for the Taiping Heavenly Kingdom, or against it?"

"I have no idea."

"Exactly. But in the southeastern states of America, where their rebellion happened, most people not only can tell you the side for which their great-great-grandfathers fought, but in which units and which battles. Many of those whose ancestors fought for the rebellion still feel the most intense bitterness toward the victors. Why? Because they were defeated, and Americans simply have no idea how to deal with that.

"That's a tremendous disadvantage, in two ways—no, three. The first is that their political leaders, when they decide to use military force, never think of asking themselves what the consequences of defeat might be. It quite literally never occurs to them that they might be defeated. At worst, they think, they might not get the kind of victory they desire. It is unimaginable to them that their actions might risk America's global position, or even its survival.

"The second is that, once they've begun a military venture, the political leaders don't have the option of backing out if they fail to achieve their goals. To do that, even to advocate that, is enough to end a career or worse, because a nation that has only known victory can't tolerate even the semblance of defeat. So, once committed, they keep on trying to achieve victory even when the only rational decision is to withdraw. Escalation has always worked for them in the past; more precisely, escalation has never caused them to lose, and so it's the only thing they know how to do.

"The third is that since American military officers are taught to expect victory, they have no idea how to direct a losing situation to their own benefit. The kind of generalship that plays for time, frustrates the opposing forces, draws out an inevitable defeat until the enemy is ready to grant generous terms in order to limit his ongoing losses—they know nothing of this; all their training blinds them to it."

"Thus what happened in Korea." Liu was nodding again, slowly.

"Or the first year of the Pacific war. If the American commanders in the eastern Pacific had known how to lose skillfully, they could have pinned down any number of Japanese naval and ground units, dangling the bait of decisive victory before the Japanese and then snatching it away again, while the American fleet recovered from the Pearl Harbor attack and prepared an overwhelming offensive. Instead, they collapsed completely, and made their nation's victory much harder than it should have been.

"Consider what happened afterwards, though. The Japanese really couldn't have done a worse job of planning the war. They started with an attack on American territory, thus uniting a nation that had been deeply divided about the potential conflict. Next, they overextended themselves tremendously, and then surrendered the power of maneuver by refusing to withdraw forces from untenable positions. Thus they allowed the

Americans to win by doing the only thing Americans know how to do: keep on hitting with more force, and still more force, until the other side collapsed. They didn't need to do any of those things."

"If you were the Japanese high command," said Liu, "what would you have done?"

"Exactly what we're doing in East Africa," Fang replied at once. "Force the Americans to play the aggressor; their national ideology doesn't allow them to be comfortable in that role. Act through allies and proxies, and maintain the good opinion of neutral countries. Let the Americans think the initiative is theirs, until it's taken from them. Anticipate each escalation they will make, have assets in place to counter each escalation, and then wait for the next one. They will throw one asset after another into the conflict, until everything they have is at risk, and then—you know the rest."

Liu sat back in the chair, considering. "And if they escalate even then?"

"We'll be prepared for that as well. And when that doesn't give them the victory they expect—why, then they'll be left with nothing at all."

SIX

Senator Bridgeport closed the door to his office, went to the bar and poured himself his habitual bourbon. Four ice cubes, this time: even with the building's air conditioning running full tilt, the air was warm and stuffy. The "new normal"—that was what the media called the brutally hot weather, when they couldn't get away from saying something about the shifting climate. Everyone else had less printable terms for it.

He sat down at his desk, clicked the trackball, started going through the daily news feed. Forecasts said there would be no letup in the drought that was hammering the western half of the country—no surprises there, most western states were in extreme drought two years out of every three these days. The states of Iowa and Georgia had just suspended payment on their debts, roiling the financial markets; the National Weather Service had just released a bulletin on a hefty tropical storm, poised off the Windwards, that could turn into the season's first big hurricane.

Bridgeport sipped bourbon, skimmed past that to the news on Tanzania. There wasn't much, at least in the US media; pundits in the major newsblogs who favored the Weed administration were making the usual noises, denouncing Mkembe as a tyrant and mouthing pious talk about America's duty to spread democracy, while those who opposed Weed were mostly avoiding the subject. None of them were rude enough to mention oil, of course. Over on social media, meanwhile, the only people who bothered to dispute the claim that the Tanzanian crisis was all about oil were the administration's paid shills. And Mel's in the middle of it, he thought irritably. Why the hell couldn't her unit have stayed stateside?

The latest Rasmussen poll was out, too. It had Weed's approval rating down to 22 percent, which was still three times what Congress could count on and well over twice what any of his most likely opponents in the 2032 election were getting. Only 7 percent of Americans believed that the country was on the right track, which was a new low. Bridgeport cupped his chin in his hand. That number wavered up and down, but the overall trend was no surprise to anybody who'd been outside the Beltway any time recently. There was a sour taste in America's mouth, no question, and a lot of it had to do with what was happening, or not happening, in Washington DC.

Down at the bottom were some of the numbers that mattered. The stock market was down hard, with financials leading the way on the news from Iowa and Georgia; unemployment was up again—real unemployment, that is; the official number had been massaged down again, but nobody even pretended to pay attention to that any more. The price of gas, which was up over $6 a gallon in May, had slipped a bit since then and averaged just over $5.50 nationwide.

Ordinary news, Bridgeport thought, on an ordinary day. He shook his head, remembering how far from normal those stories once would have been. Once this mess in Tanzania was over, he decided, it would be time to start pushing for some changes.

15 July 2029: Zhongnanhai, Beijing

Tea splashed into two cups. "Something's about to happen," said Liu Meiyin.

Liu Shenyen glanced up at his wife, startled. "Oh?"

She smiled a smile that gave nothing away, set down the teapot.

The room in which they sat and the house surrounding it could have been a good deal larger, given their joint income, and the decor was understated almost, but not quite, to the point of austerity. She'd suggested both those details when their parallel careers finally earned them a place in the guarded Party enclave of Zhongnanhai, and he'd agreed, knowing that her instinct for the appropriate gesture was keener than his.

He allowed a smile of his own as she waited for him to pick up his teacup. "Will I have to beg you for an explanation?"

Meiyin gave him an amused look. "Oh, quite possibly." Then, as he took the cup: "It's simple enough. Partly, you haven't been this quiet about your work since Xinjiang."

He nodded, conceding the point. That had been an ugly business, suppressing a Muslim insurgency among the Uyghurs; that his precise handling of the campaign had earned him his place on the Central Military Commission didn't banish his distaste for the measures the PLA had had to use.

"Partly, though, it's the news from Africa," Meiyin went on. "The only public responses from Chen so far have been rhetorical. I can't believe that he'll sit back and let the Americans take Tanzania—and nobody I know in the Ministry of Trade has gotten instructions to wind up activities there."

He met her gaze directly, and though he said nothing, she read the answer and bowed slightly in response.

Liu considered his wife, and smiled again. Their marriage had been purely a political match at first; they'd been young and ambitious, aware of the ways they could use each other to advance their careers, and sufficiently pragmatic to let that outweigh fonder and more foolish concerns. He'd assumed the two of them would be allies and occasional bedmates; he hadn't expected them to become close friends, or that he'd come to rely so often on her advice, but both those had happened as they climbed their parallel routes through the intricacies of the Party's hierarchy to their current positions, hers high up in the Ministry of Trade, his just below the zenith of the People's Liberation Army.

"I hope one question won't be inappropriate," Meiyin said then. "How much are you risking?"

"Personally?" When she nodded: "A great deal."

Her expression didn't change, but he knew her well enough to sense her concern. "If it's any comfort," he said then, "Professor Fang is advising me."

"Ah." She nodded after a moment. "I will hope for the best, then."

16 July 2029: Aboard the USS Ronald Reagan, CVN-76

Rear Admiral Julius Deckmann stepped onto the flag bridge, answered the salutes of his subordinates with a nod and his habitual "At ease, gentlemen." Below, visible through the slanted windows of the flag bridge, the flight deck of the *Ronald Reagan* and the aircraft parked on it soaked up the harsh tropical sunlight; all around, broken only by the gray shapes of other ships in the task force, blue ocean ran straight out to the horizon.

"Anything new?"

"Yes, sir," said the lieutenant at the comm console. "The ships from COMPSRON-2 are under way. *Gettysburg* and *Gridley* will meet them at eighteen-hundred."

"Good," said Deckmann. COMPSRON-2 meant Maritime Prepositioning Squadron Two, the fleet of fully loaded supply ships the US kept in Indian Ocean ports to meet the logistics needs of military operations anywhere on that side of the planet. The four freighters from Diego Garcia and the supplies they carried were essential to Operation Blazing Torch. "Hawkeye spotted 'em yet?"

"Yes, sir."

Deckmann went to the comm console as the lieutenant punched up the data feed from the E-2C Hawkeye airborne early warning plane high above the task force. Onscreen, blips from nine of the eleven surface ships in the task force moved across otherwise empty sea; to the west was Diego Garcia's ragged loop of islets, the COMPSRON ships heading northwest from there, and two task force ships, USS *Gettysburg* and USS *Gridley*, closing with them. The radar didn't show the Hawkeye and the half dozen fighters Deckmann had ordered aloft to watch for trouble, but a poke at an onscreen button would change that, and the admiral had no doubt the planes would be where they were supposed to be.

He wondered why none of that made him feel less uneasy.

A career surface-navy officer with half a dozen combat assignments behind him, Deckmann had learned to trust his intuition, and his intuition told him that something wasn't right. He went to the windows and leaned forward, hands propped against the heavy glass. Two thousand miles away lay the Tanzanian coast, already chopped up by the planners into military targets to be bombed, oil facilities to be seized, landing zones to be cleared and used, and all the rest of the ordinary geography of amphibious warfare. The operations plan was straight out of the textbook, the forces under his command more than adequate for the mission, and the other half of the operation, the Army's half, was in good hands—he'd worked with Jay Seversky on joint-force operations in Venezuela, knew he could trust the man to do his job. None of that silenced the whisper of incoming trouble, off somewhere in the back of his mind.

He turned toward the others. "I want a Global Hawk up tomorrow, and I want it to stay up until we're close enough in for tactical recon. This should be a piece of cake, but I'll be damned if I'm going to take any chances."

"Yes, sir." The lieutenant commander who handled liaison with the air wing made a note on his tablet as Deckmann looked back out to sea.

17 July 2029: The August First Building, Beijing

"The last cruise missile unit reported in yesterday morning," said the aide. "They're at Pangani, here." His laser pointer moved across the map of Tanzania, stopped well up the north coast. "All of the units are ready to launch the moment the war begins."

"Have American planes overflown those sites?" This from Ma Baiyuan, whose mouth was twisted in a hard frown.

"No, sir. Our people and the Tanzanians have both been watching for that. The Americans have satellite data, of course, but nothing else."

The table facing the screen was draped in red. Behind it sat the entire Central Military Commission. President Chen was the only one in civilian clothing.

"Go on," said Liu.

"Of course, sir," said the aide. "Our planes are all in place, and we've made all the necessary arrangements with the Russians, the Iranians, and the Central Asian republics. Russia's been particularly helpful; they've moved planes and units into Central Asia to match our buildup, for the sake of the cover story."

Yang Chao, the ground forces commander, turned to Liu. "I hope the Russians aren't playing a double game with Washington."

"We've had assets from the Ministry of State Security watching for any evidence of that, in Russia and America both. There's no sign of it—and there are the stories about Kuznetsov."

"That he has some sort of grudge against the Americans?" Yang gestured, discarding the possibility. "Rumors are no basis for sound policy."

"Ignoring them," said Liu, "is not necessarily a basis for sound strategy." He nodded to the aide, who went on.

"The Tanzanian military's done everything we requested, and units from Zambia and Mozambique are moving north to join them; our other African allies have agreed to send their own forces once hostilities actually begin. At that point, our people in northeastern Tanzania will hand over some weapons systems the Americans don't expect."

"You anticipate a ground war?" Ma asked.

Liu answered before the aide could. "Unless the Americans back down at once, yes. It's been included in our plan from the beginning. We beat them soundly in Korea, remember."

"That was a long time ago," said Ma.

"True. Doubtless they need a reminder."

Chen chuckled, but said nothing.

"As for the Americans," said the aide, "they are doing exactly what our intelligence reports predicted." The map of Tanzania went away, replaced by a satellite photo of blue water with long gray shapes moving across it. "The USS *Ronald Reagan* and its supporting ships, with four transports from Diego Garcia. They will be in striking range of the Tanzanian coast within days." Another satellite picture, which Liu recognized at once: the Kenyan countryside south of Narok, with the hard lines of runways stark against the greens and browns of the autumn savanna. "Two squadrons of F-35 fighter-bombers are being moved from the US to Tanzania via Europe and the Persian Gulf, and units of the 101st Air Assault Division are already in place."

"Which tells us," said Liu, "how they plan on conducting the invasion. American airborne and air assault units each have their own distinctive military doctrine and mission profiles. The Marine units aboard the fleet are much the same—a little more flexible, perhaps. Still, there's no question of what the Americans have in mind."

Ma made a skeptical noise in his throat, a little like a growl. "And if they change their minds and do something different?"

"They'll be handicapped by a lack of proper equipment and training. You've seen the reports from our intelligence assets in the United States; you've seen the satellite photos. The units assigned to this operation trained for it by the book."

"It astonishes me that they would let that become public knowledge," said Yang.

"Does it?" Liu turned in his chair to face him. "It's been so long since they have had to hide their intentions from anyone that they've very nearly forgotten how. I don't mean tactically—they haven't lost their wits completely; we have no idea exactly where they plan to cross the Tanzanian border, what the initial targets of the invasion will be, and so on. No." He turned back to the screen; the aide had clicked back to the map of Tanzania. "No, it's their overall strategy and military doctrine they no longer know how to hide. If all goes well, they're about to learn just why that's a mistake."

22 July 2029: The Presidential Palace, Dar es Salaam

"Look at this," President Mkembe said, flinging the paper down onto his desk. "Is there nothing too shameful for them?"

The officials gathered in the president's office glanced at each other, said nothing.

"The Tanzanian Freedom Council," Mkembe went on, irony heavy in his voice. "Whom nobody knows, and no one ever heard of, until the United States decided it wants our oil. Now these nobodies call on the nations of the world to liberate Tanzania from tyranny—as though any nation in the world is listening except the United States. As though any nation in the world has the least question about the point of this business."

Abruptly he sat down, slumped forward, put his face in his hands. "I know," he said, "I am rambling." He raised his head, considered the others. "What is the latest?"

"The riots here and in Dodoma are apparently over." General Mohammed Kashilabe, chief of the Tanzanian Army, walked over to the map on the wall. "As best we can tell, the CIA pulled its mercenaries and special forces units out of both cities yesterday, and sent them toward the Kenyan border."

"That implies," said Mkembe, "that the invasion is imminent."

"Exactly. The naval radar stations at Wete and Kilindoni have tracked unidentified aircraft out over international waters in the last two days—quite a few of them. They match the radar signatures of American naval aircraft. And of course you know about the base at Narok."

"Of course." The covert American air base had been a buzzing hive of activity for more than a week; Tanzanian air-defense radars on Mount Meru had tracked one transport after another flying in from somewhere to the north.

"All this together—" The general spread his hands. "Certainty belongs only to God. Still, I would be lying to you if I said I expected the Americans to wait another week."

"Understood," said Mkembe. "And the Chinese?"

That was the only question that mattered, he knew. If the Chinese meant Tanzania to go down under the American assault, then down it would go. If otherwise—

"I think they are preparing something," said Kashilabe. "I have no idea what. I cannot even point to any one thing to prove the thing. But our forces are ready to follow their plan—and so are those of our very good friends in Zambia and Mozambique."

"That is something," Mkembe admitted. "The others?"

Kashilabe turned to the foreign minister, who said, "They are—waiting, I suppose would be the best word. Like the rest of us, they want to know what the Chinese will do."

"I wish we had that option," said Mkembe. "Well." Then, after a moment: "If this thing could begin at any moment, it would be idiocy to stay here longer. I will be flying to Dodoma this afternoon. The rest of you have your instructions. Any questions? No? Then may God have mercy on Tanzania in this hour."

23 July 2029: The White House, Washington DC

Jameson Weed came into the White House situation room watch area, waved the staff back to their consoles, stood there as the screens brought information via satellite link from the far side of the planet. The start of the Tanzanian operation was only hours away. He walked over to the station of the information officer, asked, "Anything out of the ordinary?"

"No, sir. Anything in particular you want to see?"

Weed considered that, shook his head. "No. Keep me posted if anything comes up."

"Of course, sir."

Weed left the room, started back toward the residence. The West Wing was never quiet these days, what with the situation room staff and the other presidential offices there, but this afternoon the murmur of voices and activity he heard around him seemed hushed, tense. No doubt, he told himself. We're about to go to war.

He stopped there in the middle of the corridor, shook his head, allowed a rueful little laugh. War, he thought. In the months leading up to Operation Blazing Torch, plenty of words had been bandied about, but not that one. You didn't say "war" nowadays. You used some nice clean euphemism that didn't have anything to do with young people in uniform facing off against young people in some other uniform and going at it with guns.

He shook his head again, went to the door of the Navy Mess. Andie already knew not to expect him for dinner; the National

Security Council would be there by five, the operation would start at six, and it would be a long night after that. Might as well get something to eat now, he told himself, and tried not to think about the soldiers and sailors and marines who were telling themselves the same thing.

24 July 2029: Aboard the USS Ronald Reagan, CVN-76

The *Ronald Reagan*'s Tactical Flag Command Center, TFCC for short, was belowdecks, next to the Combat Information Center, the captain's station once the fighting started. Both were right up under the flight deck, far enough forward that when planes took off, the pounding of the catapults shook the dimly lit space like the inside of a drum. Just then, though, all was quiet. Officers bent over glowing consoles, monitoring data from the fleet and the ground units via satellite uplink. In the middle of it all, one hand cupping his chin and the other gripping a cup of coffee long since gone cold, Admiral Deckmann waited.

One of the officers swiveled around in his chair. "Sir? General Seversky. Quote good to go, unquote."

"Anything last minute from DC or AFRICOM?"

"No, sir." The digital clock above the man's console showed zero one fifty-eight local time—two minutes before go time for Operation Blazing Torch.

Deckmann nodded. So far, everything had run like a well-oiled machine. He'd spent the last hour or so of daylight on the flag bridge, watching the sun sink into red haze over the distant dark line of the East African coast, checking and rechecking the last details of the operations planning. If there was a flaw in it, it wasn't one he could find.

Zero one fifty-nine.

"Here we go," he said. "Tell Seversky we're on our way."

"Yes, sir." The officer turned back to his console. Dull sounds overhead told of planes being moved into position at the forward catapults.

Zero two hundred.

The roar of the first catapult launch boomed through the TFCC. As the sound faded, a muffled rushing announced the first round of Tomahawk cruise missiles on their way to their targets. Thirty seconds later, a second catapult fired, sending another plane into the air.

Like a well-oiled machine, Deckmann repeated to himself. I hope it stays that way.

24 July 2029: Xian satellite monitor and control center, Shaanxi Province

The duty officer turned in his seat. "Colonel."

"Yes?" Footsteps echoed in the hush of the half-darkened room. "Ah. I see."

The screens showed infrared images from three different spy satellites high above the western Indian Ocean. The enemy ships were clearly visible against the cool ocean waters. The shapes that caught the colonel's attention at once, though, were smaller and brighter: the distinctive flares of cruise missiles taking off, and the longer, redder streak as jet aircraft left the deck of a carrier.

The colonel crossed to another desk, where technicians were calculating the paths of the missiles and planes. After a brief, murmured consultation, he went to a third desk, picked up the telephone. "General? The Americans have launched their attack." A moment later: "Yes." A moment later still: "Yes, sir. I will give the order at once."

He nodded to the duty officer, who turned to his keyboard and typed rapidly for a few moments, then hit enter twice.

PART TWO

NEMESIS

SEVEN

23 July 2029: The White House, Washington DC

President Weed came into the White House situation room, glanced around. The big screens on the walls showed data and images from the Tanzanian operation. Every detail of Operation Blazing Torch was right there in real time. Gurney and Ellen Harbin were already in their seats, and Stedman was standing on the other side of the room, watching the whole process with a disapproving frown.

"Sir." The duty officer snapped to attention.

Weed waved him back to his place. "Everything going according to plan?"

"Yes, sir."

The screens agreed with him. One in night-vision green showed the flight deck of the *Ronald Reagan*; F/A-18s were being flung into the air one by one with the sudden jerk of a steam catapult. Another, fed with data rather than imagery, tracked Tomahawk cruise missile launches from the fleet. Over the next few minutes, Weed knew, the Army and Air Force would be getting into the act, and with a little good luck the whole thing would be over in a couple of days.

The door behind him opened, let in Greg Barnett. The CIA director shook Weed's hand. "So far, so good?"

"So far," Weed said; it was a private joke between them, going back to the days when the two of them were both freshmen in the House. "Let's see what the—"

"What the fuck?" It was Gurney's voice, and Weed and Barnett both turned to look. Two of the screens showing images from the fleet had gone blank. Before anyone else had time to respond, the other image feeds did the same thing, and warning texts started popping up on the screens: DATA TRANSMISSION INTERRUPTED.

Weed left the videoconference space and went into the watch area next door. The duty officer was already on the phone as the situation room staff pounded on their keyboards and tried to get a response. He set the phone down, came over to Weed. "Sir," he said, "something's gone wrong with the data downlink from the satellites. I've got technicians on it here and at SPACECOM—they ought to have it working again in a few minutes."

Weed nodded and thanked the man. Down in his gut, though, was the hard cold feeling that something had just gone very wrong.

24 July 2029: Tanga, Tanzania

The cell phone rang. One of the Chinese technicians caught it before it could sound a second time, tapped the screen, listened. The others, watching saw his face tense.

He tapped the screen again, put the cell phone down. "Lushoto's just been hit." Lushoto was the easternmost of the Tanzanian air defense stations, the logical first target for the Americans to strike, and thus the tripwire for Plan Qilin. "Our turn."

It took an instant for the words to register, but then everyone was sprinting to their stations. Lights went down, leaving only a bare minimum of task lighting, and the doors of the warehouse rolled open. Outside, the night was as quiet as a brawling port city like Tanga ever got. Somewhere in the distance, a radio was playing a popular song; closer, traffic murmured.

One of the crews wheeled a long metal shape out into the parking lot in front of the warehouse, hauled on the levers that cranked the launch tube up to the right angle.

"Go," said the chief technician.

The roar of a jet engine cut through the night sounds, and a long lean shape flung itself out of the tube, stubby wings snapping open as it went airborne. It stayed just over the rooftops until it got over the ocean and then dropped to wavetop level. By then another was in the air, and a third was about to follow.

"Hurry!" the chief technician shouted. "They could be here in minutes."

No one had to ask what he meant. The American fleet and the air base near Narok were both too close for comfort, and everyone knew that the first explosion from an American bomb or missile would be all the warning they could expect.

Twenty-seven minutes after the doors rolled open, the last of the cruise missiles based at Tanga was on its way. "Remember your orders," the chief technician shouted over the roar of the rocket. "Stay off the main roads, and watch for planes." Then he was running for his car, a few steps ahead of the others.

24 July 2029: Pangani, Tanzania

McGaffney blinked awake. The hotel room was silent, barring the soft breathing of the girl lying next to him. He lay there staring up into the darkness, feeling the edge of adrenaline, wondering what had woken him.

Then he heard it again: the sudden rush of a jet engine firing, loud at first, then fading with distance. Another followed it, another, more.

He was out of the bed and on his feet a moment later, threw on a bathrobe, headed for the balcony. Not that many hours before, he and the girl had been standing there, watching evening close in above the ocean. The view this time was different: a night sky full of stars, and beneath them lean dark shapes accelerating out of sight, a few meters above the waves, the flare from their engines the only thing he could see clearly. They were coming from somewhere in the warehouse district, moving at blinding speed, heading north and east—

Toward the American fleet. He knew that at once, knew also that the little war he was there to cover had just turned into something much more serious.

Movement behind him, a sudden indrawn breath: the girl was watching, too. "What are they?" she asked in Swahili.

He glanced back at her. "Cruise missiles," he said in the same language. "Somebody's about to get a really ugly surprise." Then: "Once the Americans figure out where those are coming from, this whole town's going to take it. D'you have people somewhere else?"

She stammered a village name he recognized, maybe an hour inland. As good as anyplace else, McGaffney decided. "Get your clothes on," he told her. "I've got a scooter downstairs. It might be fast enough."

24 July 2029: on board the USS Ronald Reagan, CVN-76

"Sir, we've lost the satellite uplink," one of the officers in the TFCC said.

"What?" Admiral Deckmann turned toward him. "Go to backup."

A clattering of keys, then: "Sir, that's not responding either."

Another officer, on the other side of the room, turned toward the admiral. "Sir, GPS has stopped transmitting."

Deckmann stared for a moment, then ordered, "Check every satellite service we've got—and make sure it's not our systems while you're at it."

"Yes, sir." A minute later: "Our systems are working fine, sir. It's the satellite network. The whole thing's down."

"Get a link—" He stopped himself, remembering that the intership data channels used satellite uplinks as well. Fortunately the Navy had been smart enough, or stubborn enough, to leave the old radio system in place as a backup. "Contact the rest of the task force by radio and find out if they're in the same fix."

"Yes, sir."

As the man was repeating the words into a microphone, Deckmann turned to another officer. "Get me Sam." A moment later he was handed a phone handset. "Sam? You've heard about the satellites?"

Captain Samuel McCloskey, the skipper of the *Ronald Reagan*, answered at once. "Yes, sir. I'm assuming it's a technical screwup."

"Might be," said Deckmann. "One way or another, it's going to mess us over good and proper—none of the GPS-guided weapons are going to be worth crap until it gets fixed, and I don't even want to think about trying to coordinate with the ground forces without uplinks."

"We'll have to—" Then, suddenly, silence.

"Sam?"

"It's not technical." The captain's voice was tight. "We've got incoming."

Moments later Deckmann was staring into a screen full of data from an E-2C Hawkeye high overhead. To the southwest, the ocean was alive with radar blips, moving low and fast toward the task force. "I can't identify them by type," said the technician, "but it's a cruise missile signal and they're coming in an evasive pattern at well over Mach 2."

"How many?"

"Heck of a good question, sir. The blips are behaving like radar ghosts, not real missiles—they don't look exactly like the radar spoofing our missiles use, but it's the same sort of thing." He tapped an onscreen button, and the screen shifted to a graphical data analysis. "The blips are up here. All this down here—" He pointed to low uneven lines at the bottom of the screen, like badly mown grass. "—is reflection from waves and spray. The actual missiles are probably in there; they've got radar countermeasures good enough that we can't follow them when they're belly to the waves."

"Any better luck with infrared?"

"No, sir."

"Damn. That's technology on a par with ours." Deckmann leaned forward. "I want to know where they're coming from."

"North Tanzanian coast," said one of the other officers. "We've got radar sign from ten positions there—probable launches."

"Get one of the F-18 squadrons down there now," Deckmann ordered. "I want those hit, and hit hard." The admiral looked around; without data from the satellite uplinks, the TFCC was more than half blind, and he'd never gotten used to the changes in naval design that put flag officers belowdecks in a fight. "How long do we have until those things get in range?"

"Under twenty minutes, sir."

"Long enough." He raised his voice so that everyone could hear him. "We're moving operations to the flag bridge. I'll be damned if I'm going to sit down here in a hole with next to no data to go on. Rashid, get Mombasa by radio and tell 'em what's happening, and then follow. George, let 'em know we're coming."

He was on the flag bridge moments later. By then the flag bridge crew had all the data there was on the screens: input from the Hawkeye and the carrier's own radar systems, and not much else. The links that coordinated radar signals and targeting data between every ship in the task force were down, along with everything else that used satellites. Down below in the radio room, technicians old enough to remember how it was done before satellite links were busy jury-rigging a data net over radio frequencies, but that wouldn't handle more than a small fraction of the flow of information that naval warfare demanded these days.

Night pressed hard against the glass of the windows, broken only by the afterburners of planes hurtling off the flight deck. After a short time, flares of light in the middle distance pushed the darkness back: SM-2 antimissile missiles launching from the cruisers and destroyers. The attacking cruise missiles were in combat range.

A long moment passed and then flashes lit up the horizon: SM-2 warheads exploding. Three of the four Aegis-equipped ships—the *Gettysburg*, the *Mahan*, and the *Gridley*—had moved southwest of the rest of the task force, leaving the *Anzio* as a final defensive screen for the carrier, the transports and the amphibious-warfare ships. Deckmann could see all three of them silhouetted against the glare, bows southwest to minimize target area, as more SM-2s and short-range Sea Sparrows surged toward the cruise missiles, and muzzle flares from the onboard Phalanx batteries, the last line of defense, blinked in the darkness.

For decades, strategists and planners had argued back and forth about what would happen if a carrier group came under attack by a swarm of cruise missiles. Deckmann had taken part in war games, and those had never gone well unless the assumptions were stacked in favor of the carrier group. Still, that was all theory. Maybe, he thought. If the damn antimissile systems do their job—

All at once, a fireball burst from one flank of *Mahan*. One had gotten through.

The hardest part was the waiting. Deckmann had learned that back in his first command, a rustbucket of a minesweeper that worked the Strait of Hormuz, chugging back and forth under the watchful eyes and itchy trigger fingers of the Iranians. He'd been lucky, then and later, but it was always hard to stand there on the bridge and wonder if this was the time his luck would run out. As the first damage reports came in from *Mahan*—she was holed at the waterline and struggling to keep the engine room from flooding—Deckmann's hands clenched on the window ledge in front of him. He took in the reports, gave what orders he could; with the limited data net, each ship's skipper had to do most of the fighting on his own.

A streak of light shot by, maybe a quarter mile ahead of the carrier. It was moving so fast that Deckmann was only sure he'd seen it when it was already well past, a zigzag of blue flame showing the cruise missile's evasive maneuvers as it closed. By then *Anzio*'s and *Ronald Reagan*'s Phalanx batteries were firing, but the cruise missile sped by and slammed into USNS *Charlton*, one of the COMPSRON-2 supply ships. The first fireball was followed by another, much bigger—*Charlton* was full of ammunition. More detonations followed, until what was left of *Charlton* vanished into the dark waters.

By then the news from the data net was getting worse; more of the task force ships had been hit. *Mahan* took a second missile a little ahead of the first, and started to sink; the order to abandon ship went out before *Charlton* was gone. *Gettysburg* was hit close to the bow, and *Saipan*, the big amphibious helicopter carrier, was struggling to control fires amidships. The harsh mathematics of naval combat were coming into play: each ship damaged or sunk meant one less ship capable of launching missiles to keep other ships from being damaged or sunk, and the cruise missiles were still coming.

The first one to reach *Ronald Reagan* hit just aft of center, above the waterline. Deckmann felt the jolt as the missile struck at twice the speed of sound, and then a second, bigger jolt as the warhead went off. Sirens screamed and the carrier's intercom barked orders; Deckmann forced himself to ignore them, and concentrate on his job.

Aft of the carrier, a missile slammed into SS *Peterson*, the COMPSRON-2 tanker. Full of fuel, it dissolved in a huge bubble of flame. One hit *Anzio* a few minutes later, and just afterwards, another fireball burst from *Gettysburg*, and then another. With brutal slowness, *Gettysburg* broke in half and sank. Aghast, Deckmann barely noticed when a second missile hit the bow of the carrier.

The minutes just after that were the worst of all. With three of the four Aegis ships sunk or damaged and antimissile munitions running low, there was little to stop the last of the cruise missiles from finding targets. *Ronald Reagan* took two more missiles in that time, one far enough aft that it did little damage, the other forward and high enough to leave the flight deck heaved up and twisted. In a darkness lit only by fireballs from missile impacts and flames from burning oil slicks, it was impossible to see what was happening to the other ships in the task force, and the flag bridge lost electricity after the third missile hit. Deckmann stood at the window, waiting. For the moment, there was nothing else he could do.

The minutes slipped past. After a certain number of them— how many, Deckmann could never be sure afterwards—he realized that the fireballs had stopped. A few more, and the lights in the flag bridge flickered back on; officers lunged for their consoles, began hammering on keyboards. When the first data came back from the Hawkeye, still circling high above what was left of the task force, the sea was clear of cruise missiles.

A little later still, the door to the flag bridge opened for a young officer in a uniform stained with smoke and fire suppressant. He saluted Deckmann, said, "Commander Johnston, sir. As far as I know I'm in charge of this ship."

Deckmann nodded after a moment. "What's her status?"

"Hull seems to be intact below the waterline, we've got the fires mostly contained, and Engineering says they can probably get 50 percent power to one of the prop shafts—the other one's junk. Let me know what you want her to do, sir, and we'll do our level best to do it."

"Good," Deckmann said. "And—Captain McCloskey?"

Johnston's gaze fell. "I've got people searching, but the CIC got ripped to shreds by that last missile—everything in that part of the boat did. Good thing you came up here, sir; the TFCC is still on fire."

24 July 2029: Camp Pumbaa, Kenya

"It's a mess," said Mahoney. "No bomb damage assessment, no photo intelligence—"

"Can you get something from your planes?" Seversky asked. They were sitting in Seversky's office in the HQ building. Outside, the scream of jets taking off and landing shredded the African night.

"We've got people working on it, but everything's been satellites or drones for fifteen years now, so it's pretty makeshift. Then there's the GPS problem. More than two-thirds of our payloads are GPS-guided, and until the GPS system's working again most of 'em won't function at all. Fortunately we've got plenty of Paveways and Mavericks, and we're reworking everything for the next couple of days to use those instead."

"Good." It wasn't, not really; the laser-guided Paveway bombs and the optically guided Maverick missiles weren't anything like as accurate as the GPS-guided munitions, and orders from Washington insisted on as close to zero collateral damage as possible. Worse, without satellite intelligence to let them know what had and hadn't been hit, the airstrikes were flying blind. Still, Seversky told himself, you do what you can. "The embassy's got a secure line to DC, and I've got a report and a request for new orders on its way. Once they get the satellite thing sorted out we can—"

A knock sounded on the door. Before Seversky could respond, a lieutenant from communications came in.

"Damn it," Seversky barked, "I ordered—" Then he saw the look on the man's face. "What is it?"

"Sir, the fleet's been hit by cruise missiles," said the lieutenant. He was holding out a sheet of paper. "Hit bad."

Seversky took the paper and answered the lieutenant's salute with a nod, but his mind was reeling, as though it couldn't accept that the words he'd heard could mean what they too obviously meant. He blinked, tried to focus on the paper. Black on white, more words spelled out the same unthinkable news. After a moment, he handed the thing to Mahoney, heard the man draw in a sharp breath, whisper an expletive.

"Well," said Seversky. He glanced at Mahoney, turned to the lieutenant. "Let me know the moment Mombasa gets any more news. I'll be in the operations room."

23 July 2029: The White House, Washington DC

The news reached the White House situation room minutes after it got to Seversky. Weed stared at the dispatch for a long cold moment, then handed it to Stedman without saying a word. As it went around from one member of the National Security Council to another, he could hear the sudden gasps and hissing breaths, the whispered profanities and Gurney's loud and characteristic "Fuck!" as the implications sank in.

"Okay," he said finally. "We're going to have to regroup. Waite?"

"Sir." Admiral Roland Waite was chairman of the Joint Chiefs; he looked as though someone had just punched him in the gut. After a moment Weed remembered that Waite had been a Navy fighter pilot, and then a carrier commander, before he'd been assigned to a desk at the Pentagon.

"Where are the other carriers?"

"The *Kennedy*'s in the eastern Pacific en route to Okinawa, sir. The others are stateside."

"Make damn good and sure they stay out of harm's way until we know what happened and can do something about it."

"Of course, sir."

"As for the rest—" He drew in a breath. "I don't want a word of this in the media—not until after the shooting's over. The fleet came under rocket fire from Tanzanian shore batteries, and there were some casualties. That's the official story, and we'll stick to that for now. Got it?"

"I'll get the media office on it right now," Stedman said.

"Please." Weed turned away. Part of him was still reeling from the shock, but reflexes honed by a life in politics were already coming into play. Play this well, he told himself, and you're Roosevelt after Pearl Harbor or Bush after 9/11; screw it up and your political career is over. Still, the first thing was to win the war, and sort out the rest of it afterwards.

24 July 2029: aboard the USS Gridley, DDG-101

By sunrise, the scale of the disaster was all too clear. Three of the task force's ships—the guided missile frigate USS *Crommelin*, the amphibious warfare ship USS *Comstock*, and against all reasonable odds, *Gridley*—had escaped damage; *Ronald Reagan*, *Anzio*, the combat support ship USNS *Rainier*, and one of the COMPSRON-2 transports, SS *Wright*, were still afloat and able to make headway; all the others were dead in the water, sinking, or already gone. Deckmann moved his flag to *Gridley* as soon as a helicopter could get him to the destroyer, and stayed on the scene to coordinate search and rescue, while the four damaged ships limped toward Mombasa and safety. The aircraft from *Ronald Reagan* were already on the ground at a Kenyan military airfield near Mombasa; what was left of the carrier wasn't fit to land a kite on, much less a Navy jet.

"A hell of a mess, no question," General Seversky said. The satellite network was still down, but radio could send encrypted data between what was left of the task force and Army GHQ outside Narok. "If you need anything for search and rescue—"

"Thanks," said Deckmann. "We should be fine. We've had choppers and boats pulling men out of the water since right after the attack."

"Good. Keep me posted. As for the operation, though, I've got a request into Washington for new orders. Without naval backup, we're in trouble; without GPS and the other satellite services, we're screwed—you never think about how much depends on those."

"If we back out now, they're going to have a lot of explaining to do in DC."

"I know," Seversky said. "I'll let you know when I hear anything."

"Thanks." Deckmann waited until the general's image disappeared from the screen, and turned to go.

"Sir?" This from a technician nearby. "Message for you from *Ronald Reagan*."

"I'll take it," said Deckmann, and turned back to the screen.

A moment later Commander Johnston's face appeared, rigid with shame. "Sir," he said, "The *Ronald Reagan* is on a sandbar off Ukunda. I take full responsibility."

Deckmann blinked, then: "Why don't you tell me what happened."

The man's face crumpled. "There were cracks below the waterline," he said, "and the bulkheads inside—well, sir, you saw what hit her. So we were taking on water the whole way, faster than we could pump it out. After a while we had to evac the engine rooms. We had a couple of commercial tugs from Mombasa by then, but they didn't have anything that can handle a ship that big. So we fought the current, and we lost."

"Casualties?" Catching himself: "Any more, I mean."

"No, sir. We got everyone safely on shore, everything classified destroyed or secured per regs, reactors shut down. All our wounded are being trucked to Mombasa right now; the rest of us will be following as soon as more trucks get here."

"What you're telling me," Deckmann said then, "is that you took command of a sinking ship and still managed to get everyone safely to shore. That's what's going in my report."

Johnston gave him a stunned look. "Th-thank you, sir."

"I'll be saying the same thing to my replacement as soon as he gets here. In the meantime, stay with your people and wait for new orders. That's all."

"Yes, sir."

Once the screen was blank again, Deckmann got up. My replacement, he was thinking. Whichever poor bastard gets handed this mess. His own career was over, he knew that—you didn't lose an engagement that badly and end up anywhere but shoreside on a pension—but there was more at stake than one sailor's bad luck. If the Tanzanians could do the same thing to any other naval force, half the military options Washington took for granted had just been kicked out of reach, and whoever got handed this operation was facing a challenge that might not have any good answers at all.

24 July 2029: The August First Building, Beijing

"Here is a satellite image of the American fleet just before nightfall on the 23rd," the aide said. Blue water appeared on the screen, with the gray shapes of naval vessels scattered across it. "The *Ronald Reagan*," the aide went on, indicating it with the laser pointer. "The helicopter carrier *Saipan*. The other ships of the carrier group, and the supply ships from Diego Garcia. You may wish to remember the shapes.

"And here is the first daylight satellite image from this morning."

Liu watched the faces of the other members of the Central Military Commission as the new image went up, and fought the urge to smile. All of them were as shaken as he had been when the image arrived at his desk earlier in the day.

"Our staff here is still analyzing the satellite data and reports from the ground," the aide went on. "A preliminary estimate is that four ships were destroyed during the battle; four more were abandoned today; one is being towed into Mombasa; three are damaged but still able to make headway; three more appear to be unharmed."

"The carrier," Ma Baiyuan said. "The *Ronald Reagan*. What happened to it?"

"Abandoned this morning," the aide said. He clicked the control, and another satellite image appeared: the distinctive outline of an aircraft carrier—but the deck was broken and marked with smoke and fire retardant, the whole thing heeled over at an angle, shadows of a sandbar just visible through the water.

Ma barked out an obscenity colorful enough that the president glanced his way with a raised eyebrow. The old general showed no sign of noticing, though. "How many hits?"

"We think it was hit by four missiles, sir," said the aide.

Liu turned in his seat. "What this means," he said, "is that the era of the aircraft carrier is over, like the era of the battleship before it."

"And the era of American global dominance?" Chen asked.

"That remains to be seen," said Liu. "The next phase of Plan Qilin is beginning as we speak. How the Americans respond to it will tell us much."

24 July 2029: Ukunda, Kenya

Something was up, that was certain. Helicopters racing south at treetop level had shaken Yamaguchi Fumiko awake a few minutes after two in the morning; she'd thrown on some clothes, scooped up her cameras, and sprinted out onto the hotel balcony. Flashes of light on the southern horizon showed that the war was on; she'd gotten fifteen minutes or so of good footage, sweated while a slow internet connection got it uploaded to the Tokyo news bureau that paid her salary, and waited for the next round.

There was no next round, or none that she could see. The next thing to light up the sky was the tropic dawn.

Nobody knew anything at breakfast, and the news media had nothing more to offer. After breakfast, Yamaguchi shouldered cameras and a tripod and headed for the beach, hoping to get some scenic shots if nothing else came up.

She was nearly at the water's edge when he saw it—a gray angular shape breaking the line of the horizon, well out to sea. Through binoculars, it looked like an aircraft carrier. She found a spot with a clear view, popped the tripod open and set it up. Video? Maybe later, she decided; first priority was to get a few stills with the big telephoto lens, identify the ship if possible, and maybe even find out what it was doing so close to shore.

The telephoto lens was as long as her forearm and heavy enough that it needed its own tripod, and it took a couple of minutes to get everything set up. Once that was done, the screen on the back of the camera lit up, blurred, and zoomed in.

It was a carrier, all right—broken, lightless, heeled over so that the deck tilted nearly into the surf on one side. The number 76 in white was still visible on the bow; further aft, black voids showed where something had punched through the steel of the hull like so much paper. In the ocean haze, the ship seemed to hover like a ghost.

Yamaguchi's finger pressed down, gently, so the camera wouldn't shift. A tiny green symbol popped up on the screen, vanished. She adjusted the focus ever so slightly, did not let herself think about what she was seeing: like a good soldier, they said back at the bureau, a good photographer keeps shooting no matter what. Another slight pressure, and the green symbol appeared again. Adjust and shoot, adjust and shoot, until the flashing light warned her that the camera's memory card was full.

Two hours later, the image of the USS *Ronald Reagan* wrecked and abandoned on a Kenyan sandbar hit the world media. For many people, it would become the definitive image of the East African War.

EIGHT

25 July 2029: The White House, Washington DC

"It wasn't a technical failure, sir," said the man in the ill-fitting suit. Weed couldn't recall his name; he was the head of one of the departments over at the National Reconnaissance Office, as close as anyone ever got to the heart of the sprawling US military and intelligence satellite net. "We've still got analysts at work reconstructing the shutdown, but our best estimate at this point is that someone managed to upload malware to the satellite network."

"A computer virus," said Weed.

"Not just one. We've got protections against malware propagation from one platform to another, and there's no sign those were breached. Someone spent a lot of time over the last five or ten years figuring out our data encryption, uploading malware in small batches, maybe even getting rogue firmware installed in satellites during manufacture—there's a lot of different ways to do it, and no reason to think whoever did this used just one."

"Whoever did this." Weed leaned forward. "Any guesses?"

"The ones that shut down first were over eastern Eurasia and the eastern Indian Ocean."

"The Chinese, then."

"They're the most likely candidate."

"If I may, sir?" This from Barnett. Weed nodded, and he went on. "What are we looking at in terms of fixing this?"

"That's the good news. We've got all our staff on this, and every contractor we can find with a high enough security clearance. They're getting a response from some of the satellites. Current estimates—" He opened a folder, checked the papers inside. "We should have at least some secure communications working again in forty-eight hours or so, the GPS system basic functions around the same time, and the military functions maybe a day later, maybe a little more depending on what booby traps got left behind. Reconnaissance is going to take a little while longer—the recon satellites really got hammered. Worst case, we have two on the ground that are being prepped for launch in a hurry."

"What's the status of the Chinese satellite network?" Barnett asked.

"As far as we can tell, fully functioning."

"That should change," said Ellen Harbin, who had been listening to the whole exchange with a savage look on her face. "We've got enough antisatellite capacity to take down their network for good."

"That's a very dangerous strategy," the man from NRO said. "Near Earth orbit is so crowded these days that any ASAT strike could trigger a Kessler syndrome."

"Kessler syndrome?" Weed asked.

"Your ASAT takes out a satellite, sir." The man mimed the impact with his hands. "The satellite basically turns to shrapnel at orbital speeds, eighteen, twenty thousand miles an hour. Any of it hits another satellite, and pow, you've got more shrapnel. Worst case, you get a chain reaction that takes out everybody's satellites and fills low Earth orbit with so much junk that they can't be replaced for years."

"A theoretical possibility," said Harbin.

"We've had three close calls in the last five years."

"There's a more immediate point," said Stedman, who had been sitting in the back of the room. "The Chinese have antisatellite weapons that are as good as ours. We could take out their network, but if they choose to retaliate in kind, ours is gone, too—not just down for a few days—and, bluntly, their military can function without satellites better than ours can."

Harbin gave him an edged look, but said nothing.

Weed looked from one to the other, then turned back to the man from NRO. "Keep me posted," he said. "And let your people know that we're counting on them."

"I'll do that, sir."

The moment the door closed behind him, Harbin was on her feet. "We can't just let the Chinese get away with this."

"We're not going to," Stedman snapped back at once. "I've got two fighter wings and the 81st Airborne on 72-hour deployment alert, with more to follow. We'll have operational plans ready in a day or so, and then it's payback time. The Tanzanians are going to find out the hard way that you don't fuck with the United States, and the Chinese are going to find out that any assets they put in our way are just going to get steamrollered."

"Good," said Weed. "But Ellen's right, Bill. Once the immediate crisis is over, there's going to have to be some kind of reckoning with the Chinese." Before either of them could respond, he held up his hands. "No more bickering, please. We've got to get this job done."

"Yes, sir," Stedman said, his face rigid; Harbin simply nodded.

As the meeting of the National Security Council broke up, Weed put his hand on the CIA chief's shoulder. "Greg, can you stay for a bit?"

Once the others were gone, Weed said, "I want to know how the Chinese did this. No, let's be honest. I want to know who the Chinese got to do this, and why your counterintelligence people didn't catch it. It's pretty much got to have been a mole, doesn't it?"

"Maybe so, maybe not," said Barnett. "China doesn't spy the way we do. They don't spy the way anybody else does."

"That's not—"

Barnett held up a hand. "Let me finish, sir. Say we and the Russians and the Chinese all wanted to know about the sand on a beach. The Russians would put a dozen elite Navy frogmen in one of their attack subs, send them ashore in the dead of night, get a couple of buckets of sand and rush them back to Moscow. We'd drop a billion or two on a satellite with special sand-viewing cameras and send it up into orbit. The Chinese? They'd get a thousand ordinary tourists to go swimming on that beach, right out there in broad daylight, and when they got back to Beijing, every one of them would just shake out their beach towels. They'd end up knowing more about the sand than anybody."

Weed took that in.

"That's what we tell new people in counterintelligence. They start out looking for the kind of spycraft we do, the Russians do, most other countries do, and we have to teach them to start looking for those towels and the grains of sand."

"Understood," said Weed. "But I want you to double-check."

"I'll have counterintelligence all over the satellite programs tomorrow morning. If there was a mole, we'll find him."

When Barnett was gone, Weed turned away from the door and found himself staring at the painting of Theodore Roosevelt. The old Rough Rider looked as though he was about to shake his head in dismay. Weed wondered if he'd ever had to worry about Spanish moles in the Department of War, then shook his own head and headed back to the Oval Office.

26 July 2029: Arusha, Tanzania

McGaffney waited for a gap between cars, then trotted across Sokoino Road. Traffic was bad, though not half so heavy as what he'd had to dodge on the way to Arusha. The American air strikes along the coast sent refugees fleeing inland with everything they could carry; he'd had to leave the highway half a dozen times and go jolting over back roads to get around jams and keep moving away from the coast toward what safety there was.

It had been a harrowing trip, but the first part of it was by far the worst, weaving inland on dirt roads in the darkness while the first fireballs erupted over the roofs of Pangani and the girl he'd been with clung to his back and cried. The fires were still visible when he got to the village where the girl had family; he waited outside the house for a moment to make sure everything was all right, then headed back onto the nearest road east and coaxed the scooter into giving him every bit of speed it could manage. Morning light showed great plumes of smoke rising here and there all along the eastern horizon: he'd watched that and wondered just how big a war this had become.

Still, he'd made it to Arusha, which was probably safer than anywhere else in Tanzania—with all the expats and international charities there, not even the Americans would be likely to bomb it without some very good reason. A few days there would give him time to figure out where the fighting was and where it wasn't, and then it would be time to head back into the thick of things and keep the editors back home supplied with stories.

He was most of the way to the old German fort when a familiar figure came toward him. "Tommy!" said Hafiz al-Nasrani. "Any luck with that tourist story?"

"Filling in a few details," McGaffney said, without missing a beat. "Should have guessed I'd find you here."

"I decided not to take my chances in Dar," said the al-Jazeera stringer. "Probably just as well, given the latest news. Have you heard about the fleet?"

"No, but I watched cruise missiles taking off at Pangani night before last."

Hafiz's eyebrows went up. "I'll fill you in, in exchange for an interview. I could use a witness who was on the scene."

"Add dinner to that," said McGaffney, "and you've got a deal."

"Done. I've got plenty of leeway in the expense account." In a low voice: "This is big. The Americans lost their carrier."

McGaffney stared. "You're serious?"

"Dead serious. It's on a sandbar off the Kenyan coast. Word is they lost half a dozen other ships as well."

"That's more than big." Then, returning to practicalities: "Let's get that dinner. You can fill me in, I can tell you what I saw in Pangani, and then we can hope the Americans don't start throwing nukes around or something."

"I wish that was funny," said Hafiz. "I honestly have no idea what they'll do."

26 July 2029: Camp Pumbaa, Kenya

"And the Paveways?" Mahoney asked.

"I've got a request in stateside," Melanie Bridgeport told him. "They're pretty sure we can fly in as many as we want in two or three days."

"Good." The brigadier general frowned, shook his head. "That'll help, but if they can't get the satellites back up and running soon, this isn't going to go well."

Bridgeport's desk was heaped with paperwork—documentation from the Navy, most of it. In theory, Navy and Air Force computers ran interoperable programs; in practice, ever since the big systems upgrade in 2024, a bug in one of the Navy logistics modules reliably crashed the Air Force system, and repeated software patches from the supplier never fixed the problem. It wasn't considered professional to discuss the fact that the supplier donated heavily to the campaign funds of half a dozen influential congressmen, and so couldn't be replaced by a firm that could actually do the job, but of course that was the score, and every logistics officer in the Air Force knew it.

Under normal circumstances, the computer glitch wasn't a problem, since Air Force and Navy units had their own stocks of missiles and bombs, but these weren't normal circumstances. With all the GPS-guided weapons useless, the naval task force out of action, and the Navy planes that made it off the *Ronald Reagan* flying out of airfields set up for Air Force use, getting the Navy fliers the munitions they needed had suddenly become a first-class mess. All her staff were busy with the ordinary work of keeping a fighter wing supplied and running in combat, so the job of making sense of the Navy system was Bridgeport's baby.

"Any other concerns?" Mahoney asked her.

"Nothing worth worrying about."

"Good." He ran a hand back through his hair. "If we can keep the air assault going until Washington pulls its head out of its ass and decides on a plan B, we can still win this thing."

26 July 2029: The White House, Washington DC

"They bloodied our nose, no question," Weed said. "The question is what we do now."

The National Security Council had just finished watching a presentation about exactly what had been done to the naval task force. Stedman, who already knew the details, spent the fifteen minutes of the presentation watching the faces of the others: Waite's as expressionless as armor plate, Weed's and most of the others appalled, Gurney's baffled and angry. Harbin, though, had leaned forward in her chair, her head tilted to one side, as though each image was a document in a language she couldn't quite read.

Do any of you realize what just happened? Stedman wanted to shout. Have any of you noticed that half our global strategy is sitting on the bottom of the Indian Ocean at this moment? Instead, he sat back, made himself stay silent.

"If we cave in, we're screwed," Weed went on. "We've got to reinforce the troops in Kenya and proceed with the operation. I want a plan on my desk first thing tomorrow."

"You'll have it, sir," said Admiral Waite. "If I may suggest, though—"

Weed motioned for him to continue.

"A plan for extracting our forces, sir. Just in case."

"We can't." Weed all at once looked older than his sixty years. "If we cave in, we're screwed. The whole country is screwed."

The plan was on Weed's desk at six the next morning: a sketchy but viable draft of an airlift operation, using most of the Pentagon's available air transport capacity to get troops and supplies from Europe and the Persian Gulf to Kenya in a hurry. By the time it reached the Oval Office, though, the unfolding situation had already rendered it hopelessly obsolete.

NINE

27 July 2029: Chahbahar Air Base, Iran

Colonel Hassan Gholadegh went to the window as the Chinese tankers began to take off. Chahbahar Air Base huddled on a coastal plain near the far southeastern corner of Iran—halfway between nowhere and Hell, they said in Tehran. You went there when someone higher up wanted to teach you a hard lesson, and when the orders came sending Gholadegh there, he'd racked his brains for days trying to figure out which of his superiors he might have offended. That was before the first advance party of Chinese officers landed, and he began to get some hint of what might be happening.

That was two months back, two months of careful preparations that no American satellite or drone could be allowed to see. Finally the big Chinese tankers came flying in over the brown mountains to the north, low and fast. Now, one by one, they were taking off, heading for a rendezvous with other planes somewhere off the coast. No one had been so careless as to mention, or so rude as to ask, where those other planes might be going, but Gholadegh thought he knew. If the rumors from Africa were more than empty wind …

That was when he saw the contrails, up over the mountains to the east: twenty of them at least. He spat out an obscenity, sprinted up the stairs to the radar room.

The radar technicians were watching them too, though with less surprise. "Word came in twenty minutes ago, sir," said the duty officer. "They're Chinese. Tehran says let them through, give them help if they need it."

Gholadegh went to the nearest screen, watched the blips. "Did they say how many—"

"No, sir."

More blips came in over the mountains. There must be at least a full fighter wing of them, Gholadegh realized, perhaps more. "They're infidels," he said, "but may Allah grant them victory."

27 July 2029: Torit Airfield, South Sudan

The J-20 came in low and fast, touched down, slowed. The ground crew sprinted out as the plane, earthbound now, turned at the runway's end and taxied over toward the hangar; by the time it was clear of the runway, another J-20 was coming in.

The pilot of the first plane hauled himself out of the cockpit, climbed down to the tarmac. Another pilot, suited up and ready, was waiting for him. "No trouble, I hope?"

"A little rough air over the mountains." His head motioned eastward, toward Ethiopia. "Nothing to worry about."

A third J-20 landed on the airstrip. Meanwhile the ground crew swarmed over the first plane, refueling, checking systems, mounting and arming air-to-air missiles for the fight ahead.

"Any word about the American fleet?" the first pilot asked.

"Al-Jazeera says they were hit by cruise missiles. Nobody else is saying anything." The relief pilot shrugged. "They have an air base south of Narok, so either way there's no shortage of them."

A bigger plane came down—a Y-8 turboprop, the transport workhorse of the PLAAF, bulging with the radomes that marked it as an aerial early warning and control plane. "Yet," said the first pilot. "Leave a few for me."

The relief pilot laughed. "Only if I run out of missiles." The crew chief signaled to him, and he climbed up into the cockpit. The first pilot waved and started across the field to the cluster of low buildings on the far side.

The canopy came down, shutting out the engine noise. Systems checks went smoothly, the routine familiar after so many months of drills and exercises. Another signal from the crew chief, and the engine roared to life behind him. A little more throttle, and the J-20 taxied out toward the runway.

The earphone in his helmet crackled, said, "Ndenge moja, akwalika kwa tekoff." It took him a moment to recall the phrase. It was Swahili, of course, since no word of Chinese could be spoken over the air, not yet. A first J-20 took off.

"Ndenge mbili, akwalika kwa tekoff." That was his signal. He pushed the throttle forward. His mouth was dry, dry as old bones, thinking of the enemy planes and pilots waiting for him in the skies over Kenya: the best in the world, or the second best. Soon he would know.

The J-20 shot down the runway, hurtled out of sight over the treetops to the southeast.

27 July 2029: above central Kenya

"Bandits," said the radar operator. Every head in the cabin of the E-3 AWACS plane swiveled toward him, and the officer in charge hurried over. Ever since word had gotten out about the fleet, everyone had been on edge, waiting for the next shoe to drop.

The radar systems on board the E-3 were the best the Air Force had, loaded with data analysis tricks that could extract a signal from the background noise that was all that the latest stealth

technology let through. The operator had shifted his screen
onto NCTR setting—Non-Cooperative Target Recognition—
as soon as something out of the ordinary showed up on the
screen. Now lines of text were appearing on the subscreen:

```
TARGET 001  PRC J20  PROB HIGH
TARGET 002  PRC J20  PROB HIGH
TARGET 003  PRC J20  PROB HIGH
```

"George, confirm that," said the officer.

One of the other operators—there were fourteen of them in
the cabin, seated back to back at big consoles—bent over his
screen, moved a trackball one way, the other. "Confirmed, sir,"
he said. "Not much else it could be."

The lines kept marching down the subscreen:

```
TARGET 014  PRC J20  PROB HIGH
TARGET 015  PRC J20  PROB HIGH
TARGET 016  PRC J20  PROB HIGH
```

The crew knew their jobs, and though the satellite link was still
down, they had other ways to get the necessary data to the Air
Operations Center on the ground and the fighters already on
combat air patrol over Kenya and northern Tanzania. At Camp
Pumbaa, hundreds of miles south, sirens howled, antiaircraft
missiles waited, and flight crews sprinted to their planes, preparing to face a contingency none of the plans for Operation
Blazing Torch had taken into account.

```
TARGET 39  PRC J20  PROB HIGH
TARGET 40  PRC J20  PROB HIGH
TARGET 41  PRC J20  PROB HIGH
```

The radar screens showed one set of F-35s turning to confront
the Chinese planes and another set roaring off the runways

and hurrying north, and the first signals from Navy fighters on their way from Mombasa added themselves to the mix. Via JTIDS, the Joint Tactical Information Distribution System, data streamed out from the E-3 to the fighters and back again. The JTIDS and the powerful radar transmitters in the radome both used Low Probability of Intercept technology to try to defeat enemy detection equipment, and electronic countermeasures gear completed the protective shell. To a sufficiently advanced sensor, though, the E-3 glowed like an electromagnetic sun— and Chinese engineers had spent most of three decades finding increasingly effective ways of detecting and targeting that glow.

As the air battle began, six J-20s broke away from the emerging fight and shot south with afterburners roaring, climbing rapidly toward the E-3. They were faster than the F-35s and equipped with equally good countermeasures gear, and five of them got clear, leaving one to dissolve in a fireball as a US air-to-air missile found its target. No one had any questions about their mission, and the E-3's fighter escort moved to intercept as the last F-35s within range hit their afterburners and raced upwards.

It would not be enough.

While three of the J-20s engaged the American fighters, two closed within missile range of the E-3 and launched high-speed radiation-seeking missiles at it. A moment later, the E-3 vanished in a ball of flame, taking with it the core of the US integrated air defense. The J-20s turned in a tight arc and plunged into the fight with the F-35s.

27 July 2029: Camp Pumbaa, Kenya

"Yes, sir." Mahoney sounded as exhausted as he felt. "That's correct; we've lost nine planes, including the E-3, and we've confirmed the loss of six of theirs."

The fight was still going on in the skies above Kenya. The Navy planes had arrived in time to tip the balance and drive the Chinese planes further north, toward their bases in South Sudan and Ethiopia, but the first wave of J-20s had been replaced by a second. Every other mission the American planes had been assigned had gone by the board, forced aside by the desperate need to keep Camp Pumbaa, its troops and stores, and its airfield from being pounded into uselessness by Chinese missiles.

"That's bad," said the voice through the headset: General Wayne Crawford, the USAF vice chief of staff. Enough satellites were working again to manage the first threads of a communications net. "I've ordered CENTCOM and AFRICOM to get you as much help as you need, as soon as they can."

"Thank you, sir," said Mahoney. "If I may, sir, we need something other than F-35s."

He could all but feel the chill through the satellite link. Plenty of senior staff in the Air Force had built their careers around the F-35 program, and still got defensive when the plane's performance problems came up. Still, it had to be said: "Six of our eight fighter losses were F-35s. The Navy lost one F-14 and one F/A-18, and they were right in the thick of it with us."

It was the right thing to say; nobody in the Air Force wanted to see Navy flyers come out ahead in a combat situation. "I'll see if I can chop you a couple of F-22 squadrons," Crawford said at once. "One way or another, you'll get what you need to win."

"Thank you, sir," said Mahoney.

A minute later he was crossing the bare dirt between the HQ building and the Air Operations Center next to it. A sound like distant thunder came whispering out of the north, echoes of the air battle; closer in, the rising note of jet engines announced a pair of F-35s coming down to refuel, reload, and swap pilots before heading back in. So far, so good, he thought.

That wasn't the mood in the AOC, though. Mahoney felt it the moment he came through the door, and went over to the duty officer's station. "What's up?"

"We've lost two more, sir."

"Lardbuckets?" A quick you-got-it nod from the younger man answered him. "I've just talked with Crawford," he said then, pitching his voice so that the others in the AOC could hear him. "They're chopping us more squadrons—he's going to try to get us some F-22s."

"Good," said the duty officer. "We'll need 'em, sir—we're bleeding."

28 July 2029: The White House, Washington DC

News of the arrival of the Chinese fighters forced the plans for resupplying the four US divisions in Kenya by air into indefinite hold. "Until we establish air superiority," Stedman explained to Weed and the other members of the National Security Council, "there are hard limits to what we can do. Even if we send them with fighter cover, the big transports are sitting ducks for their air-to-air missiles."

The president nodded. "How soon can we expect to retake control of the air?"

"Within a week, if everything goes well. I've got two fighter squadrons on the way in tomorrow, and two more following them in two days."

"What about the air bases in South Sudan and Ethiopia?" Harbin asked. "Those should get hit, hard."

"That would mean," Stedman said, picking his words carefully, "widening the war to include two more Chinese allies. Maybe more than that, if the other African countries in their camp get involved."

"They're already in," President Weed growled. "Diego Garcia's in range; I want a B-1 strike on the Chinese bases as soon as possible."

TEN

30 July 2029: Juba, South Sudan

"How bad was it?" Bill Honnecker asked. A stateside politician rather than a career diplomat, he'd nonetheless learned enough in two years as US ambassador to South Sudan to know what questions to ask.

"Bad." The CIA station chief, Stanley Fukuyama, gave his head a sharp little shake. "They nailed one of the Chinese bases pretty hard, but mostly missed the others—without full satellite data, they were flying half blind, and they had to dodge the Chinese air defense systems, which are as good as ours. At least a dozen bombs hit the town of Torit."

"Casualties?"

"Media's saying at least a hundred dead."

"Shit." Honnecker got up from his chair. "There's going to be trouble over that."

"I know. I've told my people to be ready to evacuate."

Outside the windows, the sky was still dark—maybe half an hour left until dawn. Honnecker considered the options, then picked up the telephone on his desk and punched an internal number. "Manny? It's Bill. I want helicopters on standby to get the rest of us out of here. Yeah, everyone. Let me know when they're ready. Thanks." He hung up.

Down below, in the embassy's communications-intercept center, staffers monitoring local radio broadcasts heard accounts of the bombing of Torit get worse with each retelling. When word spread that the president of South Sudan had called an emergency meeting of his cabinet, that got sent up to Honnecker in a hurry. It wasn't until just after dawn, though, that the Marine sentries on duty reported the thing Honnecker feared most: people beginning to gather in the streets around the embassy, shouting angry words up at the embassy windows.

The embassy compound was for all practical purposes a fortress, designed to withstand anything short of a military assault—most US embassies outside of Europe, and some even there, had been built or rebuilt that way over the previous decade. Even so, defending the compound against an armed mob couldn't be done without civilian casualties, and on hostile territory, that choice had risks that Honnecker wasn't willing to take. Within minutes he was on the phone with the American consulate in Kisangani, safely over the border in the Republic of the Congo, making arrangements to evacuate the embassy staff as soon as helicopters could get there.

He was barely finished with the call when a frosty message arrived from the South Sudanian government, breaking off diplomatic relations with the United States and demanding that Honnecker and his staff leave the country at once.

The next two hours were chaos, as everything that had to be kept out of hostile hands was destroyed, and whatever other packing could get done took place in the brief gaps between that urgent duty. By the time that was finished, the first of the choppers had touched down on the embassy roof, and people were scrambling aboard. Nobody had any illusions about what would happen to any American left behind.

It took four choppers in all to carry the embassy staff to safety. Honnecker was on the third. As it took off and the fourth circled in to get the Marine guard and the last civilian employees, he looked at the mob—tens of thousands of them by then, filling the streets around the embassy compound. Staring down at them, shaking his head, he found himself wondering whether Washington might just have unleashed something it couldn't control.

30 July 2029: United Nations headquarters, New York City

Staff members at UN headquarters liked to joke about the way that the US ambassador to the United Nations, Jeremiah Parks, turned red whenever he got angry. Since he did that as often as anyone contradicted the official positions of the United States, the effect was hard to ignore, and had been a common topic of late night discussions in thirty or forty languages since the early days of the Weed administration. Still, even experienced diplomats were impressed by the shade Parks turned as he listened to the third African ambassador in a row denounce the United States in heated terms for the previous night's air strikes on South Sudan.

"Three hundred twenty-two civilian deaths, your excellency," said the ambassador from Tanzania, a dignified gray-haired woman in bright-colored traditional clothing, with a voice that cut like a lash. "Why? Have the people of South Sudan engaged in acts of war against the United States? Have they attempted to destabilize the government of the United States? Have they set out to steal America's oil, your excellency? Or is it another country who has engaged in all those actions, against a nation whose only crime was to have something the United States wants?"

Parks said nothing. Only those sitting close to him could see that his beefy hands were clenched into fists at his sides.

The real action had already taken place earlier that day in the Security Council. There were two competing resolutions about the East African crisis—one introduced by the United

States, condemning China, and one introduced by China, condemning the United States—and the US resolution had come out second best. Of the permanent members, Britain and France supported the US, though with no great enthusiasm; Russia supported China, and so did India and Brazil, who had gotten permanent seats in the big 2025 reorganization of the UN; only one of the eight non-permanent members had sided with the US. Since it took a unanimous vote of the permanent members to adopt any resolution, technically speaking, neither side won, but the balance of world opinion was clearly not in America's favor.

"If an ally of the United States were attacked by a hostile power," the Tanzanian ambassador went on, "the United States would send planes and weapons; has Tanzania not the same right? If that ally had a friendly country near its borders who offered the United States the use of air bases on its territory for that purpose, the United States would gladly have accepted; has South Sudan not the same right? If the nations of some region of the world friendly to the United States—there must be such a region left somewhere, your excellency, though I confess I cannot name one—were to see a hostile power attacking one of their number, no one would challenge their right to join together to drive out the aggressor; have the nations of East Africa not the same right?

"I want to hear the United States explain to me why its actions in this crisis are justified and the actions of my nation are not. I suspect a great many people around the world want to hear that. Perhaps you'll favor us, your excellency."

She was facing Parks as she said that last sentence, daring him to meet her gaze. He looked steadily at the floor in the center of the General Assembly chamber. Weed's instructions that morning had come by phone, and were set in rock: introduce the resolution in the Security Council, Weed had said, and don't respond to anything anyone says. This will be settled on the plains of East Africa, not in the United Nations.

The ambassador from Tanzania waited for a few more moments, and then sat down. "The ambassador from Zambia," the speaker said, and Parks grimaced and braced himself for the next round.

30 July 2029: The Presidential Palace, Nairobi, Kenya

"It is my unwelcome duty to deliver this," said the Tanzanian ambassador.

"Of course." Mutesu Kesembani, President of the Republic of Kenya, waited while the ambassador took an envelope from his portfolio and placed it on the desk between them, then returned to his place at the far side of the room.

"I was not instructed to wait for a response," the ambassador added then.

Kesembani considered that, waved a dismissal. The ambassador bowed, turned and left the room. Only then did Kesembani open the envelope, extract the paper inside, and read:

To the Honorable Mutesu Kesembani, President of the Republic of Kenya:

As the Republic of Kenya has chosen to allow a hostile power to use its territory and airspace to launch an unprovoked military assault on the United Republic of Tanzania, it is therefore necessary to declare that a state of war now exists between our two countries.

Below that was a familiar scrawled signature, and then:

Elijah Mkembe, President
United Republic of Tanzania

Kesembani shook his head and reached for his telephone. "Latifa? I want Nobrike and General Kashila here in my office this afternoon. No, I don't care if they have something else to

113

do. And contact the Americans; I want to talk to General Seversky as soon as convenient."

He listened for a long moment, then, and his eyes widened. "You may tell the Zambian ambassador," he said finally, "that he may see me at four o'clock this afternoon."

He put the phone back into its cradle, stared at the declaration of war on the desk in front of him. Zambia, too—and that meant China's other allies in East Africa might join in. Not that they would dare to do much, not with the Americans already here on the ground, but it would make for difficulties once the war was over. He shook his head, wished for the tenth time that afternoon that he had never agreed to the American plan in the first place.

31 July 2029: Lunga-Lunga, Kenya

The coast road from the port cities of northern Tanzania to Mombasa, Kenya's second city and largest port, was usually thronged with trucks at every hour. Since the riots started in Tanzania, though, traffic had dropped away to a trickle, and those mostly refugees with family north of the border; since the war started, even that had all but stopped. The soldiers at the Kenyan Army base outside Lunga-Lunga and the border guards further south had little to do but try to get enough connectivity on Kenya's notoriously shaky cellular network to surf the internet, or sit back and watch birds and monkeys flit through the jungle.

The latter wasn't an option at night, and as Corporal Hassan Omumberi tapped at the cheap Chinese tablet he'd bought the month before and watched the signal bars flicker, it was pretty clear that this night, the internet wasn't going to be an option either. He sighed, put his feet up on the rail of the watch station and waited for the hours to pass and his relief to show up.

Just as his watch beeped 3 am, something like thunder rolled in the distance, off to the south. That puzzled Omumberi—the weather forecast had been for clear weather for days to come. He tapped at the tablet again, hoping to get a signal.

He was still tapping when the parade ground to his right blew up.

Stunned by the blast and the clouds of dust and smoke, Omumberi staggered over to the emergency box and pressed the switch. Overhead a siren began to wail. Moments later, another blast ripped through one end of a barracks building a hundred meters away; a little later, a third blast erupted in the middle of the compound where the company stationed at Lunga-Lunga kept its technicals.

The thunder to the south was still rumbling. It was only when he noticed this that Omumberi realized that the base was under artillery bombardment.

He left the watch station then, sprinted across what was left of the parade ground. Another shell shattered a nearby patch of jungle as he ran. Soldiers were spilling out of the barracks, some of them still pulling on their uniforms; Omumberi ducked past them, headed for the old headquarters building. If the land line still worked—.

He reached the locked door and kicked it in. Nobody used the old building except when a VIP came to visit, but it had the one landline phone on the base, and orders were to use that in an emergency so that the message couldn't be intercepted. He found the thing, nearly dropped the handset, got it to his ear, and waited for a long and terrifying moment until the dial tone sounded.

It wasn't until then that he realized that he had no idea who to call. For want of anything better, he dialed an Army friend with a desk job in Mombasa. The phone rang once, twice, a third and fourth time, and finally was picked up; a groggy voice answered, "What?"

"Nkundu, this is Hassan—"

"At three in the morning? Can't—"

"Listen to me! The base at Lunga-Lunga's being bombarded by artillery. We've taken five or six shells. I couldn't find any other number to call."

The friend was silent for a long moment, then: "God help us all. Stay on the line; I'll see who I can get at headquarters." He crossed the room, turned on a light, found his cell phone, and came back. "Hassan?"

The line was dead.

31 July 2029: Camp Pumbaa, Kenya

"Sir?"

Seversky woke slowly out of murky dreams. It took a long moment for the blur looming over him to turn into his orderly.

"Sir, there's an emergency call from Nairobi."

He blinked, sat up. "Who is it?"

"President Kesembani, sir."

"I'll take it, of course. Thank you, Sherman." He threw on a bathrobe and followed the orderly out of the bedroom, picked up the telephone in the room just outside. "This is Seversky," he said. "What can—"

"Kenya has just been invaded, General." Kesembani's voice sounded unsteady. "That was not part of the bargain I made with your government."

"What?" Seversky blinked, tried to clear his mind. "What's happening?"

"Yesterday," said Kesembani, "I received declarations of war from Tanzania, Zambia, and Mozambique. We talked about that and you insisted nothing would come of it." Seversky tried to say something, but Kesembani raised his voice and went on. "This night I am told that three of our bases and our border checkpoint along the coastal highway have been bombarded by artillery and Tanzanian forces have crossed the border."

116

The president's voice rose further, shaking: "I trust you are going to do something about this."

"Of course," said Seversky. With no time to come up with a plan of action, he did the next best thing. "I'll meet with my staff right away, we'll get a plan in motion, and—" If Kenya was being invaded, he realized, the Kenyan Army could be brought in. "Can you meet with us this evening in Nairobi? You and your general staff. We'll get this fixed."

"Thank you, General. That would be welcome."

"Eight o'clock at the Presidential Palace? Good. I'll make sure you're informed if anything comes up before then."

Once the call was finished, Seversky broke the connection, then called the HQ building and had the night crew start calling his staff. He went back to his bedroom and got dressed, trying to think of something other than the obvious, trying to shake a growing feeling that the war he'd landed in was not the one he'd been sent to fight.

31 July 2029: The Presidential Palace, Nairobi

"What you are saying," said President Kesembani, "is that the situation is far from good."

They were sitting on three sides of a long table in a briefing room in the Presidential Palace: the president, four American officers, and six of their Kenyan counterparts. Up on the screen on the fourth side was a map of southeastern Kenya, with colored rectangles marking the positions of Tanzanian and Kenyan forces on either side of a line halfway between the border and Mombasa.

Seversky shook his head. "Not at all, your excellency." He'd recovered his balance by sunrise, gotten new instructions from DC, and felt almost as confident as he made himself look. "With the help of your Army, we can handle this. I've talked to President Weed, and he's agreed to postpone the Tanzanian operation. Right now our top priority is the survival of Kenya and your government."

"That is good to hear," said Kesembani. "If I may ask, though—what is your plan?"

"Counterattack at once. Your troops are holding the Tanzanians—"

"For now," one of the Kenyan generals said. "For three or four more days, maybe."

"That'll be enough. We can have our entire force there in two. The working plan is to come straight down from Nairobi to Tsavo, then move south, closer to the border. We'll hit them on the flank, cut off their retreat, and take them out."

The Kenyans looked at each other. "That seems sensible," said the general who had spoken. "Besides holding the Tanzanians at bay, what can we do to assist?"

"You have equipment we don't," Seversky said. "Technicals, especially, and artillery—until we get air superiority back and can start using our planes for ground attack, that's going to be vital. Manpower's also an issue. We'd like as large a Kenyan force as you can assemble to join with us in the attack, push them straight into the sea, and then show the Tanzanians what an invasion looks like from the other end."

"Let us talk of that when the immediate crisis is over," said Kesembani. "For now, you have a workable plan to save us, and that is good. If the United States could bring more of its Army here, that would be better."

"We're working on it," Seversky said at once. "As soon as we regain air superiority, we can start an airlift down from the Gulf. If the Tanzanians think they can invade a US ally, they're going to be taught a very hard lesson."

ELEVEN

3 August 2029: North of Ukunda, Kenya

The technical bounced and rattled through the darkness, part of a line of trucks pushing north into Kenya, raising billows of dust that could be smelled and tasted but not seen except where the headlamps shone into it. Perched in the back of the technical, Private Kwame Mtesi adjusted the bandana covering half his face, and tried to listen above the noise for another sound, more distant, more deadly.

The Americans were on their way. That had been the word in camp that afternoon, passed down from headquarters: There would be a battle soon, something bigger than the skirmishes and brief firefights they'd had so far with retreating Kenyan forces. The Americans were looking for a fight, and they had helicopters with them, maybe airplanes as well.

That didn't bother Mtesi. He'd served in the Congo in the last two wars, and dodged bullets and rockets from enemy helicopters more times than he could readily count. No, what bothered him was the weapon they'd given him. He liked to handle the .50 caliber machine gun perched up in the front of the bed, pump burst after burst into the cabin and the engine of a helicopter until it went down. Instead, the sergeant had handed him this Chinese toy—a stubby tube half his height with some kind of rocket in it, and a grip, a shoulder pad, and a screen for the guidance system sticking out at various angles.

"Point it at a plane or a copter," the sergeant told him. "Use the screen to see with—it will see in the dark. Wait until it makes a sound like a bell, and pull the trigger. After that you can run for cover—the rocket will follow the target, and blow it up." Mtesi had rolled his eyes, but none of it mattered; Moses Olokumbe was up there next to the .50 cal, and all Mtesi had besides his assault rifle and his bush knife was the Chinese toy and two spare rockets for it.

All at once Olokumbe hauled himself to his feet, staring north the way they were going, the way a leopard does when it scents gazelles. Mtesi turned and listened, and a moment later, caught the sound—the rhythmic drumming of helicopters in flight.

They all knew the drill. The technical shut off its headlights and pulled off the road, into the bush, and everyone on board but that lucky bastard Olokumbe jumped out of the truck and scattered. All the other squads were doing the same thing, and Mtesi nearly ran into a Zambian soldier with a light machine gun who was heading for the same thicket he was. Mtesi gave the man a grin, swerved into another clump of trees and brush, got himself settled. He liked the Zambians; his company had been right up next to a Zambian unit at the siege of Likasi, and they'd been good hard fighters, men you could trust to stand beside you.

The pounding of the helicopters was close now. Mtesi got himself settled in among the brush, shouldered the Chinese toy. Whether the thing was worth anything or not, it was what he had, and he meant to see what it would do.

The little screen showed the branches of the trees above him, clear as day, and the sky beyond them. Mtesi swept the Chinese toy back and forth, waiting for something he could hit. After a moment, he got a 'copter into the screen's view, high overhead, lean and angular as an animal that hadn't eaten in too long. He got the crosshairs of the screen centered on its body, heard the sound like a bell next to his ear, and pulled the trigger.

The rocket jumped out of the tube faster than fast, straight for the helicopter. The 'copter veered, as though trying to escape, but the rocket followed it and ran right up into the middle of its body. A moment later the helicopter was gone in a great blossom of flame.

Mtesi blinked, then jumped up and sprinted for a different clump of brush—the Americans would have night vision gear, he knew, and the place where the rocket came from would no doubt take some fire from them shortly. Once he got into the next thicket and made sure he could see the sky from it, he considered the rocket launcher. Toy or not, he decided, he could learn to like something that did that much harm, that fast. He loaded another of the rockets into it, got the thing set so that the little green light went on in the right place, shouldered it again and waited for another helicopter.

3 August 2029: Tsavo, Kenya

"Call off the attack," Seversky said. His voice was heavy.

"Yes, sir." Staff officers hammered on keyboards, sending the orders that would send the surviving helicopters back to their bases and tell American and Kenyan ground units to stay put.

Seversky glanced at the computer screens in the makeshift command center. He'd planned the assault on the Tanzanian forces surrounding Mombasa by the book, making the most of the 101st's weapons and standard tactics in the main assault while the Kenyan Army and the Marines backed it up and kept the enemy pinned down. It should have worked—but nobody told the enemy that, and they were waiting with state-of-the-art shoulder-launched missiles and a defense in depth that crippled the helicopter assault and left the rest of the plan in shreds.

Twenty-two 'copters down, the screens told him. No firm number on casualties yet, but it was going to be ugly—and that meant trouble, big trouble, when the news hit the media back stateside. He shook his head; that it would also mean the end of his Army career was the least of his worries just at that moment. The critical question was how to salvage the situation.

Movement at the command center door caught his attention; it was Colonel Joe Becher, the 101st's intelligence chief. Seversky signaled him with a sharp upward move of his head, and walked over to a disused corner of the big room, where Becher joined him.

"They were waiting for us," Becher said in a low voice. "We've still got a lot of photo intel to go over, but it looks like the Tanzies started getting in position to meet us as soon as they got on this side of the border."

Seversky gave him a bleak look. "And we walked right into it."

"Basically."

"Could they have been tipped off by the Kenyans?"

"We're looking into that," Becher said. "But there's something else that's a lot more likely. If they know which units we've got over here—and we can assume that they do—that alone gives them a pretty fair shot at guessing what we're going to do."

Seversky took that in. "But—oh. Of course."

"Every unit in the Army these days is so goddamn specialized," Becher went on. "You want air-cav, you send the 101st. You want standard airborne, you send the 82nd. You want armored cav—well, you can go down the list as well as I can. So all they have to do is figure out which units they're facing, and they know what they have to prepare for. I'm not sure if the Tanzanian military has the chops to do that—but I bet you can name somebody else who does."

"In which case we may have just walked into a trap."

"Yeah."

Seversky considered, and then nodded once. "Won't be the first time the 101st's been in that situation. With a little help from Washington, we can still win this."

3 August 2029, Silver Spring, Maryland

All across the United States, in the first days of that sweltering August, Americans began to realize that events in distant East Africa had suddenly jumped off the track they'd been assigned by the Weed administration and were hurtling down a new route into unknown territory. Later on, for a while, it became a common social habit for people to discuss just where they'd been and what they'd been doing when they realized that something had gone very, very wrong.

That moment came to Pete Bridgeport late on a Sunday morning in his condo in Silver Spring. He'd slept in past eight, a rare luxury, then made up for it with an hour-long workout at the condo's little private gym three floors down. That, a shower, a shave, and toast and coffee made him feel more or less ready for the day—a quiet day by usual standards, answering emails from colleagues in the Senate and campaign contributors back home, going over the draft texts of three bills his committee would have to consider once Congress started work again in September, drafting plans for the upcoming session.

First, though, the news. He woke his computer, opened a browser and clicked on his favorite news site. Most of the stories were routine to the point of boredom. The fighting in Spain had flared again, with Catalan guerrillas staging attacks on government troops in three districts; Indonesia and the Philippines were quarreling again over gas drilling rights in the Sulu Sea; scientists on the disintegrating Greenland ice sheet reported a speedup of the melting, and warned that coastal cities worldwide would be facing three to six meters of sea level rise by century's end; closer to home, big dust storms had shut down air and road traffic in Oklahoma, Nebraska, and parts of three other states, and weren't expected to die down for at least two days. All in all, it was an ordinary Sunday.

Then he saw the headline in the sidebar: US TROOPS ENGAGE TANZANIANS WEST OF MOMBASA. It was a moment before a bit of half-learned geography from a Pentagon briefing reminded him that Mombasa was in Kenya.

He clicked through to the story: exactly the sort of bland uninformative stuff normally marketed by Pentagon-approved embedded reporters, long on cheery human-interest details about this unit or that officer and short on what was actually happening. It mentioned a couple of place names, though, and Bridgeport opened a new window and looked those up. All of them were in southeastern Kenya.

He cupped his chin in one hand, considering. The scraps of information about the war he'd been able to pry loose from the Pentagon, and from his own sources, said that all the fighting was supposed to take place in Tanzanian territory and airspace. Clearly things weren't going according to plan.

Then, a cold realization: *and Mel's in the middle of it.*

3 August 2029: The White House, Washington DC

As he sat in the White House situation room watching the latest news from Kenya, Jameson Weed didn't have to guess just how far events had strayed from the confident plans he'd approved a few months earlier. One screen on the wall showed the locations of the 101st and the Marine and Kenyan units supporting it, and the probable locations—as close as satellite reconnaissance could track them in the thick coastal forest—of the Tanzanians and their allies. Another showed the locations of American and Chinese air bases, mapped out the ongoing air battle, and kept track on which side had lost how many planes. Neither screen showed any prospect of a quick end to a war that was spinning out of control.

"What are we doing about the air battle?" he asked Bill Stedman. The two of them were alone except for the duty officers; the other members of the National Security Council weren't due there for another thirty minutes or so.

The Secretary of Defense opened a portfolio, shuffled papers. "We've rotated two more fighter squadrons to the Gulf, and four additional squadrons are on twenty-four-hour alert; they'll be joining in as soon as the logistics get sorted out. The Chinese are still ferrying squadrons of their own to East Africa—the latest intel is that they've sent J-31s to support the J-20s."

"Ouch." The J-31, smaller and more maneuverable than the long-range J-20, was designed for interception and air defense, and a squadron or two protecting the airfields in South Sudan would make the Air Force's job that much harder.

"We've also sent additional B-1s to Bahrain and Diego Garcia," Stedman went on. "As per your orders, they're going to keep hitting the Chinese air bases in South Sudan and Tanzania. That's a calculated risk—with J-31s and air defense systems guarding them, we could lose some planes."

"Get them more fighter cover," Weed said.

Stedman glanced up from his papers. "We've already allocated every operational F-35 and F-22 we've got. If anything happens right now in another theater, we're going to be in deep trouble—practically all the Air Force has left that's capable of flying are obsolete planes, F-15s and F-16s. At current rates of attrition, there's a real chance that we could run out of first-string fighters before this thing is over."

Weed simply stared at him.

"Jim," Stedman said, "the Chinese still have factories turning out fighters for the PLAAF. We haven't had fighters in production since the F-35 program wound up in '23. You'll have to ask Greg Barnett about how many fighters the Chinese can build this month, but I can tell you exactly how many we can—and we're losing three for every two of theirs. It's not pretty."

4 August 2029: Camp Pumbaa, Kenya

"A mess," Mahoney said. He and the other lead officers of the 33rd were in his office, leaning over computer screens with maps of southeastern Kenya and the latest messages from the 101st's HQ at Tsavo. "A real mess."

It was a fair assessment. Seversky's first assault on the Tanzanian forces—not just Tanzanian now, Melanie Bridgeport reminded herself; Zambia, Mozambique, and Malawi had all sent troops to join the coalition, according to the latest intel reports—had been a costly failure. Ground strikes by the 33rd's Lardbuckets might have made a difference, but every plane the 33rd and the Navy squadrons still had left was committed to the air battle against the Chinese, and that wasn't going well.

"Any word from AFRICOM?" Watanabe asked.

"They say they're still trying." Mahoney gave him a weary look. "You know the score there as well as I do."

No one replied for a long moment. So far, though they'd taken losses, the Chinese had the upper hand, and attempts to punch through their combat air patrols had run face first into the same tactics the Chinese had used on the 33rd: throw everything at tankers and AWACS planes first, then hammer the US fighters until they had to break off and return to base. The Chinese fighters could stay in the air much longer than the notoriously short-legged F-35s and F-22s, and the Chinese seemed to have no shortage of planes to throw into the battle.

"Well," Mahoney said finally, and turned to Bridgeport. "Mel, Seversky's asked me to send someone down to him to straighten out the logistics mess. They've got all kinds of Navy and Marine gear salvaged from the fleet, and it turns out the logistics people from the fleet got evacced to the Gulf right before the Chinese fighters came in. You're probably the best person for that here and now."

"I can probably take care of it online," Mel told him.

He shook his head. "Seversky thinks the Chinese can read our communications—and I don't feel like betting that he's wrong. Your staff can keep things running here for a few days, right? I want you to go to Tsavo, get their people up to speed on the Navy system, and come back. With any luck Washington will have figured out some way to resupply us by the time you get back here."

5 August 2029: North of Ukunda, Kenya

Private Kwame Mtesi crouched behind the tree, waiting, a shadow in the predawn dark. The Americans were less than a kilometer north, maybe much less than that. They had not expected to lose so many of their helicopters to the Chinese toys, or so Mtesi guessed; the first American attack on the Coalition lines had broken off in confusion within a few hours. He was certain, though, that there would be another attack, and nearly as certain that it would not be delayed for long.

His unit had been stationed along a road edged with trees, dug in against the expected assault; out beyond the trees were fields, and beyond that were the Americans. The technicals had been unloaded and taken well back behind the lines, leaving their machine guns and grenade launchers behind. Moses Olokumbe and two others were maybe ten meters off to the left, crewing the .50 caliber machine gun; some of the others had the grenade launchers. Mtesi had used all the rockets for his Chinese toy, and had only his assault rifle and his bush knife. Between brief intervals of sleep, he'd spent some time praying that those would be enough.

"Mtesi." It was the sergeant, moving quietly along the line, speaking in less than a whisper. "They're coming. Get ready— we've called for help."

Mtesi murmured an acknowledgment, felt the sergeant move on. He checked his gear, then turned the switch on the tube-shaped thing clipped to the top of his assault rifle: another Chinese toy, some kind of night-vision gear. The little screen on the butt end of the tube lit up, and he glanced down at it.

Through the screen, the scene might as well have been full daylight. He could see a farmhouse in the middle distance, a wind turbine off beyond it, and trees lining another road beyond that—and closer, much closer, masses of men moving across the fields toward him, wearing American-style helmets.

They could see him. He knew that, knew that they would open fire the moment they realized that the Coalition forces could see them. He stayed crouched behind the tree, watched them advance, waiting—.

Someone in the Coalition line, off to the right, opened fire. Reflexively, Mtesi dropped to the ground and started shooting as well. A moment later the Americans' bullets were whizzing over his head. The machine gun was hammering away, assault rifles rattled, the flash and bang of rocket-propelled grenades added to the din; it was all familiar, more than familiar, from the battles he'd fought in the last two Congo wars. The Chinese night-vision gear gave him an edge he hadn't had then, and the Americans had next to no cover to shield them; he pumped one three-round burst after another into their increasingly ragged lines.

Then all of a sudden he was lying a meter away, no longer holding his gun, and one of his legs was folded under him in a way it shouldn't have been able to go. A moment passed before he realized that he'd been hit; another moment went by before he guessed that it had been a rocket-propelled grenade. He tried to drag himself back to the shelter of the tree, but his limbs didn't seem to be working just then.

Figures ran past him in the darkness, coming up from behind the Coalition lines. He heard their voices, and grinned, recognizing the accent: Zambians, of course, the men he'd fought beside at Likasi. Everything was fine, he told himself.

Assault rifles rattled on, and the machine gun kept up its hammering. One of the Zambians crouched beside him and said something Mtesi couldn't quite make out. The Zambian repeated whatever it was, but by then he seemed a long distance away, as though he was calling from the top of a well and Mtesi was down at the bottom, in the cool water, letting it close gently over his face.

6 August 2029: The White House, Washington DC

"Ellen," Gurney said.

Ellen Harbin turned to face him with a bright bland look. The morning's National Security Council meeting, with more bad news from Africa, had rubbed her nerves raw, but she wasn't about to show that. "Yes?"

He glanced back over his shoulder, made sure no one else was in earshot in the White House hallway. "I want to know what you really think about this Tanzania business." He paused, then: "I don't buy it. I want to know why the best military in the world can't seem to win a battle against a bunch of n—" He caught himself. "Natives in trucks."

Harbin nodded, wondering what the man had in mind. "I've begun to wonder if the real problem isn't in East Africa at all," she ventured.

"Damn right," Gurney said. "You know where I think it is? Right across the Potomac." A sharp movement of his head indicated the river to the south. "In the Pentagon."

That startled her, though she kept the surprise off her face; she revised her estimate of the man. "The question in my mind is whether it's a matter of incompetence, or ..." She left the sentence unfinished.

"Or," said Gurney. "Exactly." In a low voice: "If I ever end up in this place, you and me are going to have to do some serious talking." He seemed to be about to say more, but someone from the White House staff came down the hallway. "See you tomorrow," he said, and walked away. Harbin watched him go, and allowed a slow smile.

7 August 2029: Tsavo, Kenya

Seversky looked up from the computer screen, surveyed the grim faces turned toward his. "That's bad," he said, unnecessarily. Everyone there in the command tent was all too aware of how bad it was.

"Any word from Mahoney?" he asked then.

"Same thing as before, sir," one of his aides said. "He says they've lost too many planes and can't spare anything from holding off the Chinese."

"Dammit," said Seversky, "we're bleeding to death here."

"General Seversky." It was the colonel Mahoney had sent him, the one who'd been sorting out the logistics mess; he spent a moment trying to remember her name, gave up. "If the Chinese get past our fighters you're going to have to deal with air strikes on your units, and the only things you've got to counter that are Stinger IIIs."

He considered that for a moment. "I know. Nobody told us we were going up against another major power."

The map on the computer screen showed the forces spread across southeastern Kenya: the three brigades of the 101st east of Voi, the Marines and the Kenyan forces with their backs to the Galana River, Coalition forces driving west from Mombasa and north toward Malindi—and now, another Coalition thrust across the border east of Moshi, threatening the routes that connected the 101st to its supply bases and to the possibility of retreat. Three days of hard fighting had failed to break the Coalition's grip on the Mombasa region, and the American and Kenyan losses had been heavy.

He scowled, knowing he had only one choice.

"We're going to have to withdraw," he said. "Benny, you'll be the rearguard; I want First Corps to hold Voi and cover for

130

the rest of us. Ish, you'll take Third Corps west and get a new defensive line in place as fast as possible—" He slid the map across the computer screen with a fingertip. "—right around Konza. It has to be this side of Nairobi; we can't let the Coalition take that without a fight." He turned to the Air Force colonel and, thankfully, remembered her name. "Bridgeport, I want you to head back to Camp Pumbaa and strip it to the bare walls. We need everything we can get to stall the Coalition until Washington can get us reinforcements. Anything you can free up for surface-to-surface use—Tomahawks, you name it, we need it."

"That's doable," she said. "I'll get you everything we've got."

"Good." He glanced from face to face. "Anything else? No? Okay, let's get on it."

TWELVE

8 August 2029: Expediency Council offices, Tehran

"Excellent," said Ayatollah Jahrami. "Note the delicacy of the request: should anything happen to divert the attention of the Americans from East Africa during the coming weeks, there will be concrete expressions of gratitude to those responsible. Nothing more than that. The Chinese may be infidels—"

"And persecutors of the Faith," one of the other ayatollahs reminded him pointedly.

"Granted, and for that there will be a reckoning in due time, if Allah wills. Still, for now, it is useful to deal with them."

The Expediency Council had been meeting every day or two since the East African crisis erupted. Each news bulletin from the fighting made it clearer that a balance of power fixed in place since the Second World War might be coming apart, and Iran's place in whatever new order might come out of the struggle was very much on the minds of the Council members.

"A little trouble could be arranged," said General Zardawi.

"I am inclined to think," said Jahrami, "that it would be worthwhile to cause more than a little trouble. I propose that we activate the al-Quds Force in Saudi Arabia, and make, shall we say, threatening movements on our side of the Gulf."

That got raised eyebrows around the room; the al-Quds Force was the huge covert wing of the Revolutionary Guards.

"Yes," said Zardawi. "Yes, of course. Convince the Americans that we might be ready to take advantage of their weakness—"

"Cross the Gulf, liberate the Shi'a along the Gulf coast, and seize the Holy Cities. Exactly. Not that we will." Jahrami leaned forward. "Not yet, and not in that manner. We will do all of that in our own way, and in our own time, but the Americans do not know that—and if we can force them to keep planes and ships and missiles in the Gulf, I suspect China's expressions of gratitude will be very concrete indeed."

9 August 2029: Camp Pumbaa, Kenya

By the time she reached Narok, on the way back to the airfield, Melanie Bridgeport knew that something had gone very wrong.

Getting out of Tsavo had been hard enough, with refugees streaming out of town ahead of the expected Coalition advance, and every available American and Kenyan soldier heading toward the front lines. Her driver managed the thing somehow, veering through narrow streets and dirt roads, lurching up an embankment to get back on the highway maybe twenty miles further west. Kenyan military police kept the highway clear from there on, and waved Bridgeport past; from there on it was pedal to the metal all the way to Narok.

Bridgeport noticed the cloud by the time her car went through Konza, low and dark on the southwestern horizon. The weather forecasts hadn't mentioned a chance of rain, but she had too much else to think about, too many logistics issues to try to solve, to give it much thought. It was only when the car neared Narok, and it became all too clear that the cloud was right over Camp Pumbaa, that she realized what it might mean.

Mile by mile, as the car drove south from Narok, the sky darkened and the scale of what had happened became clearer. By the time the guards at the main gate waved Bridgeport over, she could see great plumes of black smoke rising from three places along the horizon.

"Chinese got through?" she asked.

"Yes sir," one of the guards told her. "About six this morning."

Bridgeport could think of nothing to say, signaled her driver to go on.

Further in, the scale of the destruction was all too clear. The fuel depot was still on fire, the air defense batteries were scrap metal, and a couple of other buildings had been turned into blackened wreckage. Firefighting crews swarmed around the burning fuel tanks, medics hurried here and there, teams of enlisted men dug through the rubble: everything that should have been happening was happening, but the chance that the 33rd's two squadrons could make a difference in the fighting had just dropped to zero.

The car pulled up at the parking lot for headquarters and the Air Operations Center, and Bridgeport got out. For an instant she wondered if the driver had gotten lost, and then all at once she recognized what the heap of debris close by had been. "Jesus," she said out loud.

There were men standing amid the rubble. One of them heard her, turned, and came over. "Mel? Helluva time to decide to come back here." It was Watanabe, though it took Bridgeport a moment to recognize him through the soot on his face.

"Didn't have much choice," Bridgeport said. "Seversky's evacuating Tsavo."

Watanabe gave her a long blank look, then: "Shit. I hope they aren't coming here."

"What happened?"

"The Chinese just kept hammering," said Watanabe. "We tried to get another couple of squadrons in, from the Gulf, from West Africa, from anywhere and the Chinese swarmed them, went after tankers and AWACS planes—same thing they did to us. This morning they punched through what was left of our combat patrol and got some J-20s close enough to launch cruise missiles. Our antiaircraft gear took out some of them but not enough." With a weary shrug: "Our best guess is the Chinese'll be back come nightfall."

"Mahoney?" Bridgeport asked.

The operations chief looked down, answered with a little shake of the head.

9 August 2029: Qatif, Saudi Arabia

They arrived one or two at a time at the bicycle shop, greeted the proprietor with a nod and a murmured password, slipped down the stairs in back to the basement. By the time the shop closed everyone had arrived, and the proprietor locked the doors, turned out the lights, and went down the same stairs. The basement was half full of cardboard boxes and wooden crates, and the light from a single bulb shone on tense eager faces as the proprietor entered.

"Is it time?" he asked the commander.

"Yes. The orders came this morning, Allah be praised."

The men who filled the room were operatives of the al-Quds Force, the covert wing of the Revolutionary Guards. Most of them belonged to Saudi Arabia's Shi'a minority, and thus counted as second-class citizens or worse in the eyes of the Wahhabi Sunnis who ran the country; a few came from other corners of the Shi'a Muslim world. All had been trained in Iranian camps, and knew every detail of the work that was ahead of them.

The commander passed out handwritten slips of paper, one to each man. "These are your instructions," he said. "Do not discuss them with anyone but your team leader."

"And the weapons and explosives?" This from one of the men.

"Are here," said the bicycle shop proprietor. He went to the far side of the room, pulled the lid off one of the wooden crates. Metal gleamed gray inside.

"*Allahu akbar*," said the man who had spoken, in an appreciative tone. "We will set this city ablaze."

"Enough," said the commander. "Take your gear, and remember that the eyes of the Twelfth Imam are upon you."

Guns and bombs passed from hand to hand, and the first team slipped back up the stairs and out into the night by way of the back door into the alley. The others followed, one team at a time. When all had left, the commander turned to the shopkeeper. "Will you need any help getting things ready for the police?"

"No, not at all. I have already placed the charges. A few minutes, maybe, and I will be ready to give suitable hospitality to my guests. How soon do you think they will arrive?"

The commander glanced at his watch. "Half an hour, maybe; the phone calls will already have been made. It depends on how quickly they respond to the first martyrdom operations."

"Then, my friend, you may wish to hurry elsewhere."

"Of course. The blessings of Allah be with you."

"And with you."

As the commander hurried up the stairs, the shopkeeper went to another of the crates, pulled out a reel of wire and the necessary tools, and began the final preparations for his own martyrdom. He was an old man, and had lived for many years with the contempt and more than occasional brutality of the local police; it pleased him to think that some of them, at least, would shortly accompany him to Allah's throne of judgment.

10 August 2029: Tsavo, Kenya

The trucks rolled out of the parking lot one at a time and roared westwards toward Nairobi with as many American and Kenyan troops as could be crammed into them. Humvees and technicals joined them, with soldiers in the back shouldering Stinger IIIs and scanning the skies for Chinese planes. Each truck traveled by a different route, scattering across the countryside to minimize the risk of air strikes. So far, the Chinese fighters had kept their distance; maybe they were hard put to it to keep US planes from breaking through into East African airspace. Seversky didn't know. He stood in front of the temporary HQ, watching his army retreat, thinking: there are too many things I don't know.

"Sir." A lieutenant saluted. "Message from Konza."

"Isherwood?"

"Yes, sir. He says 'John Wayne.'"

"Good. Thank you, soldier."

"Thank you, sir." The lieutenant went back into the comm tent.

That was good news, at least. "John Wayne" meant that Third Brigade was in place at Konza, east of Nairobi, setting up a defensive line against the Coalition advance. The code words might not be necessary, but Seversky and his staff had decided to take no chances: if the Chinese could paralyze the US satellite system and blow a carrier battle group out of the water, they might be able to crack the Army's data encryption.

The last of the trucks rolled by: the 101st's Second Brigade and the 3rd and 7th Kenya Rifles Battalions, on their way to join the line at Konza. Seversky watched them go, then turned and ducked into the tent.

Inside, the sounds of the trucks were muffled but the diesel generator just outside more than made up the difference. Laptop screens showed incoming data: live image feeds from reconnaissance satellites and drones, weather data, reports from US and Kenyan units. He circled the room, checked each screen, stopped at one. "Anything from Martinez?"

"Yes, sir," said the lieutenant sitting there. "Messenger just came in. They're in Voi, with the Tanzies right on their asses."

No surprises there. "Time to move," Seversky said, pitching his voice to be heard over the generator. "Bill, let Ish know we're on our way. The code's 'Red Ryder.'"

"Got it," said a major on the other side of the tent, and started typing. The others began shutting down their computers and packing gear. Seversky turned back to the lieutenant. "What about Kesembani?"

"Nothing, sir." The lieutenant looked up at him. "Word is he's gone from Nairobi—him and the whole cabinet."

"Any idea where?"

"Kisumu, sir."

Seversky allowed a laugh; Kisumu was in Kenya's far west, on the shore of Lake Victoria. "Nice to know somebody has confidence in us," he said. "Well, he'll just have to wait there while we win this thing."

12 August 2029: The Kremlin, Moscow

"The Americans are trying to open a supply route by land." The speaker, a colonel from Army Intelligence, turned on his laser pointer, put a red spot on Africa's Mediterranean coast and drew it down the image on the screen. "There's no secret about the route: Libya to Chad, to the Central African Republic and northern Zaire, and then east across Uganda to their forces. Not an easy route or a safe one, and there are hard limits on how much they can bring that way."

"With Chinese planes in South Sudan?" This from Colonel-General Myshinski, the Army chief of staff. "They will get pounded."

"That's one problem, sir," said the colonel. "The very poor roads are another. There have been ground attacks on the first few American units heading through—no one's admitting responsibility for those. It might be the Coalition, or local militias—"

"Or anyone who wants the contents of a truck or two," Myshinski said. "Understood."

The colonel went on, sketching out the American withdrawal toward Nairobi, the Coalition advance, the air battles over Kenya and South Sudan, the changing fortunes of a war that everyone in the room knew could shatter a decades-old balance of power.

In his usual seat, fingers folded together, Gennady Kuznetsov watched and listened. General Bunin sat nearby, his face impassive as a stump. What thoughts might be moving behind Bunin's half-closed eyes, Kuznetsov did not try to guess, but it was plain enough which way the winds over East Africa were blowing.

When the colonel had finished speaking, Kuznetsov cleared his throat. "What you're telling us," he said, "is that the Americans are losing."

A moment of silence, and then, unexpectedly, Bunin's voice: "No."

Kuznetsov turned toward him. "No?"

"No." The general regarded him. "They've lost. They simply don't know it yet."

PART THREE

TO THE BRINK

THIRTEEN

5 September 2029: The White House, Washington DC

"Did they get everybody out of Nairobi?" Weed asked.

"Yes," Greg Barnett said. "I've talked to Miller—he was our station chief there. He's in Kisumu now, and we've got a secure diplomatic line open from there."

"Well, that's one bit of good news, at least." The president ran a hand back through his hair. "We could use more."

None of the members of the National Security Council had anything to say to that. Weed glanced around the room, and his gaze caught on the portrait of Teddy Roosevelt on horseback. Damn the man, he thought. He made it look so easy. "What about the broader picture?"

"The business in Saudi Arabia is picking up," said Barnett. "The Saudis say it's just a few protests and they've got it under control. Our people on the ground say there have been dozens of suicide attacks on police stations and government buildings, and what looks like urban guerrilla forces active in Qatif and Dammam."

"The Iranians have got to be behind it," Ellen Harbin said.

"Probably. We've got satellite photos showing three divisions of Revolutionary Guards moving up to the southern part of the border with Iraq, down near Basra. Maybe it's a bluff, maybe it's more than that. We don't know yet."

"Fair enough," Weed said. "Bill, what's the latest on the fighting in Kenya?"

Stedman didn't trust himself to answer. He nodded to Admiral Waite, who took the remote and clicked it. A map of Kenya appeared on the screen. "The new defensive line is just west of Nakuru," the admiral said. "The terrain's favorable—it's right along the edge of the Rift Valley—and Seversky thinks he can stop the Coalition forces there if we can improve the logistics situation. We've got every available resource working on that, but I'd be lying if I said we had it fixed. Between Coalition irregulars and Chinese airstrikes, getting anything through is a crapshoot."

"What about the air situation more generally?"

"Not good. They've brought in more fighters, and gotten more air-defense systems operational. We lost two B-1s to SAM fire in last night's run."

Weed gave him a horrified look. "And the crews?"

"No word yet," said the admiral.

"We tried to get Predator drones in to hit their air defense radars, but they were spotted and taken out," Barnett said then. "Chinese technology is, well, as good as ours these days."

Weed stared at him, then allowed a short sharp laugh, like a dog barking. "No," he said. "No, it's better than ours, and you know why. Everybody in this room has signed off on systems that nobody should have approved, and you've all done it as quid pro quo." He looked up and down the table. "So have I. For all these years, we thought we could afford that. Some things are going to have to change—once we finish dealing with the Chinese."

A moment of silence came and went. "The Chinese," said Ellen Harbin then. "We've talked about them every single day since this started. We need to do something about them."

"Jim, she's right," said Gurney.

"No!" This from Stedman. To Weed: "Jim, a proxy war's one thing. Going head to head with the Chinese is something else. We can't afford a major war."

"We're not facing a major war," Harbin snapped.

"We will be if we keep this up."

"That's completely unrealistic."

Weed held up a hand before Stedman could reply. "Bill, I know you've had doubts about this whole project since the beginning. I understand your feelings, but we've got to force the Chinese to back down. There's no other option." He turned to face Harbin. "What do you have in mind?"

All at once, Stedman knew he'd had enough. He slammed his folder of briefings down on the table, pushed his chair back, and stood up. "Jim, you'll have my written resignation tomorrow. I'm not willing to sit here and watch while you drag this country into a war it doesn't need and isn't prepared to fight."

"Bill," said Weed, "for God's sake, not now!"

"Personal reasons," said Stedman. "Health concerns. I'll give you all the plausible deniability you want, but I'm through." The door slammed behind him a moment afterward.

He was out beneath the West Wing portico, waiting for his car in the damp evening air, before enough of the anger drained away that he could think about what came next. After a few moments, he pulled out his cell phone and dialed his wife. "Karen? It's me."

"Are you okay? You sound awful."

"Yeah. We need to talk. Are you home?"

"Right now? Yes. What—"

"Not now. I'll be right over. Bye."

6 September 2029: Academy of Military Science, Beijing

"They will attack us on a different front shortly," Fang Liyao said. "It is simply a matter of where, and how soon."

Liu gave him a hard look. "You say that so casually."

145

"It's hardly a surprise, General. Do you remember my comments earlier about their inability to imagine defeat? Now that their forces in Kenya are in trouble, they will try to escalate somewhere else. That really is the only option their culture allows them to consider."

The two men sat in Fang's office, the desk between them a wilderness of maps and reports from the fighting in East Africa. So far, all the news was good. Nairobi was in Coalition hands, and so were the airfields there and in Mombasa, bringing PLAAF units closer to the retreating American forces and providing defense in depth against air strikes from the Americans' Persian Gulf bases. The supply route through the middle of Africa was coming under increasing pressure: slowly and unevenly, so the Americans would keep on trying to force convoys through long after an objective assessment would have discarded it and looked for new options, but steadily enough that the US force was running short of everything it needed to keep fighting.

The thought of a second front, though, was troubling. "Do you have any sense where they might attack?" Liu asked.

"Difficult to say," said Fang. "Much depends on how much international condemnation they are willing to risk. The best options strategically would be air strikes on our bases at Sittwe or Trincomalee."

"But you don't think they'll do that."

"No." A quick shake of his head denied it. "They treasure the mask of legality too much. No, my guess is that they'll attack the Motherland directly."

Liu stared at him for a long moment. "That cannot be permitted."

"It cannot be avoided." Fang leaned forward. "Nor will it work to China's disadvantage. Think of the international outcry, the reaction of the Chinese people—and the justification it will provide for a far more damaging response from our side."

"The escalation you've proposed."

"Exactly. Have orders been issued for that?"

"Of course," said Liu.

"Excellent." Then: "Their move will almost certainly be an air strike. I would encourage you to place air defenses on the highest alert."

"If the attack is serious enough, and they use their best planes, some will get through."

"Of course." Fang leaned back, folded his fingers together. "But it would be useful if they were to suffer losses. As we approach the endgame, anything that reminds the Americans of their lack of omnipotence will benefit us."

7 September 2029: Whiteman Air Force Base, Missouri

Major Jim Kroger crossed the concrete at a run, hauled himself up the ladder into the belly of the B-2. The four big turbofan engines were already cycling, filling the air with a low whine; the ordnance crew truck was backing away as the bomb bay doors swung shut.

"Good to go?" Captain Phil Bennington, "Benny" to his friends, looked up from the pilot's controls.

Kroger nodded, swung into the commander's chair. "Washington just gave the go-ahead. Straight from the White House is what the colonel said."

"I bet," Benny said. "What exactly are we supposed to blow to hell?"

"Lingshui Air Base on Hainan Island. Here's the mission order." He offered the papers.

Benny took them, read the top page, handed them back. "Lingshui? Wasn't that where that EP-3 got forced down back in 2001?"

Kroger grinned. "You do know your history, don't you? That's the one."

"Bit of a grudge match, then," said Benny.

"Yeah, but that's not the point." Kroger tapped the flight order. "They've got a big satellite intel station right next to the airfield. That's our main target—that and the airfield defenses."

Benny snorted. "They don't have anything that can touch us."

"We hope. They've got a full moon and clear skies to work with. The Creature says standoff weapons only." Brigadier General Abel Creech was in command of the 509th Bomb Wing, the Air Force's B-2 unit; nobody in the 509th called him anything but the nickname except to his face. "You heard about the Bones over in Kenya."

"Those were Bones," Benny said. "Nothing touches a Spirit."

The radio hissed and spat instructions; Benny pushed the throttle forward, and the bomber began rolling forward onto the taxiway. Three other B-2s were headed the same way: two to hit Yulin Naval Base on the southern tip of Hainan, the third to join Kroger's plane in the attack on Lingshui Air Base. Kroger shook his head; it was a hell of a show of force, that was for sure. "Well, we'll see," he said.

8 September 2029: Lingshui Air Base, Hainan Island

Major Guo Yunmen went over to the radar technician's station. "What is it?"

"I'm not sure, sir. Possibly just a malfunction, but—"

Orders had come from Beijing the day before placing the base on highest alert. "Treat it as hostile until you're certain otherwise."

"Yes, sir."

Guo turned. It was probably just a malfunction; still, orders were orders. "Get a second combat patrol up," he told the air chief on duty. "Better—"

"Sir!" It was the radar technician. Guo turned back, saw the text on the computer screen: the distinctive signature an American B-2 bomber showed during its one moment of radar visibility, when its bomb bays opened.

"Range?"

"Just over two hundred kilometers, sir."

Cruise missiles, then. "Kao—" The air chief was already on his feet. "Get every fighter into the air. That B-2 is to be destroyed if—"

"Sir." The radar technician again. "Another."

Guo turned back to him, saw the second warning. "Antimissile defenses—"

"Already engaged, sir." This from an officer on the other side of the room. "I've alerted the rest of the air defense net."

"Good." Guo looked up at the clock. "Kao, you will take charge. Beijing needs to know."

He was out of the command center a moment later. The corridor to his office seemed to stretch for kilometers. Still, he got to the door, got to his desk, found the phone and started punching numbers. The window across from him showed darkness, lit here and there by the lights of distant buildings.

"Yes?"

"Major Guo Yunmen, at Lingshui. I need to speak to General Cai at once." He forced steadiness into his voice. "We are under attack."

He could hear the orderly's breath drawn in, like a dying man's. "One moment, please."

Silence followed. Guo glanced at the clock on his desk, then wished he hadn't.

"Guo?" General Cai's voice. "What is this—"

"Forgive me, General," said Guo, quickly. "Two B-2s are in our airspace east of Hainan, just over two hundred kilometers out. Both have opened their weapons bays. Our fighters have been scrambled and antimissile defenses are engaged. The rest of the air defense net—"

The first flash lit up the sky outside Guo's office, and the phone line crackled and went dead. Instinctively, Guo ducked behind the desk; an instant later the window exploded into flying shards as the shock wave hit. He stayed crouched, and wondered whether there would be another blast, and when.

A flash a moment later answered him, and his world dissolved into flame.

8 September 2029: The August First Building, Beijing

"You were quite correct, of course," Liu said into the handset. On the computer screen in front of him were the first damage reports from Hainan and news reports from the media. There had been hundreds of deaths; he tried not to think of that.

"Regrettably so." Fang's voice was measured, soft. "And the response?"

"Already under way. I had the necessary special forces unit sent to Sittwe, and made arrangements with the naval commanders there, after our last conversation."

"I am honored by your trust," Fang said. Then: "The next few weeks will be the most delicate phase of this process."

Liu knew at once what his friend was not saying. "I will be sure to consult with you."

"I will welcome the opportunity," said Fang.

8 September 2029: The White House, Washington DC

"The damage assessment is in," said Admiral Waite. He pressed buttons on the control, and satellite photos appeared on the screen: craters and rubble, mostly, with lines and captions drawn in to indicate what had been there the day before. "The satellite intel base is a total loss, the airfield defenses likewise." Another click, showing tangled wreckage where blue water met land. "The port facilities at Yulin were pretty badly hit, though the sub base inside the cliffs is hardened against anything this side of nukes—maybe against those as well. One way or another, though, we've given them a black eye."

Weed nodded, taking this in. "And the missing plane?"

Waite turned to face him. "No trace so far."

Silence, then, as the images of crumpled harbor facilities warred with an unwelcome realization. Only two of the B-2s had returned safely to Whiteman Air Force Base; a third, half crippled by an air-to-air missile, fought its way to an emergency landing in Guam, and the fourth vanished somewhere over the South China Sea with a swarm of PLAAF fighters closing in on it.

"Who was on board?" Weed asked.

Waite glanced at his notes. "Major James Kroger, mission commander, and Captain Philip Bennington, pilot. Excellent service records, both men."

Weed grimaced. "Inform their families that they're missing, no details, we're still looking. I don't want anything about this in the media yet."

"That's not going to be easy," said Greg Barnett. "The foreign media's all over it. You'll have to call in a lot of favors to keep it out of the news here."

"As many as I have to," Weed growled. He turned to Claire Hutchison, asked the question everyone in the room wanted to ask. "Any word from the Chinese?"

Her expression was flat, unreadable. "They've lodged a formal protest with the United Nations," she told him, "broken off diplomatic relations, and recalled their ambassador and embassy staff. They've told our entire diplomatic presence to get out of China within seventy-two hours."

"They can't be serious," Ellen Harbin said then.

"I admire your confidence," Hutchison replied. Then, to Weed: "I've asked our diplomatic corps to watch for indirect approaches, third-party initiatives, face-saving maneuvers of that sort. So far, though, what I've heard back is that the Chinese aren't interested."

"What I'm hearing matches that," said Barnett.

Weed drew in a ragged breath, made himself speak. "We'll give them a few days to come to their senses. In the meantime—"

He turned to Waite. "I want the supply line to our forces in Kenya wide open. I don't care how. Make it happen."

"We'll do what we can, sir," said the admiral.

"That's not good enough," Weed snapped. "Make it happen."

9 September 2029: Russell Senate Office Building, Washington DC

Bridgeport leaned forward over the table. "Weed is lying."

None of the members of his staff disputed the point. The table in the conference room was half covered with printouts of the latest internet news from East Africa. The ones that came from US-based news sites parroted the official White House line: the US task force had come under hostile fire and some ships had been damaged, no further details at this time.

The sites from overseas told a different story. That story involved witnesses reporting scores or even hundreds of cruise missiles flying belly to the waves off Tanzania's coast in the small hours of 24 July, thousands of wounded sailors and body bags ferried into Mombasa by Navy helicopters later that morning, at least three embedded reporters with the task force who hadn't been heard from since 23 July, half a dozen ships whose whereabouts nobody was willing to discuss any more—and one whose whereabouts were all too clear. Nearly every one of the overseas news reports showed the gray ghost of the *Ronald Reagan* somewhere on the page.

"Bill, Nora, Ari, I want all three of you to get to work on the data," Bridgeport said. "Track down everything you can find about the task force. Every ship, every sailor. Whatever you can get that'll stand up in hearings."

Joe Egmont put down the printout he'd been reading. "Bill, if you try to hold hearings when the war's still going on, the media will crucify you."

Bridgeport's gesture brushed aside the possibility. "I'll call for hearings now, postpone them when Weed asks me to—and he will—and then hold them as soon as the fighting's over. I want Weed to know right now that he'll be held accountable."

"That could be risky," said Egmont.

"I know. I'll take the risk." All at once he thought of Melanie, somewhere in Kenya with the retreating US forces. "Our people in East Africa are taking bigger ones, you know."

Egmont nodded, conceding the point. "What else?" Bridgeport asked.

"The Chinese are claiming that US planes bombed a naval base on their territory," said Nora Babbitt. "The international media have some pretty convincing photos. The Chinese have called their ambassador home; the Pentagon's refused to comment so far."

Bridgeport turned to face her, aghast. "On Chinese territory? Where?"

"Hainan Island. It's in the South China Sea; they've got naval and air bases there."

He stared at her for another moment. "Get me as much data on that as you can," he said finally. "That's—stunningly reckless."

Egmont had his hand to his chin. "It's Harbin's style," he offered. "With Stedman out, I'm guessing we'll see more stunts like that."

"That's what worries me," said Bridgeport. "That, and how the Chinese are going to respond."

11 September 2029: Sittwe Naval Base, Myanmar

The executive officer saluted. "Welcome aboard, Major."

"Thank you." Major Chung Erhwan returned the salute, glanced around the inside of the submarine. The *Zheng He* was a far cry from the aging coastal-defense craft he and his team knew so well. Fast, silent, and effectively undetectable, the attack sub was the pride of the PLA Navy, and the bright metal and clean paint all around him showed that clearly enough.

Chung's pulse picked up. They would not have assigned his team to such a vessel for any ordinary mission.

"We will be under way in a quarter hour," said the executive officer then. "I trust you have orders—"

"Of course. To be opened once we are out of Myanmar's territorial waters, and under the strictest communication silence."

The executive officer's expression brightened. "Excellent. I will inform Captain Kuo at once. If you or your team need anything, please let me know."

Half an hour later, after seeing to his men and making sure everyone and everything was settled for the voyage, Chung went forward to the quarters he'd been assigned aboard the sub. The little room was spartan but neat, with ample stowage for his gear. Though he knew the sub was under way, he could barely feel the hum of the engines through the deck. He sat on the bunk, leaned back, let himself relax for a moment.

It had been a long week for him, and for everyone in Unit 6628, the PLA's special forces team for island operations. Orders had come from Beijing in the middle of an exercise, their ninth so far that year—even among China's special forces teams, Unit 6628's training schedule had a reputation for inhuman severity—and suddenly men and gear were being pulled out of the water in the middle of a simulated raid and loaded on buses and trucks for the long trip inland and south across the mountains to Myanmar. Hints and whispers from higher up the chain of command warned Chung and his men that something out of the ordinary was under way, but it wasn't until they'd arrived at Sittwe Naval Base and received sealed orders from a PLA admiral in person that Chung knew that it wasn't simply another readiness drill.

He thought he could guess what the Central Military Commission had in mind, once he had the orders and was leading his men aboard the submarine. News and pictures from the raids on Hainan were all over the media; China would certainly respond in kind, and Unit 6628's special training and weapons meant that an island or a coastal base would be the target. The only question was where.

A soft tapping on the hatch awakened him from a nap he hadn't intended to take. In the hall outside was an ensign, who saluted and let him know that the *Zheng He* would be crossing into international waters in a few minutes, and would he do Captain Kuo the favor of meeting with him in his quarters?

Chung let the ensign lead him to the captain's stateroom. It was as neat and spare as the rest of the sub, just larger enough than Chung's quarters to provide room for a table and some chairs. Kuo and his executive officer were waiting. The captain was career Navy, Chung guessed from his look, the kind who'd worked his way up from mopping decks on a coastal patrol boat. He got up to greet Chung, exchanged pleasantries, waved him to a seat.

"So," the captain said when everyone was seated and the hatch was closed and locked. "I am at least as eager as you are to find out where we are going, and—" He glanced at a clock over on one wall. "We are just now in international waters. Perhaps we can consult your orders."

"Of course," said Chung. He pulled the envelope out of the inside pocket of his coat. Red security stamps showed on both sides. "If you would prefer?"

The captain waved the offer away. "By all means open it."

The envelope, tamperproof plastic, zipped open, and Chung took out the folded papers inside. The uppermost was a folded nautical chart; he set the others down, unfolded it. It showed a section of the central Indian Ocean and an atoll with an unmistakable shape.

Chung considered it, then glanced at the others. "Of course," he said. "Diego Garcia."

FOURTEEN

15 September 2029, Endebess, Kenya

When the message came by radio, Seversky didn't need to guess what it meant. Still, he nodded, told the communications tech to go on.

"It's Hayakawa, sir. They've got a party with a white flag coming up the road from Kitale. He's asking for orders."

"Tell him to get a technical and send 'em in." Seversky returned the man's salute, walked to the front of the primary school he'd taken over as HQ after the retreat from Eldoret. Back behind the school rose the slopes of soaring Mount Elgon; beyond that was Uganda, where the last satellite photos he'd been able to download from SPACECOM showed a second Coalition force assembling, cutting off the last thin possibility of retreat.

"General?" One of his aides crossed the room. "What's up?"

Seversky didn't turn. "We're about to be offered surrender terms. Get the brigade commanders over here."

It was maybe fifteen minutes before a technical skidded to a stop in front of the school. Seversky was waiting out front. There were a couple of American soldiers in back, and another man, an officer in Tanzanian uniform.

The officer climbed down out of the truck, waited for his American guards to follow, and then walked up to Seversky. With a crisp British salute: "You are Lieutenant General Seversky, I believe? Colonel Mohammed Ilumubeke, of the Coalition general staff. I think you know why I am here, General."

"Pretty much," Seversky allowed.

"You and your men have fought very well, but—" The colonel shrugged. "There is only so much that men can do. The Coalition command has ordered a final assault on your positions. I will not say when, but soon. Maybe you will survive that. Maybe you will survive the next one, too. But—" Another shrug. "The matter is settled; now it is merely a question of how many more of your soldiers must die before this ends."

Seversky nodded, once. "I assume you've got terms to suggest."

"Of course." The colonel pulled an envelope from inside his jacket and handed it to him. Seversky opened it, glanced over the sheet of paper, and nodded again. "I'll need time to consult with my staff."

"Of course," the colonel said again. "Twenty-four hours? I think we can allow that much."

When the colonel was on his way back to Kitale, Seversky took the sheet of paper back inside. The brigade commanders were waiting, along with what was left of his staff. He handed the paper to the nearest, waited until it had circled the group.

"Anything from Washington?" This from Isherwood.

Seversky snorted. "They're, quote, evaluating options for a relief force. Unquote."

"Meaning we're on our own," Isherwood said. Nobody argued with him.

Seversky glanced around the circle of tense and worried faces. "A month ago," he said, "if somebody had said I'd be looking at a piece of paper like this one, I'd have said he was nuts. If somebody had said I'd be considering it—" For a moment, the words failed him. "You all know what we're facing. Can we beat the next assault?"

For a long moment nobody said anything. Martinez, the colonel who led Second Brigade, finally broke the silence. "Probably not. We're down to less than ten rounds per man and dead out of almost everything else. The men'll still fight, but they don't have much left to fight with."

That was true in more than a logistical sense, Seversky knew. "Does anyone disagree?"

Martinez shook his head. Nobody else responded at all, and after a moment Bridgeport realized why. They were in charge of what was left of the 101st, the Screaming Eagles, and one of the proudest records in the US Army stood between them and the choice they had to make.

"I know," Seversky said at last. "If I thought we could accomplish anything by it, I'd send back a message saying 'nuts' and we'd fight to the last man. But—" His gaze fell. "This isn't Bastogne and Patton's not on the way. We're going to have to face the fact that the US of A has just had its clock cleaned."

16 September 2029: Diego Garcia Island

The last of the boats bobbed to the surface. Chung Ehrwan, who had just hauled himself out of the sea onto another boat, wigwagged a flashlight signal to the rest of the men in the water. A few minutes later, in total darkness, Unit 6628 was on its way in.

The boats were inflatables with steeply angled radar-deflecting shields, their motors quiet as whispers. The men on board, gleaming in their wetsuits, got their gear stowed and crouched low, so that radars on shore would miss them. All the skills they'd learned in endlessly repeated drills, and tested in clashes with the Vietnamese and Filipinos on the barren, oil-rich little islets of the South China Sea, were about to face a much harsher test. Chung had reminded his men of that in the last briefing aboard the submarine, reminded them also of the Hainan bombing they were about to avenge.

There were six of the inflatables, and six strike teams, each with its own mission. Invisible in the night, Diego Garcia lay due north.

An hour later, one at a time, the men slipped off the boats and plunged into the sea to make the final approach. When it was his turn, Chung slid off the stern, hung there in the water for a moment, and then hit the button that let the air out of the boat and filled it with sea water instead. As it sank, he pushed his rebreather mouthpiece into place and pulled down his goggles, then followed the boat down, hauling out the anchor as it went. A few minutes later, with the anchor neatly wedged into the coral and the boat safe from tides and currents, Chung pushed off from the bottom and swam into shore.

The beach was narrow and steep, with plenty of cover. Chung crossed it with his bag of gear, got into the tangled tropical brush just behind. The soft click-click of a signal led him to his strike team's meeting point. As he made sure every member of the team had his silenced weapons and explosive charges, and the two men with the mortar were ready to do their part, he had to fight off the conviction that this was just another exercise.

At zero two thirty local time, they left the meeting point and headed for the nearest service road. A quarter mile up they passed a dark shape sprawled awkwardly in the ditch alongside the road: the Humvee that had been patrolling the road, with both soldiers inside neatly headshot. Chung nodded; so far, the plan was going as it should.

He passed more corpses as his team closed in on its first set of targets, one of the guarded island's main radar installations. The corpses were the work of the first two strike teams, whose job was to eliminate sentries and maintain mission security; the other four were there to destroy a set of targets and then secure the airfield. The orders did not specify what would happen after that, but Chung thought he could guess.

Zero three hundred. Chung signaled, and four of the team members headed in toward the radar installation in pairs. The two with the mortar found a good location, and Chung stayed with them. His team would regroup there, move on to the next target, keep going until the mission was completed or every member of the team was dead. He stared into the night, waiting for the flash of the first explosive charges against the radome supports.

All at once, further up the island, an explosion flared: one of the other teams had gotten to its target first. Chung signaled, and the mortar went flash-*whump*, sending the first shell on its way.

16 September 2029: Above the Indian Ocean

The flight plan they'd been given in Kunming was simple enough—southwest over Burma and the Bay of Bengal to just south of the equator, then west-southwest to Tanzania, refueling air-to-air from tankers out of the PLAAF base at Trincomalee in Sri Lanka. What bothered Captain Kwan Wenshang was the packet of sealed orders he'd been handed at the last minute, and by no less than a PLA general. He was to open them, the general told him, at a certain point along the way, and take action accordingly.

There were eight Y-8 transports in the flight, with a dozen J-20s for fighter cover—their flight path took them far too close to the American base at Diego Garcia for comfort. Each of the Y-8s contained close to a hundred PLA infantrymen and all their gear, part of an elite airborne brigade, headed for the fighting in East Africa and a potential landing under fire on a Kenyan airfield. That was the official plan, at least. Exactly what would happen after he opened the orders was much on Kwan's mind.

161

"Sir?" The navigator turned. "You wished to be notified—"

Kwan nodded his thanks, pulled out his sealed orders and opened them. He read through the packet once in disbelief, then a second time, carefully. Then he turned to the communications officer, and handed him a card.

"You will search for radar transmissions of these types," he said. "Let me know at once what you find."

The Y-8 had the latest radar-detection gear, and it took the communications officer only a few moments to find the broadcast. "Sir," he said, "we're receiving two of the signals, but not the others." A moment later: "That's odd. One of the two has just stopped."

"If the other stops," Kwan said, "inform me at once."

The transport flew on. Outside, the night rushed past. After a few more minutes: "Sir, all the radar signals are gone."

"We are under new orders," Kwan said then, pitching his voice so that everyone in the cabin could hear him. "We will be landing under fire at Diego Garcia." He handed a chart and a new flight order to the navigator, a set of instructions to the communications officer. "Let the others know." Then, rising, he turned and left the cockpit.

The soldiers looked up as he appeared in the door to the main cabin and brought his hand up in a crisp salute. Their commander, obviously surprised, stood and returned the salute. "Your mission has just been changed," Kwan told him. "Here are the new orders."

The officer glanced at the papers, at him, then read the papers and drew in a sudden sharp breath. He looked up at Kwan, then. "How long until we land?"

"Maybe forty-five minutes."

"We will be ready."

"Excellent." He saluted again, went forward into the cockpit.

Over the minutes that followed, the communications officer finished passing on the new orders to the other transports and the J-20s. Kwan, leaning forward in his seat, stared through the windscreen at the night ahead. The orders said very little about what would be waiting for them on the ground. If the airfield was held by the enemy, or their antiaircraft missiles were still in working order—

He dismissed the thought, reviewed the orders one more time.

Finally, off in the distance, dim points of light became visible. The J-20s hurtled ahead; ground attack wasn't normally a mission assigned to the long-range fighters, but Kwan had no doubt they could do plenty of damage to targets on the island, and draw out any antiaircraft missiles before the more vulnerable transports came into range. As the points of light came closer, Kwan's Y-8 sank down to within a dozen meters of the sea, and the others followed, flying low and fast toward the guarded island.

15 September 2029: The White House, Washington DC

Jameson Weed stared out the windows of the Oval Office, wishing he could take that fishing trip he'd planned months ago. The first hint of fall was in the air; it was a perfect afternoon, bright and clear, the kind of day when sitting by a trout stream and casting a fly onto the water was the best possible answer to the pressures of the world's toughest job.

No chance of that, though, not now.

The National Security Council and the Joint Chiefs would be arriving in minutes. He paced back over to the desk, read the message on the computer screen, tried to think of some way to spin it that would add up to something short of political disaster. Nothing came to mind. How do you tell a nation that's never lost a war that it's about to lose one?

No point in delaying the inevitable, though. He picked up the phone, dialed his press secretary. "Susan? I want a press conference at seven this evening." He paused, listening. "No, it's bad news—really bad. No questions afterward; there'll be a full briefing later on, time and place TBA." Another pause. "That'll be fine. Thanks."

He put the phone down. As he turned away, it rang. He picked it up, snapped, "Yes?"

Greg Barnett's voice answered, tense with worry. "Jim, we've got another problem."

Oh fuck, Weed thought. Just what I need. "What's up?"

"We've lost contact with Diego Garcia. Everything went down right after 3 am local time—four in the afternoon here."

The words landed like a physical blow. Weed guessed what that meant, flailed for an alternative. "Something technical?"

"I wish. No, NRO just got satellite images, and there are planes on the runways that aren't ours." Weed could hear the man draw in a breath. "You wanted to know when we'd get a response from the Chinese. This is probably it."

16 September 2029: Diego Garcia Island

The Marine units on Diego Garcia were as tough as any in the US military, and given any kind of warning, they might have had a chance. The problem they faced was that each blow came with no warning at all. The explosions that took out the island's radar, antiaircraft defenses, and communications links were the first sign anyone had that anything was wrong. By the time the Marines had established a defensive perimeter and started closing with the first wave of raiders, air-to-ground rockets started slamming into buildings around the airfield, vaporizing the island's fighter planes and forcing the Marines to take cover. Then the J-20s shot past at treetop level, banked and turned, fired more rockets into the American positions. As they came back around for a third pass, the first of the transports came down onto the airfield's main runway, swerved to the side as soon as it slowed to taxiing speed, and began to spill soldiers onto the airfield. Behind it came another, and another, and another, until all eight transports were on the ground and more than 700 of the PLA's best combat troops were spreading out around the airfield.

"Another force is on its way, sir," Kwan explained to Major Chung. They were standing in an undamaged maintenance building just off the main runway, the temporary headquarters of the Chinese forces on Diego Garcia. Gunfire could still be heard in the middle distance. "My orders give no details, but I was instructed to send a message via satellite as soon as I was certain the airfield could be secured."

"When did you send the message?"

"The moment we landed."

Chung grinned. "Excellent. If they're coming from Trincomalee they should be here in a matter of hours."

Voices sounded outside the building, in Chinese and American English. Chung and Kwan both turned. Three PLA infantrymen came in, escorting an American wearing a bathrobe and pajamas. "Sir," said one of the infantrymen, saluting. "Rear Admiral Wanford, the American commander."

The American looked at once dazed and outraged. He looked from Kwan to Chung and back again, apparently decided that the man in the uniform outranked the one in the wetsuit, and addressed Kwan in English. "What the hell is this supposed to be about?"

"Admiral," said Chung in the same language, "your nation launched an air attack on mine a few days ago. You may consider this a repayment."

The American's mouth opened and closed several times, but no sound came out. "I regret," Chung told him then, "that our facilities for prisoners of war are fairly primitive at the moment. We will change that as soon as more of our soldiers land and finish securing the island. Did you have anything else to say? No?" He turned to the infantrymen, and in Chinese: "Keep him apart from the others. See that he stays safe and under guard."

The soldiers saluted and led the American away.

16 September 2029: The Kremlin, Moscow

"You are absolutely certain of this?" Kuznetsov said. The president was dressed in pajamas, slippers and a bathrobe. Any other time, someone might have joked about that, but the faces that turned toward him at that moment were tense with worry.

"Yes, sir," said the duty officer at the intelligence desk, and tapped keys on the keyboard in front of him. "Here are the latest intercepts from Krasnodar."

Kuznetsov leaned over the man's shoulder, read the text on the screen, and nodded. Straightening up: "Get me Bunin." An orderly saluted and hurried away, and Kuznetsov turned to face the others. "All our conventional and strategic resources are to be put on alert at once. The Americans are not going to take this calmly."

FIFTEEN

16 September 2029: Endebess, Kenya

It had been so many years since an American army had surrendered that nobody quite knew how to do it. Melanie Bridgeport, flipping through Army manuals while the rest of the staff destroyed classified gear and paperwork, found something on how to accept the surrender of an enemy force, and somebody knew somebody who knew some corporal who was a Civil War buff, and was brought to HQ to describe as best he could how Pemberton's men surrendered to Grant at Vicksburg and Lee's men did the same thing at Appomattox. Between the manual and the scraps of remembered history, Seversky's staff figured out more or less what to do.

As the sun came up on the 16th, Seversky signed a paper accepting the surrender terms and handed it to a colonel to take to the Coalition forces. The orders had already gone out to what was left of the American force: stack your weapons, get your belongings in a pack you can carry, be ready to march to the Kitale road as soon as you're told.

As she walked out of the primary school building half an hour later, Bridgeport looked around, wondering why it seemed strange. A moment passed before she realized how quiet the morning was. It had been weeks since she'd been out of earshot of the sound of combat.

Dust was rising from the road to the east. Seversky was standing in front of the school, his face bleak. All the others were somewhere else, one clump of them over by the last of the technicals, another bunch by the trees next to the road, still another sitting in the shade and wolfing down a breakfast of MREs. Bridgeport started over toward Seversky, then saw the look the general gave her, saluted, and walked away.

Instead, she went over to the group having breakfast, got handed one of the packets, and ate fast, watching the plume of dust get closer. She was just washing it down with the last of the bottled water when the Coalition technicals rolled up to the school.

Colonel Ilumubeke climbed out of the cab of the lead truck, walked over to Seversky, and saluted him; Seversky returned the salute, crisp as if he'd been on inspection. "If you prefer, General," said the colonel, "we can spare a technical to take you into Kitale."

"I'll walk with my men," Seversky replied.

"As you wish." The colonel raised his voice. "If you will form up in column four abreast, please. It is still possible to reach Kitale before the heat of the day."

Bridgeport got up and joined the forming line. Seversky followed a few rows back. Coalition soldiers with AK-47s slung over their shoulders took up places to either side. After a few minutes, when all the Americans were lined up, one of the soldiers waved for them to start walking east.

15 September 2029: The White House, Washington DC

As details trickled into the White House situation room, what kept circling through Weed's mind was sheer disbelief. Diego Garcia was the beating heart of the entire US Indian Ocean presence, a key logistics and intelligence center and a base from which B-1s could pound trouble spots from Africa to Southeast Asia. Losing Tanzania was a problem; losing Kenya was a crisis; losing Diego Garcia ... He shook his head, tried to think.

"Sir?" An aide had come in. "The press conference."

"Yes. Yes, of course." He drew in a deep breath and went to the door.

It was by all accounts one of the best speeches of Jameson Weed's political career. Extempore—he had drawn up a draft before the news came about Diego Garcia, but it was sitting on a desk in the Oval Office as he walked up to the podium—he sketched out the situation, explained what had happened in Kenya, denounced China's behavior in thundering terms, and broke the news of the fall of Diego Garcia. "Let the People's Republic of China make no mistake," he said. "The United States will not let this unprovoked aggression stand. We will respond with all the forces at our disposal. Nothing is off the table." He leaned forward, haggard and minatory. "Nothing."

Thirty minutes later, the American ambassador in Beijing delivered a formal ultimatum to the Chinese government threatening nuclear war.

16 September 2029: The August First Building, Beijing

"This is hardly the outcome you led us to expect," said Chen Weiming. The president's voice was quiet, studied, dangerous.

"When the Committee accepted my plan," Liu answered, "I took full responsibility for the consequences. It would be absurd to attempt to evade them now."

They and the other members of the Central Military Commission sat in the same secure meeting room where Plan Qilin had first been authorized four months earlier. Outside the room, across the length and breadth of China, PLA forces and civilian defense cadres were hurrying to prepare the nation for the unthinkable. In the meeting room, though, nothing moved; the heavy red draperies muffled all sound.

Chen turned to Ma Baiyuan, Liu's equal as vice chairman of the Committee. "Ma, what exactly are the Americans demanding?"

Ma cleared his throat. "They want a ceasefire within twenty-four hours, and our forces to begin withdrawing from East Africa and Diego Garcia within forty-eight. If we do not accept their terms within seventy-two hours, or if we pursue any further hostilities against US interests, they threaten to use tactical nuclear weapons against military targets."

Chung glanced around the table as the words sank in. "Yang," he said then, "what is the current status of the Second Artillery Corps?" That was China's strategic force, some 500 state-of-the-art land- and submarine-based missiles tipped with nuclear warheads.

"On alert since the beginning of the East African conflict," Yang Chao said at once. "On highest alert since the attack on Hainan."

"Five hundred missiles," said Ma, "against how many thousands of American bombs?"

"Irrelevant." Yang leaned forward. "Five hundred nuclear blasts, or even a large fraction of that, and the United States ceases to exist as a nation. They know that. They will not risk it."

"If you are wrong," said Ma, "the history of China ends in three days."

No one else spoke. If Plan Qilin were to fail, Liu knew, it would fail then and there. A vote by the Commission to accept the American terms and withdraw the troops, and it would all have been in vain. His own dismissal and disgrace did not bother him as much as the thought of how close China stood to total victory.

Chen glanced around the table again, sighed, and spoke. "That may be so, but we cannot back down. The people will not permit it. They have watched our missiles, our planes, and our allies in Africa defeat the Americans day after day. If we bow to American blackmail now, on the brink of victory, our government will not survive, and neither will we. It is that simple.

"I intend to go before the media, refuse the American ultimatum, and inform the world that we will respond to any nuclear attack on Chinese interests with our own nuclear arsenal. Do I have your support?"

One by one, the other members of the Commission voted in favor. Chen nodded, got to his feet. "I will make the announcement in one hour. By then, I expect all of you to be on your way to your assigned bunkers. All except for you." He turned to Liu. "You have said that you accept responsibility for the consequences of your plan. Very well; you will remain here in Beijing." With the faintest of smiles: "Above ground. The civil defense program will benefit from your direct supervision."

"Of course," Liu said. "It will be an honor."

"Good." The others were rising from their chairs as well. "The rest of you know what you need to do. I trust we will see each other again. If not—" Chen allowed a shrug, turned, and left the room.

16 September 2029: Shinyanga District, Tanzania

The truck lurched to a halt. A moment later, one of the Tanzanian soldiers came around back and pulled the flap aside. "Here we are," he said. "Out, please."

Melanie Bridgeport hauled herself to her feet along with the others, headed for the back of the truck. There were trucks waiting when they'd reached Kitale, nearly all of them captured from the Americans; the Coalition soldiers had packed as many prisoners of war into each truck as would fit and sent them roaring off southwards one at a time. Bridgeport had been in the third truck to leave, in a random mix of staff officers and ordinary soldiers.

For a moment, as her eyes adjusted to the sunlight, she wondered if the Tanzanians had decided to turn Camp Pumbaa into a POW camp, the landscape was that similar. It took her a moment to notice the rundown buildings, the lines of olive-drab military tents, and the two barbed-wire fences around the lot of it. The fences looked like they had been slapped up in a hurry, and there was a crew still putting up a guard tower at one corner of the camp.

The guard walked along the line of Americans, motioned with his head to Bridgeport and the two other women who had been in the same truck. "Women's part of camp is that way," he said, gesturing. "The rest of you will come with me."

Bridgeport and the other two women looked at one another, followed the guard's gesture. Off that way was a section of the camp behind its own fence, with women in Tanzanian uniform guarding it. The guard at the gate asked their names and ranks, noted those down on a clipboard, waved them in, and another guard came and walked them down one of the lines of tents, stopping halfway down.

"This tent is yours." The guard pulled the flap aside; there were two other American women already in the tent. The guard turned back to face the newcomers. "Latrine is down there. Mess hall, in the building there. Showers? When they get here, we will find out."

She stopped, and considered them. "One more thing," she said then. "You will be told the rules here shortly. If you follow them, you will be going home as soon as this business is over. If you try to escape, or do anything else foolish, we will shoot you and then you will have to stay here forever. Please do not make us do that." She motioned them to the tent, turned and went back to the unloading area, where another truck was pulling up. The POWs stood there for another moment, and then went into the tent for lack of anything better to do.

There were eight rickety cots inside the tent, and Bridge-port and the others sorted out who was going to sleep where and tucked their rucksacks and duffel bags in what little space there was.

172

"Going home," said one of the others, a clerk in the head-quarters company named Carron. "I hope." She sat down on her cot. "God, I hope—but I wonder what they're saying back home right now."

"I don't think I want to know," Bridgeport told her.

15 September 2029: The White House, Washington DC

"They can't be serious." Ellen Harbin's expression was flat, contemptuous. "They have, what? Five hundred warheads. We have ten thousand. We could turn the whole country into ash with room to spare."

"True," said Admiral Waite, "but irrelevant. Our best current estimate, given our missile defense system and their known countermeasures, is that half the Chinese weapons will reach their targets. You might want to consider what 250 nuclear explosions would do to this country. They don't have to match us warhead for warhead; all they have to do is cost us more than we're willing to pay."

"Nonsense," snapped Gurney. "They're bluffing. They'll back down."

"They've started civil defense preparations all over the country." This from Greg Barnett, in a measured tone. "Something like five million children are being evacuated from the big cities right now. Every nondefense factory and every non-essential business has been shut down. If they're bluffing, it's a very convincing bluff."

"It's entirely possible that that's exactly what it is," Harbin insisted.

A cell phone buzzed in Barnett's pocket. He took it out, glanced at the screen, excused himself from the Roosevelt Room. "They've played a very clever game," Harbin went on, "but they can't seriously expect to win at this stage. I'm convinced that if we keep up the pressure, we can force them to the negotiating table."

Weed had been standing at his end of the table, facing away. Now he turned around. "That's my take," he said. "One way or another, though, we can't back down—not without losing our credibility around the world. I—" He stopped as Barnett came back into the room; the CIA director's face was white. "What is it?"

"Russia," Barnett said. "Kuznetsov's called an emergency press conference in the Kremlin—that's how it's being billed in the Russian media." He drew in a breath. "And their strategic bombers are in the air—not headed our way, but up. Our satellites just spotted them."

16 September 2029: The Kremlin, Moscow

Gennady Kuznetsov crossed to the podium with the double-headed eagle on it, and took his place behind it. Faces and cameras followed him every centimeter of the way. He relished that, relished the knowledge that everything that had been planned in Washington and Beijing, everything that had been enacted in the skies and sea lanes and savannahs of East Africa, had come spiraling in at last to rest on what would be done here and now.

The last tense meeting with the general staff had ended a quarter hour earlier. Final orders were already on their way to military bases across the Russian Federation, and to Russia's diplomats in the United States and around the world. Now, Kuznetsov told himself. Now it is in my hands, and mine alone.

He caught the eye of the RT video team at the back of the room, waited for the nod that told him they were ready, and began speaking.

"The Russian Federation has been informed," he said, "that the United States has responded to the failure of its military adventurism in East Africa by threatening the People's Republic of China with nuclear attack. In today's interconnected world, where the deepest desire of all peoples is to live together in peace, such threats are impermissible, and they must not go unanswered."

The eyes and camera lenses turned toward him might as well have been a million kilometers away. "It is therefore my duty as President of the Russian Federation," he said then, "to remind the United States and the world that China does not face this crisis alone. Treaties of long standing oblige us to respond to any nuclear attack on China with our own strategic forces, and those forces are ready to launch at this moment. Should the United States choose to act on its threats, we will retaliate with our entire nuclear arsenal."

He could see the shock on their faces as the words sank in, and savored it. "That is all. May God protect Russia and the world in this hour." A quick hard movement of one hand cut off the first stammered questions. Kuznetsov suppressed a smile and left the podium.

SIXTEEN

17 September 2029: Shinyanga District, Tanzania

Morning parade—that was what the guards called it—was seven o'clock sharp. The POWs in the Shinyanga camp were marched onto the parade ground in the middle of camp, lined up by tents and counted, and the guards had made it clear that if anyone turned up missing, the rest would wait there until the count came out right. Standing with her tentmates in the dust of the parade ground, Melanie Bridgeport wondered whether it would come to that; with the war effectively over and more than 1,000 miles of hostile territory between the camp and the nearest neutral country, escape didn't seem like a useful project.

The guards finished their count. The camp commandant, a portly colonel with a swagger stick tucked under his arm, returned their salutes and took the microphone. "Thank you, ladies and gentlemen." He spoke English with an Oxford accent. "Before you proceed to breakfast, I am sorry to say there is bad news—very, very bad news. Your country has threatened to drop atomic bombs on the Chinese. Of course the Chinese have said they will retaliate, and now the Russians say that they will drop their bombs on the Americans if the Americans drop theirs on the Chinese. So it is possible that we are all going to die shortly." He motioned to the guards to start marching the POWs to the mess hall, turned and walked away.

16 September 2029: Chambersburg, Pennsylvania

There were arrangements dating back to the Cold War for evacuating members of Congress and their families to one of the nuclear shelters surrounding DC, and Senator Bridgeport had been briefed on them annually by a succession of cheerful flacks from Homeland Security. When the alert went out, though, it took him less than a minute to decide that he had other plans. Like most people in Congress, he had a spare car with ordinary license plates for times when he didn't want to call attention to himself. When the call came from the Senate staff letting him know where he could meet the chartered bus that would whisk him off to the shelter, he thanked the staffer, hung up, packed a suitcase, got in the spare car and drove the other way.

The highways would be closed to anything but official traffic as soon as enough police and national guard forces could be deployed—they'd covered that in the briefings—and that meant back roads, but there were plenty of those, and once he was past the inner ring of suburbs surrounding DC it was simply a matter of staying clear of the important federal facilities. He zigzagged north and west through farm country, past fields of corn and pumpkins, past compact little towns with white clapboard churches and one-street business districts, as the hills rose up around him toward the great ragged crests of the mountains further west.

A cheery sign told him he'd passed into Pennsylvania. Another, miles later, told him just where in Pennsylvania he was, and he slowed, considered finding a motel and waiting out the crisis there. Another moment and he decided against it. Whatever did or didn't happen, nothing he'd done had earned him a place alongside the ghosts in blue and gray who waited for the trumpets there. He turned onto another state highway, and within a few minutes Gettysburg was out of sight in the rolling landscape behind him.

The next town of any size was Chambersburg, or so the sign told him; afternoon was turning toward evening by the time he got there, and cars were getting thicker on the road. He left the highway, found a motel toward the edge of town that had its vacancy sign lit, and pulled into the crowded parking lot.

The clerk behind the front desk, who must have been barely out of high school, asked for a credit card. Bridgeport handed him a $100 bill instead, with a twenty folded into it; the kid grinned, pocketed the $20, and put the other in the till. "Restaurant's open twenty-four hours," he said as he handed Bridgeport a room key. "Liquor store's three blocks that way."

Bridgeport gave him a quizzical look. "You get asked about that often?"

"Last couple of days, all the time." Sitting back down in his chair: "Need anything else, you give me a call."

17 September 2029: The August First Building, Beijing

The August First Building echoed around him as Liu got off the elevator, paced down the hall to his office. Essential staff had already gone to underground shelters scattered over much of China, and most nonessential personnel had been reassigned to civil defense duties or sent home to their families; the few who remained would be heading to shelters in Beijing before time ran out on the American ultimatum. What had been the busy heart of the People's Liberation Army a few days before was now silent, a place of closed doors and empty cubicles. He thought of the other members of the Central Military Commission, secure in deep shelters far below a dozen widely dispersed mountains; that Meiyin was safe in yet another shelter in Inner Mongolia, with the wives and families of other top Party officials, was some consolation.

In the reception area outside his office, his secretary stood and saluted. "Sir, a message for you—a professor at the Academy."

That would be Fang, Liu realized at once. "I'll take it in my office."

Outside the windows, morning light streamed over central Beijing. The air was no clearer than usual, but the familiar traffic was all but absent; evacuation orders had already been issued, every scrap of rolling stock the railways could hold was carrying children and the elderly to the relative safety of the countryside, while the vast network of shelters beneath the city built in Mao's day and indifferently maintained since then was being frantically refitted for the essential workers who would remain behind.

Liu walked to his desk, picked up the telephone, punched in a phone number and a code, and listened. It was Fang's voice, as he'd guessed. "General, I know you will have far too many duties just now, but would it be possible for you to meet me this morning at the Central Xiangqi Club? It is of some small importance."

The message clicked off, and Liu stared at the handset for a long moment, baffled. A game of xiangqi, now of all times? He wondered briefly if the crisis had somehow unhinged Fang's mind, then caught himself. Of all the possibilities, that was the least likely. What under heaven did the man have in mind, then?

There was only one way to find out. He punched another number on the telephone, waited. The phone rang once, then: "General? I hope my message was not impertinent."

"Not at all," Liu said, and drew in a breath. "I would be happy to come. Ten this morning?"

"That would be perfect, General." Was that a flicker of relief in the man's voice? Liu couldn't tell.

He finished the phone call as quickly as he could, glanced at the time on his computer, then sat down and started calling

180

up situation reports. The fighting in Kenya was over—the Americans had stopped sending planes down from their Persian Gulf bases now that their ground forces had surrendered—and Diego Garcia was quiet, with another round of PLA reinforcements on the way by air from Trincomalee. The Persian Gulf was another matter; the Iranians had kept their promise to stir up trouble there, and eight Saudi cities were ablaze with riots that looked more like urban risings with every hour that passed. Still, that was Iran's concern, not China's.

The conflict that mattered lay elsewhere. China's strategic forces were ready to launch, submarines and ground-based missiles alike. The Russians were saying nothing about their preparations, but photos from China's reconnaissance satellites showed the traces of ICBMs readied for launch and big Tupolev bombers circling over the northern coast of Siberia, waiting for the orders that would send them surging over the pole. The same satellites brought back word of similar preparations on the far side of the oceans—B-52s over Canada, missiles ready to launch, the few Trident submarines not already at sea leaving their bases and heading toward their assigned stations—as the American strategic arsenal got ready to strike.

The bleak mathematics of nuclear war played out in his head as he studied the most recent photos from above the United States. Every one of the three great nuclear powers had its own antimissile system, which could be counted on to take out some of the attacking missiles, though no one could be sure how many. Every one of the powers could assume that some of its missiles would fail to launch or go astray and tumble uselessly to earth somewhere far from its target. Even so, given the size of the arsenals in question, there would be enough nuclear fireballs over enough targets to erase all three powers as viable nations, and quite possibly to bring a sudden end to the entire project of human civilization.

Liu bowed his head, tasting his own responsibility. Were the consequences he hoped Plan Qilin might bring worth risking the survival of China, of civilization, possibly of humanity? He raised his head again, stared at the report on strategic forces until the clock on the computer warned him that it was time to leave for the Central Xiangqi Club and the meeting with Fang.

The streets of Beijing, normally so crowded, were nearly empty, and it took his driver barely half the usual time to get Liu to his destination. He'd expected the club to be as empty as the streets, but there were more people there than usual, sitting at xiangqi boards or clustered around some unusually lively match. That brought an unwilling smile; it encouraged him that not even the threat of nuclear annihilation could keep xiangqi players from their favorite game.

"General!" Fang was already in the main room of the club, and came over toward him at once. "I'm delighted that you could make time in your schedule for this."

Liu nodded, let himself be led over to a table and a xiangqi board. Fang had something in mind, he knew, and the only way to find out what was to—

Play the game. He sat, got the pieces in their places on the board, tried to copy the concentration of the players around him. That took effort at first, but as the familiar rhythm of play began, he was able to push aside everything else and let his world contract to his pieces, Fang's, and the shifting matrix of relationships among them.

Fang's opening moves were uncharacteristically aggressive. Liu chose a wary, defensive strategy, trying to draw the other man out, get him to commit his resources and reveal his plans. He shifted an advisor and an elephant to the center line in front of his general, brought a chariot forward and moved the horse on the same side over to the edge of the board: standard moves, those, freeing up pieces without showing his intentions to Fang.

The opening gave way to the middle game, and Liu stayed on the defensive, leaving no openings Fang could exploit.

The other man would be preparing some grand combination, Liu was sure; that was Fang's way, but so was concealing his intentions until the last minute. Liu studied the board. Others were watching the game, he noted, then tried to drive the awareness out of his mind and maintain his focus.

When Fang's combination finally appeared, it nearly took Liu's breath away—both horses, a chariot and a cannon, threatening a lethal quadruple check. The watchers murmured, and Liu leaned forward. Something was not quite right ...

All at once he saw it, and allowed a slow smile. The move was a bluff. Fang could not execute the quadruple check without exposing his own general to attack. Liu took one of his chariots and moved it forward, close to the river, biding his time.

Within a few more moves the momentum of the game was going the other way. Move by move, Liu closed off every remaining option Fang had, until finally the professor had no moves left and bowed his head, conceding.

There must have been fifty people watching, Liu realized abruptly. The murmurs had turned to animated conversation, and bills rustled as money changed hands. He looked up from the board to Fang's face, caught the slight raise of an eyebrow, the almost pleading look. That was when he realized what Fang was trying to tell him.

Half an hour later he was back at the August First Building. "I need a list of six or seven large civil defense installations and military factories here in Beijing," he told his secretary. "Places where there will still be plenty of people. I'll be visiting them, very publicly. You'll inform Xinhua—I want each visit broadcast, in China and internationally."

The secretary gave him a startled look, but said "Yes, sir," and started tapping on his keyboard as Liu went into his office. He woke his computer, saw the report on strategic forces, and closed it at once. There was no need to waste his time with that. Fang was right: the Americans were bluffing.

17 September 2029: Facility 6335, West of Sverdlovsk

Kuznetsov glanced around the office, nodded. Though he was nearly a mile below ground, the room was comfortable enough, with curtains covering blank walls here and there to create the illusion of windows. A smart bit of psychology on the part of the designers, or the personal quirk of some Politburo official? In all probability, no one alive still knew.

The flaws of the old Soviet government were undeniable, but it had certainly succeeded in being thorough. Eight huge emergency shelters had been excavated deep underneath the Ural Mountains, each one of them large enough to house the essential personnel of the entire national government, and built deep and strong enough that not even nuclear warheads posed any threat to those inside. These days, only two of them were still usable, and only one was kept staffed and ready for emergencies—Russia was prosperous again, with oil and natural gas revenues at record highs, but the extravagances that crippled the Soviet system were on many minds, and one such shelter was ample for Russia's current needs.

Kuznetsov went to the desk, tapped the mouse. The screen lit up immediately. He sat down, opened a text window and sent the agreed code message back to the Kremlin, letting the remaining staff in Moscow know that he had arrived at Facility 6335 and was in charge, and that they should head for their assigned shelters at once.

A few more clicks of the mouse brought up the screens he needed to watch: updates from the Russian strategic forces command center inside Kosvinsky Mountain, satellite and over-the-horizon radar data from the early warning system headquarters in Solnechnogorsk, hourly intelligence updates from SVR headquarters in the Yasenovo district back in Moscow, reports from EMERCOM on the nation's civil defense preparations. All of it argued that he'd gauged the situation correctly.

If he had not …

He brushed the thought aside, clicked on the screen with the latest SVR update. Satellite photos showed flurries of activity around American and Chinese strategic bases and both nation's fleets putting to sea. He scrolled down quickly to the reports on the world's other nuclear powers, cupped his chin in one hand as he read the report.

Britain, France and India had all gotten diplomatic notes informing them that they would not be targeted by Russia's strategic forces so long as they reciprocated. New Delhi replied within the hour, insisting that India had no hostile intentions toward anyone and offering to mediate, but there had been no word from London or Paris. Kuznetsov frowned, knowing how few minutes it would take British or French missiles to hit Moscow or St. Petersburg. Still, the report offered some comfort: spies in both countries reported that the governments and strategic forces were acting as though they wanted to survive a nuclear exchange, not to join in one.

At the bottom of the report, though, something caught his eye. One of the vice chairmen of China's Central Military Commission, a General Liu, was all over the news in China: he'd been seen playing some Chinese board game or other at a club in Beijing, then visited a civil defense facility in the city to cheer up the people sheltering there. SVR staff reported a rumor that he'd been in charge of China's end of the East African campaign, and noted that he was either the second or the third most powerful figure in the Chinese government—not the kind of man you would expect even the Chinese to leave aboveground in the country's most important nuclear target.

He sat back, considered the screen. Could the Chinese really be that confident?

18 September 2029: Expediency Council offices, Tehran

The guarded room in the nondescript building was crowded, with more than twice the usual number in attendance. Not only the members of the Expediency Council but every other figure of importance in Iran's government had been summoned. Every face turned toward Ayatollah Jahrami as he set down the latest briefing paper.

"You all know what we are facing," he said. "If the Americans follow through on their threat, it is inconceivable that they will spare us."

The old ayatollah Saif al-Shirazi considered him through thick glasses. "I trust you will excuse me if I ask why."

Zardawi, the commander of the Revolutionary Guards, cleared his throat discreetly. "In a nuclear war, your eminence, if anyone can be said to win, it is those countries that stay out of the fighting and are spared the fallout. If Russia, China and the United States destroy one another, maybe we will all die anyway, but Allah willing, some of the nations not directly involved may not perish. Which of them will dominate the world once the war is over, if anyone does? It will be those large and strong countries that take no part the war. Iran could be among those—Iran, India, Brazil, two or three others. Whether the Americans will bomb India or Brazil I do not know, but they will not miss the chance to bomb us."

Jahrami nodded. "It is simply a matter of whether the Americans are bluffing or not. And in the meantime, we have an unexpected crisis on our hands. General?"

"I suspect," the Revolutionary Guards commander said, "that you have all been watching the news from Arabia as closely as I have. I am informed by our intelligence service, though, that the situation is even more unstable than the media realizes—certainly more so than we anticipated. We hoped merely to stir up trouble for the Americans, to distract them from East Africa and foster good relations with the Chinese. None of us expected the rising against the Saudis to grow so quickly or accomplish so much."

"Do you think they can overthrow the Saudis themselves?" This from a general in Iran's regular army.

Zardawi shook his head emphatically. "With Allah, all things are possible; still, barring His direct intervention, they will be crushed. Not soon, not without a great expenditure of money and blood—but they will be crushed."

"And if that happens," Jahrami said, "we will suffer a double loss. First, all the preparations we have made to destabilize the Saudis will have to be made all over again, against a government grown wary by experience. Second, our allies will be slow to risk themselves in the future, thinking that we will abandon them as we abandoned the Arabian rebels. Yet if we act now, you know as well as I do how the Americans are likely to respond."

"Do you have a proposal to suggest?" Shirazi asked.

"Prayer comes to mind," Jahrami said.

The old ayatollah glanced around the circle of faces. "That is always wise," he said finally, "but it seems to me, along those same lines, that an important point is being neglected. Whatever the military, political, economic issues in all this—" A wave of his hand dismissed them. "There is also a religious dimension. It is possible that this is how Allah has decided to end the world He has made. If so, do you wish the last day to find you sitting at your ease here in Tehran or cowering in a shelter in the mountains?"

"That is a consideration," Jahrami admitted.

"What exactly are you suggesting, your eminence?" This from Zardawi.

"The liberation of the Holy Cities from the Sunni," Shirazi said. "The dream of the Faithful since Husayn's time." He shrugged. "I am not a strategist, merely a religious man, but it seems to me that this might be suitable for discussion."

Zardawi glanced from one ayatollah to another. "I am in favor of it," he said finally. "If we are all going to die anyway, why not die bravely? And if we are not all going to die, control of the Holy Cities—and a few other things located between here and there—might be of some significant advantage to Iran."

187

Most of the men in the room laughed, Jahrami among them. The coy reference to the Saudi oil fields, still a sixth of the world's daily production, was lost on none of them.

"We have substantial Revolutionary Guards units stationed on the Iraqi border," Zardawi went on. "It would be the simplest thing in the world to send them across the rivers, through Kuwait, and down the coastline to assist the rebels."

"Turkey will intervene," Jahrami said.

"Let them. That war has been on our doorstep for years now—who else have we been fighting in Kurdistan these last three years? When the American sun sets, either the Turks will rule the Dar al-Islam or we will, everyone knows that. And the American sun is setting. Of that, I think, there is no question."

Jahrami did not argue. "I can see the advantages of such a thing—and the risks. Still, we cannot linger over this. Do any of you oppose this project?"

No one spoke. After a moment, Jahrami nodded. "May Allah favor us, then." And if He does not, he was thinking, may He have mercy on us all.

17 September 2029: Mount Weather, Virginia

The elevator door opened and Weed and his wife got out. The hallway reminded him of official buildings in has-been nations and five-star hotels in resort towns that had fallen out of fashion; though a lot of money had obviously gone into the thing, it had an indefinable air of neglect and decay about it. He tried not to notice that. What mattered, he told himself, was that he and Andie were a mile underground, safe from Russian and Chinese missiles if the worst happened, and that he could manage the nation's response to the crisis from here.

Aside from the lack of windows and famous paintings, the rooms in this part of the Mount Weather shelter were a fair imitation of the residential floor of the White House. Weed got Andie settled in the private sitting room off their bedroom.

"They said that the staff and our luggage will be down in a bit," he told her, unnecessarily. "Will you be okay for now?" She gave him a bleak frightened glance, but nodded, and he left the room, hurried back the way he came.

Past the elevator, the elegant decor of the corridor gave way suddenly to the bare functional look of a military facility. Uniformed Air Force staff snapped to attention as Weed came through a heavy door into the National Emergency Command Center. He returned the salutes, waved them back to their stations, and went to the desk of the duty officer. "Anything out of the ordinary?"

"No, sir. Admiral Waite asked to be told as soon as you arrived. Should I notify him?"

Waite was at Raven Rock, another part of the ring of nuclear shelters that had surrounded Washington since the Eisenhower years. "Please. I'll have my office running in a few minutes; let him know he can contact me there."

"Yes, sir."

"Thank you." Weed glanced around the room, nodded and left.

On the far side of the elevator, he slowed, considered his options. He could hear a muffled sound from the sitting room that was almost certainly Andie sobbing, and he didn't want to deal with that, not just then. Instead, he went through a nearer door into what would have been the Yellow Oval Room in the White House and was more or less a facsimile of the Oval Office in this replica. The computer on the desk was already on; he tapped the mouse to wake it, waited while the screen came up, started clicking on icons to bring up the data and message feeds he needed. A quick glance over the windows as they came up showed him that everything was proceeding as it should, the nation's nuclear forces ready if they were needed.

If, he thought grimly. If the Chinese would only come to their senses, none of it would be necessary.

And if the ultimatum passed and they still refused to listen to reason?

He brushed the thought aside, hooked the chair out with one foot and sat at the desk.

SEVENTEEN

18 September 2029: Arusha, Tanzania

"Japan alone among nations has suffered attack by nuclear weapons," said the old man on the television screen, "and it is Our deepest wish that no other nation should share that same bitter experience. We ask—no, We plead—that the leaders of the contending powers step back from so terrible an abyss."

McGaffney glanced at the woman sitting next to him on the sofa, a Japanese photographer—Fumiko something-or-other; he didn't recall her family name—whom he'd met and bedded a few days earlier, just before the nuclear crisis began. She was staring at the screen in something like shock. He thought he could guess why. It wasn't every day that the Emperor of Japan called a public press conference to address the governments of the world.

The news program cut back to the anchorman, then to the United Nations building in New York. Secretary General Vo Nguyen Tranh was offering to mediate between the three hostile nuclear powers, saying most of the same things Emperor Naruhito had. A minute or so later it cut to a graphic that showed who had what nuclear weapons and delivery systems, and underlined the very real possibility that a few billion people were about to die.

"Please turn it off," the photographer said. "I can't watch any more of this."

"Too right." He reached for the remote, pressed the off button; there wasn't any point in switching to another channel, since the same news would be on all of them.

With the television off, the hotel room was startlingly quiet, the street outside the window no less so; usually Arusha in September was one big buzzing mass of activity, but not now. It was, McGaffney knew, as safe as any place on the planet; even if the Americans tossed a warhead or two at Tanzania out of spite, Arusha had no targets of military or industrial importance, just a great many tourist hotels, a great many charities and other nongovernmental organizations, and at the moment, no shortage of terrified people.

The photographer was trembling, he realized. He shifted toward her, put a tentative arm around her shoulders; she crumpled against him and clung. They would be making love again soon, he guessed. He'd seen that often enough in places hit by wars and disasters, the raw Darwinian drive to perpetuate the species shoving every other consideration out of the way.

Too right, he thought. It certainly beats waiting to see if the politicians are going to blow us all to hell. He lifted her chin with one hand, gave her a kiss.

18 September 2029: Trenton, New Jersey

Jim Lattimer, the mayor of Trenton, looked up from his desk in the emergency shelter when the police captain came in. "What is it?"

"We've got trouble." The man's face said as much. "Crowds on the streets in Central West and Chestnut Park."

The mayor gave him a tired look. "Get some people out there and tell 'em to go home."

"No dice. We've tried to get Homeland Security to release any of our guys, and they won't budge."

"Shit." The mayor thought for a moment. "Do we still have any of our choppers? Mount a PA system on one and do it that way."

"Yeah, we can probably do that. I'll get on it." The police captain went back out, leaving Lattimer to wrestle with all the other details of a city in crisis.

It was a mess, no question. All regular radio and television programming had been preempted by prerecorded Homeland Security spots hammering on a handful of points—stay home, take shelter indoors, you are safer where you are than out in the countryside or on the highways. The freeways had been closed to civilian traffic anyway, following crisis plans dating back to the Eisenhower era, and National Guard and Homeland Security forces had been called out to barricade the onramps in urban and suburban areas.

Huge swathes of the internet had been blacked out by federal order, along with most long distance telephone services, so there was basically no news other than the drumbeat of official messages. Lattimer scratched his head, glanced over the latest—he'd told one of the kids in the IT department to find a way around the internet blackout, no questions asked, and the kid had managed to get a steady trickle of news from overseas. The people out there in the streets didn't even have that much. If the feds wanted to create panic, Lattimer thought, they were going about it the right way.

An hour later, the police captain was back. "Well, we did it," he said. "We're still doing it. Care to guess how much attention they're paying?"

"Not much else we can do," Lattimer told him. "I'll see if I can get something out of Homeland Security."

He was just finishing a long and useless call with the local Homeland Security official when the captain was back;

the man's face was gray. "Big trouble," he said. "Really big. Cell phone traffic spiked."

"So you snooped."

"No shit. Phone and text both. We've got a rumor panic, big time. They're saying that somebody got news through from someplace overseas. Negotiations broke down and the missiles are about to fly. That's what they say."

"Jesus." Lattimer drew in a ragged breath. "I want the cell phone network shut down. Official business only until further notice. We can't let that spread."

"Yessir," said the captain, and hurried out of the office.

It was the logical response, but it was also the worst thing Lattimer could have done. On the crowded and gritty streets of Trenton, thousands of people who were in the middle of phone and text conversations all lost signal at the same moment, and that was enough to start the panic Lattimer was trying to stop. South of downtown, in one of the city's poorest neighborhoods, someone started shouting that the feds and the city government and everyone else were leaving them there to die; someone else started walking north; that was all it took. Before long the crowd had become a terrified mob running toward the nearest onramp to US Highway 1, the quickest route across the river into Pennsylvania.

Manning the barricade on the highway was a detachment of National Guard soldiers from the Trenton arsenal, kitted out in black riot armor. The more experienced among them looked up, alarmed, as the first dim murmur of the oncoming crowd echoed off the concrete. The sergeant in charge turned at once and went back behind the barricade. "Lieutenant, we got trouble."

The lieutenant was a Homeland Security officer with no experience handling troops in the field. "What's up, Mac?"

The sergeant motioned with his head. "Ever wonder what a mob sounds like? Listen."

The murmur was getting louder. "Get 'em ready," the lieutenant said.

The sergeant turned and started shouting orders. Soldiers scrambled back behind the barricade and leveled their guns along the highway as the mob came into view: a wall of humanity coming toward them at a dead run.

The sergeant grabbed a bullhorn and stepped in front of the barricade. "Stop!" he bellowed. "That's an order. Go back to your homes. This highway is closed."

The front ranks of the mob slowed, but the pressure from those further back pushed them forward. There were thousands of them, filling the parkway back as far as any of the soldiers could see.

"Stop!" the sergeant repeated. "Go back. You're not gonna be any safer on the other side of the river."

The crowd was mostly at a standstill by then, with its front rank less than two yards from the barricade, shouting and pleading at the soldiers. A lean young man stepped out from the crowd, and shouted at the sergeant in a voice that carried over the noise: "You fucking liar! The bombs are coming—you think we're gonna let you leave us here to die?"

The sergeant raised the bullhorn again to answer, but at that same moment the young man whipped a pistol out of his pocket and shot at the sergeant. As he crumpled, the crowd surged forward against the barricades. The lieutenant, who had been watching the exchange from behind the line, panicked and shouted an order, and the soldiers opened fire into the crowd.

The next few minutes were a chaos of screams, pounding feet, and blood. There was no second rush at the barricades, no second volley: just panic, and then the pavement spattered with blood, the bodies of the dead and wounded, and a few dozen others crouching over these latter.

As the corporal called in for a medical team, the sergeant got up, slowly, from in front of the barricade.

"Jesus, Mac," said the lieutenant, who had come forward to the line of the barricade. "You okay? I thought the kid wasted you."

"Nah," he said. "Bruised all to shit, but let's hear it for riot armor." Then he raised his head and saw the highway. "Oh fuck," he said then. "There's going to be hell to pay for this."

18 September 2029: Mount Weather, Virginia

"*How* many?" Weed asked, horrified.

"Thirty-seven dead," the aide repeated. "More than 100 wounded—they're not sure how many more. Trenton tried to send paramedics into the neighborhood, to try to get care to the walking wounded, and they got fired on."

"That's bad." Weed tried to clear his thoughts; there had still been no word from the Chinese, and the wait was chewing on his nerves. Back when the plans to close the freeways were drawn up, he wondered irritably, had anyone ever thought about how people would react?

"Have Homeland Security find out if the city government needs anything," he said finally. "But this has got to be kept out of the media. We can't afford that kind of PR disaster. Frieda, see to it."

"Sure thing, boss." The press secretary left the conference room. The aide gave Weed an uncertain look, then left also.

Ellen Harbin watched them go, turned to Weed. "Mr. President, I'd like to suggest that that's an overreaction. If anything, the news ought to strengthen our position overseas. Nobody is likely to doubt your resolve if word of this gets out."

"The rest of the world won't be voting in 2032," he reminded her. "Let it go. What were you saying about the Iranians?"

She reached for the portfolio on the table, pulled out papers she'd pushed into it in a hurry when the aide and Frieda Thaler had arrived. In a low voice: "There's a real possibility they're about to launch an invasion of the Gulf. The Revolutionary

Guards units we've been tracking since the beginning of the month—"

"The ones they moved to the Iraqi border."

"Exactly. Satellite data shows them making preparations for an assault. They may think they can take advantage of the crisis."

Weed considered that. "Or they're stone cold crazy. Got it."

"Once the Chinese back down, we may have to tackle that right away," she warned. "Having the Saudi oil fields in Iranian hands would be a disaster—and there's the risk of a general Mideast war if Turkey gets involved."

Weed nodded. "Got it," he repeated. "Get in touch with Bateson and get some options drawn up—and not a word to anybody about this Trenton thing. That could be a major mess."

Unfortunately for Weed, it was already too late to contain the news. Two decades of cat-and-mouse games with NSA and a baker's dozen other federal agencies that wanted to keep the internet under some kind of control had spawned an entire outlaw web—the Undernet, the media called it, once the phrase "dark web" became passé—that could more or less evade government censorship. Even the draconian curbs imposed at the beginning of the nuclear crisis barely slowed the Undernet down. Within minutes of the shooting, the first reports began to spread; photos taken by cell phone cameras in the crowd soon followed, and the lack of any media coverage allowed terrifying rumors to move unhindered. Somewhere in the process, the events in New Jersey that afternoon received their enduring name: the Trenton Massacre.

18 September 2029: Wichita, Kansas

The surface streets were gridlocked. Major Roy Abernethy could see that much from where he stood on the onramp; there were cars jammed nose to tail going every which way. The

Homeland Security broadcasts were still telling everybody to stay home and keep their heads down, but not too many people were listening. Half a dozen cars had come up the onramp, tried to back off, and gotten stuck between the barricade and the traffic behind. It was a real mess, no question.

He shook his head, walked back from the barricade to the field headquarters. The men of his detachment were piling out of the big National Guard trucks all along the freeway, relieving a Homeland Security unit that had been on duty for more than twenty-four hours. All the onramps to Interstate 35 had to be kept blocked, orders said, so the freeway was available for military and emergency traffic—not that there was much of that. Just one more clueless order from Washington, he thought.

"Hey, boss," said Sergeant Chip Lansberger. He was standing outside the parked truck that served the unit at a field headquarters. "Something you probably ought to read."

Abernethy climbed into the back of the truck, glanced over the shoulder of the tech at the comm terminal, stopped cold and then started reading again. "This is bad," he said to Lansberger.

"No kidding."

Abernethy turned to the tech. "Anything else come through about that?"

"No, sir."

"Let me know if that changes."

"Yes, sir."

He jumped back down from the truck, looked back down at the gridlocked streets and the desperate people—all of them dead in moments if the bombs started flying and one came down over Wichita. Exactly why, he asked himself, am I following these orders?

No answer came to mind. He shook his head again, hoped that things would somehow work out.

18 September 2029: Austin, Texas

"Fred," said Terry McCracken, "that's not good enough."

When McCracken used those words, everyone in the state government dove for cover. On paper, the governor of Texas had less power than his peers in other states—McCracken was fond of reminding people that his home state was the only territory ever admitted to the Union that fought a civil war of its own, the Regulator-Moderator War of 1839–1844, over whether to have any laws at all—but a politician with enough charisma and ruthlessness could turn the office into a powerhouse. McCracken's opponents had plenty to say about his faults, but most of them admitted that he'd managed to become the most powerful politician Texas had seen since the days of Lyndon Johnson.

He listened for a while, then interrupted the man on the other end. "Fred, I don't care. I really don't. You know and I know that this is gonna blow over sooner or later—yeah, Weed's a douche bag, but he's not enough of a douche bag to blow up the goddamn planet. You get me a line through to Trenton, and I can promise that you'll still be doing business in this state once this mess is over. You follow me? Thank you."

Earlier that day he'd fielded the first worried calls from friends and political allies here and there in Texas. There were rumors that federal troops somewhere had fired into a crowd; there were rumors that the same thing had happened in more than one place. After the first three calls, he'd done the smart thing and called his teenage granddaughter, who was able to get something off the Undernet in minutes and tell him that whatever it was had happened in Trenton, New Jersey. That was enough; McCracken had friends in the New Jersey statehouse, and all he needed was an open long distance line—for official business, certainly, though he knew the feds wouldn't see it that way.

He got through on the second ring. "Sam? Yeah, this is Terry. Look, I know you're busier'n a one-legged man at an ass-kicking contest, but I just heard about the business there in Trenton. What the hell happened?"

He was silent for several minutes, then, listening, and finally said, "Jesus Christ. I hope those sumbitches don't try that kind of thing here." Another long silence. "Jesus," he repeated. "Well, thank you, Sam. You got Laura someplace safe? Good. You keep your head down, and we'll talk once this mess is over."

McCracken hung up, stared at the desk ahead of him for a while. It was all too easy to imagine what would play out if something like that happened in proud, gun-loving Texas. He picked up the phone a moment later, and called the state Homeland Security office.

The governor's staff in the room outside knew that something was wrong when McCracken's voice got loud enough to hear through the office door. They started giving each other worried looks when they heard every word he was saying—or more precisely shouting—into the phone: "Look, goddamnit, this is serious. Your boys start shooting at Texans, they're gonna get return fire, and you're gonna be—" Then, silence. When he slammed down the phone a moment later, with a roar of polymorphous profanity impressive even by Texas standards, they knew that an epic explosion was on its way. Two junior staffers who knew they wouldn't be missed got up, without making a sound, and fled from the room. The others sat in terrified silence and waited for the blast.

The door flew open. "Brent, get me a new phone," McCracken said. "Goddamn sumbitch hung *up* on me."

He went back into his office and slammed the door behind him. The staffers gave each other another round of nervous looks, and one of them called down to maintenance, then unplugged his own phone and carried it into the governor's office. One of the others made the sign of the cross at him, as though administering the last rites. That got grins, but nobody made a sound.

The staffer with the phone came back out of the office alive and unskinned, and mimed with two fingers: the governor was pacing up and down his office. That meant something worse than an explosion was coming. The staffers gulped and got busy again, as quietly as they could.

"Maria?" It was McCracken's voice, over the intercom. "Get me Olney and Kammersdorf. Tell 'em I don't care what they're doing. I need to talk to them now."

"Yes sir," said the secretary, and started calling. General Tom Olney was an old Army buddy of McCracken's who commanded the Texas National Guard, Ben Kammersdorf a close political ally who headed the Texas Rangers. Both were under Homeland Security authority by executive order for the duration of the crisis, but McCracken had both of them on the phone within minutes, and a clash between Washington orders and Texas loyalties could have only one result.

When he was finished, the governor called Homeland Security back. "You listen to me, sumbitch," he said, stabbing the air with a finger the size of a sausage. "You're out of a job. The Texas National Guard and the Texas Rangers will be handling public safety in this state, under my command."

"You can't do that," the official spluttered.

"Try me." Another jab with the finger. "Get your thugs out of my state in twenty-four hours. You hear me? Twenty-four hours." He slammed down the phone, hard. Minutes later, on another new phone, he was calling drinking and hunting buddies of his who happened to be the governors of half a dozen Southern states.

19 September 2029: North of Khoramshahr, on the Iran-Iraq border

"Yes," said General Birjani, and hung up the phone. It was the only word he had said during the entire call. His staff expected as much, waited for orders with the serene patience of those who had long since accepted a martyr's fate. Iran's Revolutionary Guards had many such men, and the shock troops who had been hurried to the western borders in the first days of September were more zealous than most. All of them knew, as their convoys snaked through the Zagros mountains on winding roads, that they had in all probability been sent there to die.

"We have been chosen to lead the assault," Birjani said.

"The time, sir?" This from his chief of staff.

"Now."

Eyebrows went up. The men were ready, that was beyond question, and orders had been given the night before. Still, the suddenness of it …

"Allah is great," said the chief of staff.

All at once the headquarters was a flurry of activity; keyboards clattered, voices in Farsi spoke into a dozen phones. Birjani walked through the middle of it to the door, stepped out into the cool air. The first hint of the approaching dawn was just beginning to silhouette the mountains to the east. Allah would forgive him and his men for missing morning prayers; a different religious duty summoned them.

By the time he reached the armored personnel carrier that would be his command vehicle, tank engines were roaring to life and men were running to their stations. The distant drumming of helicopters told him that air cover would be in place. He allowed himself a broad smile. After so long, so much waiting, so many exercises and drills, the day was here—and if the next thing that happened after his armored division crossed the border was an American missile screaming down to lift them all into the sky in one great mushroom cloud, why, then they would be in heaven with Hassan and Husayn that much sooner.

The crew of his command vehicle were waiting for him, the engine already roaring. He climbed inside, took his familiar seat, nodded to his aides. "Ready?"

"More than ready, sir."

"Go."

The armored personnel carrier lurched into motion.

Ten minutes later, Birjani's division rolled into Iraqi territory, scattering a few terrified border guards. Scouts in fast vehicles rushed ahead, securing the necessary bridges and letting the local people know that the invasion was not directed at them— a message that, Birjani knew, was being communicated by diplomats to a stunned Iraqi government in Baghdad at the same time. The maps beside Birjani's seat told the rest of the story: across Basra province to Kuwait, through Kuwait to the Saudi border, south along the coast, west to Riyadh, and then—

Then, Allah willing, the Holy Cities in Shi'a hands at last.

EIGHTEEN

19 September 2029: Mount Weather, Virginia

"I'll take the call," Weed said, and pressed a key, muting the intercom.

The computer screen in front of him, full of details of the Iranian assault, left no question in his mind what the call would be about. He picked up the handset and said, "Prince Khalid? Yes, I've heard the news."

"Mr. President." The Saudi ambassador's voice was edged with tension. "I am glad to hear that. May I ask what you intend to do about this."

"At this moment," said Weed, "we're not in a position to be able to help you."

The line hissed softly at him for a long moment. "Do I hear you correctly, Mr. President? This is a matter of life and death for the kingdom."

"In case you haven't heard," Weed snapped, "we're facing something similar ourselves just at the moment."

"Of your own choosing," said the ambassador.

That the man was right didn't improve Weed's mood at all. "All our assets are committed to the nuclear crisis," he said. "Once that's resolved, of course we'll offer the kingdom all the help we can. I know that that doesn't help you at all right now, but it's the best the United States can do."

"Very well," said Khalid. "I will pass on your message to His Majesty. I trust you understand that the kingdom will take the actions it needs to take, whether those turn out to be in your nation's interests or otherwise."

"Of course," said Weed.

A few more formalities and the call was over. Weed put down the phone and stared at the computer screen. It galled him that the most powerful nation in the world didn't have the option of intervening when the Middle East was blowing sky-high, but that was the hard reality of the situation; with the Navy's carriers sitting ducks for anybody who had supersonic cruise missiles, the Air Force reeling from a decisive defeat, and the threat of nuclear war demanding every resource the armed services and the country had left, the Iranians and the Saudis were going to have to fight their war themselves.

He tapped at the trackball to get the latest update from the satellites, and wondered what the Saudis were going to do.

19 September 2029: Ras Tanura, Saudi Arabia

The first fireball went up just before dusk, a vast globe of flame mirroring the setting sun.

The orders had come from Riyadh earlier that day, minutes after the news from the northern border. Technicians in the vast Ras Tanura oil shipping facility blanched, but hurried to their tasks. No one had any question what to do; they'd been through the sequence in drill after drill, under the watchful eyes of government officials and princes of the royal family—but none of them thought that the thing would ever happen.

A second fireball followed, rising from the middle of one of the storage tank farms. The third came almost immediately after, a huge gout of flame from one of the pumping stations that scattered flaming debris over most of a square mile.

"Yes, Your Highness," said one of the technicians into his cell phone. He was standing by his car, several miles inland, facing the facility. "I am watching the explosions now." A shockwave hit, breaking over the technician like thunder. "Perhaps Your Highness heard that."

He listened for a few moments, while more flashes and fireballs burst over the facility. "Yes, Your Highness. The technical staff have all been evacuated to Mubarraz; the common laborers—well, there is no need for Your Highness to be concerned about them. There will be nothing here they could use anyway."

Another flash, larger, and then all at once the whole heart of the facility dissolved in a series of explosions. The demolition charges had been well placed.

"Yes, Your Highness," he said. "If you will excuse me—"

The shockwaves arrived, landing like blows. The technician waited until they were done. "My apologies—that last set of blasts made it impossible for me to hear Your Highness's voice. You were saying?" A long silence, then. "Yes. Yes, of course, Your Highness. *Salaam aleikum.*"

He shut the thing off, got into the car, drove away. If the Iranians were already well past the Kuwaiti border, it was time, past time, to get to a place of safety.

19 September 2029: Facility 6335, West of Sverdlovsk

"Anything further?" Kuznetsov glanced from face to face, nodded. "I will be in my office. If anything happens I am to be alerted at once." He turned before the staff could respond, went out the door of the situation room.

He was in his office a few minutes later. The clock on his desk showed the time: just under three hours until the American ultimatum expired.

He sat down, slumped back in his chair, allowed his eyes to drift shut, tried to push aside the pressures of the moment: the thousand and one details of the crisis, this new war just now getting started in the Middle East, and the looming threat behind it all, the mushroom clouds that might shortly reduce the world's three most powerful nations into smoldering ash. The effort failed. After a moment, he opened his eyes again, leaned forward, checked the computer screen on the desk: nothing new, and no new updates expected for another ten minutes.

Then he reached for one of the desk drawers, opened it, and pulled out a photo in an ornate little frame of silver. A flick of one finger popped out the stand on the back. Kuznetsov set the photo on his desk, considered it: a man in his thirties, dark-haired and smiling, wearing the uniform of an officer in the old Soviet Army.

Would it astonish you, Kuznetsov asked the image, to hear that the Americans are threatening to blow us all to the devil if they can't get their way? Would that surprise you at all, Father? I think not.

By then the memories were unrolling, moment by moment. His litany, he had come to call it, like the litanies the priests and *staretsi* were chanting at that moment in cathedrals and churches across holy Russia: praying to God for forgiveness and peace. He envied them, envied all those who could find it in themselves to believe in a God.

He was walking home from school. He could remember every step, talking and laughing with his friends, splashing through puddles left behind by the melting snow, the tall apartment blocks of Novosibirsk rising up above them into the pale blue sky of spring. It had been a good day, good enough that for a moment he could forget about the troubled times, the paychecks his father should have been getting and wasn't, the worried conversations running late into the night about what that drunken fool Yeltsin was doing to Russia—Yeltsin, and the plutocrats who owned him, and the Americans who owned *them*, whose babble about democracy and freedom

208

the plutocrats mouthed as they plundered Russia like a conquered province.

Stopping at the door of the apartment building, laughing and saying goodbye to his friends, waiting while the elevator clattered and groaned its way down to the lobby: all of it, moment by moment. Up to the fourteenth floor, turn left, six doors down, rattle the key just so to get the door to unlock, and then calling out, "Father, I—"

And then the dark shape in the center of the living room, not touching the floor, that resolved itself into his father's body, hanging from the light fixture. He'd put on his uniform, the one he'd worn in the Afghanistan war, pinned his medals across his chest—Hero of the Soviet Union and the rest of them—knotted the rope, climbed on the chair, and taken the only way out of poverty and failure that a proud man driven to his knees by desperation could still find.

And the scream that burst from the boy's mouth as he realized what he was seeing—

The litany ended, the memories shattered into fragments like a glass thrown against a wall. Kuznetsov drew in a long unsteady breath, released it, clenched his hands into fists, mastering himself.

If they launch their missiles, he told himself, we shall launch ours, and that will be the end of us all. And if they do not …

If they spare us and the world, then there will be an accounting. Somehow, in some way, there will be an accounting.

19 September 2029: Mount Weather, Virginia

The clock on the wall ticked quietly to itself. Weed tried to ignore it, and could not. It was old enough to have hands, and just now they traced a vertical line, the lower half thick, the top half slender and rising to a point, for all the world like a missile ready to launch.

Six o'clock, on what by all accounts was a lovely September evening up on the surface; eighteen hundred hours in the military-speak of the command facility around him. The ultimatum had exactly sixty minutes left to run.

"Sir?"

Weed looked up at the door, realized only then that the voice came from the speakers on his computer. "What is it?"

"Ms. Harbin—"

"Tell her she can wait."

"Yes, sir."

He propped his elbows on his desk, put his head in his hands. Harbin kept insisting that there had to be a way to take out the Russian and Chinese nukes, or force them to back down, or something. There had been something close to a screaming match that morning when Harbin demanded that the Strategic Command staff give her an operational plan for a decapitation strike on the Russian and Chinese leadership and the Air Force general in charge of STRATCOM told her to her face that she belonged in a padded cell. Weed had hired her because of her reputation for innovative thinking, but her kind of innovation was the last thing he needed now.

The clock ticked away: fifty-five minutes to go.

All over the world, Weed knew, tens of thousands of American servicepeople waited for his orders. A click of his trackball could bring up details of every strategic asset the United States had: Minuteman missiles in silos under North Dakota farmland, Trident submarines in the deep waters of the world's oceans, B-52 bombers with nuclear-tipped cruise missiles circling in the skies or cycling their engines at a score of air bases, two other delivery systems so secret that fewer than 100 people in the US government even knew their code names. Another click could bring up everything that was known of the Chinese and Russian strategic arsenals, with their own missiles, bombers, submarines, and ace-in-the-hole secret weapons. Behind those bare names and numbers were tens of thousands of young men and women who wore different uniforms but waited for what amounted to the same orders.

A few words into the intercom would be enough to bring the Air Force officer with the "football," the case full of nuclear launch codes, into Weed's office, and set the whole thing in motion. An hour later, something like a billion people would be dead or dying, and perhaps a billion more would be condemned to death as the fallout clouds drifted with the prevailing winds. It would be so very easy.

Fifty minutes to go.

He reached for the trackball, clicked on the icon that brought up the live feed from Mount Weather's communications center. He'd last checked it half an hour earlier, and close to thirty new messages had been sent his way since then: reports about Trenton, reports about Texas, reports from a dozen states where the National Command Authorities could no longer be quite sure that anybody was listening to their commands. In Seattle, National Guard units sent to control a riot had dissolved into the crowd, taking their guns with them; in Cincinnati, city and state police sent to keep the freeways open for emergency use had torn down the barricades and waved drivers through; something was up in Alabama but nobody knew what, because the Homeland Security director there couldn't be reached at all and the state police, National Guard, and governor's office weren't responding to messages from the federal government. The contingency plans for nuclear war covered any number of possibilities, but a collapse of federal authority even before the missiles started flying wasn't one of them.

Forty-five minutes.

He paged through the messages, looking for foreign datelines. The war in the Gulf was spinning out of control, with rebels fighting Saudi military units in Qatif and Dammam and Iranian tanks roaring across the Saudi border. Word was that the Saudis had dynamited their oil shipping facility at Ras

211

Tanura and were blowing up pipelines as they retreated. Even without an insurgency to cope with, the Saudi military wasn't a match for Iran's, and a scorched earth policy was one of the few options the Saudis had; most of what would be scorched by it was in Europe and the United States, but it wasn't as though the Saudis had any particular reason to care.

Meanwhile, rioters in Paris were besieging the Elysée Palace, demanding France's immediate withdrawal from NATO. The US embassy in Jakarta had been looted and burned to the ground by a mob and the Indonesian government had no information about the whereabouts of the ambassador and her staff. Everywhere he looked, the American position was crumbling, and the one thing that might save it—the smallest hint of concession from the Chinese—was not going to happen.

They've called my bluff, Weed thought, and realized in the same moment that it was a bluff, that the final step to nuclear war was one step further than he could go.

Forty minutes.

He drew in a long ragged breath and let it out again, knowing what he had to do. He tapped the onscreen button that activated the intercom. "Lois?"

"Yes, sir."

"Put through a call to the secretary general."

A moment's silence. "Yes, sir." Then, in little more than a whisper: "Thank you, sir."

PART FOUR

CROSSING THE LINE

NINETEEN

19 September 2029: Chambersburg, Pennsylvania

The first church bell rang at twenty minutes to seven. Pete Bridgeport, who was closing the door of his motel room, gave the air a quizzical look. Another joined it, and another; within moments, every bell in town was ringing.

He grabbed the railing of the motel balcony to steady himself. That could mean one of two things …

A car came down the street, horn blaring. The driver was shouting something out the window, and though Bridgeport couldn't make out the words he didn't think it involved Chinese and Russian missiles on the way. He made himself go to the stairs and went down.

There was a crowd gathered around the front desk, staring at a television news program. "… been confirmed by the White House," the anchorman was saying. "We're still waiting to hear from our news staff overseas, but certainly this is the most promising thing we've heard since the beginning of this crisis. Once again, the United Nations has announced and the White House confirms that a ceasefire has been declared. The US, Russian and Chinese nuclear forces are standing down, and all sides have agreed to negotiate a peace treaty. That's what we know so far. Sandy, anything yet from Beijing or Moscow?"

The sense of relief hit Bridgeport like a body blow. He managed to stay upright, though it wasn't easy. After a moment he turned, headed for the stairs down to street level.

People were spilling onto the streets, whooping and laughing and crying. The church bells were still ringing over the blare of sirens and horns; the sounds broke over Bridgeport like waves. The glow of sunset, splashed carelessly across the upper stories of the old brick buildings, seemed to shine with supernatural brilliance.

We're going to live, he thought. My God, we're going to live.

It wasn't until that moment that he realized how certain he'd been that he and everyone else in the world was about to die.

20 September 2029: Shinyanga District, Tanzania

The sound of gunshots jolted Melanie Bridgeport awake. She blinked and sat up, felt rather than saw the other women in the tent stirring. Another burst of gunfire followed, and voices shouting something she couldn't make out.

This was it, she knew.

Panic surged, and she fought it down. There was nowhere to run, and no point in trying. If the bombs were already falling, a bullet would at least be quick. She drew in a deep breath, forced herself to sit there, waiting.

More voices shouted something, further off. After that came silence, deep enough that she could hear one of her tentmates whisper, "Hail Mary, full of grace, the Lord is with thee ..."

The shouting erupted again, closer, and Bridgeport could hear the pounding of running feet. Then, all at once, the flap of the tent jerked open.

"Ceasefire!" One of the camp guards shouted the words into the tent. Even in the near-darkness, she could see the delighted look on the man's face. He went to the next tent, and the next, shouting the same message into each one.

Bridgeport sagged as the tension went out of her. If it's true, she reminded herself. Dear God, let it be true.

A few minutes later another guard came by to announce that a radio was being hooked up to the loudspeakers in the parade ground and anyone who wanted could come listen to the news. Bridgeport, still dazed, finished lacing her boots and left her tent along with the others, let the crowd pull her all the way to the center of camp, where lights blazed down from poles onto a dusty square crowded with guards and POWs.

"… Secretary General of the United Nations," the loudspeakers were saying in a clipped Oxford accent as she got there. "For those of you who are just joining us, the United States has agreed to a ceasefire. Nuclear forces around the world are standing down, and it looks like the crisis of the last few days may be over. We've just heard UN Secretary General Vo Nguyen Tranh announce the terms of the agreement. Here's Ellen Keyes in Beijing with the latest from the Chinese capital."

So it was true. One of Bridgeport's tentmates, the one she'd heard saying the Hail Mary a few minutes earlier, dropped to her knees right there in the dirt and began to murmur a prayer. For a moment, Bridgeport considered joining her there.

As the reporter in Beijing started in on the news, the first rush of shock and relief ebbed away and a cold awareness took shape in her. We lost, she realized. The war's over, and we lost. She glanced around at the other POWs, and wondered how many of them were thinking the same thing she was.

20 September 2029: The August First Building, Beijing

There must be millions of them, Liu thought. From the window of his office high above downtown Beijing, he could see the people in the streets: more of them, even, than there had been when word came from mission control that Tianlung 3 had landed safely on the Moon. He'd spoken with Meiyin on

217

a secure line from the shelter in Inner Mongolia, checked the latest news bulletins, heard beaming reporters try to make themselves heard over the cheering and the patriotic songs, watched trains full of excited children rolling back into Beijing and the other cities to rejoin their parents, taken in the footage from foreign capitals, and thought about how easily he might have blundered and killed them all.

"Sir." His secretary's voice, out of the speakers on his computer. "He's here."

"Of course," Liu said, and turned as the door opened.

Chen Weiming, President of the People's Republic of China, crossed the room to greet him. "Well," he said. "You have made quite a name for yourself, Liu."

"Thank you. I trust your flight back from Hubei was comfortable?"

"Entirely so." After a moment: "I am very glad you were correct."

"As am I," Liu admitted.

The older man chuckled. "You certainly made an impressive show of confidence these last few days. It was much discussed. And now—" A more serious look. "You are the man of the hour. As I'm sure you realize, this will require certain changes in the arrangements for the next Party Congress."

Taken by surprise, Liu managed not to show it. "I assure you that was really the last thing on my mind."

"Of course. But when the time comes—"

"I will be happy to serve the Motherland in whatever position the Party chooses for me."

"I am glad to hear it," said Chen.

The president walked to the window, considered the crowds below. "They are drunk with triumph," he said finally, "proud of their nation, their Army—proud of us. If you ordered them to march to the Moon, they would try." He turned around. "That makes it all the more important for us to step carefully to grasp our power in the world with a very light touch.

The Americans never learned that, and you see what it's cost them. We must avoid copying their mistakes."

He shook his head, then: "But we can discuss such things later. The other members of the Commission will be here shortly. Shall we go meet them?"

20 September 2029: The Kremlin, Moscow

"A most pleasant conversation." Gennady Kuznetsov was in fine spirits as he and General Bunin walked down the hallway. "Chen was as gracious as anyone could wish, and mentioned—just in passing, of course—that China will be happy to adjust the price they pay us for our natural gas and oil to correspond to market conditions."

That was enough to make even Bunin blink. "That will cost them a great deal," he said.

"They can afford it. It's not just that they own Africa now. No, Misha, they own the world. They are the superpower now—America has lost that status, and everyone knows it. And for now, at least, the Chinese have good reason to think kindly of their neighbor to the north. Those kind thoughts could be of great advantage to Russia."

"No doubt," Bunin said, "you have some use for those kind thoughts."

Kuznetsov glanced at the general, allowed a smile. "That," he said, "we will talk about another time."

They reached the end of the corridor, passed through the double doors into the press room. Hundreds of faces turned toward Kuznetsov as he and the general mounted the platform and approached the podium.

20 September 2029: Tabuk, Saudi Arabia

The planes had been coming in for most of an hour before the Saudi general got to the air base outside of Tabuk: big military

219

transports, more than two dozen of them so far, spilling out their cargoes of soldiers, trucks and tanks and then heading back out over the Red Sea toward Egyptian airspace. The planes had their markings blotted out with paint, but now that the Americans were out of the picture, there was only one power in the Middle East with the capacity to carry out a military airlift on that scale, and it was also the only power prepared to face off against the Iranian forces driving west from the Persian Gulf toward Riyadh.

The gate to the air base was still guarded by Saudi military police, but there were other soldiers with them, wearing unfamiliar uniforms, who eyed the general's car suspiciously before waving him through. All along the route from the gate to the headquarters building, the general could see the newcomers hard at work, transforming a sleepy second-rate airfield into a major military base.

The general frowned. It was a devil's bargain, no question of that, but what other choice did the kingdom have left?

The headquarters building was aswarm with soldiers when the general got there. As he left his car, an officer with colonel's insignia on his shoulders came out from the main doors to greet him effusively in tolerable Arabic. A few minutes later he was brought into the command center in the heart of the building, and introduced to General Mehmet Burzagli, commander of the Turkish expeditionary force.

"General al-Sharif." Burzagli crossed the room to meet him. "I'm glad you're here. I trust His Majesty is safe? Excellent. We are preparing to send our first units to the defense of Riyadh; perhaps you can advise us."

The Saudi general smiled and nodded, let himself be drawn over to the computer screens where maps and satellite images showed the rugged desert terrain between Tabuk and the front lines. It would have been the height of discourtesy to show any discomfort with the situation, or to make the least reference to the unquestioned fact that Turkey would expect to gain certain benefits and privileges for coming to the kingdom's rescue, possibly on the scale of those it had enjoyed in Ottoman times. He stifled a sigh, turned his attention to the nearest map.

20 September 2029: The White House, Washington DC

The White House was uncharacteristically silent as Jameson Weed settled into his chair in the Oval Office. Though the announcement had gone out to everyone as soon as the cease-fire was confirmed, and the last barricades on the nation's highways had gone down within an hour of that time, most of the nonessential staff hadn't returned to work yet. The stillness grated on Weed's nerves; it reminded him of the hush in the Mount Weather shelter in the last hours before the ultimatum expired.

He jabbed irritably at the computer trackball, and the screen brightened. A few clicks brought up the essentials from the National Security Council staff: reports from all the strategic services, assuring him that the nation's nuclear arsenal was secure; the latest briefing from NSA, confirming that the Chinese and Russian arsenals had finished standing down; and the latest news from the war in the Persian Gulf, none of it good.

Next was a preliminary report from Homeland Security on what happened in Trenton and elsewhere, along with a quick personal note from Homeland Security Secretary Mike Weissman, letting him know that his formal resignation would be on its way later that day. Weed frowned but nodded. He liked Mike, but somebody was going to have to take the heat for Trenton, and it damn well wasn't going to be Jameson Weed.

Below that, though, was a heads up from the State Department: Claire and her team were on their way to Geneva for the peace negotiations. He read the note, closed it, and tried to find something else to think about. No matter how his administration's spin doctors worked it, Weed knew, that treaty was going to mark a bitter turning point. America had finally lost a war, and there was no question at all who was going to take the heat for that.

He opened a new window on the computer screen, clicked through to one of the national news services. The headlines were full of news about the aftermath of the crisis and the war in the Gulf. Over to one side, though, a video feature was playing; some reporter was doing a people-on-the-street interview in Cleveland. The sound was off, but he could see everything he needed to know in their faces: some looked angry, some looked relieved, but all of them looked at least a little confused and lost.

What are they going to do, Weed wondered, when they realize that the war isn't the only thing we just lost?

He considered the faces for a moment longer, then dropped his head into his hands.

TWENTY

22 September 2029: Geneva, Switzerland

The room glittered with the elegance of a bygone era: lush curtains, gold trim, Art Nouveau accents. Glancing around, Claire Hayes Hutchison thought about the other peace treaties the United States had negotiated there over the years. It was a bitter thought; despite all evasions, the reality this time was that the United States had had to sue for peace.

Formalities came first, as though all the details hadn't already been hashed out over three long days by lower-level staff. Hutchison considered her opposite numbers, the bland-faced foreign minister from China, the stocky Tanzanian minister who represented the Coalition. What their demands would be was the most important question, and the one about which she had the least knowledge. If they demanded more than the United States could afford to give ...

Finally, the formal introductions were over, and each side was seated around the table. "Madam Secretary," the Chinese minister said, "may I speak frankly? When all is said and done, your nation pursued its national interests in East Africa, and so did mine. The interests of the Coalition nations were somewhat more directly affected ..."

The Tanzanian minister snorted, but said nothing.

"… but the principle remains the same. It is now, I think, in the national interests of all parties concerned to—how do you Americans say it? Draw a line under the unfortunate events of the recent past, and go on."

"A great deal depends on what you mean by that," said Hutchison.

"Under other circumstances," said the Tanzanian minister, "as a victim of aggression, my nation at least might reasonably be entitled to receive reparations. We have considered the matter, however, and decided to forego that." With a wry smile: "The recent changes in the price of our crude oil will more than make up the difference, as you doubtless know."

"Similarly," said the Chinese minister, "it strikes us as a waste of time to bicker over whose nation must accept the blame for the events of the last few months."

That took care of two of the crucial items on Hutchison's list; if the United States could emerge from this with its pride intact and its battered economy free of added burdens, there was still a good chance that something could be salvaged. "Fair enough," she said. "What I want to know, if I may be equally frank, is where's the catch."

The Chinese and Tanzanian ministers glanced at each other. "The catch," said the Chinese envoy, "if you wish to put it that way, is simply that the United States will agree to accept the status quo at present in East Africa and the Indian Ocean."

That was no surprise, though the latter half of the demand stung. Without Diego Garcia, and with the Gulf war about to make the American presence there untenable, the possibility that the United States might be shut out of the Indian Ocean could not be ignored. "Diego Garcia is the property of Great Britain," she pointed out, "and we have no right to change that status."

"Understood. Your country can, however, relinquish its treaty rights there in favor of the People's Republic of China, and we will come to our own accommodation with the British."

The negotiations would already have begun, Hutchison guessed. "I will of course have to consult with my government on that issue."

"Of course," said the Chinese minister, with a whisper of a smile, just enough to make it clear that he knew how pointless the consultation would be. The United States had no effective means to contest the demand, and everyone there at the peace conference knew it.

24 September 2029: Russell Senate Office Building, Washington DC

"I'm not going to speculate about what the hearings will or won't discover," said Senator Bridgeport. "The American people deserve to know what happened in East Africa, and the Armed Services Committee's going to do its level best to get that information for them." He raised his hand as a dozen reporters jumped to their feet. "No questions, please. My office will keep you informed about all the details as we get things set up. Thank you."

He left the podium, ducked through the door before anyone could try to collar him for an off-the-record quote. He could hear voices from the press room as he hurried down the corridor, and then the door clicked shut, plunging him into the near-silence of the old building. The hush was a comfort to frayed nerves, and he had too many of those just then.

Still, the crucial step was taken. There would be Senate hearings on the East African War, with every bit of publicity he could get for it, and a barrage of subpoenas to extract the truth no matter how many obstacles Weed tried to throw in the way. No doubt somebody from the White House or the Pentagon would be calling him within minutes, trying to talk him into soft-pedaling the hearings, making threats or promises: business as usual in DC.

Bridgeport's face tightened. This wasn't business as usual any more. And if Mel—

He forced the thought away as he got to the door of his office.

His staff gave him worried looks as he made a beeline for his office, closed the door behind him, poured himself a double shot of bourbon and went to his desk. As he settled in the chair, the intercom beeped. "Boss?"

That would be the phone call from the White House, he guessed, and stabbed at the button with a finger. "What is it?"

"General Wittkower on the phone."

The Pentagon, then. "Can he—"

"It's about Mel."

After a frozen moment: "Thanks, Anne. Put him through."

He closed the intercom circuit, picked up the phone. "Ralph? What's up?"

"We just got the POW lists from the International Red Cross," Wittkower said. "I had one of my people go through it, and—Pete, Melanie's okay."

Bridgeport opened his mouth and tried to say something, could not.

"She's in a POW camp in a place called Shinyanga in Tanzania. The IRC's got people there right now—I'll have somebody keep you posted once we hear anything else."

"Thank you," Bridgeport managed to say. "Thank you, Ralph."

"Sure thing. I figured, might as well tell you myself. Hey, let me know when you've got an evening free for dinner with Holly and me."

Bridgeport promised he would, fumbled his way through the courtesies, hung up, and sat there staring at nothing for what seemed like a long time, trying to make himself believe that the news was true.

25 September 2029: The White House, Washington DC

"It's shaping up into a major war," said Barbara Bateson, the acting Secretary of Defense.

Weed stared up at the map on the Situation Room screen, barely aware of the other members of the National Security Council around him. Yellow against blue sea, the angular shape of the Arabian peninsula hovered there, marked with the green and red symbols of contending armies. Half a world away, Turkish and Iranian forces were locked in combat on the outskirts of Riyadh.

"Who's winning?" Weed asked.

"It's impossible to call at this point," Bateson said. "The Iranian force is larger, the Turkish and what's left of the Saudi forces are better armed. It could go either way, or settle down into a stalemate—a lot depends on whether anybody else gets involved."

"So far," Greg Barnett said, "that's an open question. The Turks have cut some kind of deal with Egypt—they're overflying Egypt's airspace without anybody objecting, and we think there's more involved than that. There are rumors that Egypt's planning to send ground forces and aircraft shortly. We're also pretty sure the Turks are getting technology covertly from the Israelis. Iran's being supplied with all kinds of stuff by China—there's got to have been some kind of payoff for the use of Iran's airspace, and this is probably it."

"Do we know whether the payoff includes Chinese cruise missiles?" Weed asked.

"Not for sure, no. They've had older generation cruise missiles along the Gulf coast since the 1990s, and those have certainly been upgraded—we've had unconfirmed reports that Tehran got a shipment of Russian supersonic cruise missiles as part of the deal they cut with Moscow after the Syrian war."

"Which means that our people in Bahrain are sitting ducks," said Weed.

"With all due respect, that's overstating the case," Bateson insisted. "We've got plenty of firepower in Bahrain—enough that the Iranians would face crippling losses if it came to live fire. They can't afford that now, not with the Turks pounding on them."

"Tell me this," Weed said. "Do we have the option of intervening to help the Saudis?"

An uncomfortable silence settled over the room. "We could," Bateson said after a moment. "And it might well turn the tide against Tehran. The problem is that our losses would probably be very high. We could hit hard, but we'd take a lot of damage."

"If we don't," Barnett warned, "the Saudis aren't going to forgive us, ever—and whoever ends up in control of the situation is going to be in a position to treat everybody we've got in Bahrain as de facto hostages."

"I've been thinking about that," said Weed.

He frowned, considering the map on the screen. "Do you think there's any way we can get our people out?"

Barnett gave him a measured look. "We could, provided that Tehran was willing—and I think they'll be happy to see us go, since that's one more threat they don't have to contend with. But if that's the way we go, any hope of a US presence in the Gulf once this blows over can kiss its ass goodbye—and you know as well as I do how that's going to play in the media."

"I know," said Weed. "Will the other options play any better?"

No one answered.

"Draw up plans to get everyone out of Bahrain," Weed snapped. "Get them on my desk as soon as possible."

26 September 2029: Shinyanga District, Tanzania

McGaffney got out of the car, crossed the dusty parking lot to the front gate of the camp. The guards gave him bored looks, glanced over his papers, found somebody to escort him and waved him in. The war wasn't officially over, but with the ceasefire almost a week old and the global media chattering about the negotiations in Geneva, nobody seemed too concerned about the risk of renewed hostilities.

Protocol required a visit to the camp commandant, who shook his hand and welcomed him to the camp with an expansive gesture. McGaffney asked a few pro forma questions, noted down the man's answers, and then got permission for the interviews with American prisoners of war his editors had begged him to get.

Outside, it could have been any other POW camp from any of two dozen recent wars: dust and barbed wire, tents in rows, guards lounging about with guns slung casually from their shoulders, a clutch of Red Cross personnel scurrying about on some errand of their own, and prisoners, thousands of them, looking tired, dusty and sullen. McGaffney let his guide lead him down among the tents, then stopped in front of one at random. "How about this one?"

The guard shrugged. The tent flaps were open; McGaffney walked up to it, stooped, and said, "G'day. I'm Tommy McGaffney from All Aussie News. If I can bother you for an interview or two?"

The soldiers gave him wary looks, but made room for him, and once he made it clear that he wasn't going to ask anything they weren't supposed to answer, they loosened up. Yes, they were getting enough to eat and drink; they'd gotten the chance the day before to send notes home to their families and friends via the Red Cross; he got their names and some good printable anecdotes from them, and then thanked them and went on. Down the line of tents and over to the next row, he repeated the same performance, got more story fodder.

"What's down there?" McGaffney pointed across the way, to a section of the camp closed off behind its own fence.

"Women's part of camp," the guard told him.

"Any reason I can't go there?"

The guard shrugged, followed him to the nearest gate in the fence.

He did the same thing there, chatting with a tentful of women; one of them was an Air Force colonel, no less, and she was a looker, too. He noted down her name with the others— Melanie Bridgeport—and wondered briefly where he'd heard the last name before. Half an hour later, after another brief visit to the commandant, he was back in his car, pulling out of the parking lot to head back to Dar es Salaam.

27 September 2029: Newport News, Virginia

"In tonight's lead story," said the anchorman, "another of the Weed administration's claims about the East African war has come under fire. The issue this time? The fate of the US naval task force. Here's Bryan Tuckerman in Newport News with the details."

Rumors about the Battle of Kilindini had begun to circulate in the United States within days of the assault on the carrier group, spreading through the internet and the alternative media. The mainstream news programs and websites stayed strictly away from the story—among the rules of the game that old hands in the media taught newcomers to the business were that you didn't contradict the Pentagon when there was a war on, and you didn't contradict the president unless the other party had your back. Now that the war was over and Weed couldn't even be sure of his own party's support, though, all bets were off.

"Here's the official story," said Tuckerman, standing in front of a gray Navy ship. A clip from one of Weed's public appearances followed; "The task force came under attack from Tanzanian missiles," Weed said, "and I'm sorry to say that there were casualties on our side. Of course our naval forces responded and destroyed the missile bases." The clip ended, and Tuckerman went on: "That's true as far as it goes, but reports we've gathered from sailors who were there on the scene make it clear that what actually happened was much worse than the administration is letting on."

More than 1,000 crew members from Joint Expeditionary Task Force Three had been evacuated to US bases in the Gulf just before the Battle of Mombasa, and close to half of them were already back in the United States when the nuclear crisis began. It took a chance conversation in a Boston bar to get word to a reporter for one of the television networks, and launch an investigation. That the network in question had close ties to one of Weed's most likely rivals in the 2032 election was simply one more incentive.

"We had maybe thirty minutes' warning," said a chief petty officer from the USS *Gridley* on screen. "Cruise missiles—a lot of them, a couple of hundred—coming off the Tanzanian coast at Mach 2 or thereabouts. We had all our antimissile defenses going, and my best guess is that we took out two-thirds of the incoming missiles, maybe even three-quarters, but that wasn't enough."

"There were fifteen surface ships in the task force," Tuckerman went on. "According to eyewitness accounts like the one you just heard, four of them were sunk during the battle, three more sank the next day, and another five took enough damage to put them effectively out of action." Carrier on sandbar, the most famous image of the war came onscreen. "One volley of cruise missiles sank or crippled twelve of those fifteen ships, including the *Ronald Reagan*, the carrier at the heart of the task force."

"None of this should have been any kind of surprise," said a new face, a professor of military history from Princeton. "For years now, every time the Navy's done an exercise involving swarming attacks, they had to give the carrier group completely unrealistic advantages or this is what they got. The Navy and the nation had so much invested in aircraft carriers, emotionally as well as financially, that nobody wanted to think about what was going to happen if we kept on trying to fight twenty-first-century wars with twentieth-century thinking. Well, now we have to think about it."

"In just a moment," said the anchorman, "the latest news from Hollywood." The news program gave way to a snack-food advertisement, leaving millions of Americans staring at their televisions with shocked looks, trying to come to terms with the unthinkable.

Over the days that followed, the other television networks and the big news websites joined the feeding frenzy, finding eyewitnesses and experts of their own. Long before the story had become old news, though, the nation had something else to worry about.

30 September 2029: Wall Street, New York City

The market had been losing ground since summer, jolting down hard whenever bad news came from East Africa and never quite recovering on the up days in between. Shuttered during the nuclear crisis—not even the most diehard traders wanted to be sitting in Manhattan when a Russian or Chinese warhead came calling—it opened again on the 22nd, dropped steeply for a few days, then managed to stabilize on light trading. The same evening news program that broke the story of the Battle of Kilindini reported a 12 point gain in the Dow Jones average the previous day.

When the market opened again on Monday morning, trading on the New York Stock Exchange had opened heavy, with defense industry stocks down hard on a flurry of sell orders from institutional investors. Toward noon, a story about the upcoming Senate hearings appeared on the *Wall Street Journal* website, naming half a dozen big firms whose executives had already been served subpoenas; there had been dozens of stories like it over the previous week, but that one hit the market at a vulnerable moment, and sparked a wave of selling that spread beyond the original defense firms to include most industrial stocks. When the closing bell sounded, the Dow was down 881 points.

The next morning, 30 September, was one of the handful of days that would earn a permanent place in Wall Street's history. Traders reading the financial news on commuter trains into New York City got the first glimpse of what was about to happen, as reports from the European markets warned of panic selling in dollar-denominated commercial paper. By the time the opening bell sounded on Wall Street, the panic had spread to US treasury bills, and the dollar was down hard against most other currencies. Stock prices on the US markets opened down sharply from their lows the day before, struggled through the first half of the morning, and then plunged as traders struggled to meet a flood of sell orders at any price.

By noon it was clear that the market was in serious trouble. In Washington, Treasury Secretary Beryl Mickelson met with President Weed and the chairman of the Federal Reserve Board. "Under any other circumstances," Mickelson said, "I'd advise you to flood the market with cheap credit, but with the dollar on the ropes—"

"We can't just let the market tank," Weed protested.

"The alternative is to risk a run on Treasury paper that would send interest rates out of control, and possibly force a default on the federal debt."

Weed stared at her. "What you're saying is we're screwed."

"The stock market's expendable," Mickelson said. "The government's ability to borrow isn't. It's not going to be pretty, but a stock market crash isn't the end of the world."

Glumly, Weed nodded. Maybe it's not the end of the world, he thought, but one more blow like this and it's going to be the end of me.

Word reached the big Wall Street brokerages a half hour later that the federal government was in no condition to bail the market out. Top executives huddled with trading-floor experts, and made the only decision they could: unwind everything. As brokerages began liquidating their own stock positions, what had been a bad day turned into the worst day in Wall Street's history. By the time the closing bell sounded, the Dow Jones average had plunged 2606 points.

3 October 2029: Beijing

The little nameless restaurant just outside the Party enclave of Zhongnanhai was more crowded than usual, but Liu had had no trouble getting a quiet table out of earshot of anyone else for his lunch with Fang. When he'd been promoted to the Central Military Commission five years before, and become one of the half dozen or so most powerful men in China, he'd assumed that there was no higher he could climb. Since the war, though, it had become impossible not to notice the difference between being one of the half dozen or so most powerful men in China, and being the hero of the country and almost certainly its next president. He could sense gaps opening around him where once there had been human contact; it was by no means an agreeable feeling.

Even Fang seemed a little distant, a little preoccupied. Still, they chatted about small things, Fang's promotion to director of the Academy of Military Science among them, while the waiters brought one delectable course after another. Finally, when the meal had reached that pleasant moment when two cups of green tea made everything perfect, Fang cupped his chin pensively in his hand. "There is one other matter," he said.

"Ah," said Liu. "I wondered how soon you would move your chariot."

Fang smiled; clearly he had not forgotten the earlier conversation. Then, somber again: "Less an opening move than an inquiry about whether a game might or might not be appropriate. I have been considering the situation in the United States just now, and it occurs to me that there are opportunities that the Motherland might wish to exploit." He sipped tea. "Or might not."

Liu gestured: go on.

"I certainly don't mean to inquire about state secrets, but it is clear to me that some other country has been funding anti-government propaganda in the United States for years now."

"Good," said Liu. "Four countries, that I know of. You might be surprised if you knew which ones." In response to Fang's raised eyebrow: "I'll just say that at least one of America's putative allies has recognized that under some circumstances, it might be necessary to turn Washington's favorite game of regime change back onto its originators."

"That does surprise me," Fang admitted. "But the Americans have been preparing to deal with something of that kind for many years now—by my estimate, half their annual Homeland Security budget goes to such preparations. I don't think the same sort of process they tried to use in Tanzania could be used against them with any chance of success—but there are other possibilities, using means that wouldn't draw so much attention. Between the widespread public acceptance of antigovernment propaganda and the shock of this recent defeat, the United States is in an extremely delicate state. The right moves, or the wrong ones, could bring about a crisis of legitimacy that would destabilize it completely."

"And result in regime change?"

"Not at all." He sipped more of his tea. "In regime collapse. Perhaps partition, perhaps civil war—in any event, the end of the United States as a nation."

Liu considered that for a moment. "How would you set out to do that?"

It took Fang less than five minutes to explain the strategy. By the time he was finished, Liu was staring at him. "That is—brilliant," he said.

"Thank you," said Fang. "But I am far from certain that crushing America completely would be to the benefit of the

Motherland. That is yours to judge, General—yours with the other members of the Central Military Commission. I consider it my duty to bring the possibility to your attention."

"And for that you have my thanks," Liu said. His mind was racing, considering the possibilities. "I'll ask you not to mention this to anyone else. If we decide to proceed with this, it must be done in even greater secrecy than Plan Qilin—and if we decide otherwise, nobody must know about it, now or later."

10 October 2029: Wall Street, New York City

"You realize what this means," said the man behind the very big desk.

"Yes, sir." The trader in front of the desk was in his thirties. He wore the latest style of suit favored by young investment bankers, but his face was damp with worry.

A finger tapped on a button, opening the intercom. "Arlene, I need Jim, Vikram and Pierre up here now. Whatever else they're doing doesn't matter. Okay? Thanks." Another tap on the button shut it off.

The man behind the desk drew in a ragged breath, let it out.

Five minutes later the other chief officers of the bank were in the corner office. "You know Theo Pappas from derivatives trading, don't you?" The man behind the desk nodded at the younger man. "Theo, why don't you explain the situation."

"We got a heads up from contacts in Washington about the Tanzanian thing well in advance." Pappas glanced from face to face. "No surprises there. Back in June, once we were sure of it, we took big positions on it—really big positions, in oil and half a dozen other commodities that would be affected."

"I was informed," said the chief operations officer. "So?"

"Nobody hedged the possibility the US might lose."

The room was silent as that sank in. "We've been doing everything we can to unwind those positions for the last three weeks," said Pappas. "No dice. Even if the markets weren't tanking, it'd be a helluva job, and as it is, nobody's buying and we've run out of time."

"How deep are we in the hole?" This from the chief financial officer.

"Just north of two trillion dollars."

Another silence, and then the CFO turned to the man behind the big desk. "We'll have to get Washington to cover us. That's going to hurt."

"More than you know. I talked to the people in Treasury and the Fed when the markets tanked—just in case. They said no. With the dollar in the toilet, they've got zero room for more QE, and that means no more bailouts."

"But that means—" the CFO started, and then stopped.

"Yeah," said the man behind the desk. "How long have we got until the markets close?"

The COO checked his watch. "Three hours."

"Fair enough. We can get the press conference called, do the thing properly." Then, abruptly, the chief executive officer of the nation's biggest investment bank bowed his head and muttered, "Fuck, fuck, *fuck*."

10 October 2029: Russell Senate Office Building, Washington DC

"At least that's over with," said Senator Bridgeport. The Senate had just voted, glumly but with no significant debate, to ratify the Treaty of Geneva.

"On to the next mess?" said Joe Egmont.

"Pretty much. What's the status on the subpoenas?"

Bridgeport's staff had been working overtime preparing for the hearings on the East African War. A flurry of initial subpoenas aimed at administration officials got countered with the usual claims of executive privilege, forcing Weed to use his political capital to shelter his own people and making it harder for him to do anything about the people Bridgeport really wanted to get on the witness stand under oath.

At this point it was strategy time, figuring out who among the many possibilities would be most likely to talk. Bridgeport had been on the phone with Ralph Wittkower almost daily to make sure the Pentagon's toes weren't getting stepped on; even so, it was a political gamble for everybody involved.

"The list is coming together," Egmont said. "One name you'll want to hear is Admiral Deckmann."

"The task force commander?"

"Bingo. We've talked to him, and he's willing to testify."

Bridgeport let out a low whistle. "That could get explosive—pardon the pun."

"No kidding. The one big question we've got at this point is Stedman."

"Have you talked to him?"

"Not yet. He's a big enough fish that—"

The intercom beeped, and Bridgeport tapped the button. "Yes?"

"Heads up, Boss." Anne's voice was uncharacteristically tense. "Check the news."

"Will do." He closed the intercom, tapped the mouse to awaken his computer screen, opened a browser. "Oh my God."

"What's up?"

Bridgeport motioned him over, and Egmont came around the desk, saw the headlines, and blanched. "That's gonna hurt."

The country's largest investment bank had just announced that it was bankrupt and would be going out of business.

Over the next six weeks, US stock market averages continued to plunge, shedding half their value and erasing tens of trillions of dollars in paper wealth, and eight other major financial firms that had been considered too big to fail failed anyway.

11 October 2029: Dar es Salaam

"To peace," said Hafiz al-Nazrani, and raised his teacup. McGaffney repeated the words and clinked his bottle against the cup, then downed a good quarter of the beer at a gulp.

Dar hadn't gone unscathed. During the war's first days, when the Chinese hadn't yet secured Tanzania's airspace, American bombs and missiles had pounded government buildings and other strategic targets. Still, construction crews were already clearing away the rubble, and most of the city—including the little café south of Kingamboni where the two reporters sat—was once again open for business.

"How was Kenya?" McGaffney asked.

"Oh, fine. Nobody seems to know where Kesembani's got to—"

"Off the continent, if he's got the brains God gave a goose."

"Granted. But the Coalition bosses got somebody from Kenya's parliament to step in as temporary head of state, and they're pulling their troops out as fast as they can. It's very much 'no quarrel with you, just with the Americans.'"

"Smart." McGaffney took another swallow of his beer.

"Aside from that, and Chinese diplomats and businessmen swarming all over with pockets full of investment money—well, it's Kenya. Though I suspect it may see quite a bit of change after the first trillion renminbi."

"True enough."

"And you? Keeping busy?"

McGaffney scowled. "Out visiting offshore oil platforms. With the Gulf gone blooey, everyone back home's bent out of shape about where's the oil going to come from, so the editors wanted a nice soothing story about East African oilfields. You can bet TPC was happy to give them one, too. So I got the five star treatment, interviews with Mkembe and a couple of ministers, chopper rides out to the platforms, you name it."

"Nice work if you can get it," said Hafiz.

McGaffney finished his beer, met the other man's gaze squarely. "But not my work."

Hafiz nodded. "But of course." Then: "So where next? Spain or the Gulf?"

"Neither one." McGaffney put his elbows on the little table. "I don't go where the fighting is, I go where it's going to be."

"Sensible. The Congo, then? Now that the balance of power has changed, I can't imagine that anybody's going to be willing to put up with more trouble there—and the Chinese have got to be thinking about the minerals there."

"True enough—but that's not it either. I'm headed for the United States."

Hafiz considered him for a long moment. "You're serious?"

"Or stupid."

His expression denied it. "You think this is going to hit them that hard?"

"Maybe." McGaffney shrugged. "It's just a hunch."

But it was more than that, of course. He thought of the faces of the men and women in the POW camp up in Shinyanga District, the faces of Americans interviewed on the media: dazed and sullen, still trying to make sense of being beaten, and failing. If they can't take it out on the rest of the world, he knew—

They'll take it out on each other.

"We'll see what comes of it," he said aloud. "You got any plans yet?"

TWENTY-ONE

10 November 2029: Johnson Air Force Base,
Goldsboro, North Carolina

For some reason known only to the Air Force, the plane that was flying Melanie home was coming into an air base in North Carolina. Senator Bridgeport got word from a friend in the Pentagon on the 8th, and left Washington the next day. Traffic was light on US 95, even for a Sunday, and he made good time; by midafternoon he was in Raleigh, where he'd booked a room at a nondescript hotel. He got dinner in the hotel restaurant, and then spent the evening hunched over a laptop, firing off instructions to his staff and trying to round up support in the Senate so he'd have cover once the White House figured out just what kind of questions his committee was going to ask.

The next morning he was up early, pushed himself hard through his usual routine—shave, thirty minutes in the hotel exercise room, shower, clothes—so he didn't have time to worry. Breakfast was a bagel and cream cheese from the hotel's breakfast bar, and then he was out the door, into the car, onto the highway toward Johnson Air Force Base.

Somebody had hand-lettered a sign and taped it to the sign where the road to the air base veered off: the letters *POWs*, a crudely drawn yellow ribbon, and an arrow beneath, pointing the way. Bridgeport's wasn't the only car following the sign, either. The one ahead of his was a ten-year-old Hyundai with New Hampshire plates and as many people on board as would fit. Another hand-lettered sign directed him to a parking lot; he let some airman in a blue jacket wave him to a spot, got out. The day was cold, with gray clouds overhead; he buttoned up his coat, followed more signs and a thin stream of civilians toward the tarmac.

A crowd had gathered there already, waiting out in the open behind a bright yellow rope. Bridgeport walked down its length to the far end, where there was still space along the rope. He got there, stood looking out at the empty runway for a while, then turned to the woman next to him. "Excuse me—do you know how soon the plane's due?"

"Wish I did, hon," she said. "The website said today, is all."

"Gimme a moment," said a teenage boy with her. He had a web tablet in his hand, and tapped away at the screen, then stopped and shook his head. "Nothing yet, dammit."

"Lenny! You watch your language."

He hung his head. "Sorry, Momma."

"Your older boy's coming back?" Bridgeport asked.

She beamed. "Yes indeed. Jamie's a corporal in the 101st. What's your boy been doing?"

"My daughter," said Bridgeport. "She's a supply officer in the Air Force."

"Oh my lord," the woman said. "I'd have been scared to death to have a daughter of mine over there."

"I was," Bridgeport admitted.

They talked a little, in a desultory way, as the crowd grew. Her name was Loretta Wallace, and she was a waitress from Philadelphia, single since her boys' father stepped on a Venezuelan land mine, struggling to get by like so many Americans but managing it so far. He told her he worked for the government in DC; she nodded, didn't ask for details.

"Here we go," the teenager said after a while, and another flurry of tapping at the screen. "It's supposed to be here in—" A few more pokes. "Fourteen minutes."

"Oh, I can't wait," said Loretta.

A few minutes later, the faint sound of jet engines finally came whispering through the air. Conversations in the crowd faltered and faded out. The sound grew, and then the plane came down through the clouds: a big transport in Air Force colors, wheels and flaps down. A ragged cheer, and then silence as the plane came down onto the runway, rolled to a near-stop, and taxied over to fifty yards or so of the crowd. The ground crew hauled a boarding stairway over, the door came open, and the first of a long line of figures started down the stairs.

Bridgeport never saw who pulled the rope aside—one of the airmen, or someone in the crowd? A moment later, Loretta let out a squeal of delight and ran onto the tarmac, her younger son close behind, to throw her arms around a gaunt young man in camo BDUs. Bridgeport barely noticed. He was staring at the door of the plane, waiting, until—

There she was. He did not let himself run. He walked out, weaving around families who already had someone to welcome back, half-hearing their laughter and tears and excited words, and got within a few yards of the foot of the stairs as she reached the bottom.

"Dad." She looked tired and hungry, but her smile brought tears to his eyes. "God, it's good to see you."

He couldn't speak, simply threw his arms around her and held her. Finding words at last: "Mel. Welcome back."

Finally he drew back, still holding her by the shoulders. "You're okay?"

"Yeah, all things considered."

"Is there anything you need to do here?"

"Not a thing. They debriefed us in Germany and had us fill out the paperwork on the plane. I'm on leave until date not specified, and all my stuff's here." She patted the duffel slung over her back.

He let her go. "Good. Is there anything you want? A meal, or …"

"Oh my God, yes."

They went to his car, drove into Goldsboro, followed one of the main streets past one empty strip mall after another until he found a steak house—that was what she wanted—and settled into a booth. She put away the kind of meal he'd eaten back when he was in high school and playing tennis on the school team; he got a steak and salad, and had to remind himself more than once to eat them. It was enough to have her home, and safe.

"I'm probably going to regret that," she said as they left the restaurant, "but thank you, Dad." With a wavering smile: "It almost feels like I'm home again." All at once, she started to cry. He put his arms around her, right there in the parking lot, and held her as she sobbed.

10 November 2029: Baltimore-Washington International Airport

"Thanks, mate," Tommy McGaffney said, and pocketed his passport. The customs clerk didn't even bother to reply, just turned to the next person in line, and McGaffney took the hint and left the counter. He had the same shapeless leather bag on his shoulder as usual, and the same automatic awareness of the people around him that had kept him in one piece all over the grubbier corners of the Third World; the only thing that startled him was how natural it seemed here in the United States.

If the airport was any guide, he decided, the country was in even worse shape than he'd guessed. There were missing ceiling panels, boarded-over gaps in the walls, light fixtures gone dark, the same look of slow decay he remembered from eastern Europe in the years just before the Soviet Union crashed and burned. When he got out of the secure area into baggage claim, half the baggage carousels were closed and boarded up, and the signs yelling about this or that car rental agency on the far wall were old enough that the plastic was starting to yellow.

Somewhere not far ahead, an angry voice barked something McGaffney couldn't quite make out. The people around him looked that way and then hurried past. McGaffney paused, then went toward the voice.

It would have made a perfect snapshot: a middle-aged man with the kind of buzz cut American vets favored, shouting at a baffled kid in jeans and a tee shirt, while his wife tried to get him to shut up and go anywhere else. As McGaffney got close enough to hear, the kid was saying, "Look, it's just a joke!"

"It's not fucking funny!" the older man shouted at him.

"George," said the wife, pulling on his arm, "for God's sake, let it go."

George glared for a moment longer, and then let his wife drag him away. The kid stood there looking angry and scared at the same time, then turned a different direction and went wherever he was headed. Before he was gone, though, McGaffney got a good look at the shirt. The art on the front was a cartoonish beach scene, with the *Ronald Reagan* heeled over on its sandbar in the middle distance; in the foreground sat what looked like a big muscular American eagle, but the head had come off. The "eagle" was a heavily padded muscle suit, and from out of the neck hole rose the neck and head of a scrawny, frightened-looking turkey.

McGaffney shook his head, made a mental note to watch for more of the same sort of humor. That sort of thing was common enough elsewhere in the world, but among Americans? There it was new, and needed watching.

10 November 2029: Petersburg, Virginia

"This could be bad," Bridgeport said, as they drove past the gas station. It was the third in a row that had handlettered "Out of Gas" signs taped on the pumps.

"How much do you have left?" Melanie asked.

"Not quite down to fumes, but—" He did some math in his head. "We'd probably better find a place to stay in Richmond unless somebody has gas."

He'd planned to drive straight home that day, and hadn't thought about whether the gas stations would be open. Even with the news stories about the Gulf war and the falling dollar, even with prices going up so fast that on a drive of any length, you could just about count on seeing some kid on a ladder swapping out digits on a gas station sign, it hadn't occurred to him, or to most Americans, that there might not be any gasoline for sale at all.

They drove for another ten minutes before another gas station sign came in sight—open for business, from the line of cars at it, even though the price on the sign was $12.99 a gallon for regular. As Bridgeport turned to join the line, though, he saw a sandwich board out in front with CASH ONLY written on it.

"So much for that," he said. "I don't have more than a few bucks."

"Don't worry about it," Melanie said. "I'll cover it."

He glanced at her. "At that price?"

She grinned. "Just watch."

They crept forward, a carlength at a time, and got to a pump. The gas station had employees out to collect the money; one came over to Bridgeport's car, and Bridgeport rolled down the window.

Melanie leaned across him with a bill in her hand, held it out the window. "Will you take this?" It took Bridgeport a moment to recognize King William's face on the twenty-pound note.

The young man in the gas station jacket goggled at it. "Jesus," he said. "You know what that's worth these days?"

"A full tank of gas?" Melanie asked him.

"Lemme check." He trotted over to his supervisor, came right back. "Yes ma'am."

Bridgeport got out, filled the tank. The line was getting longer; no doubt word had gotten out on social media that there was still a station in town with gas, and they'd be mobbed until their storage tank was as dry as the other stations'.

He got back in, rolled his window up, pulled out of the station. "I suppose," he said to his daughter, "you just happened to have some British money on you."

"I heard that the dollar was tanking when we got to Germany." She glanced at him. "We all had back pay coming, so when I got mine, I cashed it out and took the money to the exchange bureau. A lot of people from the base were doing that. They were literally out of euros—they were waiting for an armored car from Dusseldorf with more—but they still had British pounds."

"Smart. Not that I'm surprised, you understand."

She laughed, sat back in the seat as he guided the car back onto the freeway.

10 November 2029: Silver Spring, Maryland

"It hasn't changed much," said Bridgeport, as he unlocked the door to his condo. "Well, except that you'll have to meet the new tenant."

The tenant in question meowed up at them as they entered. "Hello, Bus," Bridgeport said.

Melanie squatted down and reached out a hand, which the cat sniffed carefully. "I don't believe," she said, "we've met. Mr. Bustopher Jones, I presume? Colonel Melanie Bridgeport, at your service."

The cat submitted graciously to having its ears scratched and tugged, and then walked pointedly across the entry to the kitchenette, across the floor to the food dish, and glanced back over its shoulder at Bridgeport to make sure he was paying attention.

"Dogs have owners, cats have staff," Melanie said, getting to her feet. "Do you want me to feed him?"

"Not at all. In fact, I'm going to chase you out of the kitchen— I have a surprise planned."

She laughed, headed to the spare bedroom with her duffel bag over her shoulder.

Once the cat had its face in the food dish and the surprise was tucked into the oven, he went into the living room, settled on the couch. She was already curled up on the other side of it, looking tired but not half as ragged as she'd been at the airfield.

"If it's okay," he said, "I want to ask some things about—" He fumbled for a word.

"The war? I was wondering when you'd get to that." She smiled. "Yes, it's okay. What do you want to know?"

"Just how badly we got beaten."

She drew in an uneven breath, nodded. "The short version is that we got our butts handed to us. Do you know what happened to the Navy task force?"

"Yes. That hit the media a week ago."

"It wasn't quite that bad for the rest of us. No, I take that back: It wasn't quite that *fast*. The fighter wings got ground down a few planes at a time, the Army units got driven back a battle at a time. It wasn't one-sided—we took out two of their planes for every three of ours that we lost—but that's just it; none of us knew how to fight a war that wasn't one-sided. Once we didn't have air superiority any more and couldn't bring in all the supplies we wanted, nobody really knew what to do. So it turned into a slugging match, and the Chinese and the Coalition forces kept slugging until we didn't have anything left to fight with."

The cat came out of the kitchenette, licking its whiskers, and walked up to the couch. After a moment of contemplation, it leapt up, climbed onto Melanie's lap, circled twice and settled down there.

"You," she told it, rubbing between its ears, "are a worthy successor to the late lamented Macavity." Looking up at her father: "On the flight back, some of the staff officers were talking about whether the administration was going to blame us for what happened. Maybe there was a way we could have won. I don't—"

She stopped in mid-sentence, sniffed the air. "Oh my God," she said. "You didn't. Mac and cheese?"

"*With* tomatoes," said Bridgeport.

"You," she said, "are the best dad anyone ever had. I mean that."

10 November 2029: The White House, Washington DC

"Finally," Jameson Weed said, "I want to ask you and all Americans everywhere to join together with President Gurney and put an end to this unhappy chapter of our nation's history. God bless each and every one of you, and God bless America. Thank you."

They were applauding as he left the podium, kept it up as he came down the stairs and headed toward the door. Andie met him there, with an embrace and a kiss that felt less forced than anything of the kind she'd done in years. She had been crying, he could see that even through the heavy makeup she'd put on to cover it. He tried not to think of that, returned the kiss, pulled away from her and left the East Room.

And after all of it—

He tried to wrench his mind away from the thought, and failed.

—the shit he'd had to put up with—

Someone called after him—Andie? He couldn't tell, didn't want to know.

—the deals he'd had to make—

He could still hear them applauding in the East Room as he started up the stairs.

—the lies he'd had to tell—

Did they expect him to stay there, smiling and nodding, at his own political funeral?

—this.

He got to the top of the stairs, stumbled forward half blindly, turned into the Center Hall. More dead presidents looked down at him from the walls. If Nixon had been there, or Harding, or one of the other great failures of the presidency, that might have been some consolation, but of course they were nowhere to be seen: it was Washington and Lincoln, Reagan and the Roosevelts, the men whose shoes he'd tried to fill and whose pictures he'd insisted on having there as a reminder of his hopes. Well, they were doing their job now.

Enough, he told himself. Enough. There was one answer not even they could argue with.

As he got to the door of the private sitting room, he heard Andie calling up the stairs, calling his name. He paused, then hurried in, closed the door behind him, locked it to spare himself that further humiliation. She would know soon enough.

Bottom drawer of the bureau, box on the left, under the papers: blued metal gleamed. He pulled the revolver out, made sure it was loaded. Then, before he could have second thoughts, he pressed the muzzle up against the roof of his mouth and pulled the trigger.

11 November 2029: Silver Spring, Maryland

Lights sparkled in the still air as Bridgeport stared out the window. Melanie was asleep; they'd sat on the couch and talked until she could barely keep her eyes open, and he'd sent her off to bed the way he'd done when she still wore her hair in pigtails. She'd laughed then, and wept a little, and told him that she felt as though she'd finally come home.

Home, Bridgeport thought. It's a very different place these days.

He hadn't even tried to go to bed. The air around him felt brittle and bright as glass. Nerves, certainly, but it was more than that: something had changed irrevocably, maybe for him, maybe for the country or the world, he couldn't tell.

As he stared out at the lights, what came to mind was the waitress from Philadelphia he'd met at the Air Force base that morning. Just one more ordinary American, he thought. These are the people we say we're leading, the people whose votes we buy and sell. He remembered the squeal of delight she'd let out when her son appeared at the top of the boarding ramp, and asked himself: What if things had gone the other way, and she'd gotten the call from the Pentagon telling her that her son wasn't coming home at all?

We take them for granted, he thought. I've done it as much as anybody. And that it took something like this to remind me that her Jamie is just as precious to her as Mel is to me—God forgive me for that.

He half turned toward the kitchenette, thinking of the bourbon on the top shelf of the cabinet; decided against it, went to his computer instead, tapped the mouse to wake it and then walked over to the couch while the screen slowly brightened. Bus was mostly asleep, sprawled across the cushions, but stretched and purred vaguely when Bridgeport reached down and stroked his back.

Then he turned back to the computer, and saw the news.

TWENTY-TWO

15 November 2029: Silver Spring, Maryland

Bridgeport put down the telephone, stood there for one frozen moment, and then shook his head and let out a breath he hadn't been conscious of holding. Mel was watching him; she'd been typing something into her laptop on the other side of the room until halfway through the call, and had the expression of someone who wasn't sure whether to ask a question or not.

"That was Gurney," Bridgeport said. "He's offered me the vice presidency."

Her face lit up, and she started to say something, then stopped.

"I know," he said. "It's basically a bribe to head off the hearings."

"Are you going to accept?"

"I don't know," he admitted. "I told him I'd get back to him later today with an answer."

It was a tempting possibility, no question, and it also showed with painful clarity just how badly Gurney wanted to keep the fine details of the nation's military failure out of the media. No, he corrected himself, not Gurney: the offer had Ellen Harbin's fingerprints all over it. Rumors in the Senate had it that she and the new president were thick as thieves: the polite term was "close allies," though there were plenty of more scurrilous claims as well.

He frowned, shook his head again. "Well, we'll see." Turning toward her: "Any luck?"

"Not a bit." She'd been trying to get some kind of clarification from the Air Force about her status. Officially she was on indefinite leave from the 33rd Fighter Wing, and entitled to her normal pay, but there was some kind of bureaucratic tangle involved and no one could tell her exactly when to expect a paycheck.

"I'll see if I can shake something loose from the Pentagon," he promised. "I've got to talk to Ralph Wittkower anyway about this new thing. He's gone way out on a limb to help me get things set up for the hearings; I owe him that much."

Mel considered that. "What do you think he'll say?"

"I don't know. I really don't know." In Washington, those in the know referred to the Pentagon as the fourth branch of government, as influential as the executive, legislative and judicial branches—sometimes more influential, when push came to shove—and you never knew quite what game the military was playing. "I'll have to talk to Joe and a couple of other people in the office, and then we'll see."

15 November 2029: The Pentagon, Washington DC

"He called this afternoon," Wittkower said.

"And?" Admiral Waite looked up from his drink.

"We'll see. I did my best to talk him into taking it."

The two of them were in Waite's secure office, a windowless room not far from his public office but screened from eavesdropping by every technological trick the US military had at its disposal. Back when the room was built, the security measures had been directed against the agents of hostile foreign powers; these days, as often as not, the eyes and ears that had to be foiled worked for some other branch of the federal government.

Waite sipped the gin and tonic, his face unreadable. "Did you tell him why?"

"Of course not. I mentioned that we're not too happy about Gurney, and Harbin's name came up, but that's as far as it went. I promised him I'd work with whoever gets the Armed Services committee so the hearings can go forward, that sort of thing."

"Those are going to hurt," Waite said.

Wittkower said nothing. It was an open question, he knew, whether funding for the carrier fleet would survive the outcry over the Battle of Kilindini, and he remembered that Waite had been a naval fighter pilot and then a carrier officer before finding his way into the Navy's upper ranks. The flattops were probably as obsolete as oared galleys, but Wittkower wasn't about to press the point; you didn't make rude comments about a man's first love.

"The thing I wish I knew," said Waite then, "is just how far we'll have to go. Not about Gurney—he's incompetent, no question, but he's hardly the first clueless political hack that's landed in the White House. About Harbin."

"What I want to know is how far *she'll* go."

"Good question. Do you know about her papers on constitutional theory, the ones she wrote when she was teaching at Harvard?"

"I know she wrote some," said Wittkower.

"I'll have my staff send you an outline. She was banking off some of the ideas the old neoconservatives came up with twenty or thirty years ago. Her theory—unitary government theory was the label she used—is that all the powers of government belong to the president; he farms them out to the other agencies and branches of government, federal, state, local, you name it, but he can take them back any time he wants to."

Wittkower took that in. "I don't think that's quite what the guys who wrote the Constitution had in mind."

"No, but it's actually quite impressive to watch her finesse that point." Waite finished his drink. "The question in my mind is whether she'll try to act on that theory."

"In which case ..."

"Exactly."

Even in a secure office, the phrase on both of their minds didn't bear repeating. Military intervention in the US political process happened all the time, but it happened subtly—members of Congress could be lobbied or pressured, defense contractors encouraged to cut checks for one candidate or another, the votes of servicepeople and their families on military bases manipulated this way or that, and so on. Only a dozen times in the history of the republic had the Chiefs of Staff been forced to draw up plans and make preparations for something beyond that, and each time, that had been enough to panic the politicians and get the necessary policy changes made.

Someday, it might not be enough. How many of Waite's predecessors, Wittkower wondered, had to sit there and wonder: are the tanks actually going to have to head out into the streets this time?

"Have your people start drafting plans," Waite said then. "If something has to be done, we need to be ready."

2 December 2029: The White House, Washington DC

"So help me God," said Pete Bridgeport.

The East Room exploded in applause and flashing cameras. President Gurney, beaming, crossed the podium to shake the hand of his new vice president. The First Lady, Julia Gurney, followed, and gave him one of those bright Southern smiles that could mean anything or nothing. Voices, tumult, more flashes, and then he and Melanie were following the Gurneys out of the East Room, down the Cross Hall, and into the State Dining Room for the inaugural banquet.

Bridgeport still wasn't sure why he'd agreed to the job. It wasn't ambition—God knows he had enough of that, but he'd set his sights on a long career in the Senate, working his way up step by step to one of the top positions there, which was certainly more appealing than sitting around and waiting in the wings in case Gurney happened to die in office. It certainly wasn't because he owed anything to Gurney, or to poor Weed—he'd attended the funeral at Arlington Cemetery along with the rest of official Washington, of course, standing there bareheaded under bleak November skies as a presidency that had begun with so much promise ended with a flag-draped coffin sliding into the ground, but that was as far as his duty to the man went.

No, if it was anything, it was an uneasy feeling somewhere in the back of his brain that somehow, saying yes to Gurney's offer might matter more than he could imagine. You didn't get far in the political game without learning to pay attention to your hunches, and night after night, as he'd wrestled with the question, the same unformed sense had surfaced: you have to do this.

So he'd arranged for Joe Egmont to get all the plans and papers for the hearings to Rosemary Muller, who would be taking over the Armed Services Committee; he'd taken care of the remaining promises he'd made to the voters back home, and had lunch with Leona Price, who knew everyone and everything in the District, including the corner of it where he'd be living once the movers got through packing up his things in the Silver Spring condo and hauling them to One Observatory Circle. He'd had a long talk with Melanie, who would be staying in the condo but would be his hostess for official events—and now here he was, with Melanie resplendent in her full dress Air Force uniform and the movers and shakers of the

Washington establishment there to congratulate him, and still not certain why.

He helped Melanie to her seat, took his own place between her and Gurney, bowed his head while somebody with a Deep South accent said grace—Julia Gurney was a very public Christian, sitting in the pews in some church or other every Sunday without fail, and had a favorite Baptist preacher of hers in to bless the meal. Afterwards, as the waiters began bustling around with food and drink, Gurney leaned over and said, "I hope I can count on you to help me with Congress."

"That's my intention," Bridgeport told him.

"Good. You've got three days of briefings ahead—I remember, trust me. After that—well, how about Monday after the Cabinet meeting? I can fill you in on my plans then."

Bridgeport nodded, and wondered what the man had in mind.

9 December 2029: Washington DC

"Oh for God's sake," said Leona Price. "That just about figures."

Her husband Robert, who was on the other side of the living room, looked up from his laptop; he was correcting papers for one of the history classes he taught at Georgetown University. "What?"

"Gurney."

"Babe, if you can say anything about that man that I have a hard time believing, lunch tomorrow is on me."

"You're on," she said. "Care to guess what his big plan for getting America back on its feet amounts to?"

He gestured for her to go ahead.

"New aircraft carriers."

"No way."

"A new generation of carriers that can shrug off cruise missiles, to quote, regain our rightful place at the center of the world order, unquote."

He blinked, then got to his feet and came over.

On her computer screen was a transcript of Gurney's speech to Congress that day, courtesy of one of the big news websites. Reading over Leona's shoulder, Robert skimmed past a paragraph of rhetoric about getting past partisan bickering and bringing the country back together, then reached the next two paragraphs. "Okay," he said, "you got me."

"All the problems this country has right now," she said, "and his answer is spending lots of money we don't have, on new military technology that hasn't been invented yet, to keep on fighting wars the way we wish we could fight them so that we can pretend that this is still the twentieth century. Is that worth a lunch?"

"Sure thing." Then: "But I should have guessed. It's stupid, but it's a familiar kind of stupid."

"Now don't you try to back out on lunch."

"Last thing on my mind, babe. Still, this country's been trying to solve its domestic problems by boosting its military budgets and throwing its weight around globally for a long time already. This is just one more step in that direction—and it's the kind of thing superpowers on the way down usually do."

She glanced up at him. "Okay, I'll bite. Give me an example."

"You're on. The British Navy put I forget how much of its annual budget into battleships before the First World War, so they could sit in harbor straight through most of the war and then go out to fight a useless battle off Jutland. Care to guess what the British Navy did to get ready for the Second World War?"

She glanced up at him. "Build more battleships?"

"Got it in one. If they'd put their money into antisubmarine technology, they wouldn't have been at the mercy of the U-boats until we bailed them out. If they'd put it into aircraft carriers, the way we and the Japanese were doing, they wouldn't have had their clocks cleaned in the first weeks of the Pacific war. If they'd done both, Britain might still have an empire today."

"Were they just about bankrupt?"

"After the First World War? They owed us a lot of money, but they weren't as bad off as we are now. So Gurney has even less excuse than they did." He shook his head. "So where do you want to have lunch?"

25 December 2029: Pittsburgh, Pennsylvania

By all accounts, it was shaping up to be the least cheery holiday season in America's history. McGaffney himself didn't care much one way or the other—for him, 25 December was just another day—but the editorial staff back in Brisbane wanted stories with a holiday spin, and he wasn't going to disappoint them.

He strolled down the mostly empty street. The big building next to him told a story all by itself: an old factory from Pittsburgh's glory days, it had been abandoned when the city's heavy industry went offshore in the Reagan years, got turned into a block of condos when Pittsburgh hit its second wind around 2000, and now stood mostly empty again, with only a few units still occupied. The city's population was right around half of what it had been in 1970, and after the stock market crash, no one was even pretending that better days would be back any time soon.

A newspaper vending box sat on the corner, the image on the screen switching back and forth between the latest headlines. He glanced at the thing as it showed GURNEY: MILITARY BUILDUP KEY TO PROSPERITY followed by MULLER: HEARINGS TO GO FORWARD. Both those were hot stories; Gurney's plan to get America back on its feet by way of big new defense outlays was coming in for savage criticism everywhere outside of his party's tame media outlets, and even some of those were making unenthusiastic noises. How that would play out when Congress met in the new year was a good question.

As for the hearings, Rosemary Muller was the new chair of the Senate Armed Services Committee, and the media had been yammering for days about whether she'd pursue hearings on the East African War or knuckle under to whatever pressure Gurney's administration might be bringing to bear on her. The hearings would be a circus, McGaffney knew, and he'd already made plans to cover them.

He kept walking. A little further, according to the map he'd downloaded, the built-up area gave way to old industrial brownfields. The city government website insisted that those were empty—ready for development, even—but McGaffney thought he knew what he'd find there. He passed a long-vacant warehouse tagged with gang graffiti, turned a corner, and stopped to take in the scene.

Tents spilled across the open space between the street and the Monongahela River: well over 1,000 of them, a patchwork of fading colors interrupted here and there by grays and browns where someone had scavenged wood and shingles to put up something more permanent. There had been tent settlements around most large American cities for years, but never this large and never this many.

Close by, just off the road, a couple of pickup trucks had pulled over, and a crowd had gathered around them. McGaffney walked toward the crowd, and smelled the aroma of hot soup a moment before he caught sight of the folding tables and the dozen or so people handing out bowls to the crowd. A church group, he guessed, and circled around until the sign on one table confirmed it.

The church group ladled out soup, and the crowd pressed forward; a low murmur of conversation rose here and there, but that and the occasional noise of cars on nearby roads were the only sounds. No one seemed to notice McGaffney at all. He noted down the name of the church on his tablet, screening the action from view inside his coat—no need to attract attention to something that could be stolen and fenced for ready cash—then found a place to wait until the soup was gone and he'd have the chance for an interview or two. Looking over the crowd again, he thought: helluva Christmas.

17 January 2030: Arlington, Virginia

"Thank you for agreeing to meet me," said the bland-faced man.

Bill Stedman nodded. "It wasn't an easy decision," he admitted. "I'll be burning a lot of bridges if I testify—and of course there's been plenty of pressure."

"Gurney's people, I assume."

"Among others."

The little café was empty except for the two men and a single bored waitress; the clock on the wall showed three in the afternoon, too late for lunch and too early for the going-home rush. Stedman had hoped for that, for more than the usual reasons. Since Senator Muller announced that she was going to go ahead with hearings on the East Africa War, he'd been bombarded with phone calls and emails pressuring him not to testify. The administration was scared, no doubt about that, and he knew they had good reason to be: if word got out about just how many bad decisions had been made and how many overpriced Pentagon toys had failed to measure up in combat, Gurney's plans to rebuild US military superiority would go out the window, and take his presidency with them.

"But you're willing to go ahead?" the bland-faced man asked.

"Yes," Stedman told him. "I've thought it over, and I'll do it."

"Thank you," the bland-faced man said again. "Mrs. Muller will be happy to make whatever arrangements you need. She'd like to schedule your testimony for mid-April, if that works for you."

Stedman pulled out his phone, checked his calendar, nodded. "That'll be fine. The sooner you can let me know exactly when, the better—I'll need to review my files and make sure I have all the details ready."

"The committee's particularly interested in the planning stage. There'll be people from the Pentagon on the stand to talk about what happened on their end, but they'll be asking you about what happened in the White House."

"Gurney's people will try everything they can to slap executive privilege on that," Stedman warned him.

"They're welcome to try," the other man said, with a thin smile that suddenly took all the blandness out of his face. "We've got them by the short hairs, and there's not much they can do about it."

"I hope you're right," Stedman said.

6 February 2030: The Capitol, Washington DC

"Mike," said Vice President Bridgeport, "this thing stinks. I mean that."

They were sitting in the vice presidential office in the Capitol Building. Some vice presidents rarely set foot in the room except for formal functions, others used it for their legislative duties; Bridgeport had no intention of being cut out of the Congressional loop, and made it his home base, hosting meetings there with senators and representatives and trying to pull together some practical response to a nation in disarray. Gurney's fixation on the military left a vacuum in domestic policy, and Congress was being drawn into it.

Still, there were domestic policies that might help, and then there was this: the New American Prosperity Act, which established an expensive new social welfare system and loaded most of the financial burden for it onto the states. Bridgeport had frowned when he'd read the first drafts of it, and his opinion hadn't gotten any less dour as it worked its way through committee, picking up support as it went.

Senator Mike Kamanoff, Senate majority leader that year, leaned forward. "Pete, we've got to do something. Have you seen the latest polls? If we can't come up with some kind of fix for the economy, I don't know if any of us are going to survive the next election."

"I know that," said Bridgeport. "But screwing the states isn't going to help. You know what kind of budget crunch they're in."

"You know what kind of budget crunch we're in. If tax revenues drop any further we're going to have to hold bake sales to keep the lights on."

"The states are in the same bind," Bridgeport pointed out.

"They can find the money."

"Try telling them that."

"Pete—" Kamanoff gestured, palms out. "You know the situation as well as I do. One party won't accept any tax increases, the other side won't accept any spending cuts, and the economy's in the toilet, so both sides have to dig in their heels or they're going to get reamed by the voters. Everybody wants something and everybody wants the other guy to pay for it. So we spin our wheels and go nowhere, or we do something like this—" He tapped the piece of paper in front of him. "—that might actually pass."

"And won't do a bit of good," said Bridgeport. "Not if the economy's going to get socked with another round of state budget cuts and defaults. You can't just keep on piling one unfunded mandate after another on top of them. Tell you what—instead of this thing, let's get you, Phil Schick, the big names from both sides of the aisle right here in this room, put together a bipartisan commission, make whatever deals we have to, and actually do something that might make a difference."

Kamanoff considered that for a moment, then shook his head. "Too slow, too uncertain, and I don't trust that bastard Schick as far as I could throw him. No, we're going with this."

Bridgeport gave him a bleak look. If he'd kept his Senate seat, he knew, there were ways he might have been able to fight it, but as vice president he had few options. "Well, it's your call. How soon do you want me to discuss this with Gurney?"

"Soon. I'm pretty sure we've got the votes in both Houses, and if he's going to balk or want changes, the sooner I know that, the better."

8 February 2030: Nashville, Tennessee

The two of them, grandfather and grandson, walked most of a mile before either of them said a word. There were only a few cars in the lot where they left the car, and fewer people in the park around them.

"This ought to do," said Bill Stedman.

His nineteen-year-old grandson gave him a worried look. "Are you in trouble?"

"Well—" Stedman considered it. "Probably not. I'm going to be testifying to a Senate committee, and there are some people who aren't too happy about that." He glanced at the boy. "I don't think there's going to be any trouble—but if something happens, there's some stuff I want to go public in a big way. You're the family computer geek, and I figure you probably know someone who can help with that."

"Yeah," said the boy. "I've got some friends."

"Good." Very casually, in case they were being watched, his hand brushed the boy's, and a thumb drive passed from one to the other, found its way into the boy's pocket.

The boy turned to face him. "Grandpa, do you need to go dark? I mean, *really* dark?"

Stedman considered that, too. "Going dark" was hacker slang, he knew that much—it meant dropping out of sight of the authorities. There were supposed to be a lot of people who had done that, slipping into the crawlspaces of society for one reason or another.

"No," he said after a moment. "No, I don't think there's actually going to be any trouble over this. I just want some insurance in place." He gave the boy a grin. "We better get back to the car and get those groceries, so your mom doesn't start wondering if we're up to something."

20 February 2030: The Capitol, Washington DC

"Pete," said Governor McCracken, "you've got to shake some sense into these morons. Half the states in the Union are about to go broke anyway. I mean that literally; in Texas we're only getting about two-thirds the tax revenues we're used to, and we're better off than most. We can't afford the unfunded mandates we've got already, and this goddamn thing—"

"I know," said Bridgeport.

"Then why the hell is Congress going ahead with it?"

The governor of Oregon tried to insert herself between the irate Texan and the vice president. "Terry, it's not as though Pete's backing the bill."

"You're the goddamn president of the Senate!" McCracken said, right over her head.

"And if it comes to a tie," said Bridgeport, "I'm voting no. You have my word on that."

McCracken opened his mouth to say something, stopped, and said, "Thank you, Pete. That's about the first reasonable thing anybody's said to me since I got off the plane this morning." Then: "What's the chance that it'll come to a tie?"

"In the Senate? I can't be sure, but not as good as I'd like."

The governors—there were an even dozen of them, and word was that every other state governor and every state legislature backed them—didn't look pleased by the news. "I get that," said the governor of Michigan. "Everyone we've talked to says, 'Well, we have to do something.' 'Then do something,' I keep saying. 'Don't just tell us to do something, when we're doing as much as we can already.' They just look at me."

"Beltway syndrome," the governor of Oregon said. "If you want to know where Julie Blau gets her ideas, I have some suggestions."

Bridgeport tried not to wince. Blau was the hottest of the new standup comedians, and she was doing skit after skit on her nightly podcast about Beltway syndrome, an imaginary disease that infected politicians exactly seventy-two hours after they arrived in Washington and instantly reduced them to drooling, slack-jawed idiocy. The phrase was popping up everywhere from social media to the evening news just then, yet another marker of the nation's impatience with the federal government's ongoing gridlock.

"Have you talked to Gurney?" Bridgeport asked.

"Oh yeah," said the governor of Michigan. "We wasted our time there, too. He read us a little lecture about how the way to solve the country's problems is lots of defense jobs. If signing the thing gets Congress to cough up money for the new carrier fleet, that's all he cares about."

"Pete," said McCracken, "something's got to give. I mean it. Things can't keep on going the way they're going." The big Texan's voice took on a rumbling note that reminded Bridgeport uncomfortably of distant thunder. "If Washington can't get its goddamn act together, something's going to give."

2 March 2030: Camden, New Jersey

McGaffney crossed the empty parking lot toward the mall as rain splashed down around him. Ten years earlier it would have been snow, or so people had been saying all week: one more sign of the same shifting climate that had the western half of the United States hammered by drought and winter rains falling in the Sahara for the first time in millennia. One more change, he thought, in a world where more and more things stubbornly refused to stay put.

The main doors of the mall, as he'd guessed, were boarded up. He turned and went toward the next set of doors, found the same thing, and kept going. Sooner or later—

He got halfway around the complex before he saw someone step out through a little service door in an otherwise blank wall, out of sight of casual traffic. Whoever it was saw McGaffney at that same instant, and ducked back inside. McGaffney grinned, walked over to the door, and tried it. It was unlocked, as he'd guessed, and he pulled it wide open.

"G'day!" he called into the half-darkness inside. "Name's Tommy McGaffney. I'm a reporter from Australia—mind if I come in and talk to some of you?"

There was no answer for a moment, and then a gaunt young man in Army surplus clothes stepped into the light. "McGaffney? Didn't you visit the camp in Shinyanga?"

McGaffney blinked and then grinned. What were the odds of that? "Too right," he said, trying to remember the man's name. "You're—wait—Wallace, wasn't it? Corporal Wallace."

"Yeah, that's me." He allowed a smile. "I guess you travel a lot. What'cha want to talk to us about?"

"How the American economy's gone down the crapperoo," McGaffney said.

That got him a sour laugh, as he'd guessed it would. "Come on," the young man said. "You wanna know about that, you'll get an earful."

Inside was a narrow hallway, and then a court surrounded by what had once been little boutiques. The place had been abandoned for years, McGaffney guessed: a third-rate shopping mall thrown up by promoters, leased to overenthusiastic retail chains, and then left twisting in the wind as the economy slumped year after year and people who didn't have money stopped spending it. Until the stock market crash, though, nobody had started moving in. Now there were families living in the boutiques—McGaffney could see faces peering out at him from the shadows—and the long-dry fountain in the middle of the court had been turned into a fire pit for cooking what food there was.

The young man led McGaffney straight to the fountain, where a middle-aged woman wrapped in a coat that had seen many better days was feeding sticks to a fire. She gave McGaffney a wary look as he approached.

"Momma," the young man said, "this guy's a reporter from Australia. I met him at the camp in Tanzania."

"G'day," McGaffney said helpfully.

"He wants you to tell him about the economy," the young man went on.

The woman finished feeding the fire, sat up. "Do we still have one of those?" she asked. "I haven't seen it for a while."

"I think it's gone walkabout," McGaffney suggested.

That got a smile from her, and she climbed up onto the faux-stone bench around the fire pit, sat down, and motioned for him to sit nearby, which he did. The young man sat on his heels nearby. "My editors back home," McGaffney said, "want to hear about how Americans are getting on these days, and I want to make sure they hear from the people who aren't getting on too well. I'm not going to tell anybody which mall this is, or even which town it's in, and I don't need your real name. All I'm interested in is your story."

That was all it took. The woman told him about the job she'd had waitressing until the bank failures shut off the restaurant's line of credit and closed it down right before the holidays, about how hard she'd tried to cover the rent but the money just wasn't there, about the friend of a friend of a friend who knew someone who'd already squatted in that mall, how they'd found ways to barter work for what they needed, and gotten used to the taste of pigeon meat. As she talked, a few others came out from the former boutiques and sat around the fountain.

McGaffney glanced at them, gauging his chances of getting more story material from them, and turned back to the woman he'd been interviewing. "Your son doesn't get anything from the Army?" he asked.

The young man answered, with a look on his face as though he'd just eaten something spoiled. "Sure. Took 'em a while, but these days I get the same pay I got before the war, when it was still worth something. Now? With the inflation and all, it buys a little food for Mom and my kid brother and me, and that's about it." He shrugged. "We put our asses on the line for this country, and look at what we get for it."

4 March 2030: The Capitol, Washington DC

"The F-35 isn't a bad plane," the Air Force general insisted. He was visibly sweating under the bright lights in the committee room. "In retrospect, I think it was probably unwise to try to make one plane try to fill so many different missions, but you know, hindsight's always twenty-twenty. At the time, it looked like a gamble worth taking."

"Understood," Senator Rosemary Muller said. With her iron-gray hair done up in a bun and bifocals perched on her nose, she looked like a well-dressed schoolteacher. "To the best of your recollection, General, at what point in the procurement process did the first doubts about the F-35 get brought up?"

"We're proud of the open nature of our procurement process," the general said. "We solicited criticism from across the defense community, here and in our allies, and used that as input for project development. The answer to your question is that doubts were raised right from the beginning, and we did our best to respond to them."

"And would you agree at this point that the doubts were justified and the responses inadequate?"

"There was no way we could have known that at the time," the general said.

Muller nodded once, as though that settled something. "And how much, all told, did this gamble worth taking cost the American taxpayer? Counting everything together—not just the airframe cost, but all the upgrades, retrofits, and modifications that had to be done to make the F-35 fit for combat duty—how much did we spend for this plane?"

"Just over $490 billion for the whole program."

"Half a trillion dollars."

"Yes."

"And how much did it cost, let's say, the People's Republic of China for an equivalent number of the J-20 and J-31 fighters they fielded in East Africa?"

He was sweating hard by that point. "I don't happen to know that figure."

"Would you say that it was a fraction of the cost of the F-35?"

"Most likely, yes."

"Perhaps a fairly modest fraction?" Then, before he could answer: "Forgive me. You've already said that you don't know the figure." Muller turned to the other members of the committee. "Does anyone else have any questions?"

By that afternoon, every detail of the testimony was splashed over news websites across the nation and the world. There had been military-procurement scandals before, some of them far more colorful, but few of those earlier controversies had taken place in the midst of a massive economic crisis and none had come in the wake of military defeat. In response, the mood of the nation shifted further into unfamiliar territory.

10 March 2030: The White House, Washington DC

By the time the New American Prosperity Act got out of Congress, it was thicker than the Los Angeles phone book, loaded with giveaways to a galaxy of pet causes and special interests as the price of its passage: business as usual in Washington. Gurney looked at the bound copy on the Oval Office desk, flipped through a few pages without much interest, trying to remember exactly what the bill was about.

His mind was elsewhere. Half the news websites on the internet were yelling about the latest tidbits from the Muller Committee hearings. Admiral Deckmann had been on the stand for the last two days, describing exactly what happened at the Battle of Kilindini, and word was that the next witnesses would be Pentagon wonks testifying about just how many times, over how many years, that precise outcome had resulted from any attempt to model a massed cruise missile attack against a carrier group. That was bad enough—but rumors were flying that Stedman had agreed to testify, and Gurney didn't want to think about what might be made public if that happened.

The new law's Byzantine prose failed to offer Gurney any distraction, and he closed the volume again. "Okay, let's get it over with," he said to the aide who'd brought it. "Is everyone here? Bring 'em in."

"Yes, sir." The aide left.

The signing had originally been planned for the Rose Garden, but the warming climate had done nothing to tame Washington's unpredictable March weather, and rain beating hard against the windows of the Oval Office forced a change in plans. Gurney sat back in his chair, aimed an irritable glance at the rain; he'd had to cancel a round of golf scheduled for the afternoon, and wasn't pleased with that fact.

After a few minutes, other members of the White House staff brought in a bevy of senators and representatives, followed by camera crews from the media and an official White House photographer. Once everyone was in place, Gurney scrawled his name in all the right places, then got up and shook hands with the majority and minority leaders of both Houses of Congress: photo ops for everyone, a few words about how the bill showed that both parties were working hard to restore prosperity to the country, the common currency of political theater in Washington since time out of mind.

Within the hour, news stories dutifully praising the new legislation appeared on all the major news websites—and each story, as it was posted, was instantly dogpiled by swarms of hostile comments. Most of the sites closed their comments pages within minutes and deleted anything negative, but by that time political blogs and forums picked up the story and ran with it. By the time the evening news carried the story, half a dozen state governors had already held press conferences announcing that they would refuse to implement the new law.

It was the next day, though, that the real challenge began to take shape.

11 March 2030: Arkansas State House, Little Rock, Arkansas

"Mr. Speaker."

The Speaker of the Arkansas House of Representatives peered down through his glasses, identified the source of the words, and a deer-in-the-headlights look showed on his face. "The chair recognizes Representative Bickerstaff."

That got a sudden hush across the chamber. Deanna Bickerstaff was an Arkansas original, "five foot high and four wide" by her own cheerful testimony, afraid of no man and precious little else this side of Heaven. When the voters down in swampy Chicot County first sent her to Little Rock, few of the state's less eccentric politicians had any idea what to make of her, and four years of experience had left most of them none the wiser. When she got the floor, it was anybody's guess what would happen.

"Mr. Speaker," she said, "ladies and gentlemen. We've just spent the last three hours yapping about this nonsense from Washington. On the off chance that y'all are interested in doing something about it, instead of just exercising your lungs, I'd like to ask if this body is willing to consider a motion from the floor."

"Are there any objections?" said the Speaker, and glanced around the chamber. There were none. "You have the floor, Deanna."

"Thank you." She took a piece of paper off the desk in front of her. "By my count, and I may have missed one or two, this is the thirty-fourth unfunded mandate Washington's loaded onto us. Thirty-four laws that they pass and we get to pay for, whether we can afford it or not. I can't say for sure that we'd have no trouble balancing the state budget if not for those, but I reckon it's pretty close one way or the other.

"So it's not just this latest thing. They've been doing it to us for years, and they're just going to keep on doing it unless something stops 'em for good. That's why I move, Mr. Speaker, distinguished colleagues, that this body vote to have the great state of Arkansas exercise its right to call for a constitutional convention, to amend the Constitution of the United States so that Congress don't have the right to impose unfunded mandates on the states." Over the sudden murmur of voices: "And I further move that this resolution go to the state Senate on passage. Mr. Speaker, I yield the floor."

It took the speaker more than two minutes and repeated blows of his gavel to get the chamber to quiet down. "The chair recognizes Representative Haskell," he said then.

Bayard Haskell was the House majority leader that term, a Louisianan who'd married into one of Little Rock's old-money families, and looked it. "Mr. Speaker," he drawled, "I would like to second Miss Bickerstaff's motion, if I may."

The Speaker regained his deer-in-the-headlights look for a moment, and recovered. "The floor is open for debate, and the chair recognizes Representative Angerson." Then, as Phil Angerson launched into what promised to be a speech of some length and little content, the Speaker shot a significant look at Haskell, House minority leader Mary Brice, and a few others, and they converged on the Speaker's station.

The Speaker turned off his microphone, and as Haskell arrived, said, "Are you serious? That's got to be the craziest thing Deanna's popped out yet."

"Crazy like a fox," Haskell told him. "You know and I know that it's not going to go anywhere, but if a couple of other states back it, that might be enough to get Washington to back off on NAPA."

"Maybe. Depends on who supports it."

"Tell me this," said Haskell. "Can you see Terry McCracken missing a chance like this?"

The Speaker smothered a laugh; he'd gone hunting with McCracken more than once, and knew exactly how the irascible Texas governor would react.

"We have to do something," said Brice. "If this thing takes effect it's going to break us."

The Speaker nodded slowly. "Do you think the Senate will go for it?"

"We can talk to 'em at lunch," Haskell said.

They went back to their places as Angerson wound down, sat through three other speeches before Mary Brice got the floor. "The chair recognizes Representative Brice," the Speaker said.

"Mr. Speaker, distinguished colleagues," she said, "I think we all agree that something has to be done. With that in mind, I'd like to move that we close debate on the motion on the floor, put it to a vote, and go back to the more general discussion."

Haskell seconded the motion. "We have a motion to suspend debate," the Speaker said. "All in favor? All opposed? The motion passes.

"We now have a motion to call for a constitutional convention to amend the Federal Constitution, to bar Congress from imposing unfunded mandates on the states. All in favor? All opposed? The motion passes." The Speaker brought down his gavel.

TWENTY-THREE

13 March 2030: The Capitol, Washington DC

"Mind if I join you?" said Mike Kamanoff.

Bridgeport looked up from his sandwich, waved the Senate majority leader to a seat. Around them, the Senate lunchroom buzzed with talk.

"What do you think of this Arkansas business?"

Bridgeport finished swallowing his mouthful. "They've got the legal right," he said. "If two-thirds of the state legislatures vote for it, they'll get their convention, too."

"Theoretically, yeah."

"Not just theoretically." He set down the sandwich. "Did you talk to the governors when they were here lobbying against NAPA?"

"Didn't have time." Kamanoff flagged down a waiter, placed his order, turned back to Bridgeport. "I heard they were pretty pissed."

"That's an understatement. I don't think more than a dozen senators took the time to hear them out. When I met them, they were talking about Beltway syndrome."

Kamanoff grinned. "Speaking of that, did you hear Julie Blau last night?"

"No, I missed it."

"Oh, man, it was funny—the Constitution as rewritten in Little Rock. 'We-all the folks of these hyar Yew-nited States, reck'nin ta make 'em a darn sight better than they been since time out o' mind,' and so on. I don't think I've laughed so hard in weeks."

Another senator—it was Nancy Liebkuhn from Indiana, the majority whip—was walking past the table, and turned toward Bridgeport and Kamanoff. "Don't laugh too hard," she said. "Did you hear about New Hampshire?"

"No," Kamanoff said. "What's up?"

"The state legislature—both Houses—just passed a copy of the Arkansas resolution."

The grin vanished from Kamanoff's face. "They're crazy!"

"Mike," said Bridgeport, "they can do it. They really can. Calling them crazy isn't going to change that. If you don't want a constitutional convention, you're going to have to cut a deal with the states, and they're not going to settle for handwaving."

"Bullshit," said Kamanoff. "We can fight this. Calling a convention would take, what, thirty-three states on board?"

"Thirty-four," Bridgeport said.

"No way are they going to get that many. I promise you that."

Kamanoff's meal arrived, and he grabbed his sandwich in both hands and attacked it. Bridgeport glanced past him at Liebkuhn, who rolled her eyes and went off to another table.

16 March 2030: Guthrie, Oklahoma

"Well, I'll be—" Clyde Witherspoon caught himself in time, remembering who was in earshot. "A monkey's uncle," he finished, and turned to face the middle-aged woman at the other desk. "Another big check. What's that, four this week?"

His boss, Suzette Delafarge, nodded and smiled. "How much?"

"Eighteen grand."

"Ours?"

"Nah, that'd be chump change. Canadian dollars."

Her eyebrows went up. "From?"

"Some guy in Tulsa named Joe Bramwell." He handed the check over. "Heard of him?"

"No, but he'll hear from us. I'll have Suzie drop him an email when she gets in."

The storefront office of the Oklahoma Independence Party had seen many better days. Some of the decor was left over from its previous incarnation as a Chinese restaurant, and the computers and office furniture were all too clearly secondhand. A banner along one wall and a rack of buttons and bumper stickers on the other proclaimed the party's slogan: "Independence? OK!" Even so, it was just one more little group on the fringes of American politics, trying to get its message out in the face of near-universal indifference while struggling to pay the bills month after month.

Until now.

"You think it's this NAPA thing?" Clyde asked.

"I'm guessing." She tapped some numbers onto her keyboard. "I'm about ready to fall on my knees and thank the good Lord for those idiots in Congress. We've got our debts cleared, the rent covered through the end of the year, and plenty of money on hand. I'm going to ask the executive committee to okay the bus ad project."

"You got my vote," Clyde assured her. Putting ads on the sides of city buses in Tulsa and Oklahoma City had been the party's Holy Grail for most of a decade of shoestring budgets and disappointing fundraisers.

"Bless your heart. And if this keeps up—why, then we'll go to the next thing."

"Radio ads?" Clyde said, grinning.

"We can only hope," she told him, and turned back to her computer.

Over the weeks that followed, money kept flowing in, some of it in US dollars but most in the foreign currencies that were becoming standard now that the dollar was losing ground day by day. The Oklahoma Independence Party got its bus ads, its radio time, and more. So did more than thirty other parties on the far edges of American politics. Donations to extremist political movements all over the country shot up to unprecedented levels and kept rising, and their ideas flowed out into the national conversation as never before.

24 March 2030: The Capitol, Washington DC

"What do you think?" Bridgeport asked.

Leona Price considered her sandwich for a while before answering. "They're not buying it. People don't care how many big names say that it's a bad idea, and they know the polls are rigged." She looked up at him. "They think America's broken, they want it fixed, and they don't see Gurney or Congress doing anything to fix it."

Bridgeport nodded, said nothing.

Lunch with Price had become a regular part of his Monday schedule: part of his job keeping track of what Congress was doing, he would have said at first, but there was more to it than that. She was smart, smarter than most others in Congress, and working the District the old-fashioned way, neighborhood by neighborhood and street by street, gave her a finger on the public pulse that few other figures in the federal government had.

"The state legislatures agree with them," he said finally.

"Oh, they know what the score is. At this point I'm not sure it's just the unfunded mandate thing. They've been served crow by this town for years, and told to eat it up and smile. Now they're looking for payback. If they do get their convention, we'll be lucky if all they do is pass something against unfunded mandates and go home."

"I know." South Dakota had just become the fourth state to pass a resolution in favor of a constitutional convention. So far, all the states that had joined Arkansas were minor players in national politics, but word was that legislators in three of the big states—Texas, Colorado and Pennsylvania—were drafting resolutions along the same lines. If one or more of them joined in, it would be a whole new game.

"Tell me this," Bridgeport said then. "You know Congress better than anybody else in this town. Do you think I've got any chance of getting them to come to their senses soon enough to head this thing off?"

"I wish," Price told him. "You've been around here long enough, you know how many of these folks have forgotten there's a world outside the Beltway. It's going to take some really big shock to remind them—and if this is the shock, there won't be a blessed thing they can do about it once it happens." She gestured with her sandwich. "Until then, it'll be too little, too late."

6 April 2030: The White House, Washington DC

Ellen Harbin closed the door behind her, sat down at the desk, picked up the phone, punched a number. "Mr. Pohjola? I have a job for you."

"Of course, Ms. Harbin." The man's voice was all but expressionless. "What can I do for you?"

"We talked earlier about William Stedman."

"Of course."

"He's refused to be reasonable."

"What would you like done, Ms. Harbin?"

"The president has authorized executive action."

"Of course," Pohjola repeated. He said it as calmly as though she'd asked him to pick up takeout Burmese for the office. "Is there a time frame?"

"As soon as convenient."

"Not a problem. I'll take care of it."

"Thank you. Good afternoon, Mr. Pohjola."

"And likewise." The connection closed.

Harbin put down the phone. She hated to admit it, but Emil Pohjola frightened her. An operative in what was euphemistically termed the Executive Special Projects Staff, the team of off-book employees every presidential administration had on hand for those actions that were as necessary as they were extralegal, he had never been anything but scrupulously polite to her. Still, she knew with absolute clarity that if Gurney decided that she had to die, Pohjola would have her killed without a second thought or the least trace of feeling, and there would be only the thinnest chance that she could do anything about it.

She tapped her computer trackball irritably, waking the screen. The news feed had nothing new—the Iranians had just launched a major offensive in Kurdistan against the Turks, the dollar was wobbling just above four to the euro, and the New Mexico legislature had just voted in favor of a convention. She minimized the news feed, opened the latest report from NSA.

At that moment, miles away in one of the capital's Virginia suburbs, Emil Pohjola picked up a phone and dialed.

6 April 2030: Camden, New Jersey

Since the Second World War, every presidential administration had some relationship to the quintessentially American institution of organized crime, and since a certain November day in 1963, every presidential administration had taken pains to keep the relationship suitably cordial. There were limits to that cordiality—Mafia families that ran afoul of the ordinary workings of law enforcement could expect no help from the White House—but the syndicate could be confident that nobody at the top end of the executive branch would ever again try to make political hay by crusading against the mob. It was a functional arrangement, and it made room for favors to be asked and granted from time to time.

Thus Mike Capoblanco was far from surprised when he got a call from a White House staff member that afternoon. "Mr. Pohjola. A pleasure as always. What can I do for you?" A moment later: "Of course. We'd be happy to oblige."

He reached for one of the lined yellow legal pads he habitually used for notes, got a pen, noted down the details. "How soon?" He listened, then said, "Not a problem. I'll get my people on it right away. Give my best to your boss."

He hung up, then picked up the phone again and dialed a different number. "Joey? I need you up here as soon as you can make it. Yeah, it's a job." He paused, listening. "Yeah, that'll be fine. See you then."

8 April 2030: Arlington, Virginia

They looked like any of the other joggers out that cold April morning: two men in nondescript running gear pounding through a city park, packs on their backs and breath puffing out in front of their faces in little clouds. For all anyone else could see, it was sheer accident that they stayed in sight of a third jogger, a middle-aged man dressed much the same way, who was maybe a dozen yards ahead of them. It was only when they got to the only section of the trail out of sight of streets and houses that they sped up. Even then it looked casual until the two men caught up with the third.

The scuffle ended quickly as the lone jogger went limp, a chemical-soaked cloth pressed over his mouth and nose. The others hauled him off the trail, down to a park bench in a little hollow, where the third member of the team was waiting. No one spoke. They put the jogger on the bench, and one of the men held him propped up. The third member of the team, who had rubber gloves on his hands, pulled a cheap unlicensed pistol from his coat pocket, pressed it to the jogger's head, and fired. The other let the corpse fall, and the third man carefully slid the gun into its right hand, finger on the trigger.

They left at once, the two joggers back to the trail, the third man out of the park by a different route. When he got back to his car, he pulled off the gloves and put them in a plastic grocery sack, along with his coat; those and every other scrap of clothing on him would be in an incinerator within three hours. He pulled out a cell phone and speed dialed.

"Pete? It's Joey. We're finished on this end. You can go ahead with the rest of it."

Two miles away, in a silent apartment, two more men went to work. They had already found the target's computer, hooked it up to a laptop and cracked the security; now a document went into it, electronically backdated to look as though it had been written the night before. One of the men got the printer running, waited while a copy of the document printed, and took it over to the table by the couch; the other copied everything on the computer, then removed all electronic traces of his presence and disconnected the laptop. A few minutes later they were out the door, and a few minutes after that they had left the building: two ordinary-looking men in business-casual clothes, chatting to each other as they walked to their cars.

One of them pulled out his cell phone and speed dialed. "Joey? It's Pete. Everything's taken care of. You want to let Mike know? Great. See you."

It was almost four hours before another pair of joggers, looking for a quiet spot to eat their lunches, found Bill Stedman's body and called the police. Another hour passed before the police opened his apartment and found the suicide note. By then Joey and the members of his team were back home in

Pennsylvania and New Jersey, with a long list of people ready to swear that they'd been at work all morning. All in all, it was a very professional job.

8 April 2030: Silver Spring, Maryland

The TV above the bar was yammering something about the Stedman suicide—what, McGaffney didn't know, because the sound was off and the talking heads on the local news channel might as well have been mouthing empty air. It didn't greatly matter, since the same handful of facts and barrelful of rumors had been swirling through Washington since the news broke just after lunchtime.

He walked up to the bar, and glanced around at the clientele while the bartender finished mixing something for another customer. It was a quiet, upscale place, not the sort McGaffney usually frequented, full of professional types in business-casual clothes; he'd come there only because it was close to his hotel and he'd had a long day.

He spotted the woman just before the bartender came over. After bantering with the man and getting a scotch on ice, he walked over to the booth where she sat, nursing a mostly empty glass. "Don't mean to be rude," he said, "but weren't you in the camp at Shinyanga, right after the war?"

She looked up from her drink. "Yes, I was." Then, placing him: "You're the Australian journalist—I've forgotten your name."

"Tommy McGaffney. No trouble—I'll have to check my notes for yours. Are you up for a second interview? I'd be glad to stand you a drink."

That earned him a smile. "You're on. It's Melanie Bridgeport, by the way."

McGaffney flagged down a waiter with a motion of his head, indicated Melanie's glass, pulled his tablet out of his bag and got the file open. "Melanie Bridgeport, colonel, US Air Force. So what's it been like, coming back to the States after the war?"

While she answered—it was pretty much the usual thing, the long awkward journey back to something like a normal life that soldiers had been having to make since wars were invented in the first place—McGaffney watched her. A looker, he'd decided that back at the POW camp, and there was someone home behind the pretty face, too. Her drink arrived; he asked more questions, recorded the answers, took notes in case the sound files got scuppered. When the drink was mostly gone, he asked, "Can I get you another?"

That got him a quick amused look. "Is it that good an interview?"

"Nah, an interview gets one. Anything more than that is personal."

She considered that, and him. "Please."

9 April 2030: Austin, Texas

"What's your take on it?" asked Terry McCracken.

The circle of faces around the table in the state house conference room all but summed up Texas politics, or for that matter Texas as a whole: good ol' boys from the east Texas oil country, lean-faced cattlemen from the north and west, new-money types from the tech corridor between Austin and San Antonio—the Silicon Rangeland, wags called it these days—and tough Hispanic politicians whose great-grandparents had been field laborers and whose great-grandkids would probably own the state outright. They were the state senators and representatives that mattered, the movers and shakers from both parties, and in the next few minutes they would decide whether the proposal made by Arkansas and endorsed by nine other states would become a footnote in American history or something potentially much, much bigger.

"I'm in favor of it," said Maria del Campo Ruiz, the speaker of the Texas House. "Those idiots in Washington will just keep on making a mess of things unless someone reins them in good and hard. This might just do that."

"Maybe so," drawled Tom Pettigrew, the majority whip from the Senate. "But only if we can make it stick. You seen the polls? They ain't exactly in our favor."

"Canned polls," del Campo said, with a contemptuous toss of her head. "Bought and paid for by Gurney, or by Congress."

"For what it's worth," McCracken interjected, "the media polls put Texas three to two against a convention, and the polls I've had my people run are five to two in favor."

"That's about what I'm hearing," said Phil Briscoe, the Senate minority leader.

McCracken glanced across the table at him. Briscoe wanted his job, everybody in Austin right on down to the call girls and janitors knew that, and getting support from him was an unfamiliar experience. "What do you think, Phil?" he asked.

"I agree with Maria," Briscoe said. "Those bastards need their leash yanked hard. Even if it doesn't go all the way to a convention, this has got them running scared, and if it does—if we can get unfunded mandates flushed down the crapper once and for all—that's gonna make life a lot easier for us. For all the states, really."

McCracken nodded. "Anyone disagree?"

"Not enough to fight about it," Pettigrew said.

No one else spoke. "You pass it," McCracken said, "I'll sign it. I want to see the look on the face of that sad little runt Kamanoff when he gets the news."

10 April 2030: Nashville, Tennessee

I am going to fuck with you, Daniel Stedman repeated to himself. I am going to fuck with you like nobody's ever been fucked with before.

He sat down at the computer terminal in the little suburban library, entered a stolen login and password—he'd hacked the system most of five years ago, an easy job for him even then—and then hit the override codes that jammed the government snooper programs. He'd chosen a terminal where nobody else could see the screen, which was good; as soon as the override codes took effect, he was in the guts of the system, opening a piece of hackware that gave him access to the Undernet.

Whoever you are, he thought, whatever made you think you could get away with killing Grandpa, I am so going to fuck you over.

The thumb drive his grandfather had given him went into one of the USB ports, and he accessed the files, got them uploaded to the nearest Undernet server, labeled them with one-use-only forwarding codes, and sent them out of the country to servers the NSA and the Office of Internet Security couldn't close down. From there, the files propagated themselves across the planet, zigzagging from one network to another, leaving no traces behind.

He uploaded the files to a second Undernet server, gave them different forwarding codes, sent them on their way. That done, he closed the hackware window, opened a link to the Undernet chatroom he helped run, and tried to think of what to say.

That brought memories welling up—the phone call from Grandma Karen two days ago, his mother bursting into tears, her stammered words and then the bare bleak bones of the news story he'd gotten off the internet a few minutes later, pushing at the limits of his self-control. Behind those were other memories, Grandpa Bill flying out for birthdays and Christmas, walks in the woods, visits to Washington, echoes of a life that some jerk decided to snuff out.

Then, his grandfather's words: "I just want some insurance in place."

You got it, Grandpa.

He typed in: *just upped files from clean src. william stedman quote suicide unquote was murder, prob on gurney's orders. fwd fwd fwd baby.*

A few dozen more keystrokes got him off the Undernet and deleted every trace of his presence on the computer except the stolen login; he used that to look up a science fiction novel, then logged out and went in among the bookshelves.

Fifteen minutes later, 200 pages of scanned documents detailing the planning and execution of Operation Blazing Torch hit the legal internet via a site in Finland. Heading the paper was a brief typewritten note by Bill Stedman. Its first sentence went:

If you are reading this, I have been murdered.

In well under twenty-four hours, that sentence was all over the planet.

TWENTY-FOUR

13 April 2030: The White House,
Washington DC

"Deny it," Ellen Harbin said.

Gurney gave her a blank, frightened look. "But—"

"Deny it," she repeated. "Tell them that it's a pack of lies. A failed, bitter man on the brink of suicide made it up in a final attempt to lash out at his personal enemies. That's the line you need to take. Anything else and the media will eat you alive."

The president nodded, slowly, after a moment.

They were in the Oval Office, just the two of them. It usually was just the two of them at her morning conferences these days, and Harbin knew perfectly well where that was headed. The thought didn't bother her at all; it would not be the first time she'd bartered her body for political power, and if it gave her more influence in the White House, it was a bargain worth her while.

What did bother her, a little, was how easily he'd crumpled once the media circus started around Stedman's documents. She'd known for a long time that he was weak; there were plenty of people like him in Washington politics, men and women who chased the trappings of power to distract themselves from their own inadequacies. Still, there were weaklings and there were weaklings. It troubled her that Gurney had folded so easily, that he might need more time and attention than she could reasonably spare if a real crisis ever erupted.

"I've got Jim and Hannah working on your speech for the press conference tonight," she went on. That had been a risk; she didn't have any authority over Gurney's people in the Office of the President, but the speechwriters were realists and sensed the way power was shifting in the new administration. "That's the line they're taking. Give it your best, don't hesitate to get angry if anybody in the media contradicts you, and you'll do fine."

Gurney nodded again, and the blank frightened look slid off his face. He leaned forward, took both her hands in his. "Thank you, Ellen."

For a moment she thought he was going to start pawing her right there, but he released her hands, gave her a shaky smile. A few more words and she was out of the room, headed back to her own office downstairs in the National Security Council rooms.

She was most of the way there before she remembered that she'd meant to talk to him about the agitation around a constitutional convention. Not significant enough, she decided. Bridgeport could deal with that; she and the president had more important issues to face.

16 April 2030: The Capitol, Washington DC

"That's as much as I can give them," Mike Kamanoff snapped.

"Mike," said Vice President Bridgeport, "for God's sake, will you listen? They don't care. They really don't."

Kamanoff met the outburst with a bleak look. "I know. I'm the one that has to care."

The two of them and Nancy Liebkuhn, the majority whip, were sitting in Bridgeport's office in the Capitol. Both senators looked harried; the Senate had been deadlocked for two days over what to do to head off a constitutional convention. That morning, Alaska had become the twenty-fifth state to pass a resolution calling for a convention.

Kamanoff sagged, shook his head. "You know how many people in this goddamn club have pet programs that they want the states to pay for? I do; every one of 'em's been hammering on my office door for the last week." He ran a hand back through what was left of his hair. "We got NAPA repealed, and that was about as easy as circumcizing dinosaurs with your teeth."

"I didn't need that image in my mind," said Nancy Liebkuhn.

"Sorry. I think I can get the votes to pass something requiring a supermajority for any new unfunded mandate, but that's as far as it goes. Repealing the existing mandates? That's dead on arrival. Amend the Constitution? That's not just dead, it's gone to heaven and started taking harp lessons. Nobody's gonna do that."

"Then the states will do it for them," Bridgeport said. "They're not bluffing; they really can do it. Mike, you can give them the amendment they want, or they're going to play Russian roulette with the Constitution. Those are the only choices you've got."

Kamanoff's face twisted. "Look, Pete, I'd do that if I could. I can't. I could call in every favor I've got and get nowhere. The Senate won't go for it."

"Even if it did," Liebkuhn said then, "I'm not at all sure that would do the trick."

The two men looked at her. "Have either of you been keeping track of online media?" she asked. "It's not just unfunded mandates any more. People are talking about all kinds of amendments—and not just bloggers. People in politics."

"I've heard McCracken," Bridgeport said.

"Not just state politicians. You know Beidermann and Solti, in the House? They jumped on the bandwagon this week— hour-long podcast speeches, 'Let's give the people what they want,' that sort of thing. It may be too far along to stop."

"And the White House paying zero attention because it's got its head up its ass over the Stedman thing." Kamanoff gave Liebkuhn a sidelong look. "You knew Stedman pretty well. What do you think of that whole business?"

She considered that for a moment. "Bill was a decent man—well, as decent as you can be and still get a job in this town. If he'd handed me the papers and said they were genuine, I'd have believed him." She looked at them both. "And I don't believe for a minute that he killed himself. He wasn't that kind of man."

"Rosemary Muller told me," Bridgeport said, "that Stedman agreed to testify to her committee."

"I know," said Kamanoff. "Wouldn't be the first time somebody did an assisted suicide to keep the White House out of trouble." He shook his head. "Helluva town."

24 April 2030: Salem, Oregon

McGaffney peeled a couple of Canadian bills out of his wallet, handed them to the cab driver and watched the man's face light up. "This'll do?"

"Any time," the cabbie said. "Lessee, that'd be—"

"Don't worry about the change," McGaffney told him.

"Hey, thanks." The man grinned and drove off, leaving McGaffney to the rain.

For the last few weeks McGaffney had paid most of his expenses in Canadian money; you could get it easily enough at the airports, and everybody in the United States took it these days. He'd watched euros and a few other foreign currencies change hands, too. No surprises there; with the dollar still skidding against every yardstick that mattered and the federal government frozen up in something worse than its usual gridlock, taking things into some other currency was plain common sense.

One of the things behind the government's state of paralysis stared at him as he walked down the sidewalk toward the statehouse. The building across the street was an upscale retail block, not ten years old from the look of it, but every space was boarded up courtesy of the economic slump. Pasted across the plywood was a line of posters, all of them identical, with a picture of William Stedman above the inevitable slogan IF YOU ARE READING THIS I HAVE BEEN MURDERED.

Those posters were all over the country; McGaffney had seen them in Boston, Denver, New Orleans, and a dozen other cities. The mainstream media was still trying to avoid the story, but blogs and podcasts buzzed with it, and angry denials from the White House had done precisely nothing to defuse the issue. Presidents had gotten past that sort of scandal before, but something had shifted in the United States since the East African War, and McGaffney found himself wondering as he walked whether this would be one more challenge than the Gurney administration could survive.

He spotted the statehouse a moment later, with its weird ribbed not-quite-dome, and crossed the street to the edge of the grassy area around it. The building itself was surrounded by a murmuring crowd and a line of Oregon state police in riot gear. The crowd didn't look ready to start a riot just at that moment, but McGaffney stayed well back from the main mass of people. This wasn't just an ordinary meeting of an ordinary state legislature; thirty-three states had already voted to call for the constitutional convention, and if Oregon voted the same way, the Constitution's two-thirds requirement would be met.

He walked along the edges of the crowd, listening to conversations, sizing up the mood. A woman in a bright red raincoat was talking in animated tones about how she thought the Constitution ought to be amended; a man with a military buzz cut made a rude comment about President Gurney; dozens of people peered at tablets and smart phones, taking in whatever the news media had to say about the debates inside the statehouse.

When half the conversations around him suddenly went dead silent, McGaffney knew something was up. He looked around, saw the crowd clustering around those who'd tuned in to the news. Any minute, he thought—

Someone let out a high-pitched whoop. A moment later it seemed as though everyone was talking at once.

"What's the word?" McGaffney asked the air, hoping that someone would answer.

"They passed it," the woman in the red raincoat said. "Twenty-one to nine. Now maybe we can get this country back on track."

17 June 2030: Silver Spring, Maryland

"Penny for your thoughts," McGaffney asked.

Melanie Bridgeport blinked. "Hmm?"

"Okay, two pence."

She laughed. "Not worth the investment."

They were sprawled naked on her bed with the covers kicked off—with the dollar still sinking, the price of electricity had gotten high enough that air conditioning had to be saved for the worst of the heat. Melanie's military paycheck was worth less and less every month, and she'd had to ask her father for help covering expenses too many times already that year.

"No, I mean it," McGaffney said.

"Oh, just wondering about the convention again. Dad hasn't said much of anything about it, which means that he's worried."

"Let him worry," he said. "It's his job, not yours."

"And yours."

"Not hardly."

"And who just spent six days in North Dakota reporting on what special election?"

"I went for the climate."

She whacked him with a pillow, and he laughed, caught her and kissed her.

He'd originally planned to get clear of Washington once the states finished voting for the convention, and do a series of stories from all over the country, the kind of human interest stuff the folks back in Brisbane liked. That plan went out the window, though, because he had no shortage of story material in and around the capital. Congress had gone into recess but the politics were heating up faster than the summer weather; between the bitter stalemate pitting Gurney's administration against Congress, the ongoing economic slump, the increasingly frantic maneuverings over the constitutional convention, and the unexpected rise of extremist ideas in the political mainstream, Washington DC was a reporter's paradise.

And there was the girl, of course. He'd been startled enough when he figured out that she was the vice president's daughter, and that had its inconveniences now and then; he'd had to sit through three hours of polite but thorough grilling by the Secret Service in April, and she'd had to call off dates because something official had come up and she had to play hostess at One Observatory Circle. Still, she was a lively little sheila, and though she was careful not to pass on anything she shouldn't, she had an insider's grasp of Washington politics, and had helped him figure out more than once what was behind some bit of news.

"What about the convention?" he asked, after he'd finished the kiss.

"You've heard the latest bit, right? They're going to meet in St. Louis."

"Wasn't there some kind of stink about that?"

"A big one. A lot of people here tried to pressure the states into having it in Philadelphia." When he responded with a blank look: "That's where the original constitutional convention was, and it's close enough to Washington that they figured they could influence things."

"And the states said no dice."

"Exactly. It makes me wonder what they're planning, besides elections."

"Too right." There had been some talk about having all the states elect delegates on the same day, but that went the same place as so many other attempts to coordinate the fifty fractious not-quite-nations that made up the United States. Half a dozen states had already had their special elections, and the others would be doing so on a succession of Tuesdays spilling on into early August, with the convention itself scheduled for the beginning of September.

"I thought about running for a seat," Melanie said then.

"Thinking of getting into politics?"

"Not really—but this feels like more than politics." With an uncharacteristically bleak look: "This feels serious."

8 July 2030: Spokane, Washington

The little storefront north of downtown on Division Street was packed with campaign volunteers and well-wishers by the time the returns started coming in. One of the staffers had hauled in a big plasma screen and mounted it up on the wall where everyone could see it, between two signs that said *HARRIET ELKERSON* in big print across the top and *Delegate—Constitutional Convention* in smaller print underneath.

The candidate herself was in the middle of it all, short and silver-haired, shaking hands, talking with anyone who had something to say, gesturing emphatically with a half-full plastic cup of her trademark drink, which was ginger ale. That was her style; it had kept her in the thick of local politics for more than three decades, and won her an assortment of minor city, county and state elections over that time. "Listen to the people," she liked to remind her staff. "They know what they want—and they just need to know that I'll do all I can to get it for them."

Washington was a mail-in voting state, and only the inertia of old laws kept returns from being posted days before election day proper. Once nine o'clock arrived, that restriction no longer applied, and local news splashed the current vote totals on the screen:

ELKERSON 43%
MORALES 26%
BARRETT 11%

The room exploded in whoops and cheering. Elkerson beamed up at the screen for a moment, then worked her way through the crowd to the table where her campaign manager sat hunched over a laptop. "How are we doing?"

He glanced up, frowning, the way he always did when things were going his way. "You got it," he told her. "Most of the precincts that polled heavy for Vince Morales have already been counted."

She nodded, smiled, headed for the screen just as her percentage clicked up another two points. As the volunteers cheered again, she found an empty chair, stood on it.

"Thank you," she said, pitching her voice to be heard over the celebration. "Thank you all. Mick's been watching precinct totals, and it looks like we've won."

The crowd yelled and whooped. As they quieted down again, she went on. "I want you all to remember what this means. All through this race, my opponents criticized me for suggesting that unfunded mandates weren't the only issue the constitutional convention needs to tackle. The people have spoken, though, and they want change—and when I go to St. Louis in September, I'm going to do my level best to see that change is what they get."

14 July 2030: Hainan Island

Liu Shenyen leaned back into the beach chair, tried to let the tensions of too many long days slide off him. The beach in front of him stretched out golden and unoccupied to the blue surging waters of the South China Sea, sparkling with afternoon sunlight, and palm fronds rustled in the salt breeze; behind, unseen for the moment, a resort hotel that catered only to the highest ranks of the Party raised its unobtrusive roofline against a perfect blue sky. He and Meiyin had three weeks to do absolutely nothing, he reminded himself, and he needed that.

The end of the East African War and the nuclear crisis had lifted one set of burdens off him, but the PLA units involved had to return to China, and new units had to be sent out to the new permanent bases in East Africa and Diego Garcia: all of it his responsibility to manage, or at least to supervise. Then there was the trip to Moscow: officially, to negotiate a new set of mutual defense agreements with Bunin, the Russian defense minister; unofficially, to give the upper end of the Russian government a chance to meet the man who would be China's next president. After that had come three busy weeks visiting East African capitals, shaking hands, posing for photographs, meeting with heads of state, and sitting on a platform in Dar es Salaam while the African soldiers who'd taken the brunt of the fighting marched past and jubilant crowds cheered.

Liu had said all the things he knew he had to say, handed out praise and carefully chosen promises, made sure that the rest of the Chinese delegation that traveled with him did their jobs and handed out the rewards of victory with a suitably lavish hand, but all the while he'd had to keep his own misgivings in check. Tanzania stood tall; half the nations of Africa were busy negotiating agreements of their own with the Tanzanian government, and the coalition that had been created to counter the Americans was about to be deployed to end the long-running Congolese troubles once and for all. Watching the proud battle-hardened soldiers march past him in Dar es Salaam, Liu wondered whether he'd just witnessed the birth of a power that might one day challenge China for control of the Indian Ocean, and just maybe of the world.

He reminded himself to discuss the matter with Fang when he got back to Beijing; he let out a ragged breath, tried to let himself bask in the sun and the crisp salt air. From the chair next to his, Meiyin gave him an amused glance, turned back to the tablet in her lap and the daily news.

She had been radiantly happy since the end of the war, and the reason was no riddle to Liu. He knew the fierceness of her ambition, the drive to distinguish herself that had taken her from a bleak communal farm in Heilongjiang Province to an influential position in the Ministry of Trade and a home in Zhongnanhai, and knew also how passionately she longed to rise still further. Now she would be—what was the term the Americans used?—China's First Lady, the closest and most trusted adviser of the President of the People's Republic. Every one of the dreams she'd dreamed in girlhood, as she trudged through her chores or looked out across the barren Manchurian plains, was within her grasp. He smiled, thinking of the delight with which she'd greeted him on her return from the shelter in Inner Mongolia, the way they'd made love like besotted twenty year olds in the days and weeks that followed. Of all the consequences of Plan Qilin, that was the one that pleased him most.

Her breath caught then, and he turned toward her. "What is it?"

"News from America," she said, and handed him the tablet. On it was a thoughtful article from some Australian newspaper—he and Meiyin were both high enough in the Party to access foreign web pages without censorship—talking about the agitation in the United States over the upcoming constitutional convention, and the increasingly loud calls for radical change being heard across the country. Liu read it, shook his head. It baffled him that the American government would permit the rise of so obvious a threat.

An instant later, he recalled Fang's oh-so-tentative discussion of the plan that could bring the United States of America crashing down in ruins. Despite the warmth of the day, a chill moved through him.

He'd discussed the plan privately with Chen, Ma, and a few other core members of the Central Military Commission, and as far as he could tell, their reaction had been the same as his: a moment of exhilaration, thinking of the possible benefits, and then a long cold moment of horror as the other potential consequences sank in. Liu was certain that the collapse of a nuclear-armed superpower had too many possible downsides to contemplate—but had Chen and the others actually felt the same way? Had Fang mentioned the same plan to someone in one of China's intelligence agencies, and a different faction of the Politburo taken it up as a way to try to counterbalance the soaring prestige of the PLA? Or had events gone cascading down the trajectory Fang had sketched out all by themselves, hurtling toward a perilous future with no one in charge? He could not tell.

"I wonder," she said as he gave her back the tablet, "what the second most powerful man in America is doing right now."

He laughed at the implied compliment, not least because it was true. "I doubt he's sitting on a beach," he said. "Whatever he's doing, I don't envy him."

15 July 2030: Columbus, Ohio

At that moment, the second most powerful man in America was sitting in a comfortable suite at the top of a hotel in Columbus, a laptop computer on the desk in front of him, considering the speech he was scheduled to give later that day and wondering if it would do any good at all. Half a dozen members of Ohio's congressional delegation had asked Pete Bridgeport to come to their state and try to talk some sense into the state legislature, and since the Senate was in recess and he had half a dozen days free of other commitments, he'd agreed.

An afternoon reading local Ohio newspapers online and an evening reception with the state's most influential politicians had left him wondering if the trip was wasted effort. It wasn't just that the papers were full of letters to the editor denouncing the federal government for a galaxy of real and imagined misdeeds; it was that the editorials said the same thing, and so did the governor and most of the state legislators he'd met at the reception. Hostility toward the pretensions of Washington DC was a long-established American tradition, and one Bridgeport had been coping with since he first arrived in Washington as a first-term representative on his way to the House, but this was different.

He looked up from the laptop at the reason. Even from that height, he could see boarded-up storefronts, office buildings with few lights or none, streets that had half their usual traffic. The country was hurting, and the federal government had done too little about it for too long. Bridgeport shook his head, forced his attention back to his speech and tried to figure out what he could say that would balance that brutal reality.

7 September 2030: St. Louis, Missouri

The original plan had been to house all the delegates to the constitutional convention in one of the big downtown hotels in St. Louis, as close as possible to the America's Center convention venue where the meetings would be held. Well before the negotiations could get under way, though, the big media firms and a flurry of other interests had already rented big blocks of rooms in every available hotel. By the time everything was finally settled, the delegates were scattered in a dozen different hotels, in among reporters, politicians, lobbyists, and all the other hangers-on that a big convention attracts, and the buses hired at the last moment to shuttle attendees to and from the convention had to dodge downtown traffic as they veered through the streets.

303

Still, Harriet Elkerson thought, she hadn't done too badly. Her hotel was most of a mile from the America's Center, but it wasn't as crowded as some of the ones closer in, and the guests were by and large more entertaining—the Australian journalist she'd met at dinner the night before, for example. She got off the elevator, walked into the lobby.

"G'day," said McGaffney.

"Oh, hi." She glanced up at him. "Any idea how soon the bus is supposed to show?"

"Supposed to be any minute."

The bus chose that moment to roll past the big windows and stop right out in front. Elkerson got in line with the others, showed her delegate's badge to the driver, found a seat. Out the window she could see McGaffney striding out to the sidewalk and flagging down a taxi. Probably a better idea, she thought; he'd be settling into a place in the press room well before she got off the bus.

Conversations started around her well before the bus was under way. This was the big day, the one that counted. The week before had gone into the usual preliminaries—committee assignments, election of officers, jockeying over a handful of motions of no importance except as tests of voting strength— and all the while, or so the rumors had it, an unofficial committee put together by the state legislatures was putting the finishing touches on an amendment to the US Constitution prohibiting Congress from telling the states how to spend their money. The plan the state legislatures had in mind was clear enough: bring that up, get it voted in, and then vote to adjourn before any other proposals could be brought up.

Elkerson knew she wasn't the only delegate who had other plans.

The bus rolled through downtown St. Louis, past the boarded-up businesses that made up so large a part of the American landscape these days, and finally got to the convention center. There were 435 delegates—after much bickering,

304

the states had settled on one representative per House district—and so it took a good long time for her to get into the building, check in at the credentials desk, and get to her seat on one side of the Washington delegation, right up next to the seats reserved for Virginia. She'd taken the precaution of bringing her crocheting tote, and settled down to work on a baby blanket for an impending grandchild while delegates milled about, sound checks boomed over the loudspeakers, and the last preparations got made.

Despite it all, the gavel came down on time; there were more preliminaries, report of the credentials committee, reports from a few other housekeeping committees, and then the chair of the committee on legislation got the floor. Elkerson put the half-finished blanket away. The chair, a bottle-blonde lawyer from Michigan, reported on the proposed amendment and moved its adoption; someone from Idaho seconded the motion; the convention chairman opened the floor, but nobody took the bait. The question was called, and Elkerson tapped the green square on her voting tablet. The amendment passed overwhelmingly, 356 to 79.

The moment the applause died down, a state assemblyman from California was on his feet, making a motion to adjourn sine die, and before he'd quite finished talking, another state politician from Colorado was rising to second it. Debate wasn't allowed on motions to adjourn. If the states' attempt to railroad the convention was going to get anywhere, Elkerson knew, this was when it would happen.

The vote was called, and she jabbed the red square on the tablet. The numbers went up on the screen above the podium a moment later: 182 for, 253 against.

The room burst into a buzz of conversation. The chairman looked as though someone had poleaxed him. Before anyone else moved, one of the delegates was on his feet. "Mr. Chairman."

"The chair recognizes the delegate from Tennessee."

"Mr. Chairman, now that that's settled, I'd like to remind everyone that the resolution we just passed isn't the only proposal that's been brought forward. I move, Mr. Chairman, that those other proposals be referred to their proper committees and brought before this body for a vote before we pack up and go home."

Elkerson managed to press the button that called on the chair a fraction of a second before anyone else, and stood up.

"The chair recognizes the delegate from Washington," the chairman said grimly.

"I second the motion," she said.

"The motion is moved and seconded, and the floor open for debate."

This time there was no shortage of debate, but when the vote finally took place at three in the afternoon, the vote was 261 for, 174 against. When the totals appeared on the screen, Elkerson leaned back and allowed a smile. Maybe, just maybe, the hopes of the people who'd sent her to St. Louis would have their day.

15 September 2030: St. Louis, Missouri

Harriet Elkerson pulled out her crochet and sighed. It was going to be another long day.

The motion on the floor was something about the right to bear arms, yet another issue where half the country wanted one thing and the other half wanted the opposite. There had been a steady parade of issues like that since the vote eight days earlier had thrown the convention open. Old quarrels about gun ownership, abortion, and the place of religion in public life surfaced yet again, and the proponents on each side came out swinging.

Then there were the new issues, the ones nobody had thought to argue about until the possibility of amending the Constitution came into sight. Some of the proposals, she thought, were good ones—delegates from half a dozen states had called for hard limits on the power of presidents to wage war without consent of Congress, for example, and she'd decided to back a measure to do that if it was well written and came to a vote. There again, though, what sounded like common sense to one end of the country sounded like lunacy to the other end, and vice versa. It wasn't just liberals versus conservatives; choose a fault line through the middle of America, Elkerson thought, and it's on display right here.

The delegate who had the floor finished talking, and sat down. Someone else took his place and started in on what promised to be another pointless tirade.

After the first few words, Elkerson slumped back in her chair and said wearily, "I've got an idea. Why don't we just dissolve the Union and let everyone have what they want."

"I could live with that," snapped the delegate from Virginia, a lean white-haired man with a string tie, who was seated next to her.

She thought about that while the speaker ranted on. She'd meant the comment as a bitter joke, but it occurred to her that maybe there was a point to the idea. A memory surfaced: the evening when she and her second husband, on the brink of another pointless quarrel, looked at each other, realized that though they liked each other they couldn't live together, and decided that getting divorced was the only way to save their friendship. Maybe it was time to do the same thing with a country that wasn't really one nation any more.

The delegate who had the floor wound up his tirade, and someone else rose to argue for the other side of the quarrel. In the moment of quiet that followed, Elkerson turned to the man from Virginia and said, "I'm starting to think a lot of people might be able to live with that."

He gave her a long look, then said, "Ma'am, I'm not going to argue that one bit."

She considered that. "Got plans for lunch?"

His eyebrows went up. "Not yet."

"I figure that's probably long enough to draw up a resolution."

When the convention broke for lunch, the two of them walked half a block to a Burmese restaurant, got settled in a booth, and started working out the details. Both of them had decades of experience in state politics, so it took them only a few minutes to work out the text of the resolution in pencil on a yellow legal pad:

Article I: The Union of the States is hereby dissolved, and the several States shall be free to make other arrangements for their welfare.

Article II: All property of the former federal government in each State, at the time this amendment is ratified, shall become the property of that State.

Article III: All property of the former federal government outside the territory of the States shall be divided by agreement among the several States.

That afternoon, the two of them presented the resolution to the committee on legislation. The response was stunned silence. After a few minutes, the chairwoman of the committee huddled with the parliamentarian, found that the resolution was in proper form, assigned it a number—Resolution 58—and scheduled a hearing on it for the next day.

Within hours, word of the new proposal had spread through the convention, and that evening it was the one subject on nearly everyone's mind. As the next morning dawned, everyone at America's Center from the delegates to the kitchen staff sensed that something immense had happened. A line had been crossed, and there might be no going back.

PART FIVE

DISSOLUTION

TWENTY-FIVE

16 September 2030: Austin, Texas

Governor Terry McCracken leaned forward and blinked. The headline on the computer screen didn't change: *New Convention Proposal Would Dissolve Union*. The article below named the two delegates who'd introduced Resolution 58, gave the text, and then dismissed the whole thing as an edgy joke. A couple of sentences from some New York pundit, hoping out loud that the prank might bring the convention to its senses, finished it up. McCracken read the article a second time, shook his head, and reached for the phone to call the head of the Texas delegation. Some of them might be dumb enough to vote for it, after all.

Before his hand reached the phone, he stopped, and then drew the hand back, propped his elbows on his desk and rested his chin on his hands, looking at nothing in particular.

He sat up after a few minutes, reached for the phone again and punched the number. "Jack? Yeah, this is Terry. Just got the news about Resolution 58." A pause. "Yeah." Another. "Yeah. What kind of response is it getting from the delegates?"

He listened for a while, then said, "I'm thinking that it might actually be worth talking about. Take a straw poll of our people, and if they're in favor of it, I won't say no. Tell 'em that." Another long pause, then: "Okay, good. Give my best to Millie. Talk to you soon."

He put the phone back in its cradle, pushed his chair back, got up and walked over to the state flag, standing there next to the window. Neither he nor anybody else in Texas ever forgot that their state was bigger than most European countries, and that it had been an independent republic for a while and a state in the old Confederacy for a while after that. Maybe, he thought, just maybe, one or the other of those were better options than staying hogtied to Washington DC, and to forty-nine states that never could manage to see plain common sense the way Texans did.

Of course there was a personal dimension as well. In the aftermath of the crisis, he'd ended up with a hero's reputation across Texas, and in most of the other southern and western states. That was nice, but it wouldn't parlay into anything on a national level. There was a time, not too many decades back, when a powerful politician on the state level could count on a career in Congress, but these days, breaking into the hermetically sealed political world inside the DC Beltway took money and corporate connections he didn't have, and a personal life less cluttered with things nobody in Texas cared about but the national media did—say, the five kids he'd had by a string of Mexican mistresses.

But this way …

There would never be a President Terry McCracken of the United States, but of the Republic of Texas? That was another matter. He could almost taste it, and it was good. It was damn good.

He was far from the only ambitious politician thinking such thoughts at that moment. In the hours and days that followed, as their influence began to make itself felt, conversations in St. Louis and across the nation began to shift.

16 September 2030: Lumberton, Mississippi

Jim Owen stared at the television screen in disbelief, but the words refused to go away: *Delegates Say Let's Dissolve Union*. The talking heads above the banner were chattering away in their flat Yankee accents, making fun of the idea, but he gathered from what they were saying that the thing had actually been put before the convention as a serious proposal.

After a moment he hauled himself to his feet—not easy, that, with one leg still half full of shrapnel from a near miss, down near Caracas in his Army days—and went to the fridge for a beer. The floor of the cramped little mobile home creaked beneath his steps. The government made all kinds of promises about financial help for injured vets, but these days the money wasn't worth much more than toilet paper, and after the last round of budget cuts, the free health care he'd been told he would get was a joke—the nearest VA clinic was 300 miles away, and word among vets was that you could get on a waiting list for an appointment but there wasn't a chance in hell you'd get past that. Thank God he'd learned enough about engines to scrape by doing auto repair and stock-car rebuilds for friends and people in town. It was mostly barter these days, but it kept body and soul together.

He got the beer, twisted the cap off and popped it into the wastebasket halfway across the kitchen, and went back into the trailer's cramped little living room. The talking heads were still at it; after a moment he grabbed the remote and clicked the sound off. A moment later, the banner changed to *Would Make States Independent*.

He took a long pull of the beer, lowered the bottle. Not gonna happen, he told himself. Not in 100 years.

But if it did …

He downed another swallow of the beer. Without those morons in Washington getting in the way of everything sensible, maybe times wouldn't be quite so hard for a poor-ass Army vet in south Mississippi, and for a lot of other folks as well.

He shook his head, picked up the remote, switched to another channel. Across the country, as he did so, millions of Americans were thinking similar thoughts.

17 September 2030: Guthrie, Oklahoma

Clyde Witherspoon made sure the mike was switched on, handed it up to Suzette and gave her a thumbs up. The mike was new; so was the sound system, and so was the banner across the front of the platform, though it had the same slogan on it, "Independence? OK!" Of all the new things the Oklahoma Independence Party was learning to get used to, though, the most important was the crowd of people in front of the platform. A year before, they'd have counted themselves lucky to get twenty people to show up to a public meeting; over the summer, they'd had hundreds of people turn out for rallies in Tulsa and Oklahoma City, and now this.

"I want to thank each and every one of you for coming out tonight," Suzette said, and her voice boomed across the city park. "I know you had other things you could be doing right now, but you saw the news, just the same way I did. You know what's being debated in St. Louis right now, and you know just how important it is to make your voice heard.

"Nine years ago I helped found the Oklahoma Independence Party because I saw the good people of this state being treated like dirt by the government in Washington. I saw one bad law after another getting shoved down our throats because the government in Washington doesn't think we deserve a voice. And I saw it was time to do something—and now the rest of the country is starting to see the same thing."

It was true. Clyde had been fielding emails and phone calls all day, not just from Oklahomans—there were plenty of those,

314

too—but from all over the country, from people who were sick and tired of the federal government and thought the states might be able to do better. What was more, there were other parties in other states that were pulling in the same direction; just before the rally, he'd spent half an hour on the phone with a guy from Vermont who worked for an independence party there, making plans for the days ahead.

"That's why we're going to St. Louis," Suzette shouted. "We're going to St. Louis, to tell the delegates what the people want. We won't be alone, either. People are coming from all over America to tell the delegates that it's time to put the federal government out of *our* misery."

The crowd roared its approval.

"And I want you there." Her voice dropped, the way it did when she was close to the end of a speech. "I want you, all of you, or as many of you as can come, to come with us. We're renting buses for those who need a ride; we've got maps for those who don't. I want to see the good people of Oklahoma standing there, alongside the good people of every other state, to tell the world that we're fed up.

"We're fed up with the broken economy. We're fed up with a president and a Congress that can't get anything done. We're fed up with no money for our veterans, no money for our old folks, no money for anything worth doing, but plenty of money for whatever white elephant the Pentagon wants to buy this week. We are *fed* up with the *fed*-eral government. And I want you with me to tell the delegates that. Are you with me?"

They were.

The next morning, the buses loaded up outside the Oklahoma Independence Party's new headquarters, six of them, joining fourteen from Tulsa and no less than twenty-two from Oklahoma City, all rented with funds from the lavish new donors the party had attracted over the months just past. Every other political movement advocating the breakup of the United States had the same good fortune, and acted accordingly.

17 September 2030: Cincinnati, Ohio

Daniel Stedman bent over the keyboard, fingers flying. Light from a single unshaded bulb dangling from the ceiling kept a makeshift desk lit, turned the bare brick room around him into a tapestry of shadows and red-brown highlights. The space suited his mood, suited even better the job he'd taken on.

He'd gone dark months earlier, knowing just how dangerous a job that was, for himself and anyone that could be traced to him. The occasional hack-for-hire paid his few expenses; the rest of his time and all his passion went into what he'd ended up naming The Project.

All in all, what had surprised him most was how easy it had been to get this far. Figuring out who to target was the hardest part, and his grandfather's papers told him most of what he needed to know in advance. Once he'd finished sorting through those, he had a list of names, and checked those against the rumors and data thefts that filled the Undernet until the pieces started to make sense. The Gurney administration had a lot of enemies and no shortage of leaks, and that gave The Project plenty to work with.

It was more than that, though. There was new hackware available, if you knew where to look and who to ask: the kind of thing only spooks were supposed to have, really high-powered programs that could shred even top-end security systems and grab data without leaving a track. One set of rumors on the Undernet had it that the new hackware had been lifted from the US embassy in Nairobi during the war, another set of rumors denied it. Daniel didn't care where the software came from, or whose muddy fingerprints might be on it. What mattered was that the programs let him slip past firewalls, paralyze security programs, and get closer and closer to his target, until …

Now.

The trojan loaded itself into a computer in a condo in Alexandria, Virginia, burrowed its way into the operating system, then quietly copied every file on the computer and downloaded them to the Undernet. It would stay on the computer no matter what—you could reformat the hard drive and the trojan would protect itself, keep on working, and evade detection. Hookware, they called it, like a hook for a fish.

You don't know me, Daniel thought. You probably didn't even bother to find out if the man you killed had kids or grandkids. You probably don't think it matters.

By the time you find out otherwise, Ellen baby, it's going to be way too late.

17 September 2030: One Observatory Circle, Washington DC

"I'm starting to wonder if this country has lost its mind," Bridgeport said.

Joe Egmont shook his head once, sharply. "No. It's rational enough, if you look at it from their point of view. Why do the American people put up with the perpetual clown show here in Washington? Because we win wars and keep the economy more or less running. We haven't had much luck doing either of those lately, in case you haven't noticed."

"So they want to fire us."

"Basically, yeah."

For the past two days, Resolution 58 had been all over the media. Most reporters had pitched it as one more silly season story, but people hadn't taken it that way. Comments pages were flooded by posts supporting dissolution, and the online forum the constitutional convention had set up for public discussion had crashed three times, flooded with posts about dissolving the Union. Public meetings and rallies were being called, some opposing dissolution but many more in favor of it.

"The problem is," Egmont went on, "that the United States hasn't actually been one country for a very long time. I don't know if it ever was one country, really. Look at New England

317

and Texas, or Oregon and Alabama: other than the fact that they speak the same language—"

"More or less," Bridgeport said drily.

"Granted. Other than that, though, how much do they have in common? Not much. The only real bond is that they've all got the same national government, and since 1865, nobody thought that was going to change any time soon."

"And now they've changed their minds."

"A lot of people, yes. They're looking at dissolution and they're not just thinking, hey, let's get rid of those idiots in Washington—though that's part of it, and Gurney isn't helping things with this military spending thing of his. They're also thinking, hey, let's get rid of those idiots in that other part of the country that won't let us have the laws we want. And then there are the western states."

"The federal lands issue?"

"Bingo. They're looking at all the land the federal government owns west of the Mississippi, which don't pay any state taxes at all, and rubbing their hands together. There are quite a few states that could balance their budgets overnight if they could slap property taxes on what's now federal land, and don't even talk about what they could get by selling or leasing them. So everyone thinks they can get something out of it."

"And they don't think about what they're going to lose."

Egmont leaned forward. "Seriously? They've already lost most of it. This country is a basket case right now, and I don't see Gurney or Congress doing anything to change that any time soon. The arguments for dissolution are actually pretty solid, all things considered."

Bridgeport looked past him, out the window at the green lawn surrounding the vice president's mansion. A flagpole stood out in front, with Old Glory hanging limp in the still air of late summer. "There are less pragmatic issues," he said.

"Yeah, but you know how politics goes. 'What has the United States done for me lately?' These days, for a lot of people, not very much."

18 September 2030: St. Louis, Missouri

By midafternoon, word was spreading among the reporters and camera crews hovering around the convention center that there would be a demonstration that evening, a big one. As soon as he found out about it, McGaffney stepped out into the hallway, hunted up the route of the march online, and then started calling restaurants along it until he found one that could promise him a window seat overlooking the street. That done, he walked back into the media room.

"Any word yet?" he asked the woman from the BBC.

"Sweet bugger all," she replied, without looking up from the screen of her tablet. "The antis are still busy throwing every spanner they can find into the works."

"Typical Americans," the Russian from Novosti said, with a dry little chuckle. "They will spend the next week trying to avoid making a decision, and then the next six weeks blaming each other for making it."

"Too right," McGaffney said. Then, to the woman from the BBC: "Free this evening? I've got a dinner reservation with a window seat on the march route."

She glanced up, smiled. "Sorry, I'm already booked."

McGaffney grinned. "Thought it was worth the try."

He glanced up at the clock, turned toward the door, and blinked as a familiar figure came through it. "Hafiz!" he called out, crossing the room. "When did you get this side of the pond?"

"Just now," the al-Jazeera stringer replied. "Hello, Tommy." He greeted half the others in the press room by name, then glanced around. "What have I missed?"

"As I was telling McGaffney a moment ago," said the woman from the BBC, "sweet bugger all. It's all parliamentary maneuvering and backroom deals at this point."

"Any idea what chance the amendment has?"

"No one seems to know," said the Novosti reporter.

"No one at the convention," McGaffney said. "Out there?" He gestured up and back with his head, suggesting the rest of the country. "If they have anything to say about it, it's got a good fighting chance."

Hafiz considered that. "Can you fill me in?"

"I was heading for grub," McGaffney said.

"I'll buy," Hafiz responded.

"You're on."

They got a taxi from the convention center to the restaurant. "Got a call two nights ago from my bosses in Doha," Hafiz said as the taxi weaved through rush hour traffic. "They'd just heard about the dissolution proposal, and they wanted me to drop what I was doing and get here to cover it."

McGaffney gave him a startled look. "They must have dozens of people here already."

"True. They don't have anybody used to war zones."

"They said that?"

"In so many words."

McGaffney let out a low whistle.

The restaurant was crowded, but the hostess led them to a table right up against a big plate glass window, with a good view down the street. They ordered drinks—a beer for McGaffney, a cup of tea for Hafiz—and meals, as the sun sank into a cloud bank in the west and the first lights came on in the street below. After a good slug of the beer, McGaffney tried to explain what he'd seen in the months he'd spent in America: the sinking economy and the rising anger, the powder keg feel of a nation primed to explode.

"You've seen plenty of insurgencies," Hafiz asked him. "How close are we?"

McGaffney thought about that for a while. "That's a hard call," he said finally. "A lot of people lost whatever faith they had in the system they've got, and I get the sense a lot of people haven't had much faith in it for a good long time. The thing is, it'll take a spark to set them off, and I couldn't tell you when or where that's going to come. It could be here and now, or months from now on the other side of the country."

"Months? Not, for example, years?"

"If it takes years, I'll be gobsmacked. I—"

He stopped in midsentence. Hafiz read his face and turned in the chair to follow his gaze.

Down the street, filling it from sidewalk to sidewalk, came a river of marching forms. The front rank carried a printed banner with two words on it: DISSOLUTION YES. Torches blazed further back like stars, scores or hundreds of them, whipping and flaring in a wind neither of the reporters could feel. Signs and placards denouncing Gurney, Congress, and the opponents of dissolution in the convention caught the firelight, and so did faces, passionate and intense, their mouths moving in unison. A low rhythmic murmur came through the windows: the crowd was chanting something, and McGaffney thought he could guess roughly what it was.

Conversations in the restaurant dropped away to nothing, and dozens of people came over to the windows, watching the march. The front rank passed under the restaurant windows and kept going toward the convention center until it could no longer be seen. Minutes passed, the march flowed on, and the end of it was nowhere in sight.

"Fifty thousand so far?" McGaffney asked after their food arrived.

"At least." Hafiz watched the marchers, the waving placards and shouting faces, then turned back to McGaffney. "Do you recall when we had lunch in Dar es Salaam, right after the war, and you said you thought the next war would be here? I thought you'd ended up with a screw loose somewhere."

321

He speared a piece of chicken with his fork. "I was quite wrong. These people are ready to go to war."

21 September 2030: St. Louis, Missouri

"Mr. Chairman, I move to close debate."

"Second."

"It's been moved and seconded to close debate on Resolution 58." The chairman's face was hard and expressionless as stone. "Vote yes or no."

Harriet Elkerson tapped the green button on her voting tablet. The total appeared a moment later on the screen: 261 yes, 174 no.

"Mr. Chairman, I move that this body adopt Resolution 58 and submit it to the several states as an amendment to the United States Constitution."

"Second."

"It's been moved and seconded to adopt Resolution 58 and submit it to the states," the chairman said. "Vote yes or no."

Elkerson voted again, pressing the green button. The total this time was 239 yes, 196 no.

As the hubbub died down, one of the state politicians who'd tried to push through the original plan stood, ashen-faced. "Mr. Chairman," he said, "I move reconsideration of Resolution 1. If we're going to do without the United States, it doesn't exactly make much sense to raise a fuss about unfunded mandates."

Someone seconded the motion. The chairman called for debate, but no one responded, and the vote was called. By 266 to 169, the proposed amendment banning unfunded mandates was voted down.

"Mr. Chairman," someone else called out, "I move that this body adjourn sine die."

"Second."

Elkerson tapped the voting tablet one last time, and by 304 to 131, the constitutional convention closed.

The moment the final gavel came down, the floor erupted in shouting and angry words, and two delegates got into a shoving match in the aisle not far away from where Elkerson was sitting. Still, the thing was done. What would be, if it passed, the 28th and last amendment to the US Constitution was on its way to the final test of ratification.

TWENTY-SIX

23 September 2030: Spokane, Washington

The plaza in Riverfront Park was packed with people by the time the sound tech finished setting up the PA system. "Here you go," he said, handing a microphone up to the woman on the podium. "You're live."

"I want to thank you all for coming today," Harriet Elkerson said into the mike, and the words boomed out across the plaza and over the Spokane River to the other shore. "I know a lot of you have questions about what happened at the constitutional convention; a lot of you have questions about the amendment we passed and sent to the states. I want to explain why I proposed it and voted for it—why so many of us voted for it—and why I think it's the best choice we've got."

Murmurs moved through the crowd as she paused. "Most of us know what it's like to be in a relationship that just doesn't work any more," she went on. "No matter how hard you try, no matter what anyone says or does, you're not a couple any more, and the only thing you can do is accept that, make a clean break, and move on. That's what's happened to the United States. We're not a country any more; we haven't been a country for years now. We're a bunch of different countries with different values and ways of doing things, and the only thing that holds us together is habit. The amendment is the divorce that sets us free to go our own ways.

"Gurney's flacks are saying that we can't split the United States into fifty countries. Nobody's suggesting that. Once the states are free to make other arrangements for their future, they'll sort themselves out into six or eight or ten nations that make sense. New England's a country. The South is a country. Texas—we'll let them figure that out for themselves." That got a laugh, and she paused to let it die down. "Washington and Oregon; maybe Idaho; maybe Montana too—that'll be up to the people of each state. Up to you and me.

"Is it going to be easy? Of course not. Being part of the United States hasn't been easy, either. The important thing is that we'll be able to choose our own future and make our own decisions, without having to run them past people on the other side of the continent who don't understand our issues or share our values, without having everything we want blocked by that pack of idiots in Washington DC. I think that's worth a little extra trouble."

She paused to drink from a bottle of water on the podium. Someone in the crowd called out to her, "If Gurney gets his way, it's gonna be more than a little trouble."

Elkerson put down the bottle. "I know," she said, "and we're going to have to be ready to deal with that. I don't think he's clueless enough to try to tell the people that they can't exercise their constitutional rights, but we have to be prepared for that—one way or another."

25 September 2030: The White House, Washington DC

"They can do it," said Janice Kumigawa, the president's legal adviser. "That's just the problem. Everything the convention did is legal according to the Constitution, and if the state conventions vote to ratify, the amendment takes effect and that's all there is to it."

"What about the Supreme Court?" Gurney demanded.

"They don't have a say in it. Neither does Congress, and neither do you. I'm sorry, sir, but it really is that simple."

The picture of Teddy Roosevelt on horseback loomed up behind Gurney; Ellen Harbin tried not to think about the contrast. She, Gurney, and Kumigawa were the only people present in the room. That was one too many for what Harbin had in mind, but she was prepared to wait.

"The president," she said, "needs a legal justification for having a say."

Kumigawa glanced at Gurney, and when he nodded, turned to face Harbin. "That won't be easy—not if it has to stand up to legal challenge."

"Find something," Harbin told her. "It doesn't have to be ironclad; it just has to be plausible."

"You're asking for a fig leaf."

"Essentially."

"I can probably manage that." She pushed her chair back. "Is there anything else?"

Gurney looked at Harbin, then shook his head. "No, that's it. Thanks, Jan."

"Sure." She got up and left the room, closing the door behind her.

Once she was gone, Gurney turned his chair to face Harbin. "Do you think we can make it stick?"

"I'm sure of it," she told him. "The agitators who are pushing this nonsense have momentum on their side right now, but that's all they've got. Once they find out that you're not going to sit on your hands and let the country go down the drain, this dissolution fad will pop like a bubble, and people will come back to their senses."

"If they try it again—"

"They can't be allowed to try it again. It's long past time to make some significant changes to the way this country is governed, and this gives you the opportunity to make those."

He swallowed visibly. "One thing I want to see changed—this stupid every-four-years election business."

"Exactly." She allowed a bright smile. "That and other things."

She got up, walked over to the painting of Roosevelt, knowing that Gurney would follow. "This is the twenty-first century," she said. "We don't wear powdered wigs or ride in carriages any more; There's no reason why we should still be saddled with an eighteenth-century system of government. Especially when all it takes is someone strong enough to take charge and make the changes that have to be made."

He came up behind her, put a hand on her shoulder. She let her hip slide up and down against his stiffening flesh. "Feeling strong?"

"Strong enough," he said, and pulled her to him.

2 October 2030: Lumberton, Mississippi

The pickup rattled to a stop on the county highway, turned into Jim Owen's driveway, and nosed up to the mobile home. Jim looked up from the stock car engine he was rebuilding as two young men piled out of the cab: the Wilcox boys, sons of a friend of his. "Afternoon," he said. "I'd 'spect to see you two fishing on a day like this."

"Most days, sure," said Bobby Lee, the oldest. "Mr. Owen, can we talk? Someplace private, maybe?"

"Sure thing." He put down the torque wrench, wondered what the boys were up to.

A few minutes later they were sitting around the kitchen table with a cold beer each. "So," said Owen. "What's on your mind?"

"The amendment," said Bobby Lee. "They're saying Gurney's not gonna let it go to a vote—that he's gonna send in federal troops to stop any state that tries it."

"Who's they?"

"Everybody in town."

"Like they know what the president's thinking."

"You hear the speech he made Tuesday?" This from the younger brother, Nate. "That's what he said himself."

"Yeah, I heard it." It had been all over the news the next morning: Gurney blustering about the convention. He'd used the word "consequences" so many times there were jokes about it all over the media.

"Cal Parker told me today that the boys at the armory just got word they'll be on call starting the first of November," said Bobby Lee.

"Cal told you that?" Owen leaned forward, propped his chin on his hand and his elbow on the table.

"Yessir. And we been talking about doing something if it comes to that." Bobby Lee swallowed visibly. "That's why me and Nate want to talk to you. You were with the Army Rangers in Venezuela, weren't you? That's what Daddy said."

"Yeah," said Owen. "Yeah, I was."

"We can get fifty or a hundred boys together easy, the kind who been shooting and hunting since their mommas taught 'em to walk," said Nate. "Once we do that, can you teach us the rest of what we're gonna need to know if it comes to a fight?"

Owen considered that for a long moment, weighing conflicting loyalties against each other. "Yeah," he said finally. "I can do that."

29 September 2030: The White House, Washington DC

"The plan goes into effect," said Ellen Harbin, "as soon as the first state ratifying convention votes for dissolution. Before that happens, we don't have legal justification."

"Technically speaking, shouldn't that wait until the amendment is ratified?" This from Blair Murdoch, the head of Homeland Security.

Harbin shook her head. "That raises legal issues we don't want to have to deal with—and that's when we can expect organized rebellion to get under way, if there's going to be any. No, we need to stop this thing the moment it's clear that the Union's at risk."

She'd considered scheduling the briefing in the Roosevelt Room, but the stark modern lines of the National Security Council briefing room were better suited to the hard decisions that had to be made. The audience was a select one: Murdoch and two of his top aides, three senior planners from the National Security Council staff, two people from the Executive Special Projects Staff, and one from the black-budget end of the Office of the President: the inner circle of Gurney's administration, or as much of it as would take an active role in the transfer of power to the new unitary government. Gurney himself was off giving a speech in Pittsburgh, safely out of the way.

"Here's what needs to happen," Harbin said, and pushed the button on the control. The screen behind her lit up, showed a series of bullet points. "Homeland Security forces, backed by Army and Marine units wherever that's necessary, secure all fifty state governments—that means occupying the buildings and removing governors, department heads and members of the state legislatures to FEMA shelters, where they can be interned for as long as necessary.

"Mayors and city councils of the fifteen largest cities get the same treatment, and so do delegates to the constitutional convention and the ratifying conventions. Every figure who might provide a scrap of legitimacy to an opposition movement has to be rounded up. If we run out of room in the FEMA shelters, military bases in isolated rural areas can be pressed into service as internment camps.

"Once that phase of the operation is over, appointed administrators take charge of the state bureaucracies for the duration of the crisis, and Homeland Security and military units

330

move to the second phase, the neutralization of any attempts at armed resistance."

"Any idea how much of that we can expect?" Murdoch asked.

"No," Harbin admitted. "I wish we did. If it's just a little sporadic violence, that can be taken out promptly with ground units, or even police. If it's significantly more than that, we need to be prepared to use whatever it takes—air strikes, special-forces units, the whole spectrum of military operations. It's crucial that any armed resistance be crushed as fast as possible, before it has the chance to organize into a sustained insurgency.

"Once that's taken care of and any survivors have been interned, we enter the third phase, which is stabilization. Once no one has any remaining doubt that the federal government will defend the Union with whatever force might be necessary, military units return to their bases, and Homeland Security police and militarized units deal with any further unrest as it occurs."

"What about the internees from the first phase?" one of Murdoch's aides said. "Are they released during the third phase?"

Harbin gave him a blank look, then said, "Of course. Subject to the president's orders."

She turned back to the screen, clicked the button to bring up the next set of bullet points. Behind her, the Homeland Security aide who'd spoken glanced at his colleague, who met his gaze briefly and then looked away.

10 October 2030: Wichita National Guard Armory, Wichita, Kansas

"Got a moment, Chip?" Major Roy Abernethy asked.

"Sure thing, boss." The sergeant was sitting in the open back gate of an armored personnel carrier, entering data on a laptop; he scooted over, motioned to Abernethy to sit. "What's up?"

The major glanced both ways, made sure nobody else was in earshot. The APCs in the armory lot spread out to either side, angular shapes beneath the pale autumn sky. "Orders from DC," he said. "Got 'em yesterday."

Lansberger glanced at him. "And?"

"They want us on twenty-four hour standby as of November 1," he said. "Reason not given—but I got told, unofficially, you understand, to make sure each squad has street maps of Topeka with the state government buildings marked."

The sergeant watched him, said nothing at all.

After several minutes: "Chip, I can't do it. I joined the Guard to help people and do my bit for the country." Looking away: "Not to stomp the crap out of the Constitution because that toad in Washington says hop."

"A lot of us," said Lansberger, "have been saying the same thing."

Abernethy glanced back at him.

"When those orders come in, boss," said the sergeant, "if you tell us to sit right here and ignore 'em, you won't get any argument."

"And if it's more than that?"

Lansberger gave him a long slow look. "If it's more than that, talk to the guys. Tell 'em that anybody who can't go that next step can leave his gear and go home, no questions asked. Some'll take you up on it—but not many. If push comes to shove, not too many at all."

11 October 2030: The White House, Washington DC

The only people in the West Wing on Sundays were essential staff, duty officers down at the situation room, and janitors, and that suited Ellen Harbin well. She needed privacy just then, time and space without interruption to finish working out the last and most secret details of the transfer of power to the new unitary government. She'd come in via the walkway from the Executive Office Building, locked herself in her office, and silenced the phone. Gurney was in Kansas City giving yet another speech against dissolution, so that was one interruption she didn't need to guard against; everyone and everything else could wait.

She pulled a thumb drive from her purse, stuck it in her computer's USB port, waited until the security screen came up and typed in username and password. A moment later, her desktop displayed more than a dozen documents: the presidential order that would launch the transfer of power, the orders that would go out to Homeland Security and the military, and the rest of it. It was nearly ready, but nearly wasn't good enough; the first state ratifying convention had been scheduled for 11 December, and everything had to be in place by then, down to the last legal formality and the last extralegal action.

One of those latter still had to be arranged. She opened a new document and typed at the head of it: *Subjects for immediate executive action on enactment of Presidential Order 18827.*

She paused, then, considered the options. Certain people had to be removed for the plan to work as it should, and it would be convenient to use the same opportunity to remove others; the risk was that too many disappearances too suddenly would draw attention too soon to the wider agenda. A case could be made for patience ...

No, she told herself, not this time. Every plan she'd tried to carry out so far, from the beginning of Weed's administration right up to the convention, had been crippled by those who weren't willing to see things done with the ruthlessness and force that each situation demanded. Finally, she had complete control of the planning; this time, finally, she could do the thing right, and that meant striking hard and fast.

That settled, she started typing, listing the names of those who were to be killed. Before she was finished, there would be more than 100 names in the list.

12 October 2030: The Pentagon, Washington DC

Admiral Waite paced down a Pentagon hallway to "the tank," the soundproof conference room where the Joint Chiefs met. Guards at the door saluted and let him in.

Wittkower and the heads of the service branches were already there. So was the CIA director, along with key officials from elsewhere in the executive branch. That wasn't usual for a meeting of the Joint Chiefs, but then this wasn't a usual meeting; most of the federal government's remaining power to make things happen was concentrated in the tank that morning, with one crucial decision to make.

"You've seen Gurney?" This from Alberto Mendoza, the Marine Corps commandant, once the pleasantries were past.

"Yes." Waite settled into a chair at the long table in the room's center. "Every time I go there these days, I wonder if I'm the only adult in the building." That got an uneasy laugh from the others. "He's still dead set on this plan of his," Waite went on, and the laughter stopped. "Today he ordered me—his word—to get things rolling: troop movements, logistics, everything. He's got Justice busy manufacturing legal excuses."

"They'll need 'em for martial law," said Wittkower.

"It's not just martial law." Waite leaned forward. "He wants the whole country under military rule. Homeland Security's working on a list of people to round up, internment camps, that sort of thing."

"Jesus," said Wittkower. "Dictatorship, then."

"Basically," said Waite.

"Do you think we can make a military takeover stick?" Mendoza asked. "That would be a tough job at the best of times."

Greg Barnett answered. "I've had people working on that for more than a month now, running simulations with every scenario we can think of. If everything goes our way, yes, we can make it stick, but we get a major insurgency out West backed with arms and money from China—there's no way Beijing would be dumb enough to miss an opportunity like that—and any other country that wants to make trouble for us chipping in whatever their budgets can bear. If any significant number of National Guard units side with the states, though, we get civil war, again with China et al. backing the other side. Could we win? Heck of a good question."

"That got asked a lot in 1861," said Mendoza.

"In 1861," said Wittkower, "one region wanted out and the rest of the country said no you don't. Now? The North wants to get rid of the South just as much as the South wants to get rid of the North, and let's not even talk about the western states." He leaned forward, elbows on the table. "And it's not just civilians. How many of you have had your intelligence people check out what the rank and file of your branches are saying? The Army's best units will follow orders, but there are a lot of second- and third-string units that might not, and the National Guard is a real risk. They're as likely to end up on the other side if it comes to shooting."

"The Marines will follow orders no matter what," Mendoza insisted.

"Bill, what about the Navy?" Waite asked.

"I've had our security people all over," said Admiral Gullickson, the Chief of Naval Operations. "Morale's been in the crapper since the war. We've done our best, but if I ordered them to fire on American civilians I'm honestly not sure how many would do it."

"Same for the Air Force," said General Braddock, who headed that service. "Or worse. There's been a lot of loose talk, and a lot of—well, propaganda, basically, at some air bases and the towns around them. There are units I'd trust, but others I wouldn't—and don't even ask about the Air National Guard."

"There seems to be a lot of money backing dissolution," said Waite. "Chinese money?"

"Heck of a good question," Barnett said again. "America's made a lot of enemies, and China's only one of them—the Russians, the Iranians, you name it, and you can bet the Saudis aren't feeling too charitable toward us right now, either. Of course you've got Texas oil families, old money down South, various others domestically who might be backing this. We've tried to trace the funds, but whoever it is knows how to hide their tracks."

"What does Wall Street think?" This was from Wittkower. That mattered a great deal, and the room went quiet.

"Depends on who you ask," said one of the civilians, a career bureaucrat from Treasury. "Some firms are scared to death of dissolution and some think they can get rich off it. Military government? That's no problem, they know they can work with us. Insurgency or civil war is another matter. Even if we win, they're saying, that'll trash what's left of the economy and hand everything we've still got in the rest of the world to Beijing. If we don't win, they're going to be hanging from lampposts and they know it."

"Right next to you and me," Mendoza said. No one laughed; they all knew the commandant was right.

"Here's the question that matters." Waite looked from face to face around the table. "Do any of you think we can make it work, without tearing what's left of the country apart?"

Nobody answered. After a long moment, Waite said, "Well. Then the question is what to do about it."

"Until Gurney acts," Barnett said, "it's all he said, she said— you saw what happened with the stuff that hit the internet when Stedman died."

"So we wait?" Wittkower said.

Waite nodded. "Until Gurney moves—or something else happens."

12 October 2030: Alexandria, Virginia

Harbin sat down at her desk, fished around in her purse, pulled out a thumb drive and stuck it into the port of her computer. The finder window popped up, showing a security screen she didn't want; she scowled, ejected that thumb drive, found the one she wanted and jabbed it into the slot.

Five minutes later, she had forgotten about the mistake. By that time, though, the files that had been on the first thumb drive were already listed on a screen in a half-derelict building in Cincinnati, Ohio.

Daniel Stedman got the files stashed, then started opening and reading them. A few screens later, his eyes had gone wide as he began to realize how big of a fish his hookware had just landed. He got the files forwarded to three offshore Undernet servers, then accessed a chatroom and typed: *just upped files from clean src. code red political!!! fwd fwd fwd baby.*

When that was done, he sat back, stared at the screen for a while. The Undernet would get it to the legal net in a matter of hours, but that wouldn't necessarily have the impact he wanted; the administration could simply dismiss these papers as they'd done with the papers on the East African War, and try to weather the new controversy as they had the older one. That wasn't good enough. If the documents could only get to the right people ...

He considered that, then leaned forward again and started to type.

TWENTY-SEVEN

13 October 2030: One Observatory Circle,
Washington DC

Bridgeport couldn't sleep that night. After three or four hours of futile effort, he pulled himself out of bed, threw on a bathrobe and slippers, and went into his sitting room. Rain drummed against the windows as he scratched Bus behind the ears and waited for the computer to finish waking up.

Once that was done, he checked the news. There wasn't much. In the Middle East, the Kurdistan front had settled into the same stalemate that had gripped the Arabian front months earlier, with Turkish and Iranian armies hammering each other repeatedly over the same narrow strip of bloodsoaked sand. The dollar had fallen to just under 12 to the euro and 6 to the yuan; an American oil company had been caught trying to smuggle crude oil out of the country in order to sell it at market prices overseas, and was facing draconian penalties; Governor McCracken of Texas had made a speech in Atlanta calling Southerners to support the 28th Amendment. An ordinary day's news, Bridgeport thought, and caught himself, remembering how little time had passed since news stories like those hadn't been normal at all.

He closed the news and opened his email. There were a dozen ordinary messages, and then one with the subject line *Dear Mr. Bridgeport* from an address he didn't recognize. He considered sending it to the spam filter, thought better of it, clicked.

You don't know me from Adam, the email read, *but you knew my grandfather, Bill Stedman, and he told me once that he thought you were an honest man. That's why I'm sending you a link to some papers that came from a hacked White House computer; it's gone to some other people as well. If you look about halfway down the list of names in the document labeled ExAcList you'll know why. Sincerely, Daniel Stedman.*

Bridgeport read the email a second time, his chin cupped in his hand. Of course it could be a clever new way to get spam or spyware past his computer's filters, or some subtler trap, but his gut feeling said otherwise. He compromised, clicked on the last email in his inbox, which was from Joe Egmont and had no subject line.

The message was stark: *Pierre—call me. J.*

Bridgeport leaned forward. The use of his real name was a private signal between them, and meant serious trouble. He paused and frowned, then reopened the email from Daniel Stedman and clicked the link. A privacy-screened browser window opened, and showed him a directory of documents. He clicked on the one labeled ExAcList. It read:

Subjects for immediate executive action on enactment of Presidential Order 18827.

Below that was a list of names, and *Pierre Bridgeport* was about halfway down it.

Bridgeport reached for the phone to call Joe Egmont, then thought better of it; the phones at the vice presidential mansion were monitored, that was a safe bet, and it was at least as certain that Gurney's people had immediate access to the intercepts. Instead, he opened three of the other documents. One of them turned out to be the text of Presidential Order 18827, which declared martial law, suspended the Constitution, and gave Gurney unlimited power to rule by decree. The other two were orders to Pentagon officials sending the US military into America's streets with orders to shoot to kill in case of resistance.

That was enough. Bridgeport considered the possibility that the whole thing was a well-crafted fake, but it all made the most unpleasant kind of sense of the rumors that had been flying around Washington for weeks, and there was Egmont's email to weigh in the balance. One way or another, it was too plausible to dismiss, and that meant there might be very little time left for him to act—if there was any at all.

He scribbled the URL for the link to the stolen documents on a scrap of paper, deleted both emails, triggered the program that cleared and overwrote everything in his trash bin, then shut down the computer and left the room. The moment Gurney's people knew about the leak, all hell was going to break loose, and when that happened, there was precisely one place on the planet where he would be safe.

Maybe.

The clock in his bedroom said 4:11 am: late enough, he decided. He dressed quickly, got his briefcase, threw a coat over his shoulder, and made himself slow down as he went to the elevator and hit the button for the basement level. The Eisenhower-era private subway that linked government buildings in the core of the city had been extended out to the vice president's residence back in 2002, at the same time the deep underground bunkers there had gone in. That was his ordinary route to the Capitol, and everything depended on Gurney's people not realizing that anything was out of the ordinary.

The Secret Service guard at the subway station looked up from a half-finished crossword puzzle as the elevator opened and Bridgeport came out. "Morning, Mr. Bridgeport," he said.

"Morning, Jim," Bridgeport said. With a shrug: "I couldn't sleep, and figured I might as well head in and get some work done before the shouting starts up again."

The guard chuckled. "I bet. Have a good day, sir."

"Thank you. You too."

Bridgeport got into the subway car, punched in the code for the Capitol and took a seat. Back when it was first put in, the government subway system still had drivers and conductors. He missed that bit of human contact—especially now.

Especially when his route took him right under the White House, and it would be child's play for Gurney's people to stop the car, have him dragged out by hired goons, and treated the way they'd treated Bill Stedman.

He drew in a ragged breath as the car started moving, and hoped he'd still be alive when it got to the Capitol.

13 October 2030: The Capitol, Washington DC

"Mr. Bridgeport!" The night watchman at the subway station in the Capitol basement gave him a startled look. "Mighty early, sir."

"I know. Too much to get done. Thanks, Fred."

"Thank you, sir," said the watchman, pocketing the tip.

Bridgeport's footfalls whispered off the stone walls as he went through the silent building to his office. Security guards looked surprised, but then greeted him with a friendly "Good morning, Mr. Bridgeport, sir." He returned the greetings, got to his office, and unlocked the door, more than half expecting to find someone waiting for him inside with a silenced gun.

The office was empty. He turned on the lights, locked the door behind him, went to his desk and picked up the phone. That line was probably monitored, too, but at this point it was almost too late in the game to matter.

The first call went to Joe Egmont. "Joe? It's Pete."

"Thank God. Have you seen—"

"The list? Yes. I'm in my office."

"I'll be there in a few minutes."

"I'll let the security people know. Joe, I'm going to call the Pentagon next."

"Do that," said Egmont. "I've been on the phone with my contacts there. Waite's expecting your call."

Bridgeport blinked. "Your idea?"

"Seemed like the right thing to do."

"Thank you. See you in a bit."

Bridgeport closed the line, dialed the security desk and told them about Egmont, then called Waite's office at the Pentagon. "This is Vice President Bridgeport. I was told that Admiral Waite's there."

"Yes, sir," said the voice on the other end. "I'll put you right through, sir."

A click, and then a familiar voice: "This is Admiral Waite."

"Pete Bridgeport. I don't know of an easy way to say what I have to say."

"I do," said the admiral. "You've seen the leak of Presidential Order 18827 and the other documents that go with it, and you want to know if they're authentic."

"Basically."

"Yes," said Waite at once. "Some of them have already been sent to us here and to NORTHCOM."

Bridgeport paused, taking that in, then said, "I need to know where you stand, Roland."

It was the admiral's turn to be silent. "I don't want to see this country torn apart," he said. "I want to see the Union saved—but not this way. Not at the cost of everything the United States used to stand for. And there's another detail, of course. Did you read the whole list of people Gurney wants taken out?"

"No," Bridgeport admitted. "I probably should have."

"My name was on it," said Waite. "So was Ralph Wittkower's, and half a dozen other people at the top end of the military. They're planning a clean sweep."

Bridgeport took that in. "What I need to know now is whether you'll back me."

"What are you planning?"

"Congress is going to do what the Constitution says we're supposed to do. I need you to make sure nobody stops us."

"We can do that," Waite said at once. "What exactly do you need?"

"Enough troops in and around the Capitol to keep Gurney from trying anything stupid."

"You'll have it. I can offer you something else."

"Go ahead," said Bridgeport.

"I'm prepared to resign as Chairman of the Joint Chiefs and testify before Congress."

Bridgeport's mouth fell open; it took him a moment to recover. "Thank you, Roland."

"We were debating what to do," said Waite. "You've just given us the best available answer. I'll be there at 8 am sharp."

Bridgeport thanked him again and set down the phone, then drew in a deep breath, picked up the phone again, and started dialing senators.

13 October 2030: The White House, Washington DC

Ellen Harbin arrived at the West Wing at 8:30, after fielding a panicked phone call from one of her aides. "What's happened?" she demanded as she came into the National Security Council office.

"The president wants to see you," said one of her senior analysts. "Right away."

She took that in, nodded, turned, went straight to the Oval Office past knots of tense and whispering staff, and knocked on the door.

Silence.

She knocked again, and when there was no answer, opened the door and went in. She found Gurney staring at a flat screen with a face the color of putty and the expression of a man who had just been strangled.

"Lon?" Harbin asked. "What is it?"

Gurney kept staring at the screen and said nothing. Harbin came around to see for herself. A TV newscast showed Admiral Waite in uniform in one of the Capitol briefing rooms. ADMIRAL: GURNEY PLANS MILITARY COUP was splashed across the bottom of the picture. "—a terrible idea," Waite was saying, his face bland. The words at the bottom of the picture shifted: RESIGNS AS CHAIRMAN OF JOINT CHIEFS. "But if this is how the American people decide they're going to exercise their constitutional rights, the military's job is to salute and say, 'Yes, sir; yes, ma'am.'"

Harbin stared at the newscast for a long moment, and then swallowed. "Lon," she said, "we can cope with this. Get on the line to Wittkower and tell him to do his job."

He looked up at her then, and though he still said nothing his face was bleak and pleading. "Okay," she said. "I'll call him. If he wants to hear it from you, you'll have to back me." She turned and left the Oval Office before he could respond.

Back in her own office, she all but threw herself into her chair, picked up the phone and dialed. "This is Ellen Harbin," she said when a receptionist picked up the other end. "I need to speak to General Wittkower at once."

"I'm sorry, ma'am," the receptionist said. "The general's not available."

"That wasn't merely a request," Harbin snapped. "Put me through to him."

"I'm sorry, ma'am," the receptionist repeated. "The general's not available."

"That's not good enough," said Harbin.

"I'll see to it that your disapproval is reported to the proper authorities, ma'am," the receptionist told her. The boredom in his voice was so evident that she disconnected the call with a jab of one finger.

Three calls to three other top Pentagon brass got her no further, and she slammed down the phone and went back to the Oval Office, entering unannounced. "Lon," she said, "the Pentagon is stonewalling me. You've got to call Wittkower and talk some sense into him."

It took her twenty minutes of pleading and bullying to get Gurney out of his funk and on the phone, and she stood there listening while he made the call. "This is President Gurney. I need to talk to General Wittkower at once." A silence. "Dammit, this is an emergency. Get him on the line." Another silence. "I don't care. Get him on the line!" Another. "What do you mean, 'No, sir'? I'm the goddamn president. Get him on the fucking line." Still another silence, and then Gurney lowered the handset and stared at it. "He wouldn't put me through."

"You'll have to try someone else," Harbin said.

"Ellen—" He looked up at her. "The news is saying that there are Marines surrounding the Capitol."

It was the first good news she'd had all day. "Good. Somebody's come to their—"

"No. Ellen, listen. They're protecting Congress." He swallowed visibly. "From me."

She stared at him for a long moment, then said, "We'll find a way around that. You stay right here. I'll get Homeland Security on this."

He nodded vaguely, and Harbin hurried out of the room.

13 October 2030: The Capitol, Washington DC

"Any word from the White House yet?" Bridgeport asked.

"Nothing directly," Wittkower said. He was in BDUs, looking every inch the field commander he'd been in the Venezuelan war. "Gurney's people are talking with Homeland Security—we've intercepted transmissions, and I've got people working on decrypting them. They've got the White House pretty well guarded, but we can take 'em if we have to."

"I hope you won't have to," Bridgeport replied.

They were in his office in the Capitol. Outside, Marines in full battle gear guarded the Capitol grounds, and the sound of helicopters overhead could be heard all through the Capitol like a distant drumbeat.

Wittkower nodded. "I wish the House would hurry up."

"They're working as fast as they can. This has got to be done the right—"

The intercom buzzed, and Bridgeport poked the button. "Yes?"

"On the floor," Joe Egmont's voice said. "Four hundred thirty-eight in favor. I've got the articles. Kamanoff and Schick just appointed the committee."

"Good," Bridgeport replied. "I'll be over in a minute." He poked the button again and glanced up at the general, who was giving him a quizzical look. "The House just voted to bring the articles of impeachment to the floor, with a big majority in favor. It's all over now but the shouting—well, on their side." He got out of his chair. "It's the Senate's turn now. Keep us safe for another couple of hours, and we'll finish this."

"I can do that," said Wittkower. "The Marines can hold off anything they can throw at us until the 82nd gets here, and then it's all over. Keep me posted."

"Of course." The two men went to the door.

The hall outside the vice presidential office was full of senators and staff. Wittkower hurried through them to the elevators—his command post was in the basement levels—and Bridgeport watched him go, then turned toward the Senate chamber.

"Pete!" Mike Kamanoff, the Senate majority leader, saw him and hurried over. "You've heard about the House."

"On the floor."

"It's a slam-dunk at this point. I wish we had some other choice."

"So do I. Where's Phil Schick?"

"Last I saw—"

347

The sound of hurrying feet hushed the talk in the hall, and both men turned. A staffer came up the stairs at a run. "Impeached," he said, panting. "Vote just passed the halfway point."

"Well," said Bridgeport. "Ladies and gentlemen, I believe we have a job to do." He started walking toward the Senate chambers. One after another, the senators in the hallway broke away from conversations and followed him.

13 October 2030: The White House, Washington DC

"Ignore it," Harbin snapped. "Lon's still in charge."

"The Constitution gives them—" the aide began.

"The Constitution is a scrap of paper 250 years out of date. Lon's still in charge. If you want to argue, there's the door."

The aide gave her a dubious look, but subsided.

"I'll be back in ten minutes," Harbin said then. "I'll expect a list of the military and Homeland Security assets we've got close enough to DC to get here first thing tomorrow or sooner. This nonsense has gone far enough." She turned and left the National Security Council rooms; the aide watched her go.

She'd expected Lon to be in the Oval Office, but the room was empty. She waited, one hand on the brown wood of the famous desk. Get through this, she told herself. Get through this crisis, bring things back under control, use the excuse to take care of Bridgeport and the other people in Congress who needs to be removed, and then there's just one more obstacle in the way.

Just one more heartbeat, and she'd have the biggest prize of all.

Five minutes later, when Gurney hadn't returned, she let out an annoyed sigh, sat down at the desk and woke his computer. She'd sent the orders for Homeland Security to his mailbox, having gotten the password from him months earlier; a few clicks of the mouse and she had them on his desktop, added the presidential signature, then sent them on their way.

There, she thought. That should take care of it. She got up, left the room, flagged down a member of the White House staff, told her to find Gurney for her, and then hurried back to the National Security Council offices.

The aide she'd assigned to make the list was nowhere to be seen. She blinked, startled, and walked over to his work station. There was a note:

On second thought the door sounds like the better option. I've cleaned out my desk and cleared my files from the computer. Happy trails.

Harbin grabbed the note, crumpled it, flung it into the nearest wastebasket, and went to a phone to get someone up from the Executive Office Building in a hurry.

13 October 2030: Homeland Security headquarters, Bethesda, Maryland

"Sir." The colonel in black Homeland Security BDUs saluted. "We just got word from Andrews."

Blair Murdoch glanced up from the computer screen. "And?"

"It's the 82nd Airborne. They've secured the airfield, and more transports are coming in."

"Whose side are they on?"

"Nobody knows yet, sir. I've got our people working on communications intercepts."

Murdoch hauled himself out of his chair. Crunch time, he said to himself. Aloud: "Good. Any trouble with our people in Camp Springs?"

"No, sir."

"Good. Tell 'em to sit tight. No shooting unless they're fired on."

"Yes, sir." The colonel waited a moment, then saluted again and hurried out of the room.

Murdoch paced over to the big plate glass window that made one wall of his office. The Capitol and the White House were less than ten miles away; he couldn't see either one, but the helicopters hovering around the Capitol were visible, small as gnats in the distance.

Damn it, anyway, he thought. How the hell did we end up in this kind of mess?

He went back to his desk and gave the computer screen a morose look. The orders checked out as authentic, straight from the National Security Council, and they were over Gurney's signature, though he had a pretty fair idea who had actually written them. There were only two problems with them: the first was that Gurney wasn't technically the president any more, and the second was that they ordered him to throw everything Homeland Security had in the DC area into a frontal assault on the soldiers guarding the Capitol the following morning—an assault that would almost certainly plunge the country into civil war.

And if the 82nd wasn't on Gurney's side …

Murdoch paused a moment longer, then picked up the telephone. "Torrey? Get me a secure line to Bridgeport's office in the Capitol. Thanks."

He waited, pressing the handset to the side of his face. After a long moment, a flurry of electronic beeps, and another long moment, a ringtone sounded on the other end.

Someone picked it up on the second ring. "Hello?"

Necessary though it was, it took Murdoch an effort to say it. "This is Baird Murdoch at Homeland Security. I need to talk to President Bridgeport."

Dead silence. Then: "Just a moment, Mr. Secretary. I'll get him on the line."

13 October 2030: The Capitol, Washington DC

"So help me God," said President Bridgeport.

Camera flashes went off around him like gunfire, recording the moment, chasing shadows around the Rotunda.

It had taken more than an hour for someone to find the chief justice and get her to the Capitol, and by then the first reporters were showing up, begging for a story. Everybody in Congress who'd been able to make it to the Capitol that day was there; so was Ralph Wittkower in full Army dress uniform, and half a dozen top Pentagon brass; so was Claire Hutchison, and so were a couple of assistant secretaries of cabinet departments. Bridgeport's staff had hurried over from One Observatory Circle, and Melanie had managed to drive in from Silver Spring in time and get through the Marine cordon. All in all, it was a motley crowd: suitable witnesses to one of the least orderly inaugurations in American history.

The chief justice closed the Bible and handed it to an aide. She looked almost as dazed as Bridgeport felt.

Someone handed Bridgeport a microphone. "For obvious reasons," he said, "I haven't had time to write an inaugural address. I'll have something to say to everyone as soon as we get a live TV crew here. Until then, I want to ask all Americans—wherever they stand on the issues that have divided us—to stop, take a deep breath, and join together with me to make this nation work again. Thank you."

That got a round of applause. "We didn't have time to plan for an inaugural banquet either," Bridgeport said then, "but if you'd like to join me for a buffet, I'd be honored."

He handed the microphone to an aide and turned. Melanie was waiting; she threw her arms around him, kissed him on the cheek, and whispered, "Dad, I am *so* proud of you."

The Senate catering staff had a reputation for being able to cope with anything on next to no notice, and they lived up to it that evening. Long tables elegantly draped showed off a sumptuous spread framed by the opulent china and silver of an earlier day, and immaculately dressed servers moved noiselessly around with trays of hors d'oeuvres and champagne. Bridgeport led the way with Melanie on his arm, then motioned

351

to the guests: help yourselves. They'd had, he guessed, as long and harrowing a day as he had.

Once everyone was tucking into the buffet, Bridgeport got a glass of champagne and let himself drift to one side of the hall. He could see Melanie over by the door to the Rotunda, talking with her Australian reporter. Joe Egmont and a couple of members of Bridgeport's staff positioned themselves unobtrusively nearby to fend off the media if necessary. Wittkower crossed the hall, talked with Egmont briefly, then came up to Bridgeport.

"Mr. President," he said. "Couple of things. We got through to the Secret Service unit in the White House."

"And?"

"They're standing down and waiting for your people to come over. Gurney's gone—he boarded a private jet around three this afternoon."

"I wish I was surprised," said Bridgeport. "Where's he headed?"

"South. Nobody's sure of anything beyond that. The place is almost empty—most of the staff bailed hours ago. Harbin's still there, and Julia Gurney—"

"Good God. He didn't even take Julia with him?"

"What the staff said is he didn't take anything but money."

Bridgeport stared at him for a long moment, then: "Harbin should be behind bars as soon as possible."

"I've got people on the way there."

"Good. I'll have my people follow, and make sure Julia's safe and has anything she needs. None of this is her fault."

"Granted." Wittkower paused. "Technically speaking," he said then, "is Gurney still supposed to be under government protection?"

"Heck of a good question. If he formally requests it, Congress will probably have to vote on it. Until then—" He drank the rest of his champagne. "Probably not."

"That's what I thought. Thank you, sir." Wittkower went away, got something from a waiter that wasn't champagne, and downed the whole glass at a swallow.

Bridgeport envied him the drink, and considered flagging down a waiter, but just then the conversations stopped and faces turned expectantly toward him. Before he could wonder why, the familiar blare of trumpets and tubas sounded off to one side. Someone had tracked down a military brass band and gotten it to the White House, and it launched into the one tune everyone in Washington DC knew by heart.

It was only then, as the opening bars of "Hail to the Chief" rang off the stone walls of the Cross Hall, that the events of the last few hours finally felt real.

13 October 2030: The White House, Washington DC

Ellen Harbin stood by the window of her office, cell phone at her ear. Outside, the sky was the color of iron, fading to black as evening came on; a few brown leaves whipped by on the wind; Harbin didn't notice them. All her attention was focused on the ringing sound on the other end. Two rings, three, four, click: "Hi, this is Lon. I can't take your—"

"... appalling abuse of power." It was Bridgeport's voice, of course, live from the Capitol. "It's one thing to try to save the Union, and quite another to use that as an excuse to violate everything the Union stands for ..."

She jabbed the screen with a finger, hit the same auto-dial again. One ring, two, three, four, click: "Hi, this is Lon. I can't—"

"... thing I want every American to realize is that our system worked. Congress did what it's supposed to do, according to the Constitution; our armed forces did what they're supposed to do; the other branches of the government did their jobs, and stopped this thing in its tracks ..."

There was someone behind her, standing in the door. She could feel the presence there, looming. She refused to turn and look, jabbed at the phone again, listened. One ring, two, three, four, click: "Hi, this is—"

"… left the country in a private jet earlier this afternoon …"

Bridgeport, she thought. Bridgeport, you fucking *liar*.

"Ms. Harbin." A man's voice, unfamiliar, came from the door. She turned, finally, defeated. A Marine colonel was standing there, with others she couldn't see out in the hallway behind him.

"I'm speaking with President Gurney," she said coldly.

The colonel wasn't impressed by the bluff. He stepped into the office, and men in the uniform of the Capitol Police came past him. "Ms Harbin," said the colonel, "Gurney's been removed from office. These officers are here to arrest you."

It took a moment for that to register. When it did, she darted for the computer on her desk. One of the policemen got there first. Another caught her by the arm, got handcuffs on her.

"I stand by everything I've done," she said then.

The colonel's expression said "whatever" more clearly than words could have done. He nodded to the officers, who led her out. One of them began reading her the Miranda warning in a monotone as they went out into the hallway.

13 October 2030: Above the Amazon rain forest

Gurney glanced out the window at the darkness. The lights of a small town flickered in the middle distance, sliding slowly past as the executive jet he'd chartered flew steadily south. Paraguay was still hours of flying time away, but at least he was clear of the United States. He'd watched satellite news broadcasts for a while, once the jet was safely out over the Atlantic, and there was no question in his mind that he'd gotten out just in time.

He tried not to think about everything that had gone wrong. At least he'd had the good sense to make sure he had a way out, and the slush fund he'd learned to keep on hand from the first days of his political career more than paid for itself this time. A couple of suitcases full of money—euros, mostly—and a stash of precious metals heavy enough that two of his aides had to haul it on board the plane would make life a lot easier once he got safely to the family property south of Villarrica.

He was still thinking about that when he noticed the red and white lights in the middle distance. They weren't sliding back behind the plane, the way the lights of the town were doing. They were—

The cabin door opened in front of him, and the copilot came aft, his face pale. "Mr. Gurney," he said, "there are two planes flanking us. They've ordered us to land."

Gurney stared at him for a moment. "Whose are they?"

"They won't say."

"Not a chance."

"Mr. Gurney," the copilot said, "they say they'll shoot us down unless we land."

No, Gurney thought. No. This can't be happening.

Almost ten years later, a Chilean entomologist chasing exotic butterflies in the part of the northern Amazon basin where Colombia, Venezuela, and Brazil come together stumbled across an abandoned one-strip airfield in the middle of the jungle. Delighted by the stroke of luck—two of the species he was seeking were most often found in natural clearings—he searched the landing strip, and found at one end, under camouflage netting half overgrown with vines, the rust-streaked hulk of a corporate jet.

The entomologist contacted the local authorities, who surrounded the site with a police cordon and sent for detectives. Nobody was surprised that the plane turned out to be

Gurney's, but there was no sign of what had happened to the ex-president or his aircrew, except something that might once have been a bloodstain in the rotting carpet of the main passenger cabin. Of the fortune that Gurney was said to have taken with him—by then a matter of legend—no trace was ever found.

TWENTY-EIGHT

13 October 2030: The White House, Washington DC

"Mr. President." It was a White House staffer, a middle-aged woman with hair the color of iron. "She's ready to see you."

"Thank you," Bridgeport said.

She led him to the top of the stairs, around a corner and down the Center Hall, then stopped at a door and knocked. "Ma'am? Mr. Bridgeport."

He could just barely hear the reply: "Please let him in, Molly."

The West Sitting Hall was the First Family's living room, and looked like it, done up in the faux-Western decor Gurney fancied. Julia Gurney was sitting on a couch with a half-full glass in her hand. Her hair and makeup were flawless; only the blurred look in her eyes told Bridgeport just how much she'd been drinking.

Still, she got up easily enough. "Pete. Thank you for coming to see me—and I should congratulate you, too, shouldn't I? Can I get you something to drink?"

He considered that. It wasn't yet nine in the morning, and gray light was streaming through the windows of the adjacent rooms. Still, he said, "Please, and thank you. Bourbon, if you've got some."

That got him a dazzling if not entirely steady smile. "Of course." She went into the family kitchen with her glass, came out again with two glasses on a tray, both full. Bridgeport went to intercept her, got the tray safely onto the coffee table and helped her sit.

"Julia," he said, "I'm so sorry about all of this. I can't imagine what it's been like for you these last couple of days, with the crisis and—" He picked up his glass of bourbon, gestured with it. "All the rest of it. If there's anything my staff or I can do to make things easier for you, please let me know."

"Thank you. I really do appreciate that." She sipped at her bourbon. "I spent a couple of hours last night on the phone with my brother. I'll be going back to Baton Rouge as soon as my family can arrange things. The one thing I'd like to ask, if it's not too much trouble—could I have a few days to get everything of mine packed here?"

"As long as you need. It's going to take me a while to get everything packed at One Observatory Circle, you know."

"Thank you, Pete." She took another sip. "I'll be sure to let your staff know just as soon as I get my things cleared out of here. I'm sorry to say that you'll have to have someone else get rid of the rest. Do you know when I found out that Lon had flown out of the country? When it got on the evening news."

Bridgeport looked away. "Oh my God."

Her lip trembled, but then she raised her chin and controlled it. "I'm sorry, Pete. I don't mean to burden you with my troubles. I know you have way too much on your plate as it is. But—but I want to know one thing." Without the least change of expression or tone: "What happened to that whore of his?"

That made him look back. "Harbin? She's in jail."

"Really? What for?"

"Conspiracy to overthrow the Constitutional government," said Bridgeport.

That got another smile, just as dazzling, but edged like a knife. "You know, that's the first bit of really good news I've heard in days. Thank you. Thank you, Pete."

He finished his bourbon, got up. "If you need anything else, be sure and let me know."

"I certainly will. Pete, you're a real gentleman—unlike some I could name. Thank you."

He extricated himself from the room, found Molly waiting just outside. "If there's anything she needs," he said, "let my staff know at once."

"I certainly will, Mr. President."

14 October 2030: The White House, Washington DC

"You want to know how bad it is?" said Beryl Mickelson, the Secretary of the Treasury.

"Essentially, yes," President Bridgeport replied.

"Bad. For all practical purposes, the federal government is bankrupt."

They were in the Cabinet Room, where Bridgeport had called the first official meeting of the cabinet he'd inherited from Gurney—there had been an unofficial meeting in his office in the Capitol the night before. He'd considered replacing some of them with his own nominees, decided against it for the time being. If the nation survived the dissolution crisis, there would be time to consider that.

"Tax revenues are just over 11 percent of what they were before the war," Mickelson went on, "and that's without correcting for inflation. Of course part of that's simply a matter of how many people are out of work, but a lot of people and a lot of businesses have simply stopped paying federal taxes. They're gambling that the federal government isn't going to be around long enough to make trouble for them.

"And then there's the inflation. The official rate is 20 percent per year, but that's just so that cost of living raises don't kill us. The actual rate is close to 130 percent per year, and it's been accelerating for the last six months or so. Quite a few businesses have stopped accepting payment in US dollars entirely—Canadian dollars, euros, and barter arrangements are all pretty common these days. I've been told by people in the General Services Administration that they're having trouble finding suppliers for some goods and services who will still take federal checks at par."

Bridgeport nodded. "I don't blame them. I assume that at least some bills aren't being paid at all."

"Almost half," Mickelson admitted. "But some of the departments were also ordered to keep issuing checks even though we don't have anything to cover them."

Bridgeport blinked. "You're saying the US government is kiting checks?"

"Not exactly. You kite checks when you've got money coming in to cover them. This is uncomfortably close to check fraud."

An uncomfortable silence filled the room. "Okay," said Bridgeport finally. "So that's where we stand. We'll be spending the next few months figuring out what to do about it, but there are some things we need to do right away." He turned in his chair to face Barbara Bateson, the Secretary of Defense. "Barbara, you know what's coming."

She nodded unhappily. "Pretty much."

"The carrier groups are history. I want two carriers mothballed and the rest scrapped. We'll settle later what's going to happen to the rest of the surface fleet. If the nation is still around come spring, we can start figuring out what a navy looks like in the age of supersonic cruise missiles—but you know as well as I do that it's not going to look like the one we've got.

"And we need to bring the troops home. We can't afford to keep military forces all over the world any more, and if dissolution goes through, I don't want any of our young people left overseas."

He glanced over at the others. "Domestically, I need a list of all the federal programs that aren't actually authorized by the Constitution. I'll get the attorney general's office and my staff working on that. Once I've got the list, those programs are going to get cut."

Another silence. "Mr. Bridgeport," said Anthony Bellarmine, the Secretary of Health and Human Services, "that amounts to about three quarters of all federal expenditures."

"I know," said Bridgeport. "If we cut federal expenditures by three quarters, that might just be enough to convince the credit markets and the American people that we're serious about change." He leaned forward. "I know it's going to hurt, but the survival of this country is at stake, you know."

16 October 2030: Washington DC

"Yes," said Leona Price. "Yes, I'd be honored." She listened to the phone for most of a minute, then said, "Sure. I can be there first thing tomorrow, if that'll work." A pause. "Fair enough." Another. "Thank you, Pete." Then: "Goodbye."

Her husband was staring at her as she put the phone back down. "Baby, what is it? You look like somebody just clobbered you over the head."

"More or less." She blinked, turned to face him. "That or I'm dreaming. That was Pete Bridgeport. He's just asked me to be his vice president."

His mouth fell open. After a moment, he shut it. "You're— no, clearly you're not kidding. Baby." He crossed the room to her, threw his arms around her and gave her a kiss. "Baby, I'm so proud of you!"

She beamed. "Ready to be Second Hubby?"

"Any day of the week."

Her expression twisted, then. "For as long as it lasts. You know, it just about figures that the first person from the District to get this would be the last vice president this country is ever going to have."

"You don't think Bridgeport can pull things together."

"Hundred to one against it."

"Maybe so," Robert said, "but you're still my favorite vice president."

She kissed him back. "Sweetie." Then: "Who knows, maybe I can still make some kind of a difference."

17 October 2030: The White House, Washington DC

"If we can pull this off," said Joe Egmont, "it's going to be the biggest political upset since Truman trashed Dewey."

He and Bridgeport were in the Roosevelt Room. On the table in front of them were printouts of the latest polls and projections from across the country. In state after state—not all of them, but enough that the exceptions didn't matter—voters were leaning toward pro-dissolution candidates for the state ratifying conventions, and the elections for delegates were only weeks away.

"How are we doing for money?"

"Fair to middling. Some of the big corporate donors are coming through; I'm pretty sure they're also handing cash to the other side, so their bread is buttered whoever wins. Still, they're donating. We're getting a good response from the patriotic groups—American Legion, DAR, that sort of thing, and there's enough old money there that it matters. We should be able to run a decent national campaign."

"And the PAC?" Political action committees were the bread and butter of American political fundraising, and getting one established to help fund the anti-dissolution campaign was a necessity.

"Up and running. You should see the first United PAC ad buys hitting the internet tomorrow or the next day."

Bridgeport nodded.

"How much do you want to know about the other end of the campaign?"

"No more than I have to." Election fraud had been a normal part of American elections since George Washington's time, Bridgeport knew; everyone did it, and the only reward you got for keeping your hands clean was a string of lost elections.

"What you need to know," Egmont told him, "is that we're in trouble on that front. Usually the state and local party organizations handle the payoffs, and most of those aren't interested in helping us out on this—they're on the other side if they're taking any position at all. And—" He glanced up at Bridgeport. "There's big money on the other side. Really big money."

"Whose?"

"That's the frustrating thing—nobody seems to know. Some of it's not too hard to trace. There are some Silicon Valley millionaires who are funding the California pro-dissolution campaign, and some serious Texas oil money going into the same thing all over the southwest. That sort of thing only accounts for a fraction of it, though."

"I'm wondering whether it might be foreign money," Bridgeport said.

"Very possible. The United States has a lot of enemies, and this would be a helluva good investment for any spare cash they've got." Egmont shrugged. "But there's no proof."

Bridgeport looked at the polls again. More than once, as he'd tried to figure out what was happening in a United States that might not be united much longer, he'd felt as though he was grappling with an opponent he could almost but never quite see—as though there was a mind and a focused will behind the rising spiral of crises that was overwhelming the country. The problem was that the intuition never went any further, never gave him anything he could use.

"There's one bit of good news," Egmont said then. "Your personal approval ratings are way up there. People like you personally."

"For whatever that's worth," said Bridgeport.

"It's a handle," Egmont said. "It might get a few people to vote the right way."

19 October 2030: Silver Spring, Maryland

Melanie Bridgeport stood there looking at the telephone for a long moment. On the other side of the room, her laptop screen had just switched over to the screen saver, hiding an article from the local newspaper. Tommy McGaffney was off chasing an interview with one of the leaders of the pro-dissolution movement in New England; the lights of Silver Spring sparkled in the autumn night. She was alone with the decision she knew she had to make.

No point in delaying, she told herself, and picked up the phone and dialed.

Three rings, and then a familiar voice: Joe Egmont, her father's chief of staff and sometime campaign manager. "Hey, Mel! What can I do for you?"

"I—I need your professional advice," she told him.

"Shoot."

"I want to run for a seat in the Maryland ratifying convention. I don't know anything about how to do that, but—I want to do it."

Egmont was silent for a few moments. "Okay," he said then. "That ought to be doable. You'll need somebody experienced to run your campaign—I can think of a couple of people who are mostly retired, but might be game for a local campaign like that. Do you know the cutoff date for registering as a candidate?"

"The 23rd," she said. "I just read it in the paper."

"Gotcha. Does your dad know about this?"

"No. I haven't had a chance to talk to him."

"Hey, that could be a great media handle—president's daughter enters race, doesn't tell him about it." He considered it for a moment. "If I wasn't too busy I'd do it myself. Ought to be a fun campaign. No worries, though; I'll get you set up with somebody who knows what to do. Get yourself registered first thing tomorrow if you've got the time, and we'll get it rolling. Good enough?"

"Yes. Thanks, Joe."

"Any time. You take it easy, Mel."

She finished the call, put the phone down, went back to the laptop and looked up the details. I can do this, she told herself. I have to do this if I'm going to live with myself.

4 November 2030: The Capitol, Washington DC

President Bridgeport got out of the limousine and walked up the steps to the Capitol, Secret Service agents in tow. Camera crews from the media lined his route, taking pictures and video footage: business as usual, but there was even more of a point to it than before.

The weeks since Gurney's attempted coup and the Congressional countercoup had gone past in a blur of meetings, phone calls with world leaders, speeches to the media, and late night planning sessions trying to figure out how to bring stability to a nation on the brink of collapse. A major policy speech to both Houses of Congress, though it was one of the normal rituals of presidential power, had to be postponed until immediate necessities had been dealt with, and it so happened that the nearest date that fit Congress's crowded schedule was the day after the 2030 midterm elections.

"Those are crucial," Joe Egmont had said, in one of those late night planning sessions two weeks earlier. "It's not a matter of who wins—it's a matter of how many people vote. If we get anything like a decent turnout, that's a sign that we're starting to turn things around."

So much for that, Bridgeport thought sourly as he entered the Capitol. The people have spoken: 22 percent by voting, the other 78 percent by staying home.

Party leaders from both Houses were waiting for him, and the obligatory greetings and handshakes followed, with more cameras flashing. Bridgeport could see the worry behind the practiced smiles, though. They knew, just as he did, that things weren't going well.

The worst of it was that by most measurements, the economic crisis had already passed its crest and was receding. The plunge in the dollar's value, devastating though it had been, had made American goods and services more affordable than those of foreign competitors for the first time in most of a century. Exports were up, job creation was up, and small businesses were springing up all over the country, cashing in on rock-bottom rental costs. He would be talking about all those things in a few minutes, but the media had been talking about them for most of a month now, and it hadn't made a noticeable difference in the country's mood.

He threaded his way through the familiar corridors, nodded greetings to familiar faces, got up onto the podium behind the Great Seal—familiar, too, though he was still getting used to being on the other side of it. Senators and Representatives, reporters and camera crews faced him, waiting—and that was when it struck him, hard as a physical blow, that in a few months all of it might be over and done with forever.

He kept the realization off his face, got ready to begin his speech.

9 November 2030: Spokane, Washington

Harriet Elkerson looked troubled. "I don't want this to turn violent," she said. "That's the last thing that anybody needs right now."

"I know," said one of the young men sitting across the table from her. "But you may not get to choose. If the Feds send troops—"

"I don't think Bridgeport would do that."

"I hope you're right, Mrs. Elkerson." The possibility hung there in the air between them.

In the weeks since the convention, more by accident than by plan, Harriet Elkerson had become one of the leaders of the dissolution movement in the rural eastern half of Washington state. The storefront office she'd opened to run for a delegate's seat stayed open, though the banners had changed, and the volunteers who gathered there and then went doorbelling through Spokane neighborhoods were chasing votes for pro-dissolution candidates for the state ratifying convention in January. In private moments now and then, Elkerson felt twinges of uneasiness about the whole business, but she felt sure that it was still the best option the country had.

But if it came to civil war …

"I'm willing to support civil disobedience, if it comes to that," she said firmly. "I've already talked about that, you know, and if the federal government sends troops, I'll be right out there confronting them. But I'm not going to give any encouragement to violence."

The young man nodded. "I can get behind that. My question is, what are you going to need if it comes to civil disobedience?"

Elkerson thought about that for a moment. "That's an excellent question," she said. "It shouldn't be too hard to find out what's worked in the past. One way or another, though, it's going to take a certain amount of money."

"That's not a problem," the young man said. Elkerson gave him a quizzical look, and he leaned forward. "There are some Seattle tech millionaires backing dissolution," he said in a low voice. "Names you've heard of. I know people who have connections. If you can let me know what you're going to need, I'll see what I can do."

"I'll have my people get to work on it," Elkerson said. "If we can get some funding in place now, get the things we need in place before anything happens, it might be possible to head off any trouble before it happens. I'd prefer that, you know."

11 November 2030: Lumberton, Mississippi

"That wasn't half bad," said Jim Owen. "There's a lot y'all still need to learn, but we're getting there."

There were almost 150 of them, young men in hunting gear, shouldering a motley collection of rifles. They were bedraggled and muddy from a long day training in the Mississippi woods, and looked nothing like an army—not any army the South had seen since 1865, at any rate—but Owen remembered the Venezuelan irregulars who'd made life so hellish for his unit, and nodded. If it came to fighting, these boys would do right well.

"We'll call it good for today," he told them. "Y'all be here tomorrow, oh nine hundred sharp, and we're gonna do it again. Got it?"

"Yessir!" they shouted back, and Owen thought of the boys who'd marched off from Lumberton in 1861, the last time dissolution was in the air. That was a sobering thought; how many of those boys ended up in the clay at Antietam, Gettysburg, or all those other places on the long road from Manassas to Appomattox? He pushed the question aside, said, "Get out of here."

They laughed and started back to their cars, parked all anyhow on the side of the road a hundred yards away. Owen turned and went the same direction. He'd gotten most of the way there before he noticed an unfamiliar car, with someone in it. Some of the others had noticed it, too, and were hanging back, watching.

Owen was maybe five yards from the car when the driver's side door opened and a familiar figure got out: Ray Muldoon, the county sheriff.

"Afternoon, Ray," Owen called out. "How's life treatin' you?"

"Fine as frog hair. You and the boys been havin' a good day out here?"

"You bet."

"Glad to hear it. You got a minute to talk?"

"Sure thing," said Owen.

They walked across the road and a short distance into the pine woods on the other side. "I just got a call from the governor's office," Muldoon said. "They want to know about militia groups getting organized in the state—like this one you've got going."

"I bet," said Owen, grimly.

"No, not like that. They want to know what you need."

Owen stopped and stared at him.

"Jim," the sheriff said, "dissolution's gonna happen. You know what the polls are running right now? Better than 70 percent in favor, and down here in Dixie, it's more than that. Word is the state government's planning on it—and if the Feds send troops ..."

"Yeah." With a sideways look: "Last I heard, the state government don't have enough spare change to buy buttwipe."

"There's money for this," Muldoon told him. "There're supposed to be some old-money families backing dissolution, names you've heard of. I know some people with connections. You let me know what you need, I'll get it."

Owen considered that. "A few mortars and machine guns. Some Stingers and antitank rockets, and ammo—plenty of that. As long as we're fighting on our own ground, that's what we'll need."

"No problem," said Muldoon. He lowered his voice. "Aside from whatever I can get now, when Mississippi votes for dissolution, or the Feds do something—whichever comes first—as county sheriff, I'll be taking charge of the National Guard armory in town. You won't get everything—you know Billy Briscoe, don't you?"

"Billy? Sure."

"He's drilling a bunch of boys up north of town, and they'll get a share. But you'll have everything you need."

"I'll give him a call," Owen said. "We'll get things sorted out."

17 November 2030: Silver Spring, Maryland

"Permit me," said President Bridgeport, "to congratulate the successful candidate."

Melanie blushed, and then threw her arms around him. Everyone else in the room whooped and clapped. The little storefront space Melanie had rented as headquarters for her campaign had already been crowded before the president made his unannounced visit; now, with a couple of Secret Service agents hanging back dutifully near the door and a flurry of reporters who'd been tipped off, the room felt as though it was about to burst and spill everyone onto the wet street outside.

It had been a wild ride. The state legislatures had scheduled their ratifying conventions with scant regard for the realities of American politics—or, perhaps, with all too clear a sense of what would likely happen if the political establishment had time to respond—and so she'd had only a little more than three weeks to make her case to the voters of the Silver Spring area. A capable campaign manager had been one huge advantage, but Joe Egmont had been right. Once the media started going on about the president's daughter, Air Force officer and former POW, running all on her own for a delegate's seat, she'd had all the publicity she needed.

She let go of her father, turned to face the reporters. "I want to thank everyone who helped make this happen. Gretchen Hayes, my campaign manager." A plump white-haired woman, who looked like everyone's favorite grandmother and had the instincts of a shark, stood up and smiled and sat back down. "All my volunteers, and especially the voters of this district, who listened, who encouraged me, and who chose the right answer and not the easy one."

Two weeks earlier, when it was anyone's guess who would win the election, she'd put some time into writing out what she'd say if the voters chose her. How did it go? "This coming January," she said, "I'll be meeting in Annapolis with the other delegates to decide whether Maryland is going to ratify the 28th Amendment. You know how I'm going to vote—but this is going to take more than voting.

"I want to ask each of you to remember what this country is supposed to stand for. I want you to talk to your friends and neighbors, and remind then what this country is about. We don't have to fall for the easy answer of dissolution. We can make the United States work again, if we work together at it. Thank you."

The others in the room were clapping and cheering again. Melanie looked at her father, though, and saw right past the smile. He knows we won't work together now, she realized. He knows we're going to lose.

19 November 2030: Falls Church, Maryland

Emil Pohjola considered the list of names on the screen. All things considered, it had taken him far too long to find time to read the leaked documents that detailed Gurney's failed takeover. The new administration had made a clean sweep of special-projects staff and the other less-than-legal dimensions of the White House machinery; that was business as usual—most new administrations did the same, and Pohjola knew he would have no difficulty at all finding new employment if he needed it—but the delay had kept him from discovering a vulnerability, and that touched his professional pride.

The document open on the screen, already well on its way to lasting notoriety, was the list of people who had been slated for execution as soon as Gurney's takeover began. It included a great many major public figures and no shortage of minor ones, but down near the bottom was a name known only to a select circle of Washington operatives: Emil Pohjola.

That had been an unpleasant surprise. What it might mean, now that Ellen Harbin was in jail awaiting trial, was even more unpleasant. Pohjola's harsh trade had its own code of ethics. Part of it was you didn't turn on your own people without very good reason, and if you did, you didn't expect them to cover for you, because they knew you wouldn't return the favor.

After a moment, he picked up the phone, dialed a familiar number in Camden. "Mr. Capoblanco? This is Emil Pohjola." He waited through Capoblanco's effusive greeting, then: "I'm sorry to say we may have a problem. I was just tipped off that last April's transaction will be getting some unwelcome publicity in the near future." He listened. "No, I don't think the new team has anything to do with it. Someone with a grudge, or so I was told." After another pause: "Exactly." Another: "You're most welcome. Good luck."

The call finished, Pohjola put the phone down and stared at nothing in particular for a while. The logical next step was to go to ground, the way Capoblanco and his people would be doing, but there was at least one other option, and his name on the ExAcList document made that other option tempting. Finally, with a thin smile, he minimized the document, looked up a phone number on the internet, and dialed.

TWENTY-NINE

11 December 2030: North Charleston, South Carolina

"Another beer, if you don't mind," McGaffney said.

"Sure, hon." The waitress gave him a smile and went back inside the restaurant. Out in front, though summer was long past, outdoor tables and big umbrellas splashed with liquor logos had been pressed back into service. The day was warm for December, but that wasn't the reason for the crowds that packed downtown Charleston.

"Dammit," somebody said a few tables away. "They know what they gotta do, what's keepin' 'em?"

McGaffney tapped the words into his tablet—local color, always good for a story—then brought up a window, checked the newsfeed from the convention. No word yet; he minimized it again, kept typing.

Just over a mile away, in the Charleston Convention Center, the delegates to South Carolina's ratifying convention were deciding whether their state would be the first to vote for dissolution. It was a fine bit of irony, since their state had been the first to vote for an earlier attempt at the same thing, back in 1860. The session was under tight security; there were state troopers in riot gear all around the convention center, and helicopters up above, reminding McGaffney of nothing so much as Dar es Salaam during the riots before the war. Word was on the internet that President Bridgeport had asked to be allowed to address the convention, and been told to go away.

All at once the man who'd spoken a few tables away jumped to his feet. "Woohoo! They did it!" An instant later others were up, shouting one thing or another. Their voices blurred into a roar that set the air shaking. McGaffney clicked on the window again, saw the news: the vote had gone for dissolution, 103 to 21.

As McGaffney went back to typing, someone at the next restaurant along the street started singing loudly:

"We are a band of brothers and native to the soil,

Fighting for our liberty with treasure, blood and toil …"

The man who'd jumped up a few tables away from McGaffney whooped again, and joined in, off key:

"And when our rights were threatened, the cry rose near and far,

Hurrah for the Bonnie Blue Flag that bears a single star."

By that time dozens of others had joined in:

"Hurrah, hurrah! For Southern rights, hurrah!

Hurrah for the Bonnie Blue Flag that bears a single star."

The crowd was still singing—they were onto another verse, something uncomplimentary about the Union—when the waitress came back with McGaffney's beer. He paid, then asked, "What's the song?"

She gave him an incredulous look. "Where y'all from?"

"Brisbane, Australia," McGaffney told her.

"Oh! Well, then, of course you wouldn't know. That's 'The Bonnie Blue Flag,' one of the old songs from the Confederate days."

McGaffney nodded, noted that down. "What do you think of all this?"

"I don't know," the waitress admitted. "I hope it turns out better than it did the last time. You let me know if you want another, you hear?"

She went back inside. McGaffney took a swig of the beer, glanced around, and frowned. Something had changed, though it took him a moment to realize what it was. Before the singing started, the crowd had been the usual mix of American faces, white and brown and black.

Now every face around him was white. He hadn't noticed any of the others leaving, but they were nowhere to be seen.

13 December 2030: Silver Spring, Maryland

"They kept it up all night," McGaffney said. "That song and a dozen others. Thousands of 'em, just in the parts of Charleston I saw, singing and drinking and waving a couple of flags—the blue state flag, and one I don't know."

"Red," Melanie Bridgeport said, "with a blue cross like this—" She crossed her forearms in an X. "—and stars."

"Too right."

"The old Confederate flag."

He let out a whistle. "Much of that going on in the other states down south?"

"That's what I hear."

They were sitting in the kitchenette of her condo, takeout Burmese spread across the little Formica-topped table between them. His luggage was in the living room, still sporting airline tags; he'd flown back into Dulles that afternoon, and hadn't mentioned a next flight. Melanie wondered if that meant anything, and decided to ask. "And now?"

"For me?" He looked at her, tilted his head to one side like a cockatoo, a mannerism she found delightful. "Depends on whether you can put up with me. Not much point in hopping from state to state while the conventions make up their alleged minds. If that's the Confederate flag—" His hand cupped his chin. "I could play that angle. Get some interviews up in that town in Pennsylvania, the one where they fought the big battle—"

"Gettysburg."

"That's the one. Other places around here, where some of your history happened. They'd eat that up back home."

"I think I can put up with you," she said, smiling.

"Now that's a compliment." He helped himself to two more scoops of kat kyi hnyat.

4 January 2030: Annapolis, Maryland

"The chair recognizes the delegate from Silver Spring," the PA system boomed.

Melanie got to her feet, took the microphone, drew in a deep breath.

"Ladies and gentlemen," she said. "I think most of you know that I'm a colonel in the Air Force, and I was in East Africa during the war. I did time in a POW camp, and I got to see a lot of people I cared about get killed, because people in our government were more concerned about their careers than the quality of the weapons systems your tax dollars paid for, or the sanity of the plans they sent us there to carry out.

"I'm saying this so you know that I have as much reason to be bitter about the government in Washington as anybody in this room. I want you to remember that when I tell you why this convention and this state needs to vote against the 28th Amendment."

She could hear voices murmuring in the balconies, ignored them. "When I was in the POW camp in Tanzania, I had a lot of time to think about patriotism. All these years we've acted as though patriotism is all about the sort of chest-thumping arrogance that shouts 'We're number one!' even when we're not. That's not what patriotism is.

"Love for your country is like love for your family. If your family has problems—your dad's having an affair with somebody at work, your mom's drinking herself under the table

376

every night, your kid brother's starting to run with a gang—you're not showing love for your family by insisting that there's nothing wrong and if anybody disagrees, there's the door. There's another alternative, which is sitting everybody down and saying, look, we've got problems, and we need to work together to fix them.

"That's what we need to do as a country. That's what the convention in St. Louis was supposed to be about, before it ran off the rails. America has problems. We all know that. But there's an alternative to storming out the door.

"We've heard delegates insisting that it doesn't matter if Maryland votes against the 28th Amendment, that it's a done deal. That's not true. If thirteen states vote against this thing, it dies, and then we can actually sit down together as a nation and do the job they were supposed to do in St. Louis. Five states have already voted no. Let's make Maryland the sixth, and turn this thing around, so this country can solve its problems instead of running away from them. Thank you."

A whisper of applause stirred the air around her as she sat down. "The chair recognizes the delegate from Hagerstown," the PA system boomed.

Whether or not her speech made any difference in the outcome was anyone's guess; informal polls of delegates just before the Maryland convention showed narrow majorities against the 28th Amendment. When the delegates balloted that evening, though, the vote was 59 in favor of dissolution, 93 opposed.

"I don't know," said Melanie later that night. She'd agreed, laughing, on dinner with McGaffney at one of Annapolis's best restaurants, in exchange for an interview on the convention. "Maybe it was just wasted breath. Still, I think we did the right thing."

"To the State of Maryland," McGaffney said, raising his glass with a smile.

"To the State of Maryland," she repeated. The glasses clinked.

Over the next week, four more states voted for dissolution.

29 January 2030: Lincoln, Nebraska

"Whaddya think?" said the man in the plaid wool coat.

"Haven't the least idea," McGaffney answered genially. "I'm with the media."

"No kidding?" The man shook his head. "A damn shame, I call it. A goddamn shame."

They were standing outside the Nebraska statehouse, in a crowd the news websites estimated at 20,000. Two feet of snow and a brisk wind off the prairies further west were no obstacle to the locals, McGaffney gathered, and not much more to the media—there were dozens of camera crews present and scores of reporters, waiting with everyone else for history to happen.

"It's a goddamn shame," a woman not far away said, "that this didn't happen a long time ago. We'd have been a lot better off without those idiots in Washington screwing us over." A murmur of approval circled through the crowd.

"Look at that," said the man in the plaid coat. He waved a gloved hand at one of the flagpoles in front of the statehouse, where the American flag snapped and stretched in the wind. "Doesn't that mean anything to you folks any more?"

"Oh, give me a break," the woman said, in tones of utter contempt.

Before anything else could be said, a buzz went through the crowd. McGaffney looked up to see one of the doors of the statehouse opening. A single figure came out, bundled against the cold, and walked to the podium that had been set up on the front stairs.

Already? McGaffney thought. They've only been at it for two hours.

"Ladies and gentlemen," said the man, "the convention has made its decision. Nobody saw any point in revisiting the same arguments, so as soon as the preliminaries were over, the convention voted unanimously to close debate and go straight to a roll call vote."

The wind rushed past, setting the flags snapping.

"The final vote on the 28th Amendment was 118 in favor and 32 opposed."

Whatever else he might have wanted to say went unspoken. A wordless roar went up from the crowd; it sounded, McGaffney thought, like the cry of a dying animal. A moment later some of those around him were whooping and cheering, while others had tears running down their faces; still others stood there with mouths and eyes wide, trying to grasp what had just happened.

The door to the statehouse opened again, and two men in the uniforms of the state police came out. They went to the flagpole with the American flag flying from it and began lowering it. As it got within reach of the ground, the crowd surged forward; there was a scuffle McGaffney couldn't see clearly, and then more whooping and cheering. A few moments later people came pushing past him from the front of the crowd, shouting something he couldn't make out; one of them shoved something into his hands.

It was a scrap of blue cloth with a bit of white on one side. A moment passed before McGaffney realized that they'd torn the flag to pieces for souvenirs.

He turned to go. The man in the plaid wool coat was behind him, clutching a similar scrap of cloth. As McGaffney watched, the man crumpled to his knees and doubled over, pressing the scrap to his chest and bawling like a child.

McGaffney looked down at the scrap in his own hand and tossed it aside in disgust. He tried not to notice when someone else dove for it.

29 January 2031: The White House, Washington DC

President Bridgeport was in the library on the ground floor of the White House when the news came. The old building was silent around him; there had been staffing cuts, part of the desperate effort to bring costs down to what federal tax revenues would support, but it was more than that. He guessed that everyone else in the White House was watching the same thing he was: the news feed from Nebraska, where a bunch of farmers and local politicians meeting in the Lincoln statehouse were about to decide whether the United States of America was still going to exist when the sun came up the next morning.

No surprise if it ends that way, he thought, since the whole thing began with a bunch of farmers and local politicians meeting in a hall in Philadelphia. He recalled the men who'd gathered there, in their coats and smallclothes and powdered wigs, to try to invent a country like no other in history out of a bundle of colonies on the shore of a mostly unknown continent. What would they have thought if they'd guessed how their experiment would end?

He had no shortage of other things to attend to just then. The latest statistics on the economy had come in that morning, with another slight uptick in employment and job creation; the Iranian and Turkish governments had started negotiations in Geneva, aimed at ending the stalemated fighting in Arabia and Kurdistan, and oil prices were down as a result; a consortium of banks had tentatively agreed to settle the US debt for much less than face value, though details still had to be worked out and plenty could still go wrong; the Council on Economic Advisors had come up with a plan to issue a new, more stable currency, and get the inflationary spiral under control for good. Under any other circumstances, those would have taken up Bridgeport's attention. As it was, none of them mattered, unless …

The words BREAKING NEWS scrolled across the news feed banner at the bottom of his computer screen. Then: NEBRASKA VOTES 118-32 FOR DISSOLUTION.

He'd wondered many times how he'd react if—when—the news finally came. As it was, he stared at the headline as it advanced across the screen and tried to make the words mean anything at all.

After a moment he got up and walked out of the library into the Center Hall. His footsteps sent quiet echoes whispering off the walls, past the paintings of dead presidents and the trophies and mementoes of 250 years. It's over, he thought. After all the hopes and the struggles and the blood that was shed for it, it's over.

The reporters would be arriving soon, he knew. After a moment, he drew in a deep ragged breath, made himself go to the stairs.

THIRTY

The little nameless restaurant just outside the Party enclave of Zhongnanhai was quieter than usual when Liu arrived. The doorman and the hostess greeted him as effusively as ever, and he chose the same little table where Plan Qilin had first been discussed most of two years before.

He had just settled comfortably into the chair when a familiar voice spoke. "General! I trust I have not kept you ..."

Liu got up. "Not at all, Fang. It's good to see you."

"Likewise," said the professor.

The waitress appeared the moment they both sat, and for the next hour the two men ate dim sum and talked about irrelevancies: the doings of their wives, the latest projects at the Academy, the latest gossip from the upper circles of the PLA. Finally, when the meal had reached that pleasant moment when two cups of green tea made everything perfect, they fell silent, looking at each other. They had discussed the events in America more than once over the months just past, and noted the faint but unmistakable signs of overseas funding and planning.

"Apparently," Liu said at last, "someone else recognized the same opportunity you did."

"It has been fascinating to watch." Fang sipped his tea. "I am far from sure that whoever funded and directed it had the entire plan worked out in advance. I would have expected to see propaganda for dissolution start circulating well before the convention in St. Louis, for example, and there was little of that. Still, if there were improvisations, they were done quickly and well. Whoever directed this has a first-rate mind." Glancing at Liu: "I certainly don't mean to inquire into state secrets, but I wish I knew which nation funded and planned this."

"I have my suspicions," Liu said, "but nothing more."

They were both silent for another long moment, sipping their tea. "It will be a very different world without the United States," Liu said then. "Different, and I'm by no means certain it will be any safer."

"Granted," said Fang. "Much depends on what happens in the future. If the states are able to gather into viable regional groupings and establish functioning governments, we can hope for a peaceful outcome. If fighting breaks out among the states, or the attempts to form new nations fail—" He shrugged. "And that depends, above all, on the intentions of those who fed the collapse. If their goal is to turn America into a war zone, then a war zone it will likely be."

"If there were reason to try to stop that process," Liu asked, "could it be done?"

Fang gazed into his teacup. "Possibly. It would be very difficult. If you wish, I would be happy to draw up a tentative plan."

"Please do," said Liu. Then, after another silence: "I pity them."

"The Americans?"

"Yes. To have to come to terms so suddenly with the fact that they aren't the masters of the planet—it cannot be easy."

"The Motherland will face the same experience someday, you know," Fang said. "No nation remains a superpower forever."

"True." Liu drained his teacup. "When that time comes, I hope our people are able to meet the decline with some measure of grace."

2 February 2031: Alexandria Detention Center, Alexandria, Virginia

"I believe you wanted to see me," said the warden.

They could as well have gotten someone from Hollywood central casting to play a Southern prison warden, Ellen Harbin thought sourly: big belly, big jowls, little black eyes that would resemble a pig's if they weren't so cold, and the Virginia accent with too much mountain twang to even try to pass for tidewater. "Yes, I did," she said.

He motioned her to a chair, waited until she sat before settling behind his desk and motioning her to speak.

"I want to know," she said, "on what legal basis I'm still being held."

The warden blinked. "Excuse me, ma'am?"

"The arrest warrant cited a federal crime. The federal government no longer exists, and its laws no longer have any force. I want to know why I'm still being held here."

The warden looked at her for a long moment. "That, ma'am, is a very interesting point of law. Ain't you the one that was arguing that unitary-government theory?"

That startled her; he didn't look like the kind of person who would know about that. "That's correct."

"Under that theory, the president's the law. So if there's no more president, there's no more law, and I ought to just let you go. Right?"

"That's correct," she repeated.

He got up and went to the bookcase on one side of the office, looked at the law books there. "That's a very interesting point of law, " he repeated. "I can see only one problem with it, really, where you're concerned. If there ain't no law for you—"

He walked over to the room's one door and turned his back to it. "—then there ain't no law for me, either. And that means that I can do whatever I happen to want to do to you, right here and now."

He smiled, then, and it wasn't a pig's smile; it was a shark's. Harbin blanched, and pulled herself out of the chair, looking around for an escape, a weapon—

"Sit down," the warden said. "Fortunately for you, your theory ain't worth two buckets of warm piss. The state of Virginia had its own laws more'n 100 years before there was any such thing as the United States, and it's still got its own laws now that the United States is gone. You follow me? You're a legal resident of Virginia, you're subject to the laws of this commonwealth, and that's the basis on which you're going to stay right in this here jail."

"And what Virginia law," Harbin said coldly, "am I supposed to have broken?"

"Now that's a reasonable question," said the warden. He walked over to his desk, pulled some papers off it and handed them to her, then went back to his seat. "This came in from the grand jury last week. You've been charged, ma'am, with arranging the murder of William Stedman."

The indictment had all the usual paperwork attached; she flipped from page to page, stopped cold on the one that listed the witnesses the grand jury had called. The one name that mattered was at the head of the list: Emil Pohjola.

"That's absurd," she made herself say.

"That's up to the jury to decide," said the warden. "Now if you'll excuse me, ma'am, I have work to do."

3 February 2031: Silver Spring, Maryland

He had his suitcase packed when Melanie got back to her apartment: Not a surprise, but it still hit hard. She tried not to let the hurt show. "When's the flight?"

"Just before midnight." McGaffney was sprawled on the couch, his tablet on his lap; he finished typing something, shut it down. "Only bloody seat I could get."

She could see past the casual smile to the wariness in his eyes, guessed at the reason. "You're wondering if I'm about to—what's that phrase you used yesterday? Spit the dummy."

That got a laugh. "Too right." A moment later: "Are you?"

"No." She put her purse on the end table, went to the couch; he made room for her, and she sat. "No, I figured that you'd be on your way as soon as things quieted down here. Do you ever think of settling down?"

"Tried it a couple of times. It never worked out for long. If I was minded to try it again, you know, we'd talk."

He was lying, she knew that much at once, but it was some consolation that he cared enough about her feelings to say it. "So where next?"

"Back to Africa. Things are heating up in the Congo again, with the Coalition gearing up to settle things, and my bosses want stories about that."

She thought of the latest headlines and felt cold. "Be careful."

"Oh, I will," McGaffney said. "And you? Any plans yet?"

"Nothing worth mentioning." She half-turned on the couch, facing him. "I don't think anybody knows what's going to happen next. Once the states decide what they're going to do, there'll be armies and air forces, and—" A little helpless shrug. "I'll have to decide then where I belong. That's not a decision I ever thought I'd have to make, but—"

"You could move in with your dad, if it comes to that."

She laughed. "For the time being. Nobody's even talking about what's going to happen to the White House." After a moment: "One way or another, I hope I see you again someday."

He took her hands, then, all at once dead serious. "Don't wish for that," he said. "Where I go, there's going to be blood

387

in the streets. Don't wish for that here. It could happen too bloody easily, if too many people get stupid."

Taken aback, she thought about that, then said, "Maybe in a war zone somewhere else, then. That's my trade too, remember."

He blinked, relented. "True enough." His hands moved to her face. "That'd be corker."

"I'm going to take that as a compliment," Melanie said, and kissed him.

It wasn't much later that the taxi arrived. She gave him another kiss at the door, heard his footfalls fade to silence in the hallway, turned away from the door. The condo was mostly dark, the curtains still open: the lights of Silver Spring sparkled in the winter night.

And now, she thought? What am I going to do now?

The lights had no answer for her. Looking out at them, she wondered how many others were asking themselves the same question that night.

5 February 2031: The Kremlin, Moscow

Glasses clinked together. "I suppose congratulations are a waste of breath," said Bunin.

"Not at all." Gennady Kuznetsov allowed a smile, sipped at the vodka. "Not at all, Misha. Besides, it's not as though I can expect to receive them from just anyone."

"True. *Za nashikh uspekh.*" The general raised his glass, and everyone else did the same and repeated the toast—"To our success."

There were fewer than a dozen men in the room, all of them belonging to the innermost circle of the Russian Federation's government and military: the only men in the world who knew the whole story behind the headlines that had shaken the world now for a week, and would keep shaking it for months and years to come. The waiters had brought in vodka and hors d'oeuvres and made themselves scarce; here and here alone certain things could be discussed openly.

"You will have some explaining to do if questions come up in the Duma about all that money," said Igor Vasiliev, the intelligence chief.

"Lost in foreign exchange markets when the dollar crashed," Kuznetsov replied at once. "All the documentation's in place at the Ministry of Finance. Yes, I'll be flayed alive for hiding the losses, but that will blow over after a few months."

"And if anyone ever traces any of it to America?" Vasiliev persisted.

Kuznetsov's smile went away. He took another sip from the glass, considered it, and drank the rest. "Don't even suggest that. I spent far too many sleepless nights thinking about the consequences."

It was a rare admission of weakness, and no one pressed the issue. Bunin picked up a bottle of vodka and refilled the president's glass. "And now?" he asked. "The rest of it?"

The question hovered in the air. It would be easy, Kuznetsov knew, so easy, to take that next step—to fan America's old hatreds and new grievances just the little bit further that would be needed, put the state governments at each other's throats, and then set off the acts of violence that would send the no longer United States tumbling downhill into a future as the world's largest and most intractable failed state. Eventually the United Nations—based in Geneva by then, or Hong Kong, or just possibly in St. Petersburg—would have to send in troops; there would be a ceasefire, then partition, with Russia, China, and the European Union all carving out their own spheres of influence from the corpse of the former superpower. The plans were already drafted, the money could be found somewhere: All that would be needed was a nod of the head to Bunin, a few words to Vasiliev, a few orders issued over the next week, and the wheels that would crush what was left of the United States would begin to turn.

He savored the thought, and then sighed. "No," he said. "No, I think our little project has gone as far as it should go."

The others regarded him, said nothing. After a moment, Kuznetsov laughed his dry little laugh. "You're too polite to ask why, but I'll tell you anyway. First, the risk of detection. We've been lucky so far, but it's never good to trust too much to luck—and if the Americans ever find out what has been done to them, we could lose everything we've gained."

"True," said Vasiliev.

"Second, the money. You're right about the Duma, of course: There will be hard questions. The arrangements I've made will cover what we've spent so far, but to go on—" A quick expressive shrug. "—that would cost many billions more, billions we don't have. It can be done if necessary, but not without serious risk, and I'm not convinced the risk is worth taking."

"Also true," said Vasiliev.

"Third ..." Kuznetsov stared at the vodka in his glass, watched reflections shimmer in it. "Third is another matter entirely. Tonight, Misha, there are millions of infants sleeping in their cradles in America. If we go ahead now, one of them, or more than one, will grow up as I did, learn what I did, decide—" He drank. "—what I did. Could become Gennady Kuznetsov."

He glanced up from the vodka to find Bunin looking at him with that flat, unreadable peasant's look. "Also true," Vasiliev said, "and that would be a danger to Russia."

"I know," said Kuznetsov. "But that's not what I was thinking of."

A moment of silence, and then Bunin slapped the president on the shoulder. "Gennady, you think too much." Then: "But you are doubtless right." He raised his glass. "*Za vas.*"

"*Za vas.*" Kuznetsov raised his glass as well.

18 February 2031: The White House, Washington DC

Pete Bridgeport came down the stairs, stopped when he heard voices. "—is off limits," someone was saying. "Remember, this is still a residence. Now this way is the East Room ..." The voice faded into a rustle of footfalls on carpet. It was Nora playing tour guide, of course, leading a gaggle of tourists through the building. Tours on the hour, pricey lunches served in the State Dining Room five days a week: it had taken only a few days for the remaining White House staff to come to terms with the obvious ways to keep lights on and paychecks covered, now that the government they used to serve wasn't there any more.

A half-remembered article in a magazine nagged at Bridgeport's memory: didn't European aristocrats fallen on hard times do the same thing, cooping themselves up in a corner of their mansions and letting tourists roam through the grand halls and salons of an older and more lavish day? Doubtless the White House could do well for itself that way; the staff had already fielded the first handful of inquiries about weddings in the Rose Garden once spring came.

Once the last whisper of the tour group faded to silence, Bridgeport went down the stairs, ducked through the entrance hall and left the building. The day was cold and clear, and snow crunched under his shoes as he crossed the lawn to Pennsylvania Avenue—the barriers had all been taken down, and the security guards were looking for other jobs—and started walking toward the Capitol. Passersby stopped and stared if they weren't locals, or greeted him with a wave and a friendly word or two if they were; he smiled and nodded, finished the walk.

These days the Capitol was wide open, without even someone to take tickets at the door. He walked inside, ducked past a family of Japanese tourists who were snapping pictures of everything in sight, went to the elevator and punched the floor for the Senate lunchroom. That had redefined itself after the first few days into a restaurant open to the public, serving the famous Congressional bean soup and sandwiches named after dead presidents. Tourists liked to eat there, but so did those politicians from the old government that hadn't hurried back home to try to find places in one of the new ones.

He knew the regulars at lunch, but this time Bridgeport found most of them gathered around three tables that had been pushed together.

"Pete!" Senator Liebkuhn from Indiana—former senator, Bridgeport reminded himself—waved him over. "Your timing's good," she said. "We're inventing a country."

"No kidding." He went to join them, ordered a bowl of soup and half a Harry Truman when the waiter came by. The senator's words were no surprise. New England and Texas had just declared themselves republics, and eleven southern states had delegates in Montgomery hammering out what wags were already calling Dixie 2.0.

Liebkuhn filled him in. "We've been at the Senate Office Building on the phones with the states all morning. The seven eastern states that voted against ratification are in. So are Ohio and Delaware—they called off their conventions once Nebraska made it moot. New Jersey only ratified because of Trenton, they want in, and the Kentucky legislators talked it over and decided they'd rather be with us than with the South. So what we're saying is, okay, the rest of you don't want the Union, that's fine. We still do."

"Thinking of using the old name?" Bridgeport asked.

"It's got a nice sound to it, doesn't it? Here, take a look at the map." She handed him a printout of the old United States, with a new border drawn in yellow highlighter. Inside the line were twelve states forming the eastern core of the continent, from New York and the mid-Atlantic westward through Ohio, West

Virginia, and Kentucky to Illinois, Michigan and Wisconsin, reaching from the Atlantic to the Great Lakes and the upper Mississippi. Highways and rail lines, harbors and waterways, farmlands and urban centers: it was, Bridgeport realized, a viable country.

He glanced up to see another familiar face, also a lunchtime regular. "Hi, Leona. You might want to pull up a chair."

"What's up?" Price fielded a chair, and the others made room for her.

The senator filled her in, and asked, "How about the District of Columbia?"

"How about the *state* of Columbia?" Price replied.

That stopped conversations at the table for a moment, but only a moment. "Rhode Island's gone," said a New York congressman down the table, "so, yeah, we've got an opening for a little bitty state. You want the position?"

Price grinned. "Have to put it to the citizens, but I'm guessing yes."

"Just a moment," said Bridgeport. He left the table, found another lunchtime regular, a former Senate staffer, and talked to him in a low voice. The staffer left the lunchroom and was back five minutes later with a bundle of cloth. Bridgeport stood up, and said, "Can we clear some space in the middle here? This might be useful." He and the staffer unrolled the bundle. Thirteen stars in a circle, thirteen red and white stripes: a tourist-shop copy of the original US flag lay spread in front of them.

No one said anything for a moment. Around the lunchroom, conversations fell silent and necks craned as the other diners began to notice what was happening.

"It was a good country," said Bridgeport, "back when there were just thirteen states, and we didn't think we were supposed to run the rest of the world. Thirteen states could make a good country again."

"It'll take a lot of hard work, Mr. President," said Liebkuhn. She emphasized the last two words. "A lot of hard work."

They were all looking at him, Bridgeport realized: not just the senators and representatives, but people all over the lunchroom. He drew in a long uneven breath. "I know," he said. "Let's get on it."